Praise for The White Road

"*The White Road* is an action-packed and terrific read—enjoy. Flewelling is at the top of her game, and her game is very, very good indeed."

—Patricia Briggs, *New York Times*
bestselling author of the Mercy Thompson series

Praise for Shadow's Return

2008 Romantic Times Reviewers' Choice Nominee for Best Fantasy Novel

"The fourth book in Flewelling's superb Nightrunner series picks up right where the last book left off with nary a hiccup. Seregil and Alec continue to be entertaining, while Flewelling pulls off the near impossible in this compelling page-turner."

—*Romantic Times* (4½ stars)

"Excellent! . . . This (is a) terrific fantasy thriller that can stand alone, but is enhanced by the other tales in the Skalan saga." —BookReview

"Flewelling presents a well-developed fantasy world with faie from many clans, wizards, alchemists, and ambitious humans. Love and jealousies abound and drive the story."

—SF Revu

Praise for The Tamir Triad

"Some of the most inventive and emotionally gripping fantasy to come down the pike in years . . . Flewelling's writing is both intelligent and visceral, with unflinching detail that compels readers to turn pages in wide-eyed fascination. . . . At the same time, however, a sense of poetry runs through her narration. . . . Flewelling takes the stock trappings of the sword-and-sorcery genre and turns them into a riveting epic story that is unique, disturbing, and enthralling."

—*Mythprint*

"Perhaps the deepest psychological novel I've ever read—the fantasy makes the unconscious issues real. Gorgeous but dark." —Orson Scott Card

Praise for The Oracle's Queen

"A splendidly stirring coming-of-age tale."
— *Romantic Times* (4½ stars)

"It is a great book!" — *Affaire de Coeur* (4½ stars)

"I've been looking forward to *The Oracle's Queen*, the third volume in The Tamír Triad, with eager anticipation and it doesn't disappoint. Central characters remain true to the previous volumes, and at the same time we see new facets to their personalities. The inexorable flow of events drives the narrative forcefully onward while unexpected twists keep us guessing. . . . I can recommend it and indeed the whole series to lovers of intelligent contemporary fantasy that nevertheless keeps faith with all the strongest traditions of the genre."
— JULIET E. MCKENNA, Emerald City

"This novel delves deeply into the psychological effects of razzle-dazzle magic, thrones, swords, and the rest, and makes for a terrific read. . . . Magic, mystery, politics, emotions, and rare golden threads of the numinous all make this book a rich tapestry of a read right through the climax. . . . There is never an easy answer in *The Oracle's Queen*: the characters gain so much dimension that they linger in the mind long after one reads the last page. This trilogy is a must for those who love fantasy with all the Good Stuff stitched together by intelligent world-building and a wise eye for the frailties, and the greatnesses, of the human spirit." — SF Site

"A fine conclusion to an above-average series . . . Flewelling does an excellent job of adding depth and texture to the story of a young person thrust onto the throne of Skala."
— *Contra Costa Times*

"Lynn Flewelling's *The Bone Doll's Twin, Hidden Warrior,* and *The Oracle's Queen* are brilliantly original and moving. This story still haunts me, months after reading the books. There's plenty of gritty realism to make this a book for adults and mature teenagers, but what it definitely is not is 'escapist.' This book drags you through so much emotionally painful territory that you're almost relieved when it's done and you can escape to your safe regular life."
— ORSON SCOTT CARD

hated for it to end and it did. That's how good books are supposed to make you feel: like you're living in another world, with people you really care about, and you don't want to close the book and go home. If these books hadn't turned out to be excellent, I wouldn't be reviewing them, of course—because I rarely review books I didn't finish, and I rarely finish books that I don't enjoy. I loved these."

—ORSON SCOTT CARD

"*The Bone Doll's Twin* is a great read. Lynn Flewelling has outdone herself with this vibrant tale of dark magic, a hidden child, and the demon ghost that haunts it. She builds a convincing, colorful world with carefully chosen details, and her characters are memorable because their dilemmas are vividly drawn and heartbreakingly believable. This is exactly the kind of fantasy novel that will keep you up long past your bedtime."

—KATE ELLIOTT

"A fascinating read, both intellectual and haunting."

—BARBARA HAMBLY

"A dark and twisting enchantment of a book, a story of deception and loyalty and heroism that will magick its readers along with its characters."

—LOUISE MARLEY

"Lynn Flewelling is one of the best at creating complicated stories peopled by diverse characters, each with his own agenda, and each absolutely believable. This tale of a girl disguised by magic and brought up as a boy is engrossing and compelling as it explores the honorable reasons behind dishonorable deeds—and the dark consequences that follow a single desperate act. Flewelling accompanies her skill at storytelling with an exquisite level of detail that brings her entire world to life. A most satisfying tale for readers already familiar with her Nightrunner series—for others, an excellent introduction to the joys of a Flewelling fantasy."

—SHARON SHINN

"You liked Lynn Flewelling's Nightrunner series? This novel is even better. *The Bone Doll's Twin* is a sharply honed, powerful story where good and evil are as entwined as two children's lives, and salvation carries a very high price. Highly recommended."

—ANNE BISHOP

turns poignant, spooky, and earthy. . . . A moving and thoroughly recommended read."   —Starburst

"This terrific tale is dark and exciting, and the magic in it is truly wonderful."   —*Booklist*

Praise for the Nightrunner series

Luck in the Shadows

"Memorable characters, an enthralling plot, and truly daunting evil. . . . The characters spring forth from the page not as well-crafted creations but as people. . . . The magic is refreshingly difficult, mysterious, and unpredictable. Lynn Flewelling has eschewed the easy shortcuts of cliched minor characters and cookie-cutter backdrops to present a unique world. . . . I commend this one to your attention."

—ROBIN HOBB

"Part high fantasy and part political intrigue, *Luck in the Shadows* makes a nice change from the usual ruck of contemporary sword-and-sorcery. I especially enjoyed Lynn Flewelling's obvious affection for her characters. At unexpected moments she reveals a well-honed gift for the macabre."   —STEPHEN R. DONALDSON

"A new star is rising in the fantasy firmament . . . I am awed by the scope of the intricate world. It teems with magic and bustles with realistic people and spine-chilling amounts of skullduggery."   —DAVE DUNCAN

"A splendid read, filled with magic, mystery, adventure, and taut suspense. Lynn Flewelling, bravo! Nicely done."

— DENNIS L. McKIERNAN

"An engrossing and entertaining debut . . . full of magic, intrigues, and fascinating characters. Witty and charming, it's the kind of book you settle down with when you want a long, satisfying read."   —MICHAEL A. STACKPOLE

"Exceptionally well done and entertaining." —*Locus*

"Lynn Flewelling has written a terrific first novel, a thrilling introduction to this series. . . . Highly recommended."

—*Starlog*

STALKING DARKNESS

"Flewelling is bringing vigor back to the traditional fantasy form. In this highly engaging adventure novel, the most powerful magic is conjured out of friendship and loyalty. The author has a gift for creating characters you genuinely care about."

—TERRI WINDLING, *The Years's Best Fantasy and Horror,*
Eleventh Annual Collection

"Events move forward in this second adventure. . . . It's up to four companions to stop Mardus's schemes. Things get very violent and there's also a strong emotional undercurrent . . . an amusing twist on the old 'damsel in distress' scenario."

—*Locus*

TRAITOR'S MOON

"What most fantasy aspires to *Traitor's Moon* achieves, with fierce craft, wit, and heart. It is a fantasy feast—richly imagined, gracefully wrought, and thrilling to behold. An intoxicating brew of strange and homely, horror and whimsy, lust and blood, intrigue and honor, great battles and greater loves. It is a journey through a world so strange and real you can taste it, with companions so mysterious and memorable you won't forget it. Lynn Flewelling is a fine teller of tales who delivers all she promises, cuts no corners, and leaves us dazzled, moved, and hungry for more. *Traitor's Moon* is a wonderful book." —PATRICK O'LEARY

"While fans of Dungeons and Dragons–style lore will find enough wizardry, necromancy, swords, daggers, and devilishly clever traps here to satisfy the most avid, this book also provides entry to a complete and richly realized world that will please more mainstream readers." —*Bangor Daily News*

The White Road

LYNN FLEWELLING

BALLANTINE BOOKS • NEW YORK

A Spectra Mass Market Original

Copyright © 2010 by Lynn Flewelling

Published in the United States by Spectra, an imprint of The Random House Publishing Group, a division of Random House, Inc., New York.

SPECTRA and the portrayal of a boxed "s" are trademarks of Random House, Inc.

Map by Virginia Norey

ISBN 978-0-553-59009-8

Printed in the United States of America

www.ballantinebooks.com

9 8 7 6 5 4 3 2 1

For my terrific kid sister, Susan.
Thanks for your love,
support, and enthusiasm
all these years.

Acknowledgments

I would like to thank my wonderful editor, Anne Groell, for her insight and care with this book, and my wonderful husband, Doug, for his unwavering support.

Thanks also to heavy metal cello band (that's right—cellos) Apocalyptica, for making such great music to write to.

✖
Safe harbor

DYING—even for just a little while—took a lot out of a person. Alec and his companions had arrived in Gedre last night and Alec had managed to stay on his horse as they rode up from the harbor to the clan house, but he'd spoiled it by fainting in the courtyard. Mydri had taken one sharp look at him and packed him off to bed in a room overlooking the harbor. And when their host saw Sebrahn, Riagil í Molan had ordered that the *rhekaro* stay hidden, too. Given Sebrahn's strange appearance, Alec could hardly blame him.

Winter rain lashed against the window across the room and the wind moaned in the chimney. Gedre harbor was barely visible, the ships anchored there just dark smudges in the mist. After their stormy crossing from Plenimar, it was rather nice to be in a soft bed that didn't roll under him. He had no idea what time it was. When he'd awakened, Seregil was already gone, no doubt to speak with his sisters or their host, the *khirnari*.

Sebrahn was curled up on the cushions of the window seat, gazing out—though at what it was impossible to say. The rhekaro might have Alec's childhood features, but it was impossible to pass him off as an ordinary child. His pale, silver-white hair hung nearly to the floor behind him. His white skin looked ghostly in the grey light, and his silver eyes were the color of steel. Riagil's wife, Yhali, had replaced the rags Sebrahn had arrived in with soft Aurënfaie tunics, knitted stockings, and shoes that fit him, though

Sebrahn seemed confused by the latter and kept taking them off. Just as any little child might do—

But he's not a child, is he?

Pushing that thought away, Alec reached for the mug Mydri had left on the bedside table and sipped the medicinal broth. His hand shook a bit, spilling a few drops down the front of his nightshirt.

He and Seregil had been in desperate condition when Micum and Thero had found them in Plenimar, but Sebrahn had been even worse. He was made of magic and had used a staggering amount to kill their pursuers in the Plenimaran wilderness, bring Alec back from Bilairy's gate, and heal both Seregil and Alec. For the first few days of the voyage they feared that the wizened, depleted little rhekaro might have used himself up. Too weak to get out of his bunk, Alec had fed Sebrahn several times a day, squeezing blood from his fingertip onto the rhekaro's little grey tongue. After a few days of this Sebrahn grew more alert and continued to improve. And today he seemed nearly himself again.

Alec wondered how long Riagil and Mydri were going to keep him shut away up here. His long linen nightshirt was fresh, but he hadn't had a proper bath since they'd escaped from the alchemist's villa almost two weeks ago. He sighed and ran his fingers through his hair, which hung halfway down his back—lank and dirty. His fingers caught in snarls and tangles. Stretching out one long blond strand, he wondered—not for the first time—whether he should just cut it off, as Seregil had sacrificed his during their escape.

Sebrahn was squirming around now. One by one, the borrowed shoes fell to the floor. The alchemist, Charis Yhakobin, had created the rhekaro to be nothing more than a sexless, voiceless tool—one whose unnatural flesh and strange white blood could, according to Yhakobin, be distilled for some kind of potent elixir. But Sebrahn and his ill-fated predecessor had been much more than that. Sebrahn might be sexless, but he was not voiceless, or mindless, either.

"What do you see?" asked Alec.

Sebrahn turned to look at him. "Ahek."

Alec chuckled. His name had been Sebrahn's first halting word. Since then, he'd managed a few more for people, things, and a few actions. Understanding was another matter. Strangely, it didn't seem to matter whether you spoke Skalan, 'faie, or Plenimaran to him. Tell him cup, *tyxa,* or *kupa,* and if there was one in the room, he would fetch it.

Sebrahn left the window seat and joined Alec on the bed, leaning against his side. Alec touched the rhekaro's soft, cool little hand, noting the thin scars that ringed the base of several fingers where they'd grown back after Yhakobin cut them off for some experiment.

Why didn't you sing to save yourself?

Alec gathered him close again, his heart beating a little faster. "No one is going to hurt you again, or take you away. If they try, we'll leave."

Sebrahn looked around the room, then pointed out the window and said in his raspy little voice, "Leeeve."

"That's right. On a ship. Can you say 'ship'?"

Sebrahn was not interested.

"Chamber pot."

The rhekaro slipped off the bed and pulled the required vessel from under the bed. Alec made use of it and had Sebrahn put it back for the skutter to deal with. Now what? There didn't appear to be anything he could do but watch the rain. It was a relief when he heard someone coming up the stairs to his door.

Micum looked in and grinned. "That's a long face!"

"Where is everybody?"

Micum came in and pulled a chair up beside the bed. "At breakfast. I came up to see if you're awake. Hungry?"

"Not really."

Micum held out his hands, and Sebrahn abandoned Alec for the big man's lap.

"Traitor," Alec grumbled. Sebrahn had warmed to their tall, red-haired friend during the voyage. Sebrahn reached up to touch Micum's thick, grey-streaked moustache, apparently puzzled that the big man had something on his face that his two beardless protectors didn't.

"Uncle Micum," Alec said with a smile.

Micum laughed and kissed Sebrahn's hand, just as if he were one of his own brood. "I like the sound of that. What do you say, little sprout?"

Sebrahn didn't say anything, just leaned against Micum's broad chest and fixed his gaze on Alec. It was too easy to imagine anything he wanted in those eyes. What Sebrahn was really feeling—or if he could—remained a mystery.

Alec and Micum were in the midst of a game of cards when Seregil came in with the wizards. Magyana looked most of her two centuries today; under a fringe of grey bangs, her lined face was pale and tired, but her eyes were kind as always. Thero, still in the youth of his first century, was tall and dark, with a thin beard and dark curling hair pulled back from a long, somewhat austere face. But his pale green eyes were warm, too, as he took in the sight of Alec and Sebrahn.

"We need to talk," Seregil said, sitting down on the bed beside Alec.

"I'll leave you to it," Micum said, putting Sebrahn on the bed and rising to go.

"Please, stay," said Thero. "We have no secrets from you in this matter."

This sounded serious, and all the more so when Magyana threw the latch and cast a warding on the room to keep out prying ears.

"Now then, this creature—" she began, her lined face somber.

"Please don't call him that," said Alec. "He's a person and he has a name."

"He is not a person, my dear," Magyana told him gently. "You may be right about the rest of it, but he's not human, or 'faie, either."

"There's something we need to tell you," said Thero.

"What is it?"

"Thero sensed it, but not clearly, when he first saw Sebrahn in Plenimar," Magyana explained. "It's true that the rhekaro has been given the semblance of a child, but another form radiates beyond the physical. I don't understand it, but what I see around him is the form of a young dragon."

Alec stared hard at Sebrahn, squinting his eyes, but saw nothing unusual. "A dragon? That's impossible! Sebrahn was made from bits of—me!"

Seregil was frowning at the younger wizard. "Why didn't you tell us, Thero?"

"I wasn't sure what I was sensing. It's Magyana who sees it clearly."

Magyana took Alec's hand in hers. "Seregil has told me something of how Sebrahn was made. I believe you can tell me more. Do you know what materials he used?"

Alec shifted uneasily; it was a time he didn't really want to remember. "Sulfur and salt, tinctures—"

"Nothing of dragons?"

"I saw dried fingerling dragons hanging in his workshop, but I didn't see him put any in."

"Very well. What else do you remember?"

"There was something he called the 'water of life'—some kind of silver, I think."

"Quicksilver?" asked Magyana.

"Yes, that was it. He put that all in with my tears, blood, shit and piss, hair, and my . . ." He faltered, blushing under the weight of their collective gaze.

"His semen," Seregil finished for him. "How in Bilairy's name do you get a dragon out of all that?"

Thero shrugged, his pale green eyes serious. "We don't know yet. But they did."

"It was my Hâzadriëlfaie blood that *Ilban*—" Alec faltered, horrified to have the slave word for "master" slip out so easily. "That's what Yhakobin claimed he needed the most. He said that it was the only thing that would work to make a rhekaro. But since I'm *ya'shel,* he did a long purification process first, trying to get rid of my human blood, he said."

"Ah, that would explain it," Magyana murmured. "I thought you looked different, more 'faie."

That was a sore topic. "I had to drink tinctures of metals and wear amulets; seven of them, I think: tin, copper, silver, gold—I don't remember the others. And he kept taking drops of my blood and making them burn to see what color they were. When it got to the right shade, he used more of my blood to make the mixture do whatever it did."

"Right out of his chest," Seregil growled. "They tapped him like a keg and hung him up to bleed on their mess." He paused, then leaned over and pushed the hair back from Alec's left ear, showing them the small blue dragon bite tattoo on his earlobe. "Could this have something to do with it?"

Magyana raised an eyebrow. "It's possible, I suppose. But it's such a tiny bite. There wouldn't have been anywhere near as much venom from it as there was from yours, Seregil."

The dragon that had bitten Seregil had been the size of a large dog, and the *lissik*-stained teeth marks spanned the back of his hand and the palm. His arm had swelled up like a sausage and he'd been damn sick for a few days, but lucky to survive all that with no more long-term damage than the mark.

"If that's what Yhakobin really wanted, then he'd have used Seregil instead," Alec mused. "Besides, he didn't know I had the mark until after he'd bought me, and didn't know what it was once he did. I told him it was just decoration." He looked to Thero. "What about the Orëska? Nysander knew about the Helm. Maybe there's some wizard guarding this rhekaro secret, too."

"It's doubtful," said Magyana. "Skala barely existed when the Hâzad went north. And even if there is someone, it's quite possible that he or she is sworn to utter secrecy, as Nysander was. Or dead. We lost so many during the assault on the Orëska House."

"Maybe so, but don't you think that somewhere, down in all those vaults, there might be *something* about this?" Seregil gave her a winning look. "If anyone would know where to look, it's you. You know those cellars better than anyone."

"I'll look around as soon as I go back, but it's likely to take a long time, since I don't know what I'm looking for. There are a few people I could speak with, but you shouldn't get your hopes up."

"It would be an easier task for two people," said Thero. "I had a message spell from Prince Korathan's wizard, Norubia, last night. The prince is losing patience waiting for us to come back and account for ourselves. If I don't bring you back, then I'd better have a good story. Otherwise it's likely to raise questions you don't want asked."

"I hate to put you in that position," said Seregil. "But there's no way we can take Sebrahn to Rhíminee. It would be damn near impossible to hide anyone with a 'dragon aura' or whatever it is in a city full of wizards, and if Queen Phoria ever got wind of what Sebrahn is capable of, she'd have him and Alec caged like a pair of chukarees to use against the Overlord's armies in her endless war."

"Do you think that was the real reason Sebrahn was made?" asked Magyana.

Alec shook his head. "If Yhakobin had known about the killing power, he and his slave takers wouldn't have made a head-on charge against us. We have that secret in our favor, at least."

"Do you know anything more about the Hâzadriëlfaie, Seregil?" asked Magyana.

"Only that they took their reasons north with them when they left. Everyone in Aurënen knows the tale."

"Isn't it obvious?" Thero said, pointing at Sebrahn. "If I knew someone was going to use me for that sort of thing, I'd run, too." He paused, then gave Alec an apologetic look. "I meant no offense."

"None taken." Alec was too busy wondering how many people had been hung in cages and bled to make the white creatures before the prophet Hâzadriël had her mysterious vision.

"Thero's right," said Seregil. "I've been up around

Ravensfell Pass. It's the ass end of nowhere, and about as far from Plenimar as you can get. This must be why they've been so insular."

"They killed my mother for bearing a ya'shel child, and tried to kill my father and me, too," Alec told Magyana. "He spent the rest of his life on the move. I didn't know why at the time, but it must have been to keep them from finding us again."

"He never spoke of any of that to you?"

"No. He wasn't much of a talker, my dad. And if I asked about my mother, he'd just say it was better for me not to know. As I got older, I wondered if she'd broken his heart, maybe by running off with another man." He shook his head. "After the vision the Dragon Oracle showed me at Sarikali, I'm ashamed to have thought of her that way."

"You had no way to know, dear boy." Magyana patted his hand. "Your father was a wise man. He must have loved your mother a great deal to risk so much for her. And for you, as well. As for the Hâzad, consider the consequences of a person of their blood finding his way south again."

"A dragon oracle, and a dragon child . . . ," murmured Seregil, wandering over to the window.

Alec suddenly gave a great yawn. Magyana laughed and held out a hand to Micum and Thero. "There's nothing to be gained by dwelling on such things now. Come along, you two, and let Alec rest. Thero, you must compose your response to the prince and send word to the captain of the *Lark* that we mean to sail tomorrow."

Seregil turned and headed for the door with them. "I'll be back in a little while."

"Where are you going?" asked Alec.

"To talk to my sister."

Before Alec could get more of an answer than that, Seregil was gone again.

It was still raining, so Seregil brought Adzriel up to one of the rooftop *colos.* Its domed roof kept them dry, but the tall window openings hadn't been shuttered and the wind off the sea was raw. Sitting down on one of the stone benches, Adzriel pulled her cloak about her and looked up expectantly.

"I have a favor to ask of you," he told her.

"Are you speaking to me as your sister or a khirnari?"

Seregil smiled slightly. "Both?"

She patted the seat beside her and took his hand. The familiarity of it make him feel like a child again, just for a moment. "Go on, then."

"I believe that Sebrahn is the child the Dragon Oracle at Sarikali told Alec about."

"That would make sense."

"Did Magyana tell you what she sees when she looks at Sebrahn?"

"No," said Adzriel, "but I assume you mean the strange aura about him. I thought you must know, but since you didn't speak of it . . ."

"Ah. So you see the dragon, too?"

"A dragon? No, it shifts and glimmers. Can Alec see it?"

"No, and neither can I. Magyana and Thero just told us." He paused, looking down at their joined hands. "I'd like to take Sebrahn to Sarikali, since it was the oracle there who foretold it. Perhaps the *rhui'auros* will know what he is." The temple mystics—the only permanent residents of sacred Sarikali—were renowned for their knowledge and visions, and the Dragon Oracle was theirs—or they were its. No one knew for sure.

"You know I don't have the authority to give permission for you to take something as strange as Sebrahn onto sacred ground, little brother, even if I went with you. That would require a vote by the entire Iia'sidra Council, and that could take a year or more."

"We can't wait that long." He thought a moment, trying to come up with some other option. "Is Tyrus still around?"

"As far as I know, he's still up in the hills."

"Then, speaking to my khirnari, may I bring Sebrahn to Bôkthersa?"

Adzriel considered this for a long moment. "I don't suppose Riagil will let you stay here much longer. It's clear that Sebrahn scares him."

"He's a smart man."

"Then Sebrahn does have some darker power?"

Seregil looked up into grey eyes identical to his own. "Sebrahn can kill. With a song. He heals with his blood, and he can kill with his voice."

She didn't appear surprised. "Who has he killed?"

"The men who caught us in Plenimar—Yhakobin's slave takers."

"He killed them because they attacked you and Alec?"

"Yes. And that's the only time. Then again, we've only had him for a few weeks. I have no idea what else he's capable of."

She raised a disapproving eyebrow at him. "I can still tell when you're lying to me, Haba."

"Yes, I suppose you can. All right then, here's all of it." Seregil lowered his voice, though it would have been difficult for anyone to hear them over the wind. "He can raise the dead."

"Raise the dead?" This time she was clearly surprised.

"Yes. Alec wasn't just hurt in Plenimar. He was killed." The words came out in a rush now. "We were totally outnumbered by Yhakobin's men. Alec was struck by two arrows and that's when Sebrahn sang; it killed every man left standing. I killed Yhakobin myself." He rubbed at his eyes. "But Alec was dying when I got back to him. That's why he's in such bad shape now, and I'm not." Tears stung his eyes; the memory was too raw. "Sebrahn brought him back from Bilairy's gate."

"But—are you certain he was actually dead?"

"Yes!" Seregil's voice was suddenly a little unsteady. "I held him in my arms and watched the blood stop flowing from his wounds. I saw his eyes fix. I *know* what death looks like, Adzriel. He was dead."

"I see." She was quiet for some time. At last, she laid a hand on his arm. "Then, yes, you must come to Bôkthersa and speak with Tyrus. If Sebrahn is somehow a dragon, then Tyrus will know. Even if he doesn't, then at least you'll be safe for a time with us. You can rest and decide what to do next."

"Sebrahn may be a danger to the clan, you know."

"That is my responsibility. And what about Alec? Don't you want him safe?"

"Of course." He squeezed her hand. "Thank you, eldest sister."

"Then that's settled. But you haven't said who kidnapped you. Micum and Thero spoke of finding the slavers who took you, but they seemed to think there was more to it."

"Indeed. The slavers told them that Ulan í Sathil ransoms slaves from Virésse and Goliníl."

Her grey eyes widened in dismay. "You don't think that Ulan í Sathil had something to do with this?" If true, it was an unforgivable breach of *atui*—Aurënfaie clan honor—and could spark a bloody feud with Akhendi, in whose *fai'thast* they'd been ambushed, as well as with Bôkthersa and Gedre, whose people had been killed along with the Skalan escort. "Do you have any proof of this?"

"No. But the slavers who took us were not the ordinary lot. They struck too far inland, and they had a necromancer with them." He paused, weighing his words. "I wouldn't have thought of Ulan, except that Yhakobin mentioned to Alec that he traded with him."

"It's no secret that Virésse trades with Plenimar. Who can blame the khirnari for saving his own people any way he can? I'd do the same, in his place."

"Yes, but it's also no secret here that Alec is half Hâzadriëlfaie. Ulan could have told his friend Yhakobin about Alec to buy favor."

"That is conjecture, Seregil, not proof."

"It just seems like too many coincidences."

"I'd like to see Sebrahn again," Adzriel said, rising and going to the door of the colos.

Seregil smiled as he followed; she'd spoken more like a khirnari just now than a sister.

Together they went down to Alec's room. Sebrahn was on the bed at Alec's side. Magyana and Thero were with them, too, and there were *bakshi* stones and coins strewn across the quilt.

Sebrahn retreated closer to Alec as Adzriel sat on the bed next to him.

"Give me your hand, Sebrahn," she said softly. Sebrahn let her clasp it. She continued to look at him intently, and Seregil knew she was seeing whatever it was that the wizards did.

"I feel no evil in him. Riagil mistakes power for that," she murmured. "Alec, can you control his singing?"

"You told her?" Alec asked, surprised and none too pleased, either.

"I had no choice," Seregil explained. "We need to go to Bôkthersa, and she deserves to know the whole truth. There's a man named Tyrus there who might be able to help us; he knows more about dragons and their lore than anyone I've ever met. He's called Dragon Friend."

"Why?"

"Because he lives with the young ones, and talks to the old ones."

"There are dragons in Bôkthersa?" Alec's eyes were as wide as Micum's little daughter's when Seregil brought her a present.

"Don't you remember what I told you when we first met, when I was trying to talk you into staying with me?"

"That you'd seen dragons flying under a full moon?"

"You'll see them, too, *tali.*"

"How? When?"

Seregil grinned and exchanged a look with his sister. "I'd rather have it be a surprise."

"Have it your way," he said, bemused. He turned to Adzriel. "You think Sebrahn is actually a dragon?"

"No, but he seems to be connected to them in some way, if only through the oracle. Since Sarikali is out of the question, you must bring him to Tyrus."

"Why can't we go to Sarikali?" asked Alec.

"I'll explain later. What do you say, talí?" asked Seregil.

"I say we go!"

Seregil smiled. "Then it's settled. Thank you, sister."

She rose and kissed them both on the forehead. "I'll send word to my captain to get the ship provisioned. It will take some time, but Alec must have more time to regain his strength."

"I'm fine!"

Adzriel laughed as she went out. "That's for Mydri to say, little brother."

Seregil chuckled, too, knowing that Alec was heartily sick of people fussing over him. The promise of Bôkthersa was probably more than enough to make it bearable, though.

Going home at last, he thought with a mix of excitement and concern.

Micum and the wizards came back soon after Adzriel had gone. Micum limped over to the bed and sat down. "We overheard your sister speaking with our host. I take it we're not settling down here?"

"'Guests and fish stink after three days,' as they say," Seregil told him with a crooked grin. "Are you all going back to Skala together?"

Micum raised an eyebrow. "If you think you two are going anywhere without me, you'd better think again. I'm not letting you out of my sight until you're both safely settled, since you can't seem to keep out of trouble."

"What about Kari?" asked Alec.

"Thero's already taken care of that with one of those message spells."

"What did she say?" asked Seregil, though he had a pretty good notion.

Thero grimaced. "That she'd skin both me and Micum if we let anything else happen to either of you. Even allowing for the auditory limits of the spell, I had the impression that she meant it quite literally. She won't be happy if she finds out I've deserted you. To be honest, I wish I was going with you." Thero grinned in a way Seregil never would have imagined him capable of.

Micum laughed. "He's finally gotten a taste of nightrunning and likes it. Don't worry, Thero. I've had years of practice managing Seregil, and Alec's not half the bother."

"I suspect it will be easier than facing the prince and

lying," the young wizard replied. "I've never done that before. I don't think Nysander ever did, either."

"With Sebrahn's powers, perhaps the rhekaro could end the war," mused Magyana.

"Or wipe out the court and a lot of innocent Skalans," said Alec. "As you said, Thero, you and Magyana can best protect us by convincing everyone there that we're still recuperating."

"When we're not rummaging about in the Orëska vaults," he said as he and Magyana rose to go.

"I'm rather looking forward to it," said Magyana. "It's been a while since I poked around down there."

Seregil closed the door after them, then pulled off his boots and stretched out beside Alec, frowning.

"You're worried about taking him to Bôkthersa, aren't you?" asked Alec.

"Yes." Seregil took Alec's hand and absently rubbed his thumb over the scar on the palm. "But if Tyrus does know what Sebrahn is, that may go a long way to figuring out what to do. In the meantime, we need to keep a tight rein on him." He looked at the rhekaro, who was now watching them from the foot of the bed. "No more singing, you. Understand? Bad."

"Baaaad."

"That's right," Alec said. "And now, I need a real bath!"

"Yes, you do." Basin baths could only accomplish so much, but Seregil didn't really mind; when he was locked in that cold cellar room under Yhakobin's house, beaten and sick, Alec's unwashed scent on a pillow had saved his sanity and reaffirmed his resolve. It affected him the same way now, but this time Alec was safe beside him.

Never again!

"Talí?" He smoothed a hand over Alec's back, letting his fingers count the knobs of the younger man's spine.

His only answer was soft, even breathing. Alec was fast asleep. Seregil smiled and settled back against the pillows. Baths could wait.

"Ahek. Sleeeeping," Sebrahn rasped.

"Yes, sleeping. Go to the window."

The rhekaro slowly slid off the bed and went back to the window seat. Once there, he fixed his gaze on the two of them. Perhaps it was a trick of the rain still beating against the windowpanes, making the light cast weird shadows, but Seregil could have sworn that Sebrahn looked resentful.

Can't be helped, he thought. *I had him first and you're going to have to be the one who makes do.*

CHAPTER 2
✄
Wizard's Work

THE WIZARDS were at their door early the following morning.

Magyana reached into her coat and gave Seregil a handful of small, painted willow wands. "Here are your message sticks. Break one and Thero and I will know you need us and where you are. And do try to hang on to them this time."

Seregil gave her a wry look as he pocketed them. "Thank you."

"I have something for you, too," said Thero. "Actually, it's an experiment of sorts. I was up all night designing it. Nysander excelled at transformation spells, and he passed that on to me. I think I *might* be able to give Sebrahn a more normal appearance. I'd be happier attempting it in a proper casting room, but here we are. First, Alec, make Sebrahn understand that I mean no harm."

Alec reached out to Sebrahn and took his hands. "Thero is a friend, remember? He's going to help you, so don't be scared."

Looking somewhat less than reassured, Thero took a lump of blue chalk from his belt pouch. "Move the bed against the wall and roll back the carpet, will you?"

Seregil and Micum pushed the heavy rope bed out of the way with Alec still in it, and drew back the carpet. Thero drew a wide circle on the bare floorboards and inscribed a complex ring of symbols around the inside rim. Standing in the center of it, he ran a critical eye over his handiwork. "There. That should hold in the damage, if it all goes wrong."

"Goes wrong how? And what do you mean, 'should'?" demanded Micum.

"Well, I've never attempted magic on a being of this nature. Don't worry, I'll start with something simple. Bring Sebrahn into the circle, Seregil. And I need a few strands of Alec's hair, since Sebrahn was made from him."

Alec gave him the hair and the others joined him, sitting on the edge of the bed.

Thero took out his crystal wand and wrapped the hairs around it. With his free hand he gathered Sebrahn's long hair together, then ran the wand over the length of it from crown to ends. When he was finished, the rhekaro's shining hair was the same rich honey gold as Alec's.

"That's better," said Seregil, "but he's still too pale. The hair only makes it more obvious."

"I'm not done." Thero pulled out a small pouch and took out a pinch of some kind of brown powder. Bowing his head, Thero murmured a spell and sprinkled it on Sebrahn's head. In the blink of an eye the rhekaro had the sun-browned skin of a peasant boy. The only things not affected by the spell were his eyes. Those remained the same unnatural silver.

"That's the best I can do, I'm afraid. I don't want to risk blinding him." Thero drew a small knife and cut through the edge of the protective circle. The design disappeared in a flash of light and Sebrahn scampered back to Alec.

"He looks good," said Micum. "He really could be Alec's boy, now."

"His eyes are still a giveaway to anyone who knows what to look for, though," Seregil mused.

"Cut his hair into long bangs," Thero suggested. "It doesn't all have to be magic. You're the great master of disguise, as I recall."

Alec, who'd been cutting Sebrahn's hair several times a day for months now, went to work at that, and in a moment Sebrahn had a ragged fringe of hair hanging into his eyes. "That will have to do. How long will it last?" Thero asked Alec, brushing Sebrahn's hair back from his face to inspect the changes.

"Hopefully until I spell him back to normal. But again,

there's no telling what effect Sebrahn's unusual nature will have on the magic. It might all wear off tomorrow."

"What happens when his hair grows?" asked Micum.

"The spell is on his body, not just the hair. It should be fine."

"What about your magic? Couldn't that attract attention if we run across the wrong sort of people?" asked Seregil.

"Not with transmogrification spells like these. His skin and hair really are that color for now."

Seregil clasped hands with him. "Thank you. This will make a tremendous difference. Really, you're invaluable, as always."

Thero grinned. "Take care of yourselves. I hope you find what you're seeking."

"I hope you do, as well."

Everyone went to see the wizards off except Alec and Sebrahn. Left behind in their continuing seclusion, they stood together at the window and watched the *Lark* set sail.

"Leee-ving," said Sebrahn.

"And so will we. Soon."

Alec felt a bit stronger today. Since he was up already, he decided to attempt a walk around the room, keeping an ear out for Mydri's heavy step on the stair just in case.

He was dizzy and unsteady on his feet, and took a few falls in the process until Sebrahn came over to walk beside him. Then Alec kept a hand on the rhekaro's shoulder to steady himself, and they walked slowly back and forth between the bed and the door. It felt good to move, even if occasionally the floor seemed to pitch like the deck of a ship under sail.

He grinned down at Sebrahn. "I hope I don't need one of your healings today."

Sebrahn immediately held up a pale forefinger. Alec gave it a gentle squeeze. "Thank you, but I was just joking."

Sebrahn cocked his head slightly to one side, and his eyebrows drew down just the slightest bit.

Alec stared at him in surprise. On a normal person's face, that look would have indicated confusion. "Joking. I didn't mean that I did need . . . Oh, hell. Never mind."

Sebrahn stared up at him for a long moment, held out his finger again, and then brought it back to his chest. "Jok . . . king."

Alec laughed. "Well, sort of."

Sebrahn did it again. "Joking." This time his face twitched as he tried to approximate Alec's grin.

"I've often found that a sense of humor is a sign of an intelligent mind."

Startled, Alec turned to find Seregil leaning in the now open doorway. "Sneaking up on me?"

"I came to warn you that I can hear you staggering around up here. Lucky for you, Mydri got caught up in conversation down at the quay. You're looking a little pale. Let's get you back to bed."

"I can do it!" Alec protested, then turned too quickly and fell on his face before Seregil could catch him. Sebrahn sprang to his side and crouched there. When Seregil reached down to help Alec, Sebrahn hunkered lower and hissed at him.

Seregil stepped back in surprise. "It's only me. He's the one who fell over."

Alec sat up and gathered a handful of Sebrahn's hair, giving him a not-so-gentle shake. "No! Bad! Go to Seregil."

Sebrahn's face was blank again as he rose and walked to Seregil's side. The older man took the rhekaro's face between his hands. "I wouldn't hurt Alec. I never will. I love him. Love?" He looked to Alec, who only shrugged. Seregil gingerly gave Sebrahn a hug. "Love. You can trust me, little one." He pointed to his own chest, then to Sebrahn's. "Trust."

Sebrahn cocked his head again, then touched Seregil's chest and rasped out, "Serigl."

Alec laughed. It was how he'd taught Sebrahn his name, and others—by pointing. Apparently that was the only way Sebrahn was going to interpret the gesture from now on.

Seregil lifted the unresisting rhekaro in his arms and deposited him on the window seat. Then he did the same with Alec, lifting him onto their bed and stretching out beside him. "So," he drawled, sliding a hand down Alec's side, then up again, rucking up the rumpled linen nightshirt as he went. "Getting our strength back, are we?"

Alec shivered under his touch. "Yes, but it's still daylight outside, Sebrahn is staring at us, and you left the door wide open. Again."

Seregil nuzzled his neck. "I'll close the door."

Alec grabbed him before he could make good on that. "And I need a bath."

"All right. You shall have one." Seregil sighed. "We really are going to have to do something about Sebrahn, though."

"I know. Now, bath?"

"Yes, my lord. At once, my lord." Seregil laughed as he headed for the door. "But I still say we're going to have to find some way of dealing with Sebrahn, and not just because I don't want him staring at my ass when we're—"

"I know!"

"It's like having a dog around. Always underfoot."

"Don't say that!" Alec called after him, but Seregil was already headed down the stairs.

Within the hour servants brought up a small brass tub and steaming cans of hot water from the kitchen.

"Sebrahn first," Alec insisted, fully enjoying handing out a few orders after all the ones he'd been suffering.

"Let me, then," said Seregil. "You're too wobbly and you have more than enough bruises."

The rhekaro had no bodily functions, and no particular smell, but he still got grubby. This was his first real bath, but he showed no sign of fear as Seregil mixed cans of warm and cold water and poured it over him. Sebrahn just sat there while Seregil washed him with the cloth, then lathered his hair. When the bath was over and he had Sebrahn wrapped in a flannel, they both smelled nicely of rose-scented soap.

Seregil gave the rhekaro an uncommonly fond look, surprising after their earlier exchange. "I forget, sometimes, how much he resembles you. And even more so now, thanks to Thero. I suppose it's almost like seeing you at that age. Now then, your turn."

With Seregil's help, Alec sank into the warm water and rested his head on his bare knees, letting Seregil scrub his back and wash his long hair. "Don't you think I should cut some of it off?" he asked yet again as Seregil's finger caught in a tangle.

"It's up to you, talí, but I like it," Seregil told him, as always.

"Then you have to grow yours out again, since you seem to have forgotten the problems."

"I am, but I can't do it quite as fast as our little friend can." He pulled the chair over to the side of the tub to keep him company as Alec took over with the cloth.

When Seregil sat down, Sebrahn climbed into his lap. Seregil smiled down at him.

Sebrahn is as much pet as child, thought Alec. *A pet that can kill.* Seeing the two of them like that, he wondered, *What do I call this? A "family"?*

But he knew better, and that brought a now familiar tightness around his heart. He brushed it aside. Later. They'd figure things out later. Right now he was just going to enjoy the damn bath!

"Are you all right, talí?"

"The water's just getting cold."

Seregil helped him out and wrapped him in a large flannel. Alec leaned against him, the water dripping from his hair onto the floor around his bare feet and soaking the front of Seregil's shirt.

"I do feel better."

"You smell better, too."

Seregil's warm, deep chuckle vibrated against Alec's heart. Taking him by the hand, he drew Seregil back to the unmade bed. "Sebrahn, go look out the window."

The rhekaro obeyed the now familiar order at once.

Alec glanced at the door, making sure it was closed. Satisfied, he gave Seregil a push and tumbled them both into bed, pulling Seregil on top of him and holding him tight.

"What's this?" Seregil asked, smiling down at him.

"If you have to ask, then it's been too long," Alec said

with a chuckle of his own. "I keep telling you, I'm getting better!"

And Alec must have trained the rhekaro well during the long days up here, Seregil thought later, for Sebrahn never took his gaze from the harbor as they rolled and surged and moaned together, tangled in Alec's long wet hair.

When Alec woke up again some time later, it was still light out, Seregil was gone, and Mydri was looming over him. "My, aren't you energetic."

The look in those dark eyes left him completely tongue-tied as he waited for another upbraiding, but she just shook her head. "How do you do that nightrunning business with such a guilty face?"

Sebrahn squatted at the end of the bed, eyeing the healer with an intensity that made Alec nervous. Sebrahn had already been told that the various household members were friends, but if he'd turn on Seregil, all bets were off.

Mydri shook a colorful little rag and yarn doll from her sleeve and placed it in Sebrahn's hands. "A gift for you, little one. Be a good—rhekaro and let me see how your Alec is healing."

Sebrahn regarded the doll for a moment, then tried to stuff it into his own sleeve as Mydri began her examination.

She ran cool fingers over the delicate new skin covering the wounds on Alec's chest and throat. Then she went about feeling his pulse, listening to his heart and bowels, and clucking her tongue over the bruises on his arms. All the same, when she'd finished at last, she seemed pleased. "You're healing faster than you have any right to, you know." She glanced over at Sebrahn, who had given up on the sleeve idea and was staring at the doll again. "Whatever he did, it was powerful, and it's clear he's devoted to you."

She pulled another doll from her sleeve and got Sebrahn's attention. "Don't I have a nice baby?" she asked, holding the doll against her chest and patting it gently. "Will you take good care of your baby, too?"

Slowly, Sebrahn copied her, cuddling his own doll. "Baby?"

"You see?" said Alec. "He does understand things."

Mydri watched closely as Sebrahn brought the doll's painted linen face up to his own, silvery eyes crossing a little as he studied it. "I've seen how he mimics what he sees you doing. Show him gentleness and he'll be gentle." She paused, still watching Sebrahn. "I doubt this change of appearance will hide him well enough. His aura sometimes extends beyond this room, and there are those in the house who can feel it."

Alec waited for her to go on, to tell him she didn't want him to go to Bôkthersa. Instead she surprised him with a smile that made the blue lines of the healer's marks under her eyes tilt up. "Our family owes you a great deal, little brother, for all you've done for Seregil. There was so much pain in him at Sarikali. Yet even then I could tell that you'd given him back some of what Ilar í Sontir took from him, all those years ago. What was it like, meeting that man?"

"Seregil told you?"

"About how Ilar duped you with a false name, and the way he treated Seregil? Yes."

Suddenly uneasy, Alec sat twisting the edge of the quilt between his fingers. "It was—strange."

"It hurt, I'm sure. Both the betrayal, and Seregil bringing him with you."

"Yes. I still don't understand why he did that. Ilar treated him like filth once he had Seregil under his thumb, and he was nothing but trouble after we escaped."

"But according to what Seregil told me, he helped you. Something about a secret way?"

"Well, yes," Alec admitted. "But in the end he just ran away. We might as well have killed him."

"Could you have done that, Alec í Amasa?"

He thought about it, then shook his head. "No. He was too pathetic and—well . . ."

"Let me tell you something that you're probably too young to have learned yet. Love and hate aren't so far apart."

Alec shook his head, remembering. "Seregil told me he

used to love Ilar, and now he loves me, but that there was no one else in between, among all the people he bedded. And I could tell that Ilar wanted to make things up with him."

"And did Seregil let him?"

"No." Alec didn't want to think about his own jealousy and doubts. He didn't want to remember the sight of Ilar naked and trying to kiss Seregil by the stream that day, or the way Seregil had appeared unable or unwilling to stop him.

Mydri smiled and patted his hand. "You can't change his past, Alec. Neither can he. Let it go and turn your thoughts to the journey home. Now, please listen to your healer and stop throwing yourself around."

When she was gone he disregarded her admonition and went back to the window seat, bored and wondering where everyone else was. Sebrahn climbed into his lap. The rhekaro still had the doll, and he picked curiously at it as he rested his head against Alec's chest.

Alec rubbed his cheek against that cool, silken hair and stared out the window. It had finally stopped raining, but the sky remained dreary with low, dark clouds. The harbor beyond was nearly empty today; the fishermen were taking advantage of the break in the weather. Adzriel's ship, a sleek caravel, rode at anchor like a dark swan.

"Bôkthersa!" he murmured with a thrill of excitement that swept away all the dark thoughts. He'd forgotten to ask if Adzriel would keep him locked away there.

That afternoon Seregil, his sisters, and Micum came to his room. Micum caught Alec's eye and gave him a warning look. Seregil and the women looked like they'd been arguing. Seregil's mouth was set in a stubborn line, and Mydri seemed furious.

Adzriel closed the door behind them and locked it.

Mydri was glaring at Sebrahn; it was as if their gentle conversation earlier had never happened. "Adzriel told me about the rhekaro's true powers, Seregil." She turned on Alec. "And you said nothing, either!"

"I meant for them to tell you once we were under way," Adzriel explained, interceding for them.

Mydri was not mollified. "Adzriel, how can you possibly bring something so dangerous to our own fai'thast?"

"Seregil is our brother, in blood if not in name. Since Alec is his *talímenios,* he's our responsibility, and through him, Sebrahn." She gave her sister a stern look. "Whatever Sebrahn is, he's theirs, and thus ours. Isn't that so?"

"Well, yes, but—"

"Then it's settled. They'll be safe there, and can take what time they need to discover more about Sebrahn."

Mydri stood up, angry now. "Adzriel, as your sister, and as a ranking member of the clan, I protest. I love these two as much as you do, but—"

Adzriel gave her a look that cut her off midsentence. "I don't speak now as your sister, or his, but as your khirnari. And I say that it is safer by far to have this rhekaro within our control than to lose him to those who would use him for ill in the world. I have spoken!"

It was amazing to see Mydri cowed. Alec was a bit shaken himself, and Micum, too. No wonder Adzriel had been elected by her clan, in spite of her relative youth.

"As you wish then, Khirnari," Mydri said, throwing up her hands. "I only hope you don't come to regret your decision."

So do I, Alec thought, sending up a silent prayer to Illior.

"So, what route are you planning?" asked Micum, deftly changing the subject.

"We'll put in at Chillian and ride from there," said Adzriel.

"We can cut the ride by half if we go north to Half Moon Cove and go by way of Smuggler's Pass," said Seregil. "I can travel that road home with my eyes shut."

Home. Alec thought he caught a suspicious glitter in Seregil's eyes and felt a small tightness in his own throat. If Adzriel meant all she'd said, then it was his home, as well.

CHAPTER 3

❧

A Rude Awakening

ALEC DRIFTED off to sleep that night feeling less of an out-cast. To the Bôkthersans he was family, rather than an unwanted guest. With Seregil beside him and Sebrahn curled at the foot of the bed, he drifted off into a deeper slumber than he had in days.

So it was a nasty shock when someone yanked him off the bed and onto the cold floor and stuffed something into his mouth. The shutters were open and by the faint moonlight he could make out several darkly dressed men, one of whom was holding a struggling Sebrahn. They'd stuffed a rag in the rhekaro's mouth, which explained why Sebrahn wasn't singing a killing song. In a way that was a relief, since Alec had no way of knowing if he'd kill only their assailants or everyone else within earshot, as well.

Seregil, naked and armed with one of the swords they'd brought from Plenimar, was fighting off two more men by the door.

How in Bilairy's name did they get in without us or any-one else hearing them?

No sooner had Alec taken that in than the two men hold-ing him dragged him to the open window and thrust him out feet first, keeping hold of his hands, and he found himself dangling above the cobbled courtyard. There was no ques-tion of pulling free—Bilairy's Balls, he hated heights!

And falling even more so—which he was. But he hardly had time to panic before two men caught him and pinioned his arms. Both of them wore hoods and black cloth across their lower faces. He struggled in earnest now, though to little avail as they half dragged, half carried him toward the courtyard gate, where more dark figures waited. Where were the watchmen?

Suddenly someone came close enough to try to force a bag over his head. Seeing one slim chance, he struck out wildly, finding the bag man's belt and the knife hanging there. Wrenching it free, he slashed at anything he could reach and succeeded in stabbing the man holding the bag and driving the two who'd been holding him back long enough to assess the situation. They were too big to be Aurënfaie, armed with long knives and dressed in leathers and boots. He, on the other hand, was barefoot in a nightshirt and badly overmatched. He was wondering if he could outrun them in his current condition when armed men burst into the court-yard and attacked his attackers, Micum in the lead.

Alec got out of the way fast and bolted for the house. Shouldering his way through a crowd of alarmed women, he ran up the stairs, still clutching the bloody knife.

Where was Seregil and why hadn't Sebrahn sung? He was grateful for the latter, but at a loss to understand.

He found Seregil on the floor by the bed, bloody but still alive, with a struggling Sebrahn in his arms, one hand clamped firmly over the rhekaro's mouth. Three men lay dead around him, bloody enough to be Seregil's victims rather than Sebrahn's.

"Tell him," Seregil gasped. "Hurry! He won't listen to me."

Alec dropped the knife and took Sebrahn's face between his hands, putting his mouth close to the rhekaro's ear. "Don't sing, Sebrahn! That would be bad now. Very bad!"

The rhekaro went still. Seregil waited a moment, then slowly removed his hand and pulled out the gag.

"Baaaad," Sebrahn whispered.

"By the Light, what happened here?" Adzriel exclaimed, pushing through the excited little crowd that had gathered in the doorway. Mydri was close behind.

Alec was doubly glad of Thero's transformation magic

now, though he could hear others whispering about the color of Sebrahn's eyes. Mydri shooed the onlookers away and closed the door.

"So?" she asked, hurrying to the bed.

"Assassins and kidnappers, I'd say," Seregil panted, pressing a hand to his side. Blood was seeping through his fingers, and there was already a small pool of it on the floor by his hip.

Alec looked around frantically. The washstand had been spared in the scuffle. Grabbing the pitcher, he knelt in front of Sebrahn, who'd already slashed his own palm with the knife that Alec had dropped. The rhekaro held his hand over the water, then quickly lifted out the dark blue lotus blossom that formed there.

"Here." Seregil took his hand away and Alec saw a deep slash across Seregil's ribs. "Bastard stabbed me while I was asleep. It's a good thing his aim was off. He should have slit my throat. Bilairy's Balls! Those sons of whores were good."

Mydri gave him a light cuff to the back of the head that made him wince, then stifle a grin.

It took four blossoms to close the wound, and Sebrahn laid more on it, sending the healing deeper. When he was finished, Alec cut his own finger more deeply than usual and let the drops fall on Sebrahn's tongue. The wound across Sebrahn's palm closed before their eyes.

"It can't heal itself?" asked Mydri.

"Not that we've seen," Seregil told her.

"Yhakobin made me feed him like this, and the first one, after he sliced them up," Alec told her. "I saw a hand grow from the stump of Sebrahn's wrist, and an eye for the first one."

Mydri stroked Sebrahn's hair, her expression softer than he'd ever seen it before. "Poor things. Poor, wretched little things! But why didn't he sing and protect you?"

Seregil shrugged. "Who knows? As it was, he killed Yhakobin only when it was clear that Alec was in severe danger."

"How in the world would he know?"

"He just does," said Alec.

Mydri cupped Sebrahn's chin and looked deeply into his eyes. "So strange!" she murmured. "There is a mind there, but not a normal one, just—like fragments floating around."

Alec hadn't realized how badly he was shaking until Adzriel knelt and put her arms around him. "Are you hurt, Alec?" There was blood on his nightshirt.

"No. Where's Micum?"

"Here," Micum said, pushing his way through the crowd gathered in the doorway. He was wearing breeches and nothing else. The blood spattered across his chest was someone else's.

"Get the bodies outside and put them with the others!" Riagil ordered, storming into the room. "The rest of you go back to your rooms. There's nothing for you to do here."

"Please, leave us alone to tend our wounded," said Adzriel.

"I'll have tubs prepared at once," Yhali said as calmly as if she dealt with such intrusions on a regular basis, yet Alec very much doubted that she did.

Riagil shooed the others out, then righted a fallen chair and sat down, clearly intending to stay.

Mydri and Micum helped Seregil and Alec back to the bed. Sebrahn climbed up and nestled in between them.

"Are you sure you're not hurt?" Mydri asked Alec, taking in his bloodstained nightshirt. It had been torn and hung off one shoulder.

"Yes, I'm fine. Seregil?"

"Much better. Thank you, Sebrahn. So much for keeping him secret, though," Seregil said, frowning. "Micum, are any of them still alive?"

"Not a one," Micum replied. "Khirnari, your swordsmen are well trained but a bit too quick."

"Perhaps, but the invaders killed two of my watchmen," Riagil replied, looking shaken and angry. "I have men out looking for more of them and any boats they came in on."

Seregil rose and grabbed his breeches and coat from the top of the clothes chest. Yanking them on, he pulled on his tall boots and headed for the door. "We can search the bodies, anyway. Alec, you stay here with Sebrahn."

Alec was in no condition to argue.

"Mydri and I will stay, too," Adzriel sat down on the edge of the bed and took Alec's bloodstained hand in hers. Her hands were trembling.

Seregil paused in front of Riagil. "I am sorry we brought this trouble into your house."

"I regret that I did not keep you safe," Riagil replied. As Seregil hurried off after Micum, Riagil turned to Alec. "Who were these assassins?"

"That's what Seregil and Micum are trying to find out. It all happened so fast, and their faces were covered. If they'd spoken, I might have known the accent, but no one did. But they were damn good, whoever they were. If they had managed to kill Seregil before he woke up, Sebrahn and I would probably be gone." Unless they'd uncovered Sebrahn's mouth, of course, and that really would have been the end of their secrets. Too many people had witnessed Sebrahn's healing, and word was probably spreading through the house.

"I see. Then I will leave you and see what your friends can find." He rose and gave Adzriel a small bow. "I give my regrets to you and your clan, as well, Khirnari."

"The fault is not yours, I'm sure," she replied graciously, and Alec suspected the exchange had something to do with Aurënfaie honor, because Riagil looked relieved as he went out.

The dead were laid out in a row just outside the gates. Men held torches for Seregil and Micum as they began their examination. With help from some of Riagil's men, they stripped the bodies and studied the clothing.

Riagil joined them, looking on intently.

"They're certainly not 'faie," Seregil said. These men had hairy chests and were too bulky in their build. Seregil shook his head, wondering how Alec had managed to hold off so many of them in his weakened state.

"Pretty damn plain," said Micum, looking over one of the leather vests.

"Let me see the stitching." Seregil turned it inside out, then checked some of the other clothing. "Most have crossed stitches instead of slanting. That could be Mycenian work, or north Plenimaran."

"The knives may be Plenimaran, too."

They turned their attention to the bodies now, looking for any sort of guild mark or other tattoo that would indicate who they were or where they had come from.

None of them carried a purse, so there were no coins to tell them anything, either.

Seregil took one of the lamps and held it close to one of the dead men's faces. "The lower portion of the face is considerably lighter."

"He shaved his beard."

"Yes."

Several of the others showed the same pale jawline.

"Looks like Plenimarans to me," said Micum.

"There are dark-haired, bearded, hairy-chested men in Skala, too, and Mycena."

"True."

Micum examined the man's hands. "Callused, but no dirt ground into them or under the nails. And more callused on one hand than the other. They were swordsmen by trade."

Seregil did the same with several others, inspecting palms and fingers. "This one was left-handed. And this one was an archer."

"If they were assassins, then why didn't they kill Alec and Sebrahn, as well?" asked Riagil.

"Because they weren't," Seregil replied, still at work. "They were kidnappers, and very well-informed ones, too. They not only knew that we're in Gedre; they knew which room we were in. And they meant to kill me, not take me. You probably have a spy in your house, Riagil."

"I will make inquiries, of course."

Good luck with that, thought Seregil. *If your spy is good enough not to be noticed before, then he's likely to just lay low now.* "Have you had anyone new come to live in your household in the past month? A guest? A new servant?"

"No."

"It could be someone who visits the house," said Micum.

"We're a trade port. People come and go every day!"

Seregil stood up and wiped his hands on his breeches. "Well, if I had to wager on it, I'd say they were Plenimarans who somehow managed to track us here, sent by someone who knew the alchemist. I think it may be time for us to move on."

Yhali had the tubs set up in the kitchen, and Alec was forced to swallow his modesty in front of the servants as they tended to him and the others. Sebrahn remained calm when a pretty young maid gently sponged the blood from his face and chest, though he wouldn't let go of Alec's hand.

By the time they returned to their room, someone had cleared away the wreckage of the fight. The carpet was gone, too. Micum came in as they settled into the freshly made bed with Sebrahn safely between them.

Seregil fell back against the pillow beside Alec with a groan.

"Does it still hurt where Sebrahn healed you?" asked Micum.

"A bit. His flowers work wonders, but it's not an instant cure."

Micum was quiet for a moment, looking pensively at Sebrahn. "Do you think he could do something for this game leg of mine?"

"Probably," said Alec. Someone had left a cup of water on the righted night table. He handed it to Sebrahn. "Show him the scars, Micum."

Micum stripped down his leather trousers, showing him the ropy mass of scar tissue the *dyrmagnos* had made of the back of his thigh and calf.

"Go help him, Sebrahn," Alec coaxed. "Can you heal his leg?"

Sebrahn slipped from the bed and squeezed blood from his cut finger into the cup. It took a lot of flowers.

"I wonder why he didn't try to heal him sooner?" said Seregil.

"I don't think he notices old wounds," Alec replied, holding out his left palm, the one with the round shiny scar in the middle. "He's never paid any attention to this. That first girl he healed had an infected foot, and you were covered in blood tonight. I don't know—maybe he knows by smell. Is it working, Micum?"

Sebrahn sat back. Micum flexed his leg, then stood up. "By the Flame, sprout, that's a damn sight better!" The scars remained, but it was clear that Micum had more use of that leg than he had before. He picked Sebrahn up and kissed him on the nose, then put him back in bed with Alec. "Well, I'm past sleeping tonight. If you two don't mind, I'd like to sit here for a while."

"You'll get no argument from me," Seregil said with a yawn. "I've had enough excitement for one night."

The following day Seregil and Micum went out with Riagil's men to continue the search along the waterfront. Just after midday they found an abandoned longboat at the far end of the beach to the west of town. It was of Skalan make. Leaving the Gedre men to make inquiries in the area, Seregil and Micum walked back to the clan house, sunk in thought and frustration.

"Well, what do you think?" Micum asked as they neared the house.

"The boat could have drifted off from any Skalan warship or trader that's dropped anchor here. Or it could be like the clothing—something to throw us off."

"I still think the assassins are from Plenimar."

"So do I, but how did they get here? Fly?"

"Never mind that. Who sent them?"

"Someone who knows about Sebrahn, obviously. The alchemist's kin? The Overlord?"

"The Overlord? If that's true, my friend, you've really put your foot in it this time, and deep!"

"Then let's hope I'm wrong. Still . . ." He rubbed at the

healing wound on his side. "Yhakobin knew the secret of making them. What if he's not the only one?"

"And that person would know what Sebrahn really is."

Seregil walked on in silence, hands clasped behind his back. It looked like they hadn't quite escaped, after all—which made their presence here a continuing danger.

Visions

IT TOOK Seneth ä Matriel Danata Hâzadriël, khirnari of the Hâzadriëlfaie people, and her escort several hours' steep riding to reach the Retha'noi witch man's hut, which stood in an ash grove near the edge of his mountain village. Seneth had started after an early breakfast, and now the midday sun was glinting harshly on the distant crags framing Ravensfell Pass.

The hut was a small, round structure made from sticks and withy, and covered in stretched deerhide. There was no sign of Turmay, except for a thin plume of smoke rising from the hole in the center of the roof.

"Stay here," Seneth ordered the other riders. Going to the low door, she pulled the long fronts of her coat and tunic back from her trousered legs and crawled on hands and knees into the dimness of the witch's hut. The change from light reflecting off snow left her nearly blind for an instant, except for the column of light shining through the smoke hole and the glow of the fire beneath.

"Welcome, Khirnari," the witch greeted her, and now she could make him out, sitting cross-legged on the far side of the fire, wearing nothing but a crude loincloth.

"Thank you for word of good news, my friend." It was hot and close, too. She shrugged off her fur-lined coat and sat down on a pile of furs across the fire from the witch. Turmay's eyes were closed, his stooped body so still that he appeared not to even be breathing. His grey curls hung motionless over his shoulders.

She'd seen the witch marks on his hands and face the night that her friend, Belan ä Talía, had brought him to her after both had seen visions of a *tayan'gil*—or "white child," as he put it—far away in the south. Someplace where a tayan'gil had no business being made.

Half naked as he was, she could see the elaborate witch marks that covered his shoulders and chest. Other marks circled his shins like the patterns on the *oo'lu* lying silent across his lap. Seneth had known generations of Retha'noi over the course of her long life. Only the male witches used the oo'lu—a long, intricately decorated horn made from a hollowed-out sapling. Each had a unique pattern of decoration, except for the black handprint somewhere along its smooth polished length. Turmay must have been playing it quite recently; the tingle of Retha'noi magic hung in the air, enveloping her like a scent.

Which was better than the smell of the hovel: sweat and hides, sour milk, pungent smoke-dried meat, and a body that would not see a proper bath until spring.

"Did you find the ride difficult, Khirnari?"

Seneth started as Belan ä Talía leaned forward into the circle of firelight. "What have you learned, my friend?" she asked them both. Belan was a seer, a rarity among their kind and probably due to her mixed blood. The rare intermarriage with the Retha'noi had gradually become tolerated, since the hill folk had proven to be staunch allies and kept to the valley as jealously as the 'faie, if not more so. Breeding with an outsider, though? That was unthinkable, and strictly prohibited.

"The tayan'gil is in Aurënen," Belan replied. Belan and Turmay had been searching together ever since they'd had their first visions of the tayan'gil.

"Aurënen? Are you telling me that the Aurënfaie would create such a creature?"

"Who can say, Khirnari? We only know that one is there."

"Where in Aurënen?"

The witch opened his eyes at last, and she saw that they were red-rimmed and bloodshot. "I can show you, though I don't know the name of the place."

He lifted the wax mouthpiece of the oo'lu and settled his lips inside it. Puffing out his cheeks, he began to play. This horn was almost four feet long, and he had to shift to keep the end of it out of the fire.

It was not music, though the strange buzzing, hooting, booming drone produced by the oo'lu was not unpleasant. If you listened attentively, you could hear the sawing song of summer cicadas, the bellow of a bull, the peeping of tiny marsh frogs, and birdcalls. The patterns were complex, when played by an expert. It was impossible for those not trained to it to get more than a breathy farting sound out of it.

Turmay played a soft song this time, with the hiss of wind over snow and owl calls mingled with the slow drone.

"Close your eyes and touch the oo'lu," Belan told her.

Seneth did so, and the horn, smooth and warmed by the witch's breath, vibrated against her palm.

Light flared behind her closed lids as if she'd stepped outside again, then she had the dizzying sensation of flying up through the smoke hole.

Confused images tumbled across the surface of her mind—the blurred glimpses of brown steppes, mountains less jagged than those that protected her fai'thast, and the flash of sunlight across a great broad expanse of water.

The Great Lake, near the Tirfaie town called Wolde. Years ago she'd ventured from the valley as an *Ebrados* rider, and they'd stolen through the sleeping town. She could still remember the reek of the place, and the filth. But that lake! Standing on the shore under a full moon, she'd never seen anything so beautiful.

Yet Turmay's magic carried her on, farther and farther from anything familiar, over forests and grasslands, and over a body of water that made the lake seem no more than a puddle.

The sea, the witch whispered in her mind through the droning of the oo'lu. *My people once lived all around its shores, until the light-skinned people drove us into the mountains. We were fishermen and sailors, and the cries of the gulls are still in our bones.* The oo'lu song shifted to a strange, high-pitched call, like that of the white birds she'd seen circling the lake. *Beyond, and beyond again lies your true homeland, Seneth, daughter of Matriel.*

They passed over a mountainous island, and then over the sea again to a land unlike her own except for the spine of mountains bleak against a dark blue sky.

"Aurënen," Belan told her, sounding very far away.

The swath of land between the mountains and the sea was pale and dry like a bone. Turmay's magic carried her to a town on the shore. The tiny houses along the water looked like nubs of white chalk set in sand, with familiar domed roofs.

The white child is here.

Can you show it to me?

I cannot see it, but I feel its presence like a canker in my mind.

"I can't see its face in my dreams, Khirnari," whispered Belan. "It has some magic about it that I can't break through. But it is small like a child, and it has no wings."

"But you're certain our blood runs in its veins?" Seneth murmured. The blood of the First Dragon, the one from whose blood the 'faie had sprung, ran deeper in her people, giving them strong magic. Since coming here and marrying among themselves, a few children had even been born with tiny appendages like wings on their backs, or eyes the color of moonlight on steel. Somehow the Tírfaie dark witches in Hâzadriël's day had discovered the secret of their blood and found a way to use it to make tayan'gils, whose powers of healing surpassed anything seen before. Rumor had come down through the centuries of other uses the witches made of the creatures and their white blood—the White Road, as they called it—to create elixirs with great powers, though no one knew what, exactly.

"Yes, there is no doubt," Belan told her. "But it's not pure. It's not right."

Not pure. Seneth's heart quickened at the possibility that those words embodied.

"It will take months to reach Aurënen," Seneth mused, concerned. Who knew what disasters might happen by then? There was no way of knowing what the power of this strange tayan'gil would be, but the uneasiness that had plagued her since Belan had first come to her was stronger now. If a tayan'gil born of impure blood somehow harmed an Aurënfaie, the shame would rest with her and her clan. The gulf of centuries that had opened between them and their Aurënfaie ancestors could not change that. Atui could not be circumscribed by time or place.

This tayan'gil must be reclaimed and so the Ebrados would ride—no matter how long the trek, no matter what the risk. It was the way of her people—one that had preserved them down all the centuries since Hâzadriël had brought the chosen to safety in the north. It was the honor and the burden of the Ebrados, guarding the White Road, and there was no other way.

Slowly, the vision faded, and the hot, heavy air closed in around her again.

"Thank you, my friends," she said, anxious to get outside again. But something had been niggling at the back of her mind since the first night Belan had brought the witch to her.

"Turmay, why did you see this 'child'? It's nothing to do with the Retha'noi."

The old man shrugged. "The Mother sends the visions. I follow them." His fingers moved over the oo'lu, tracing a patterned band. "It's written here, in the journey path. So I will go with your seekers."

Seneth regarded him in surprise. As far as she knew, the Retha'noi never left the valley. Then again, they kept to themselves and did not answer to her. Who knew their comings and goings? Moreover, she reasoned, a witch with such powers would certainly be an asset for the search. "Thank you, my friend."

Emerging from the hut, she pulled on her mittens and shielded her eyes for a moment against the glare off the snow, inhaling deeply. The sun had moved less than an hour across the sky.

The unpleasant odor of the hut clung to her hair and clothes. Mounting her shaggy mare, she led the way down the trail and through the Retha'noi village, then took the steep, packed snow road beyond at a gallop, enjoying the rush of sharp, clean wind against her face.

Turmay sat staring into the fire for some time after Belan and the khirnari had gone, running his fingers around the journey band; the balance must be kept. The length of the journey between the doors of life and death was for the Mother to decide, and those journeys—like a river—flowed in only one direction. The white child changed this. The Mother was angry.

He regarded the oo'lu sadly. It was a fine instrument. He'd woven many healings with it, many births, as well as other, less kind magic when necessary. He'd had this one almost ten years, and waited for the time its patterns foretold.

No witch made his own oo'lu. No, you searched for a hollow branch or sapling large enough to play well, preferably one hollowed by ants. Then you took it to the oldest witch you could find, for him to make it and sing it into being. It was the old one who had the visions and painted them into the rings of the oo'lu, and he who sang the fire song and tossed the new horn across the campfire for you to catch and mark the part of your destiny that would happen next. When the destiny of that oo'lu had been fulfilled, the instrument cracked. Then it was time for a new oo'lu, a new path. On this oo'lu, the old witch Rao, long dead now, had painted one ring that had never been painted before in Turmay's lifetime, perhaps never before ever. This was one of the ones his handprint had spanned, together with Wanderer, Uniter, and Father of Many. Not even Rao had known what this other ring was called, or why the Mother had put it into his dreams.

"You will know when you know," the old witch had said with a shrug.

So far only Father of Many had come to pass; not only his own, but the babies he played into men's loins and women's bellies at the moon festivals. He had not wandered nor united anyone in a way that had cracked this oo'lu, but ever since he'd dreamed the white child, he didn't expect to carry it much longer. But the Mother had not yet shown him how to accomplish her purpose—to destroy the white child.

Seneth arrived home to find the captain of the Ebrados riders waiting for her in the hall. Rieser í Stellen, who was also a carpenter when the Ebrados were not needed, rose from his seat by the hearth and bowed respectfully. Tall Rieser he was called, for the fact that this lean stork of a man stood half a head taller than anyone else in the clan, and favored dark clothing, which made him look even taller. He was also known as Rieser the Grim, for reasons just as obvious; he was not a joyful man. All the same, his keen grey eyes betrayed his anticipation as she handed her coat to a servant and sat down by the fire to pull off her boots.

"What news, Khirnari?" he asked.

"It's time to gather your riders, my friend. I know where you must go."

"We can be off at dawn."

Seneth leaned forward to warm the chill from her hands. "Sit with me, and I will tell you the route. And you'll have a guide, one whom I think will prove most useful. Do you know a Retha'noi named Turmay?"

"I do. He's an honorable man—and a powerful witch, by all accounts. But how will he guide us?"

"He and Belan have worked out where the tayan'gil is. It is in Aurënen, in a town on the northern coast."

"Really?" He looked at once surprised and uncharacteristically pleased. "It will be good to see that land. I still have my grandmother's green sen'gai." He absently touched the blue-and-white sen'gai all Hâzadriëlfaie wore: blue for the sky, under which Hâzadriël and her people had wandered for so long, banded with white for the White Road they'd traveled, and which ran in their veins. It was time to follow that road again.

He paused, then said, "Could it be *her* child who's behind this?"

"Or the White Road blood has appeared again in Aurënen, but I think it more likely that you are right."

Rieser shook his head with a grim smile. "If I am, what should I do with the ya'shel?"

"Bring him back if possible. If not, then kill him."

Rieser rose and bowed with a hand to his heart. "I'm honored to ride again, Khirnari."

Seneth smiled up at him. "You have never failed me, Rieser í Stellen. I wish you a safe journey and a successful hunt."

For as long as the followers of Hâzadriël had lived in this valley, there had been Ebrados—the Hunters of the White Road—and for the past fifty-eight years Rieser í Stellen had been one of them. The Ebrados weren't called upon often anymore; the generation that had settled this valley was long dead, and most of the people now didn't look past the mountains that guarded them for anything they wanted. Occasionally a few adventurous youngsters tried to sneak out through the pass. If the guards didn't see them, the Ebrados went to bring them back. There had been only a few serious cases in the last hundred years, and all but one successfully hunted down.

Ireya ä Shaar had been the exception; her name was a bitter taste on the tongue of the clan. She had lain with a Tírfaie, a fact revealed at the child's birth; no 'faie child had yellow hair and eyes the color of dusk on a winter's night. No one knew how she'd met the man, or why she had betrayed her own people to bear a forbidden half-breed son, only that she had given him to his father to save. Her own brothers had killed her, and the Tír man had killed them. He and the child had never been found.

Syall í Konthus had been captain then, and they'd spent the whole summer trying to track down the mysterious Tír and the baby, but to no avail. Month after month, Syall rode out, even after the khirnari called off the hunt and none of the other Ebrados would go with him, until one spring day when his horse found her way back to the clan stables riderless. The dried blood crusted on her withers and the saddle were evidence enough to guess that he might have found his quarry, after all, or some other misadventure in the outer world. Whatever the case, he never came back. Scouts went out periodically, but none had found a trace of him, or the half-breed child, who must be nearly man-grown by now, in the way of mixed bloods.

Rane and Thiren, Syall's eldest sons, had been elected to the Ebrados for this trip, and they were the only ones among all his riders about whom Rieser had any concerns, suspecting that theirs was a duty born of vengeance. Emotion had no place in this work.

The rest—Nowen, Sona, Taegil, Morai, Relian, Sorengil, Kalien, Allia, and Hâzadriën—had ridden with him for years. They were among the best riders, swordsmen, and archers of the clan, chosen for their prowess and bravery. Hâzadriën was the exception, but this old friend had other skills. There wasn't a man or woman among them about whom Rieser had the least doubt.

The trail they were to follow this time was two decades cold, and retraced that journey five centuries ago. Rieser liked a good challenge.

He gathered with the others in the main courtyard of the clan house the following morning. The khirnari and Turmay were already there waiting for them. The Retha'noi was dressed in thick sheepskin garments, his coat decorated with animal teeth sewn on in patterns like beads. Turmay's horse had a 'faie saddle and one small bundle hanging from it, and he carried his oo'lu strapped across his back. Rieser had never seen any witch man without one.

Rieser nodded to him. "It's good to see you again, friend. So you're to be our guide?"

"Yes. Together we will ride your white road, and find the white child."

Rieser blinked in surprise. The white road was never spoken of to outsiders. Then again, Turmay was a witch—a hard person to keep secrets from, it seemed.

Seneth gave them her blessing, and Rieser led his riders out of the courtyard and down the river road at a gallop. Turmay rode beside him, as at ease as any of them in the saddle.

Sledges had packed the road smooth, making for an easy ride down the long slope of the valley to the mouth of the pass. There they all dismounted to drink and bathe their hands and faces at the sacred spring, and touch the stony head of the dragon above it for luck. It had died long before they'd come here and turned to stone, as the old dragons did. Most of the body had crumbled away, but the huge head was perfect, down to the sharp spines on its muzzle. Even in winter it was still warm to the touch, as was the water. Hâzadriël had taken this as a sign that the valley was to be theirs—they who had the blood of the Great Dragon in their veins, their gift and their curse. That heritage was proven through the tayan'gil, made from some evil distillation of Hâzad blood, who had dragon's wings and great powers of healing, as the dragons of their homeland were said to.

The Retha'noi people had been here already, but they kept to the heights with their herds and witches, and welcomed the lowlanders when the Hâzad proved to them they meant no harm.

Turmay didn't drink, but instead sprinkled spring water on his oo'lu.

"Why are you doing that?" asked Rane.

Turmay rubbed his wet hand up and down the long horn. "So your moon god will help me find the white child, too. My Mother doesn't mind if I pray to your Aura for guidance, since it is one of your kind that we seek."

"You call it a child. Why?"

Turmay shrugged. "Because it's small like a child."

"You can tell what it is, even without the wings?"

"The Mother knows and she tells me."

This was very strange. The last tayan'gil they had hunted down had been tall and winged, like all the others.

The younger riders talked excitedly among themselves as they began the long ascent. This hunt, their first, would lead them far beyond the world they knew, perhaps all the way back to Aurënen. Rieser himself felt a thrill of excitement at the thought of seeing that lost homeland, even if their purpose in going there was a grim one.

Rieser glanced over at Hâzadriën, riding to his left as always. The glamour was a good one; he looked as normal as the others and would be safe while it held. "Ready for the hunt, old friend?"

It was habit, of course. Hâzadriën never answered or smiled, or showed any emotion for that matter. He just twitched his shoulders, settling pale, leathery wings more comfortably under his loose tunic. The glamour hid the rest.

CHAPTER 5

Luck and Deep Water

THE DAY of their departure from Gedre, dark rumpled clouds hung low on the horizon and the cold wind promised rain and swift sailing. The wind whipped their cloaks around their legs and pulled at their hoods as Alec and the others said their farewells to the khirnari. It had been a week since the assassins' attempt, and there had been no trouble since.

"Thank you for the chances you've taken, harboring us here," Seregil said, pressing a hand to his heart. "And for the care and friendship you've extended to my talímenios. If ever you need our help, we'll be here like the wind."

"If you can manage not to get yourselves killed in the meantime," Riagil said.

Holding a closely bundled Sebrahn by the hand, Alec managed a grin. "We have so far." The khirnari seemed happier today; Alec suspected Riagil was glad to see the back of them. "And thank you again for this," he added with genuine gratitude. Riagil had given him a bow and quiver when he learned that Alec's famous Black Radly had been lost to the slavers. It was a flat bow made of lemonwood from southern Aurënen and backed with vellum. It was as fine a one as he'd ever handled, well balanced and as light as it was strong. The limbs pulled evenly and true, with nearly the same weight as the Radly.

With the last of the farewells said and gifts given, they boarded the ship and soon got under way. The salt-laden breeze caressed Alec's face and pulled little tendrils from his braid as he stood at the prow with Seregil, Sebrahn between them, savoring the familiar tug of excitement as the clustered white houses and then the harbor slid away into the mist behind them. The start of any journey filled him with anticipation, and this time he was going to Bôkthersa.

Seregil covered Alec's gloved hand with his own and leaned close. "Deep thoughts for deep water?"

"Not really. I'm just excited to finally be—"

"Don't say it!" Seregil exclaimed, grey eyes going comically wide. "You'll jinx us."

Alec grinned. "Well, I hope Astellus will smile on this voyage. How's that?"

"I wouldn't tempt fate."

"You don't believe in fate."

Seregil stared out at the flock of red-winged terns winging along beside them. "Maybe I'm changing my mind about that. I've been thinking a lot about what happened in Plenimar."

"It's over, talí," Alec murmured, raising Seregil's hand and kissing the back of it—a bold move for the reticent northerner, here on deck where anyone could see.

"Not the enslavement and humiliation, Alec; how we got there in the first place. A man I knew nearly five decades ago, the man who changed the entire course of my life—and there Ilar was in Yhakobin's house, at the center of the web that caught us!" He plucked one of Sebrahn's long hairs from Alec's shoulder. "And the bastard has changed my life again, hasn't he?" He let the wind take the strand. "And yours."

"I've been thinking about Ilar a lot, too. The first time you ever told me about him, you swore you'd kill him on sight, but in the end you took pity on him instead."

Seregil rested his elbows on the rail and heaved a weary sigh. "Are you still jealous? Do you think I was weak for saving him?"

"Weak? No, you were merciful. I know I was angry at the time, talí, but looking back, I'm glad."

Seregil raised a skeptical brow. "So you're *not* jealous anymore?"

It was Alec's turn to stare out across the waves. "That pathetic eunuch? What is there to be jealous of?"

"As I recall, you weren't so philosophical at the time."

"Not when I caught him trying to kiss you down there by that stream. And he betrayed me, too, just like he did you, after making me trust him all that time in Yhakobin's house."

"But before you knew the truth? What did you think of him when you still thought he was 'Khenir'?"

Alec looked away, suddenly uncomfortable. If he was honest with himself, he had to admit that he had liked the man. But only because Ilar had been kind to him—a seeming friend in a friendless place. "He was still lying," he said, stubbornly shaking off the thought. "So what do you think? Is he alive?"

"Maybe."

"Maybe he died with Yhakobin and the others when Sebrahn sang. He couldn't have gotten that far away."

Seregil looked down at Sebrahn thoughtfully. "Maybe. We still don't know what Sebrahn's range is. Either way, I doubt we'll be seeing Ilar again. Let it go, talí."

Alec turned and looked landward. The mist was thinning, and he could make out a line of jagged, snowcapped peaks. The Ashek range followed the northern curve of Aurënen, embracing the deep blue Osiat like a giant's necklace. Bôkthersa lay deep in the mountains to the west, a fai'thast of green valleys and sweet water. The sen'gais Adzriel and Mydri wore were that same green, the long tails of them fluttering in the wind.

"How many tries does this make?" Micum asked as he joined them at the rail.

"This makes three," said Alec.

Micum grinned. "Three's a lucky number. Still, it wouldn't hurt to make an offering. A coin over the right shoulder for Astellus should do the trick."

Alec fished a sester coin from his purse and held it a moment on his open palm, letting the sunlight catch the finely stamped design. A crescent moon with five rays cradled a flame: moon and fire; Ilior and Sakor, the patrons of Skala and the royal family. The first time he'd seen one of these was soon after he and Seregil had met, and Seregil had taught him some sleight of hand. He smiled to himself as he rolled it expertly across the backs of his fingers, then palmed it and shot it up his sleeve.

Micum chuckled. "No wonder you are such a terror at the gaming tables."

Alec cast the coin over his shoulder into the water.

Seregil produced a small owl feather from his purse and let the wind take it. "Luck in the shadows."

"And in the Light," Alec murmured.

The Old Sailor was on their side this time. They sailed through a few small squalls and were pelted with sudden hail, but the wind remained at their back. Alec loved the storms, the wind, the pitching of the ship. It was exciting. But even on clear days, the Osiat was rough and they had to put in near shore each night. Alec, Micum, and Seregil sang for the crew as the ship rode at anchor, and listened to the others tell tall tales and old sorrows.

They passed the time at cards and dice and bakshi, too, and the money washed back and forth between the travelers and the sailors. Seregil was particularly lucky, and narrowly avoided a fistfight one night when a crewman accused him of cheating, which—for once—he wasn't.

In the quiet of their cabin another night, Seregil's thoughts turned to home and he spoke of old friends there, including his childhood friend, Kheeta í Branin.

Alec had met Kheeta in Sarikali and liked him well enough, once he got past wondering if Seregil and he had been more than friends. Seregil referred to Kheeta as "cousin," but that was common within a clan, especially among social equals; it seemed everyone was addressed as "cousin," "aunt," "uncle," "brother," or "sister." It was hard sometimes to figure out if it was to be taken literally or not.

Seregil chuckled warmly. "I wonder what my uncle Akaien will make of you?"

"I hope he approves." Alec was only half joking. Akaien

was one of the few family members Seregil had ever mentioned in their early days together. This uncle, a swordsmith by trade, had also been a smuggler. Under Aurënen's Edict of Separation, Virésse had been the only legal port for trade with the Three Lands. However, that hadn't stopped clandestine trade, and Akaien had brought his young nephew along. Seregil had told him stories of sailing out under a dark traitor's moon to meet and trade with Skalan ships. The fondness in his voice made Alec think that this Akaien í Solun must be a very different sort than his brother, Seregil's father.

It was then that Seregil had first met Tírfaie foreigners and learned something of the wider world. Seregil also joked that it was this early criminal behavior that had shaped his character.

"He will approve, talí. Of that I have no doubt," Seregil assured him. "But my other sisters? Well, I'll make you no promises there."

Sebrahn was as insistent as ever about staying with Alec. Since there was simply no way Alec could remain cooped up in the cabin, it wasn't long before the crew got a look at what lay under the voluminous cloak and hood. Even Seregil couldn't come up with a plausible explanation for Sebrahn's silver eyes, and many warding signs were made in the rhekaro's direction.

Alec found himself alone with Adzriel one day as they both stood at the rail, watching porpoises leap along beside the ship. She was still keeping her distance from Sebrahn, he noted.

"If you're so scared of Sebrahn, why are you letting him come to Bôkthersa?" he asked at last.

Adzriel said nothing for a moment. Alec had always marveled at how much she resembled her brother, both in looks and in being tight-lipped as blue mussels when the mood took her. When she spoke at last, her voice was devoid of its usual warmth. "As I said in Gedre, he is our clan's responsibility. And if you cannot destroy a dangerous beast, then it is best to know where it is."

"A beast." The word hurt.

"A dragon, but not a dragon. His outward appearance is so deceiving. You know better than I how dangerous he really is."

"So you're going to lock him up somewhere forever? You'll have to lock me in with him."

"No, of course not." She took his hand between hers. "Little brother, I would not harm you for all the world, or any that you love. It's my hope to find a way for your little one to somehow find a safe life, harming none and free from harm. Or as free as he can ever be." She turned Alec's palm up and looked at the stippling of pinpricks across his fingertips. "Can you spend the rest of your life like this? What sort of nightrunner carries a child about on his back?"

"I don't like to think about that, but—"

"But you and my brother must have your lives back," she finished for him with a kind smile. "I promise you, I will use all my power and influence to seek out some solution to this. Are you certain he cannot drink the blood of another 'faie? It's such a tiny little bit that he needs."

"Seregil tried, but Sebrahn just spit it out."

"Well, then we must discover something else."

Late-afternoon shadows stretched across the water to meet them as they sailed into Half Moon Cove. Thick pine forest encircled it and spread to the feet of the distant mountains. Somewhere beyond those mountains, thought Alec, lay the place of Seregil's birth.

"So this is where you and your uncle plied your trade, eh?" asked Micum, standing with them at the rail.

"Yes," Seregil murmured. "Just like the old days, except it's daylight."

Gazing at the green mountains, the words of Seregil's haunting song of exile came back to Alec once again, and he began to hum the tune. Seregil gave him a sidelong smile, and then sang it aloud. This time it was a love song, filled with warmth and joy.

My love is wrapped in a cloak of flowing green
and wears the moon for a crown.

And all around has chains of flowing silver.
Her mirrors reflect the sky.
O, to roam your flowing cloak of green
under the light of the ever-crowning moon.
Will I ever drink of your chains of flowing silver
and drift once more across your mirrors of the sky?

When he was done, Alec saw Adzriel and Mydri both dabbing at their eyes.

CHAPTER 6

❧

An Unexpected Guest

ULAN Í SATHIL, khirnari of Virésse, was at work in his study when his kinsman Elisir í Makili came in and closed the door softly. He was still in his salt-stained cloak and boots, and his red and blue sen'gai was a bit awry.

"Ah, you're back," Ulan said, laying his pen aside by the crumpled handkerchief on the desk, and extending a hand. "I fear I sent you on a fool's errand. Your quarry turned up in Gedre a week ago." No one needed to know that he'd sent another pack of well-paid Plenimaran assassins after them there—an unsuccessful venture, as it turned out.

"That's good news, Uncle! I thought I'd failed you," the younger man told him. "I did bring you someone, though. Thanks to Soran í Brithel and his long-sighted magic, I found Ilar í Sontir of the Chyptaulos clan out in the wilderness east of Riga. He was half dead and he's quite mad. He cowered in the cabin the entire voyage and wouldn't let anyone near him, but I got enough out of him to think that he knows something of the disappearance of Yhakobin."

"Excellent, nephew! Bring him to me at once." Ulan would much rather have had the rhekaro, but this was better than nothing.

Elisir returned with a slight, hunched man bundled up tight in a ragged wool cloak. The hood was pulled down almost to his chin. He stopped just inside the door, trembling violently. Ulan could smell his unwashed odor and hear his labored breathing. The khirnari rose slowly, trying as always to ignore the pain in his joints and chest, and went to him.

Ilar's hands were wrapped in the folds of the cloak so tightly, Ulan could count his knuckles through the cloth.

He took Ilar gently by the elbow and led him to a chair. "Welcome, Ilar í Sontir. Come and warm yourself. Elisir, has he eaten anything?"

"A little bread and gruel during the crossing. The cook judged that's all he could hold down in his condition, and he had trouble with that. The skutter boy was kept busy, cleaning up after him."

"Go down and ask Moriea for some water and broth." Ulan gave the trembling man a kindly look. Ilar's hood had fallen back a little, revealing a chapped red nose and chin, and the way Ilar was biting his lower lip. "You'll feel better once you're settled here. I assure you, you are quite safe, my dear fellow."

One thin, shaking hand emerged from the cloak, and Ilar pushed his hood back enough for Ulan to see his eyes and the dark circles under them. The neck of the cloak wasn't tied. Ulan could make out the white ring of skin on his throat where a metal collar had rubbed for so many years.

Ulan remembered him well from that summer gathering years ago, and had seen him often in recent years, while visiting Yhakobin. The change in him was shocking. There was most certainly the glaze of madness in those shadowed eyes, and some recent hardship had taken its toll. Yet in spite of that, some of his beauty survived.

Ulan went to the sideboard and half filled a cup with water from the ewer, then mixed a little brandy into it. When he tried to give it to him, however, Ilar eyed it with obvious fear, and asked in a quavering voice, "Don't I get two?"

"Two? Why?"

"*Dwai sholo.* It's always two! It's not fair!" Under Aurënfaie law, the ultimate punishment was to be imprisoned in a small room and given two bowls of food or drink a day, one poisoned and one not. If the prisoner chose well and survived a year and a day, he was set free. Not many lasted that long.

"This isn't poisoned, my dear fellow. You have nothing to fear here. You never did any wrong to Virésse and you are welcome, as I told you. Please, try to drink a little. It will calm you."

Ilar's hood fell back as he clasped the cup in both hands. His dark hair was full of dust and sticks and lay lank against his scalp. He took a cautious sip, then a long gulp. Water ran from the corner of his mouth to darken the filthy tunic he had on under the cloak. That appeared to be his only garment, aside from a pair of shoes that were coming apart at the seams. When he was done he gave Ulan the cup and curled more deeply into the armchair.

"I never expected to see you on these shores again," Ulan told him as they waited for the broth.

"I had nowhere to go," Ilar replied dully, rubbing at his throat where the collar had been. "They left me. I think . . . Ilar who ran away all those years ago is dead."

"Life changes us all, dear boy. And yours has been very difficult."

Elisir came in with the broth on a tray and set it down on a small table by Ilar's chair. "She sent this up tepid, Uncle, so he wouldn't burn himself."

"Give her my thanks, Nephew. You should go see to your crew. I'll take care of him now. You did well."

The brandy water was doing its work; Ilar's hands were a bit steadier as he lifted the bowl to his lips and drank.

"Slowly now," Ulan told him with a smile. "I don't want you spoiling my fine carpet."

He watched Ilar finish the broth, and when it appeared that he wasn't going to be sick, he poured him a little more diluted brandy and put the cup in his hands. "Are you warm enough? You're still shivering."

"Warm . . . no, I'll never be warm. The stars were so cold . . ." A tear spilled down one dirty cheek, leaving behind a trail. "I was lost . . . alone. All alone . . ." He grew more agitated. "They'd see the mark! And the collar . . . And my brand! The slave takers . . ."

"You're safe from them here, my poor friend. We will take care of you from now on. No one else needs to know you're here." He leaned forward and took Ilar's hand. "I think you've suffered quite enough for your crimes."

The empty cup tumbled to the carpet as Ilar covered his face, sobbing hoarsely. It was a calculated risk to take the man in, but Ulan doubted anyone would recognize this wretched creature as the dashing young man who'd disappeared so long ago.

"I was alone," Ilar whimpered. His mind was badly unhinged, but this was different from the fear and despair shown by most rescued slaves.

Ulan leaned forward to squeeze the weeping man's shoulder. "You just need rest and good food. And a bath, of course. Shall we go now?"

Ilar recoiled in terror, as if Ulan's touch had burned him. "No! I can't. No one can see . . . Please, don't let anyone *see*!"

"Very well. I'll have a tub brought to your room, and some proper clothing. You can wash yourself and dress without anyone seeing you. Come now, there's a guest chamber just down the hall, and quite near my own room, should you need me."

Ulan rose and took Ilar's hand to help him up. Cloak and sleeve fell back from the thin arm, and Ulan saw four long, scabbed scratches on the underside of the forearm, but no brand. Ulan had seen Yhakobin's mark on his arm many times. There would be another on the back of Ilar's left calf, as well. Or should be. But the skin of his forearm was unblemished above the scratches.

Ilar managed to stay on his feet as Ulan helped him to the guest chamber, and waited with him until the tub was prepared. The servants brought soap and healing oils and scented the water properly when the bath was ready.

"There now," Ulan told him, motioning the others out. "One servant will wait outside, should you have any difficulty, but no one will come in unless you call. Just let him know through the door when you're ready to see me again."

Trembling in his rags, Ilar mumbled, "You are very kind."

"You are an Aurënfaie in need, Ilar. I won't turn my back on you."

"But you left me there." He sounded more like a lost child

than a man betrayed. "You ransomed so many others, but you left me in slavery."

Ulan sighed. "Your master treated you well, and held you in high regard. Look at yourself, Ilar. I don't mean to be cruel, but where can you turn, so scarred and broken that you can't even bathe properly for fear of someone seeing the marks of slavery on your body? I've seen too many returned slaves kill themselves. Truly, I trusted your master to take better care of you."

Ilar shivered and mumbled something Ulan didn't quite catch.

"Bathe and rest, Ilar. You are safe here." Ulan could feel the sudden tightening in his chest again. "Go on. I'll come see you in a little while."

Ulan controlled his breathing by will alone until he was safely behind the closed door of the next room. Then, collapsing into a chair, he pressed his handkerchief to his lips as he began to cough. It was no ordinary cough, this one. When the fit came upon him, it felt like an eagle tearing at his lungs. No one knew the severity of his condition except his personal healer, and she was sworn to silence. No one must know. As the coughing eased at last, he tasted blood. He spat into the linen handkerchief and saw with dread but no surprise that it was stained faintly pink.

He rested his head against the back of the chair and tried to relax as the pain slowly subsided. When he could stand again, he went to the wall adjoining Ilar's chamber and moved a small tapestry aside to uncover the peephole there.

Ilar paced for a while, shivering and muttering to himself too softly for Ulan to hear. Finally he stopped with his back to Ulan and let the cloak fall, then pulled the tunic over his head.

The reason for Ilar's plea for privacy was immediately apparent; the scars of severe floggings covered the back of his emaciated body from neck to knees, and quite a number of them were recent enough to still be scabbed over in places. Ulan had never known Charis to treat his slaves cruelly, and certainly not Ilar, whom he'd valued above all the others, and even spoke of freeing someday. No, something had happened—something to do with Ilar's escape, no doubt.

The brand on Ilar's calf was missing, too, just like the one on his forearm. While that would make keeping him a bit easier, it begged the question of how the marks had disappeared.

Perhaps some sort of obscuration spell? he wondered, though he'd heard nothing of Seregil or the other one having any particular skill of that nature.

If he could only find them, he'd have an answer to that.

Ilar turned around by the tub, reaching for a sponge on the bath tray.

Aura's Light! Ulan stared, deeply shocked. Charis had never mentioned that Ilar had been castrated; Ulan had always had the impression that he was a kind master. Then again, the scars that remained were old ones, and Ilar's manner toward his master had been respectful, not fearful. No, one of Ilar's previous, less gentle masters had done this to him some time ago.

Ilar lowered himself unsteadily into the tub and began to cry again. Satisfied for now, Ulan let the tapestry fall back and returned to his study. His evening dose from the healer had been left for him there. The herbal potion still helped to ease the pain, but she'd had to make it much stronger of late.

At last, the boy came with word that Ilar wanted to see him. Ulan found him in the large bed, propped up against the bolsters with the comforter pulled up under his chin, his long wet hair soaking the silk of both.

"There now, that's better isn't it?" Ulan said, sitting down in the chair beside the bed. "Can you tell me how you came to be in such a state? Did Seregil í Korit do this to you?"

Ilar shook his head vehemently. "No . . . he would never . . ." But his gaze was vague now, and his attention clearly wandered.

"Do you bring news of the rhekaro, and the others?" Ulan knew he should let the poor man sleep, but he was too anxious for answers.

"Rhekaro?"

"Is it—" Ulan covered his mouth quickly with the stained

handkerchief as another fit of coughing overtook him. This was as bad as the previous one. "Please go on," he wheezed when it passed. "Tell me of the rhekaro," he urged gently, trying to recapture Ilar's attention.

"His child . . ."

Child? That was an odd way to look at it. "Did your master discover the elixir he promised me?"

Ilar gave him a blank look. "It can heal."

Ah, yes! This was what Charis Yhakobin had promised in return for so much Virésse gold.

Ilar let out an hysterical little laugh. "They aren't supposed to speak!"

A speaking elixir? The man was mad.

Ilar's eyes went vaguer still. "Ilban would have—But there was a terrible sound! It hurt . . . stinking in the sun . . . but not Seregil and Alec . . . so beautiful under the sky!" Ilar's twisted smile sent a chill up Ulan's spine. "But the bodies! Oh, the bodies and the birds!"

"Whose bodies?"

"Ilban . . . all of them . . . Seregil . . . So beautiful!"

The way Ilar spoke of the Bôkthersan told Ulan that this wreck of a man still had strong feelings for Seregil, even after all these years. He'd guessed as much when Charis had sent word, asking that Seregil be delivered to him, as well as the boy.

"Seregil is not dead," Ulan told him. "He is in Gedre."

"Alive? Seregil is *alive*?" Something like joy momentarily lit that gaunt face. "Alive. But . . ." He reached out from under the comforter and pulled back the sleeve of his linen nightshirt to show Ulan the scratches, even as his eyes began to drift shut. "Beautiful."

That word again, so incongruous with his actions. The man's mind was obviously as fragile as his ruined body, skipping between thoughts and memories. Ulan took his hand and felt the delicate bones through the chapped skin. "Rest now, my friend. Sleep well, and we will talk more tomorrow."

Ilar was asleep before Ulan reached the door.

The khirnari made his way slowly down to his private bath

chamber. Hot needles of pain shot through his arthritic knees and feet. He was an old man, with the afflictions of age as well as sickness, but he couldn't let that stop him from carrying out his duties. He'd been khirnari of Virésse for two hundred and seventy years—longer than any person in any clan had ever served. He'd never given his people any reason to feel worry or doubt about his leadership, and he had but one regret. The reopening of the port at Gedre had cut into the business of his fai'thast far more deeply than he'd anticipated when he'd struck the bargain at Sarikali, and this was largely the doing of Korit í Solun's brat, Seregil, the exile. If the council that had judged Seregil all those years ago had been held anywhere but in that sacred haunted city, Ulan would have seen to it—quietly and skillfully, of course—that Seregil was given the proper sentence of dwai sholo. As it was, he'd discovered at Sarikali the sort of man he'd grown into—a spy and sneak thief of the highest order, and therefore a potential threat and one to be watched. For that reason Ulan had men in Rhíminee, and even one on the privateering ship Seregil owned, the *Green Lady*. Little happened on the water that Ulan í Sathil did not know about. He'd thought himself well rid of Seregil when he'd given him into the hands of the slavers.

He reined in his wandering thoughts. Another affliction of age.

The bath servants were waiting for him, and helped him disrobe and climb into the sunken black marble tub. He sank gratefully into the soothing hot salt water. It felt silky against his skin, and was redolent with the aromas of sage and lugwort. Pink autumn crocus petals floated thick on the surface. It was a twice-daily ritual now, and one that offered him ease, but only temporarily. He looked down at his body—the withered arms and legs, hollow belly, and swollen joints. And how long had it been since he'd needed a woman in his bed? None of that mattered to him, really, only the subtle changes in his mind and the not-so-subtle ones in his lungs. The rest was discomfort and dwindling time. If he did not find the rhekaro, then time would have its way with him.

Yhakobin had promised him a healing elixir, one that

would take the eagle's talons from his chest, the hot sand from his joints, and the fog from his mind. And, he'd claimed, it might prolong life, as well. Ulan would not give up.

He tried to piece together Ilar's ramblings as he soaked. His spies in Plenimar had already sent word that Charis Yhakobin had disappeared and there were rumors from Benshâl that one of the Overlord's favorites, a friend of Charis's, was missing as well. If Ilar was sane enough to speak the truth, then the alchemist was dead, probably at Seregil's hands—though what the "sound" had been he could not guess. The clash of battle, perhaps? But Ilar had said that it hurt him. Whatever the case, this was a major calamity. As far as Ulan knew, only Charis Yhakobin had possessed the skill to create a rhekaro. And unless he'd had an apprentice Ulan didn't know about, the knowledge had died with him. Perhaps another alchemist could complete the process. It would take some delicate intelligence gathering to find one, though, as the Plenimaran Overlord must be searching the land just as thoroughly. After all, it had been made for him.

Ulan stirred the sinking petals with one finger. Men like this didn't simply go missing. And Yhakobin had no reason to run away, so Ilar's account probably contained some element of fact.

At least Ilar í Sontir had been properly dealt with all those years ago. Suspicions had run rampant in the wake of the young man's disappearance; most did not connect his amorous pursuit of the khirnari's son to the murder Seregil had committed. Most assumed that Ilar had run away out of shame over his young lover. Members of Ilar's own clan, the Chyptaulos, were relieved—though the dishonor he'd brought upon them had left an indelible blot, since they could not punish him for the seduction to satisfy the honor of Bôkthersa. In order to avoid a blood feud, the old khirnari of the Chyptaulos had stepped down and Dendra ä Arali, who had no strong blood tie to Ilar, stepped into his place. As Ulan had hoped, with Ilar out of the way, speculation had quickly died down.

It was very fortunate that young Seregil had known nothing of Ulan's hand in those events—and when he'd come to Ulan as a grown man in Sarikali and put the question to him, Ulan had happily lied, resisting the urge to tell him that his betrayer was still alive. He'd had no particular plan for either Seregil or Ilar at the time, but he was not a man to give up a secret.

Ilar had known about Seregil and his talímenios; Ulan took a certain degree of pleasure in keeping the miserable slave informed now and then, once he was broken and in the possession of Charis Yhakobin, a man Ulan knew well. He didn't particularly like the man, but he'd been a trustworthy business partner and ransomed many slaves over the years.

But now Ulan would care for Ilar like a son. It was thanks to the poor creature that the alchemist had learned of young Alec's bloodline in the first place. Ulan been rather surprised when Charis had contacted him so eagerly, asking after the young half-breed. Once the man made known something of the reason, however, Ulan began to plot. All attempts to set up a kidnapping from Skala had failed; there was no one there except his own spies he could count on, and that would have been too obvious. And there was, of course, simply no way for a Plenimaran to gain access to them.

So he'd waited, and seen his chance when word had come that the exile and his talímenios were returning to Aurënen on business for Queen Phoria. For the sake of his clan, Ulan had risked the collective honor of Virésse by facilitating the raid and capture of Alec of Kerry and, according to the alchemist's request, Seregil as well. It was capture or kill him outright, anyway, given Seregil's devotion to his talímenios. Under different circumstances, Ulan would have admired him for that.

And just when the whole gamble was about to fall his way, this disaster.

"Khirnari?"

Ulan started slightly, not having heard Elisir come in; it wasn't the first time he'd gotten caught up in memories when he should be concentrating on the present. The body was not the only thing that lost strength with age. "What is it?"

"They told me downstairs you've made a guest of that wretch."

Ulan smiled. "I offered him kindness, but no formal pledge of hospitality. That can wait until I find some use for him."

"I see. Well, what do you want me to do now?"

"Keep watching. Use every resource. They've left Gedre. I want to know where they go and if they have a child with them. If they're dead, I want proof."

"Yes. But, Uncle, if I may? Why is this child so important?"

"Nephew, have I ever given you cause to doubt my judgment?"

"No, of course not. I was simply curious."

"I understand. However, I must rely completely on your trust in me, and your best discretion. Now, where do you think they'll go from Gedre?"

"Bôkthersa, or perhaps back to Rhíminee? According to my Skalan spies, there's no love lost between him and the current queen, so it's more likely he'll go to ground among his own."

"I cannot afford to take any chances. Rally your spies in Skala, as well. Capture them if they are in Skala, but simply send word if you find them in Bôkthersa. We can't risk making Adzriel ä Illia our enemy. Seregil may be *teth'brimash,* but his sister will never consider him so."

"As you wish, Uncle."

Ulan waited until his nephew was gone, then had the servants help him out of the water. His body moved more easily now; the bath had eased his swollen joints, allowing him to sleep tonight, but the pain would be waiting for him in the morning.

Ilar was sitting up in bed when Ulan entered and took his seat the following morning. Ilar looked no better today, still haunted and gaunt, eyes wild and filled with distrust, but he seemed a bit more lucid.

"Good morning, my dear fellow. And how are you today?"

Ilar glanced nervously around the room. "Am I really in Aurënen?"

"You are indeed. If you're feeling up to it, can you tell me more of what happened in Plenimar?"

Ilar closed his eyes as if he was in pain. "It was Seregil. He escaped somehow—and he saved me. People died— Ilban was going to sell me, flogged me—"

Ulan waited patiently, trying to piece together what he was hearing. Clearly Ilar's memories from that time were still painful and disjointed.

"Seregil came back—not for me . . . I don't know why. Alec hates me, but he—And Ilban . . . He's dead."

"How did they kill your ilban?" Even free, Ilar still called Yhakobin "master." Some of the slaves Ulan had ransomed back from Yhakobin never lost the habit; their very souls were crushed. Many of them killed themselves soon after their return. Only the ones who hadn't been in captivity more than a few months ever really recovered. "What about the rhekaro?" Ulan prompted.

"Stole it, stole me."

"Who did? Seregil?"

But Ilar did not seem to hear him. "I showed the way. *I* did!" he cried angrily. "We walked for days and days." He subsided as quickly as he'd angered, and his gaze began to wander, taking on that vague, glassy look tinged with panic. "It rained so hard! There was no . . ."

Ulan quelled an impatient sigh. "The rhekaro, Ilar. What does the rhekaro look like?"

Ilar shuddered. "The moon. A bone . . . No, the moon. Alec called him that . . ."

"And the wings?"

Ilar shook his head.

This was not good news. Yhakobin had been concerned about the first rhekaro he'd made and its lack of wings. It had apparently been useless, and he'd destroyed it. "Tell me more."

"It eats Alec's blood," Ilar whispered. "And the magic flowers—" He shuddered again as he held out his arm, the one where the brand should have been. "It . . . Sebrahn! He *hurt* me!"

"Sebrahn? Is that his name?" It was the Aurënfaie word for "moonlight." "The rhekaro, Ilar. Tell me more of it."

Ilar closed his eyes, as if remembering was an effort. "Silver eyes."

"He certainly fits his name," Ulan said with a smile. "Now, can you tell me how your ilban and his men died?"

"I don't know. I ran away and only heard the noise."

"What noise?"

Ilar shook his head. "I don't know. It was a terrible sound." He went silent, and Ulan could tell that he'd lost the thread again. "There are always slave takers. Always, and I didn't have my brand. And they stole my collar, too. I had to wait, then I went back to see." He paused, eyes brimming with sudden tears. "Like they'd fallen asleep . . . Just—lying there . . . Except Ilban. I suppose it must have been Seregil. He—" Ilar paused and wiped his eyes. "Did you really say last night that Seregil is alive, or did I dream that? It's so hard to tell."

"Yes. He and Alec are safe. Why did you think they were dead?"

"Everyone was dead . . ."

Had Seregil and Alec managed to kill Ulan and all of his men? It seemed so, and that they must have been badly wounded. Yet Ilar kept insisting that they looked "beautiful."

Ilar wrapped his arms around his chest and rocked miserably. "The birds! I should have known. I should have stayed."

"And what about Sebrahn? What happened to the rhekaro?"

But Ilar just picked at the scabs on his arm, whispering, "I should have stayed. I should have stayed, I should have—"

"Calm yourself, Ilar. They are still alive, so you might meet them again someday."

That got his attention. "Would they come here?"

"Perhaps." Not willingly, of course. "We'll speak more when you are stronger."

Ulan left him to rest and made his way out to the balcony

overlooking the harbor. Already the heat of the morning bath was fading away, and the pain creeping back. A cough shook him and he sank into a chair, handkerchief pressed to his mouth.

If all went well, that would cease to be a problem.

CHAPTER 7

※

Bôkthersa

THE BÔKTHERSAN FAI'THAST encompassed a broad swath of mountains and foothills in the western spur of the Ashek range, and forests that swept from the heights right down to the sea. It was two weeks' ride to the Bôkthersan capital, but Alec looked forward to it—in part because it was his new homeland since he'd been accepted into the clan by bond, and partly for knowing that Seregil and his uncle had ridden these roads and mountain trails together years before.

They'd seen no signs of habitation since they'd left Half Moon Cove, and their only road was a succession of twisting game trails. It was just the sort of place to meet up with bandits. Adzriel assured them that there was no cause for worry, but she had brought an escort of twenty men from the ship.

Seregil's exile song had truly captured the beauty of this land. There were sweet cold springs along the way, and tumbling cascades that glittered in the sunlight. The forest was a mix of tall evergreens, oaks, beeches, and trees Alec didn't recognize. The few remaining leaves still clinging to branch tips—gold and yellow, and fiery orange and red—stood out against the dark firs and clear blue sky.

Seregil was their guide. They slept rough in clearings, singing and drinking around the fire as the moon rose overhead. During the day there was little to do but talk and hunt. And if their escort was anything to go by, the Bôkthersans were a friendly, easygoing people, though most of them remained a bit leery of Sebrahn.

* * *

Smuggler's Pass was a narrow track between two towering stone faces, barely two horses wide in places.

"What did you smuggle through here anyway? Snakes and candles?" Micum grumbled, sweating in his heavy coat and hauling on his horse's reins to get her through one of the narrower spots. Sebrahn was perched on the saddle, holding on to the pommel with both hands as Alec had taught him. Given his nature, the rhekaro would cling there until Alec told him otherwise.

"Leather goods, swords, and horses, mostly," Seregil replied, walking just ahead of him.

"What happened if you were caught?"

"This is our fai'thast. No one has authority here but the khirnari, and my father turned a blind eye. We did have to watch out for other clans near the coast—and pirates."

They emerged at last onto a high plateau strewn with boulders and scattered, wind-twisted pines. If there was a trail, it was covered with snow, but Seregil knew the way, using boulders of different shapes as way markers. The peaks in the distance were stark against the cloudy sky, and the only life they saw here were the flocks of small ravens, which circled them now and then, calling out in their croaking voices.

It was much colder now, and the wind cut through their clothing. Their skin chapped and Mydri handed around a vial of beeswax and goat fat salve to keep their lips from splitting and bleeding when they smiled or yawned too widely. Alec kept Sebrahn bundled under his own cloak; the rhekaro might not feel the cold, but it was possible that he could freeze.

They made camp that night in a circle of huge boulders Seregil referred to jokingly as the Sky Inn. As they carried their gear in from the horses, Alec saw that there were names, short messages, and crescents of Aura scratched all over the face of the rocks, from the snow line to as high as a man could reach. Seregil showed him his own name there, and Akaien's, etched close together. From the difference in height, Seregil had been a child when these marks were made. Alec added his name near Akaien's and had Seregil put his there, too.

Alec went around reading more, and saw dates that went back centuries. Suddenly his toe caught on something and he went sprawling, arms sinking up to the elbows in snow, filling his mittens.

"Ah, I see you've found the woodpile!" said Seregil.

While Alec and Micum dug out the pile of twisted pine branches and small logs, some of the others dug down through the snow at the center of the circle and uncovered a large stone fire pit. The haunches of venison they'd brought on one of the packhorses were frozen solid, so they shaved off thin slices with their knives and either cooked them over the fire on a stick or, like Alec, just ate them raw. They passed around the dwindling bags of hazelnuts and dried apples, and boiled snow for water, since the last of the tea had been used up. As always, Alec found a moment away from the others to feed Sebrahn and trim his hair.

Even in their heavy clothing, the cold sapped strength away. They bedded down early around the fire on cloaks spread across packed snow, and everyone shared blankets with someone.

Alec lay awake for some time, looking up at the night sky. The stars looked as big as half-sester pieces up here, so bright they cast shadows among the boulders. That, and the crackle of the smoky fire, made him think of his father again, and the winters they'd spent trapping in the Ironheart Mountains. When he fell asleep, he dreamed of his father— a tall, taciturn figure striding confidently on his long snow-shoes, the varnished rawhide webbing leaving a pattern like serpent skin for Alec to follow. In the dream his father never turned around, but Alec knew him by the ragged blond hair sticking out under his fur hat. Sometimes they'd gone on like that in silence for hours—or all day, if the traps were empty. Then the vision he'd had of his parents and his mother's death crept into the dream, and he saw his father through his mother's eyes—a handsome young hunter whose dark blue eyes were filled with anguish. In this dream, his mother turned into a dragon and flew away, only to be brought down by the arrows of her own kinsmen. Drops of her steaming blood fell on the snow, leaving a line of red spots like trail markers, leading north. Grief-stricken, Alec watched her fall in the distance, then turned to find her faceless murderers leveling their bows at him.

The sky was overcast at dawn, and large, fluffy flakes of snow began falling as they ate their cold breakfast. It fell more thickly as they set off, capping the rocks with white and muffling the world in that eerie quiet that only snow can create.

It got colder as they went on, though they were going downhill gradually now, and into sparse forest. Snow lay thick on the ground and crunched under their horses' hooves as they rode slowly down a steep, winding trail only Seregil could see.

As they rode today, Seregil told funny stories about his exploits with Alec and Micum, including how Alec's first test as a nightrunner had been to break, unsuspecting, into Seregil's own villa in Rhíminee.

Alec ignored the laughter at his expense and lifted his face to the pale white sun showing dimly through the clouds. Some memories of his father didn't hurt; fresh snow had always meant easy tracking.

"Spotted cat," Micum said beside him, pulling him from his reverie.

Sure enough, the unmistakable pattern of paw pads and tick marks of the claws crossed their path in a wandering line. For the rest of the afternoon they made a game of identifying tracks in the snow to break up the monotony. They saw the spoor of rabbit and deer, great Aurënen stags, bear, and mice, along with a strange pattern Alec thought he recognized. It was a sort of hand- and footprint combination, and always appeared in great numbers, seldom far from a stand of trees. It looked like a whole family of tiny people had crawled along on all fours. Tiny people with tails.

"Are those porie tracks?" he asked, surprised to see them this far north.

"Red ones," said Mydri. "They're on their way to the lowlands. They come down to forage in the winter. The village children coax them in to eat from their hands."

"Not just the children," Adzriel said with a chuckle. "I watched your grand wizard sit outside for hours with apple slices and bread crusts."

"Thero had them climbing up on his shoulders by spring," Mydri added. "There aren't many who can do that! He swears he didn't use any magic on them, either. But it takes considerable patience and gentleness."

Seregil raised an eyebrow in mock surprise. "I can imagine the first, but gentleness?"

"The children loved him," said Adzriel. "He did little magics for them, too. Mydri, remember the time he made a pastry rabbit get up and run around the table while the dishes floated around in circles?"

Seregil looked over at Alec with a smirk. "Thero?" It was the sort of playful magic Nysander had delighted in at feasts, especially if there were children present; the very sort that a younger Thero had held in such disdain.

Adzriel shook her head, smiling. "One time I said I looked forward to his next performance at some feast. He went a bit stiff and told me, 'I don't perform, I entertain.' But you could see the twinkle in his eye."

It wasn't long before Alec heard a familiar rustle and chirping in the branches overhead. Not all the pories had gone south yet, he was glad to see, just as he was glad that none of his companions considered them game. These had reddish brown fur rather than grey, like those in the south, and were the size of a large cat. Otherwise, they had the same clever little hands, golden eyes in blunt-nosed faces, and long, bushy ringed tails they used like rudders as they leapt among the branches overhead, or ventured cautiously down to snatch away bits of bread the riders held up for them.

While they were at it, Alec spied a small black squirrel on a branch overhead. It froze for an instant, then decided it had been seen and darted away up the trunk.

"Haba!" Alec exclaimed. It was the first one he'd seen.

Mydri smiled. "Are you speaking to Seregil or the squirrel?"

"The squirrel. Seregil doesn't like being called that."

"Why not?"

Alec shrugged and said nothing. The fact that Seregil could only associate it now with Ilar was no one's business but his own.

They were riding along through a stretch of forest the following day when Seregil suddenly reined in. "Look what I've got!"

He held up his left arm, showing them the tiny fingerling dragon clinging to the sleeve of his coat. It scuttled up to his shoulder, switching its tail and fluttering its tiny brown wings.

"First dragon! Little brother's the luck bringer," said Adzriel, leaning over to touch her brother with mock reverence. According to custom, Seregil was the luck bringer until they reached their destination.

Sebrahn leaned out from Alec's saddle to see it.

Seregil held out his arm so the rhekaro could have a better look. The fingerling immediately took flight to land on Sebrahn's knee.

Sebrahn pointed to the little creature and looked up at Alec. "Drak-kon?"

Seregil sidled up to Adzriel and asked something in a low voice. Adzriel looked at Sebrahn for a moment, then shook her head.

Sebrahn touched the dragon's spiny head with one finger as two more fingerlings fluttered down to his shoulders, tangling their tiny talons in his hair. A fourth and fifth joined them.

"Sit still," Alec warned, but suddenly all five dragons took flight like flock of ducks on a lake.

Sebrahn held out his hand as if to stop them. "Drak-kon!"

"Maybe he's the luck bringer," said Micum, shaking his head.

"I've never seen them do that before," said Adzriel. She gave Alec a meaningful look.

"They probably want some of his hair for their nests." Several of them had flown off with long blond strands clutched in their claws.

She nodded as she watched the rhekaro hold out his hand for another little dragon to land on. "Maybe he really is one of their own."

The fingerlings became a common sight as they went on, scuttling through the snow and up trees, darting across the road and startling the horses, and crawling into the warmth of bedrolls that night. Since it was taboo to kill a dragon in anything but outright self-defense, everyone was careful not to slap at any sudden itches or step on a fingerling on the way to take a piss.

Sebrahn showed a surprisingly childlike interest in the little creatures, squatting down to watch them scuttle around, even picking one up.

"Sebrahn, no!" Seregil said quietly, so as not to startle rhekaro or dragon.

But the dragon just perched on the back of Sebrahn's right hand with its tail wrapped around the rhekaro's thin wrist.

"If it bites him, do we put lissik on it?" Alec wondered.

But as before, the fingerling flew away without nipping Sebrahn. The rhekaro followed it with his eyes as it fluttered into the trees.

CHAPTER 8

❦

Following the Oo'lu's Song

TURMAY PLAYED his oo'lu every night. It could set wet wood on fire, charm rabbits from their holes into his snares, and who knew what else? All Rieser cared about were the nightly visions of their quarry, but by the time Rieser and his Ebrados reached the great lake called Black Water, the answer was always the same—south—and vague enough to make the captain wonder how they would find them in a whole region—especially one in which they were almost certain to be recognized as outsiders.

They avoided the little Tírfaie hamlets they passed, but weren't above stealing from sheepfolds and root cellars, and finding oats for the horses in unattended barns. They took shelter where they could, in deserted byres or cottages when they could find them, but more often in hastily made branch huts. Hâzadriën was very skilled at their construction, and Turmay knew a song to keep out the snow and wind.

As the weeks drew out, Rieser was proud of his riders, especially Thiren and Rane, the youngest. So far they hadn't complained or shirked, though they and the others were a good deal leaner than they had been when they left the valley.

As 'faie, they stood out in this part of the world, and drew curious looks from the Tír they met when deep snow forced them onto the highroad. It was best to keep their hoods up and their mouths shut, and they did just that, though the two brothers couldn't help looking at the women.

The glamour hiding Hâzadriën's true features was holding well; he appeared to have dark hair and ordinary blue eyes, rather than his true silver. Silent, ancient, and bone-pale, he was neither male nor female, but since he had no breasts, it had been the custom from Hâzadriël's day to call him "he" and "him." Clothed, and cloaked in the khirnari's magic, there was nothing remarkable about him.

The land around the lake called Black Water was more heavily settled, and avoiding the Tír was no longer an option. The deerskin map, which Seneth had commissioned from the clan archivists, began here. Following it, and Turmay's visions, they forged ever south and west.

As captain of the Ebrados, Rieser had learned the Tírfaie tongue and studied their ways. He'd even spoken to a few, when the hunt for wayward 'faie had taken him to some remote village near the pass. So he was able to barter in the markets of the small towns they passed through, south of the huge lake. He got by well enough in the towns, exchanging game for vegetables and dried fruits.

In the smaller villages, however, people hunted their own dinner and weren't interested in any bartering, so he used some of the silver coin he carried, though he kept his gold well hidden. The small silver pieces were made like Tír money, blank and rectangular, and valued by their weight. Farther south the money changed to round coins stamped with designs, but the shopkeepers still took his silver gladly.

It was here that he first overheard people talking of some war to the south. The countries of Skala and Plenimar were shown on his map as two large islands separated by a sea called Inside, and seemed to be waging perpetual war, judging by what he was hearing in the marketplaces.

Beyond the lake, they entered a thick forest and followed a road leading in the right direction. Exhausted and filthy from sleeping rough, they finally gave in and stopped for the night at a lonely inn. Hopefully they wouldn't draw too much attention to themselves. He wondered what the local folk would make of Turmay.

The inn was built of timber, with a thatched roof. The sign hanging over the door showed what was apparently meant to be a dragon, painted a garish red.

Ducking his head under the low doorway, Rieser entered a

large room with a broad hearth and half a dozen tables. A handful of fellow travelers were scattered around the room, eating stew and bread, and drinking from large clay cups. Everyone was talking loudly and he found it hard to understand them. He caught a few familiar words, but the accent was very different from what he'd learned.

At the back of the room a thin, grey-haired woman stood behind a sideboard, serving up mugs of some drink—probably turab, judging by the smell and the state of inebriation of some of the patrons. A harper sat by the fire, plucking out a lively tune, while a young boy carried out food from a kitchen beyond. The room stank of sweat and smoke and ale, but he and his little band had no room to brag on that account. It had been weeks since they'd had a chance to bathe in anything more than an icy stream. He and the others stomped the snow from their boots by the door, but they didn't attract much attention until they pushed back their hoods. The room went quiet and suddenly all eyes were upon them.

The old woman came around the board to greet them, smiling wide. "Welcome!"

As for the rest of it, he was fairly certain she was saying that no 'faie had passed through here for many years, and that they were to go warm themselves by the fire.

"Thank you, old mother," he said, bowing. "Your hospitality is much appreciated."

The silence was finally broken by loud laughter, apparently at what he'd said, or how he'd said it. More likely the latter, given the difference in accent.

She gave Turmay a curious sidelong glance as she urged them toward an empty table by the hearth. Turmay's witch marks weren't visible now, of course, the way they were when he played his oo'lu; it was more likely his short stature, strange clothing, and the long horn he refused to be without even for a moment. He even slept with it by his side.

The woman called out shrilly at the open door at the back. Moments later, the boy reappeared with a tray of mugs. It was turab, and a fine brew, too.

"It's good!" Taegil whispered in surprise.

Turmay took a sip. "Yes. And I smell venison."

The food proved good, as well. The venison stew was thick and well seasoned, with chunks of carrot and onion among the meat, and the bread was sweet and hot from the oven.

As they were eating, one of the other patrons sauntered up, thumbs hooked in his sword belt, and looked them over. "Where are you from, brothers?" he asked Hâzadriën in passable but strangely accented 'faie, though he certainly was not of that blood.

"My friend is mute," Rieser explained tersely. "We are from Aurënen."

"I don't know your accent. Which part of Aurënen?"

"The far south." Rieser went back to his food, hoping the fellow would go away.

"What clan?" the man persisted, appearing genuinely pleased to encounter so many of them at once. "You're the first I've ever seen not wearing any sen'gai."

"We're from a small clan in the south. How do you come to speak our language so well?" Rieser asked, hoping to steer him clear of where they were from, in case he'd been there himself.

"My wife," the man said proudly. "She's what you people call a ya'shel, from Skala. Pretty as the morning sky and as good a woman as ever trod the earth."

"Is that so?" Rieser suppressed an inward shudder at the thought of this malodorous Tír—or any Tír, for that matter—rutting with a 'faie woman, even if she was only a Tír-begat half-breed.

"Where you headed? Up to Wolde?"

"No, we're going south."

The man laughed. "South's a big place."

"We are going home," Rieser told him.

"By land or river?"

"River?"

Their inquisitor seemed surprised by his ignorance—not a good thing. "The Folcwine. Part of what we call the Gold Road up here, though a good stretch of it is the river. It's been a mild winter, and last I heard there was still open water all the way to Nanta. By the last reports, the Skalans were garrisoned there, keeping the peace." He gave Rieser another curious look. "The river's your fastest way south."

"We took a different way." This was something he didn't know before, though he'd seen a river marked on his map. A boat would mean close contact with these people, but he could probably stand it if it meant getting to their destination faster. River travel would save them weeks, if not months this time of year. It might be worth the risk and discomfort.

The man directed him to a town where they could find a boat south, then said, "If you came up from the south overland, you must have seen something of the armies, eh?"

Armies? Was there no end to this man's curiosity? "Only from a distance," Rieser replied.

"Which side? Skala's or Plenimar's?"

"I don't know. We were too far away." Rieser clenched his left fist under the table, resisting the urge to shout at the man. He was standing too close, making Rieser tilt his head back to look him in the eye.

"Well, it will be better if it's Skala, friend. You don't want to run afoul of any Plenimaran marines. They're a rough lot."

The man talked on, but Rieser's increasingly brief answers finally got the message across and he left them alone, as did the others, though there was much staring. Perhaps it was because of Turmay, who was dipping his stew up into his mouth with his fingers, or of Nowen and the other three women of his company. They were comely, he supposed, and Sona and Allia looked young enough to be of interest. He was glad of the weight of his sword against his thigh under the table, in case things turned ugly.

But the night passed without bloodshed and they pressed on for the river.

The river town turned out to be a fair-sized place, no doubt because of the trade that went through it. The waterfront was a warren of warehouses and long wooden platforms that extended out from the shore. He saw stacks of wool bales everywhere, and tufts of the stuff blew about on the ground.

There were also soldiers. There was an encampment just

outside the walls, and there were many uniformed men—
and women, too—in the streets. They wore chain mail under
tabards emblazoned with the shape of a red bird in flight,
and many were armed with long swords.

Rieser paused at a stall where a man was selling roasted
chestnuts. "Who are these soldiers?" he asked.

The man gave him much the same look as the Tír back at
that tavern had. "Why, the Skalan Red Hawk regiment, of
course."

According to the man back at the tavern, this was a good
thing. Encouraged, Rieser led his company down to the
waterfront.

Boats were tied up beside the long wooden platforms,
many of them little more than huge rafts, like the ones children played with on the lakes back home.

After some confusion he was directed to someone called the
dock master. This turned out to be a friendly man with dishon-
est eyes whose palm had to be crossed with silver before he
would take them to something called a "flat boat" that could
carry their horses. Rieser paid the captain in gold for passage
on one of the larger ones, what the master called a "barge."

For the next week they kept to themselves as much as possible, but it was difficult. The bargemen picked up other passengers along the way, and stopped to let others off. Some of
these people felt it necessary to pester Nowen and the other
women with unwanted attentions, and Rieser and the rest of
them with pointless questions. Young Rane and his brother
Thiren were excited and curious, and a few times Rieser was
forced to act as their interpreter, but he soon made it clear
that they were to keep to themselves.

They began to see signs of the war now. Some of the villages they passed had been burned, and dead sheep and
horses floated at the river's edge.

"Who has done this?" he asked the barge captain.

"Damn Plenimarans, of course!" the man replied. "You're
in Mycena now, and they've always been Skala's friend."

"What are they fighting about, these two lands?"

"This river, for one thing. Surely you've heard it called the

Gold Road? What do you think we carry down from Boersby, eh? It ain't all Wolde cloth and apple wine."

"They don't have gold in the south?"

"Damn little of it, and they're not content with silver." He grinned and put a finger to the side of his nose. "But then, who is?"

This made sense. The mountains surrounding the North Star clan's fai'thast were rich with metals, and some gems and rock crystal, too.

Just then Rieser caught sight of a large camp in the distance on the western shore. There were hundreds of tents and shelters, and what looked to be twice that in horses and men.

"There's some of the Skalans, in winter camp," the captain told him. "A good thing for us, too. The Plenimarans raid our boats whenever they can when they're this far west."

"How do the Skalans feel about the Aurënfaie?"

The man gave him a surprised look. "You ought to know better than me, what with the 'faie trading with them for horses and all the rest."

Rieser cursed himself for breaking his own rule of talking too much. "We're from the south. I don't pay much attention to such things."

"Ah, well, that'll be why you don't sound like any 'faie I've met, then," the captain said, not looking entirely convinced. "As for the war, Skala still holds Nanta, so I won't have to put you ashore before that. At least that was the last news I had. By the Old Sailor, it can change in the blink of an eye! You'll do well to find a ship to make the crossing, rather than going overland. The two armies will start up again pretty soon and you wouldn't want to get caught in the middle of that, believe me."

"I thank you for this knowledge," Rieser said. For once, a talkative Tírfaie had proven useful.

There had been no question of Turmay playing the oo'lu during the voyage, or in the teeming city of Nanta, when they docked at last. None of them had seen a city of this size before, or a body of water as large as the Inside Sea, and the young ones drew smiles from passersby as they gawked.

The harbor was full of huge ships with red sails—Skalan warships, the captain said—and there were soldiers everywhere, wearing long tunics with different emblems on their chests. A good many wore the sign of a white horse and walked with the swagger of horsemen.

As soon as their horses had been unloaded, Rieser led his people away from the city. They camped in a small copse overlooking the sea. It was much warmer here than in the northlands; there was hardly more than a dusting of snow on the frozen ground.

The map showed this sea, but being beside it was far different. The water stretched west to the horizon, covered in whitecaps in the evening breeze, and was undrinkable, as they soon learned. The waves surged against the rocks below their camp, sending up clouds of white spume. It smelled different than lake water, too. There was a sweet tang to it, and he could taste salt on his lips as the wind carried the spray up to where he stood.

As soon as the moon was up, Turmay took his place by the fire and began to play. The song was rich and deep, nuanced with sounds like the calls of birds and croaking of frogs. Tonight it also growled like a mountain bear.

The witch stopped suddenly and looked across the fire at Rieser. "The tayan'gil has left the place where it was. It journeys west, with many companions. One of them is a ya'shel with your blood."

Rieser nodded. It made sense. The half-breed infant he'd pursued with Syall would be a young man by now. Somehow the dark witches had found him and made the tayan'gil. How they had gotten all the way back to Aurënen was as much a mystery as why the tayan'gil existed at all.

"Can you see their faces, Turmay?"

"Not yet. I just know that he and the tayan'gil are still together."

Rieser gave him a rare smile. "Thank you for your help, my friend. Without your visions, we would not have come so far so quickly."

"Thank the Mother," the witch replied with a grin.

* * *

Turmay lay awake after the other 'faie had gone to sleep. The tayan'gil Hâzadriën did not sleep, and the witch suspected that Rieser had ordered it to watch him at night.

Turmay had not lied to Rieser. He just hadn't told him the whole truth.

Curled up by the fire, he clutched his oo'lu close and silently prayed to the half-moon above.

Beautiful Mother, giver of life and death, shine your face on me and guide me to this white abomination. Guide my hand to kill it before it acts again!

home

SNOW was falling gently as Alec and the rest reached the mouth of the home valley.

Seregil had tried to describe his home to Alec, but when they finally reached it just before sunset, Alec found it more vast and beautiful than he'd imagined. The lower end of the valley was rolling and broad, with plentiful water from several rivers. Acres of meadow promised lush hay in summer.

The valley was dotted with horse farms that reminded Alec of Watermead, and others raising sheep, goats, and chickens, and still others that looked like they were tilled for grain and vegetables in summer. Farther up, the valley narrowed and the sides grew steeper, but Alec could make out the dark shapes of herds there, too.

Seregil kept his hood up as they neared the final crossroad. His kin and the escort riders greeted friends by name. Four decades weren't a lot in a 'faie lifetime, and he recognized quite a few people. Some of them were his age, and it was bittersweet to see how young they still looked compared to him.

Though he kept up a cheerful façade, he felt an increasing inner turmoil as they reached the final turn onto the steep road that led up to the town of his birth. To their left he could already hear the roar of the lower river churning in the gorge below. The Bôkthersan clan house and central town lay on the eastern shore of a large mountain lake. The Silver River cascaded down from the peaks to feed it, and then continued down the valley in a rushing torrent.

The sigh of the breeze in the boughs soothed him a little, as it always had, and the deep snow brought back happy memories of snowball fights and ice fishing on the lake, and hot drinks around the bonfires afterward as the feeling came back like pins and needles to cold fingers and toes.

To be riding up this road again was gift enough, but to be in the company of Alec and Micum and his kin brought a lump to his throat.

He wondered if his other two sisters, Shalar and Illina, would be there to greet him. They'd shunned him since his first exile, sending no words of comfort and staying away from Sarikali when he'd been there. According to Adzriel, there were others among his kin and clan who would not welcome him warmly, either.

Nudging his horse up beside Seregil's, Alec gave him a knowing look as he said quietly, "That's not a very cheerful expression, talí. Aren't you happy to be back?"

Seregil forced a smile, not wanting to spoil this first visit for Alec in any way.

Alec's heart beat faster as they approached the town. The houses here were very like those in Gedre, square and solid with domed colos on top, but built of timber and dressed stone, and decorated with intricate carvings.

The valley was breathtakingly grand, bathed in the golden light of the setting sun. The frozen lake was nowhere near as large as the Blackwater, but it was large all the same. There were little islands out there, too, and Alec could imagine camping out on one of them some summer night.

People waved and called greetings as they headed down the main street toward the clan house. Alec was thrilled to see so many green sen'gai in one place. Everyone wore the graceful traditional clothing here; men and women alike wore trousers and boots or slippers. The main difference in the tunics, which were split from hem to belt on either side, was that the women's were longer. They were made of soft wool, and dyed in every color for everyday use, with patterns of embroidery at the neck and cuffs.

The clan house stood on a hill overlooking both town and water. Beyond it, the forest closed in again, thick and dark. Protected by water and mountains, the rambling clan house sprawled across the high ground, windows glinting and smoke rising from scores of chimneys.

"Welcome home, Haba," Adzriel said, leaning in the saddle to clap Seregil on the shoulder. Alec was the only one who noticed the brief flash of pain in his lover's grey eyes before the forced smile appeared again. The closer they came to this place, the more tension Alec felt along the talímenios bond, though Seregil was keeping up a bold front, as usual; he'd said next to nothing about his feelings about coming back here. Even after all this time, Alec had to rely on the bond and intuition. Fortunately he could read Seregil like a scroll. He might not always know the cause, but he knew what Seregil was feeling, especially when he was unhappy or fearful. The latter was a rare occurrence, but that's what Alec was picking up now. He caught Seregil's eye again and gave him a reassuring smile. Seregil gave him a nod and a hint of a smile, then turned his face for home.

Word spread and people shouted and waved to their returning khirnari from rooftops and street corners. Adzriel led the way through the central square, where the ancient temple of Aura stood, its walls brilliant white against the darker buildings, its carved lintel painted silver and blue.

As they neared the outer gates of the clan house, it looked to Seregil as if the entire household had turned out to meet them. Adzriel's husband—tall, plain Säaban—was in the forefront, and another tall man was with him, the sight of whom made Seregil's heart beat so hard it hurt and his eyes sting. It was his uncle.

Adzriel waved to her husband, eyes bright and cheeks flushed.

"And mind you call him Säaban, and not by his formal name or 'sir,' as you did in Sarikali," he overheard Mydri reminding Alec. "He's kin."

"I don't imagine he liked me dragging you away from home again, sister," Seregil said to Adzriel, adding with a small grin, "Unless you two are already a settled old married couple."

"I still know how to cut a switch, Haba," she retorted without so much as a sidelong glance.

Micum burst out laughing. Seregil actually blushed, but suddenly his heart felt lighter.

Alec let out an ill-concealed snicker and whispered, "Sorry, I was just imagining her chasing the Rhíminee Cat around with a switch."

"I can count on one hand the times she made good on that threat," Seregil retorted with a grin.

Adzriel laughed. "I've always said I should have beaten you more."

"You're probably right."

To his surprise, old friends and relatives crowded in around his horse as soon as they reined in at the gate. As he'd expected, his other two sisters weren't among them. But his uncle was, and Akaien smiled and waved to him as if he'd only been gone a few days. He hadn't changed much. He was tall and dark like Seregil's father, but with a ready smile and warmth in his grey eyes that Seregil had seldom felt from Korit í Solun.

Kheeta's mother, Aunt Alira, was the first to embrace him when he dismounted. "It's about time you came back, you rascal!" she cried, tears rolling down her cheeks. She made a show of feeling his arms and shoulders. "And skinny as ever!"

"You haven't changed a bit either, Auntie," he replied, hugging her tight.

"And this must be the golden-haired lover I've heard so much about," she said, looking Alec's way just as he lifted Sebrahn down, then staring as she saw the rhekaro's eyes. Her fingers twitched as if she resisted making a warding sign.

Alec hitched Sebrahn up on one hip. Sebrahn clung to him like a porie, his large eyes alert and darting from face to face.

Not an auspicious beginning.

And what if he starts singing?

But then Akaien was right there in front of him and all other thoughts fled as he grabbed Seregil in a fierce hug. For just an instant Seregil was surprised that he was nearly as tall as his uncle. Akaien's arms were as hard and wiry as ever from his smithing work, and his large hands scarred and stained. Seregil could smell lingering traces of smoke in his hair.

"Uncle!"

"My boy!" Akaien pulled back and looked at him. "Look at you, Seregil, still the image of your mother."

"Just the thing a man wants to hear," he replied wryly as Kheeta í Branin claimed him for an embrace. He was Seregil's age but looked younger, even with the distinctive white streak in his dark hair showing under his sen'gai.

"You look better this time around, except for this mess," his friend said, roughing Seregil's ragged hair. "Is this some new Tírfaie fashion?"

"Plenimaran, actually," Seregil told him with a laugh, then noticed that Alec had hung back, still holding Sebrahn, while everyone else was greeting friends and loved ones. "Alec, talí, come meet our uncle. Uncle, I present to you my talímenios, Alec í Amasa of Kerry."

"I'm glad to meet you, Uncle Akaien," Alec said, setting Sebrahn on his feet and clasping hands with the older man.

Akaien smiled as he looked Alec over. "Well, I like your braid better than my nephew's style. Apart from the color of it, you look as 'faie as Seregil. Adzriel said you looked more Tír but I don't see it."

No one but Seregil caught Alec's slight wince; Alec was as sensitive to that well-meant observation as Seregil was to his own old nickname. Some effects of the alchemist's purifications still lingered. Alec had looked completely 'faie when the man was done with him, and although the magic or whatever it had been had faded a bit, he still looked more Aurënfaie than he had.

"Who is this little one?" asked Akaien.

"This is Sebrahn." Alec pulled back Sebrahn's hood. The

rhekaro's hair had grown out halfway down his back since the last trimming, and he was dressed in a white tunic and trousers of 'faie cut that Yhali had given him. He was still barefoot, though, refusing all efforts to make him wear shoes.

"Well, now." Akaien held out his hand, showing no surprise at the color of Sebrahn's eyes. "Greetings, little stranger."

Sebrahn slowly reached out and brushed his fingers against Akaien's, and Seregil breathed a sigh of relief. Akaien was a highly respected member of the clan; if he and Adzriel accepted Sebrahn in front of the others, then perhaps this would be an easier stay than he'd expected. Indeed, others were already crowding around quietly to get a better look, as if Sebrahn were a newborn babe being presented to the clan.

Seregil waved Micum over. "And this, Uncle, is my oldest friend in Skala, Micum Cavish."

He watched in amusement as the two men sized each other up. They were of a height, but where Micum was heavy-boned and ruddy, Akaien was wiry and fair-skinned, his hair long and dark brown like Seregil's. All the same, there was a similarity about them that Seregil hadn't really put together until now: at once highly honorable but not above stretching the laws for a good cause—or when it suited them.

"Well met, Micum Cavish," Akaien said in Skalan as he clasped hands with him. "Adzriel speaks warmly of you. You have my thanks for your family's hospitality to my wayward nephew. I've felt easier in my mind since I heard about you. I hope he hasn't been too much trouble."

"We've gotten into our share of scrapes over the years, but we got each other back out, too," Micum replied in Aurënfaie.

Säaban released Adzriel at last and greeted Micum. "Welcome, Micum Cavish."

"And you, sir."

"I hope they have a proper feast prepared," Adzriel said with a laugh, putting an arm around Alec's waist and pulling

Seregil by the hand. "The one who was lost is with us again, and brings his talímenios and—this little one. Now, come along out of the cold!"

The crowd parted, but many people reached out to pat Seregil on the back and shoulders as he passed, and their warm greeting loosened the knot of tension in his chest. All the same he kept close to Alec and the rhekaro, who was looking back over Alec's shoulder now, those black pupils still a bit wider than Seregil liked to see. He was aware of Micum at his back, too, and grateful for his friend's presence.

Inside the gates, the gardens were buried in snow and the mossy old fountain silent for the winter, but the great double doors were open wide, spilling out firelight like a carpet for them. As he passed under the lintel carved with Aura's crescents, he was startled to find both of his estranged sisters waiting for him by the hearth.

Shalar, the older one, favored their father, right down to the lines of disapproval around her mouth. She wasn't smiling, but Illina, who could have been his twin, came forward and took his hands in hers. "Welcome home, brother." And she kissed him on both cheeks.

Seregil hugged her close, swallowing around the new lump in his throat. "Thank you, sister."

Shalar was somewhat warmer with Alec, taking his hand and admiring Sebrahn's strange beauty. "What unusual eyes. But bare feet in winter?" she chided as she chafed the rhekaro's feet between her hands. "Why, he's like ice!"

"He doesn't like to wear shoes. And he doesn't feel the cold," Alec explained, and got a look of disapproval equal to any he'd seen from Mydri.

Turning away, he saw that Akaien í Solun had his arm around Seregil now, laughing about something with Kheeta. Seregil had always been closemouthed about his past, especially in the early days. Since they'd become talímenios, he'd talked more, but not a lot. It was just his nature, and Alec had long since given up wishing he were different. Still, meeting this uncle at last, and witnessing the deep bond of

affection between them, he wondered how Seregil could
have put him out of his mind for so long.

After seemingly endless introductions to kin and friends,
Seregil led Alec through a warren of corridors to his old
room, which Mydri had assured him was still his to use. It
took a moment to remember the way, but he found it at last.
Setting his pack down by the door, he looked around, trying
to see it through Alec's eyes. The bed was the same, with its
golden oak headboard carved with pinecones and rabbits,
and neatly made up with the colorful silk counterpane, a bit
faded now and sweet with the scent of lavender and cedar.
The same blue pitcher and basin were on the washstand,
below the mirror he'd cracked playing a forbidden game of
ball here with Kheeta one rainy day.

Outgrown toys were gone from the top of the clothes chest
and windowsills, but his books and scrolls were still on their
shelves, and the sword rack stood under the window, holding the wooden blades he'd used, tutored by his father,
Akaien, and various older cousins. They ranged from the
first tiny one that had been put into his hands when he'd only
just learned to walk, up to the scarred, deeply notched
wooden long sword with which he'd beaten nearly every
challenger. From the very beginning it had felt right and
good to have a sword in his hand, and swordsmanship had
become his first passion. His quick reflexes, determination,
and rapidly developing skill had earned him the respect of
his elders. All except for his father, of course.

Alec closed the door and hugged Seregil. "Bilairy's Balls,
we finally made it!"

Seregil laughed softly. "It's certainly better than where we
ended up last time."

Sebrahn was already at the window, standing on tiptoe to
see out past the sword rack. Seregil picked the rhekaro up so
he could see the empty garden outside, and the leafless trees
that cast lacy, dancing shadows across the far wall over the
bed at dawn. Seregil sighed, remembering himself being
held the same way, in the strong loving arms of his sisters or
uncle, when he was very small. That felt like someone else's

life now, and he supposed it was. Then strong arms embraced Seregil and Sebrahn together, and Seregil knew that Alec wouldn't let him go until he was sure of his mood. Seregil turned and kissed him. "I'm fine. Lots of good memories here. I was a happy child, believe it or not. I had good friends, and kin who loved me."

"They still do and so do I, talí," Alec said, looking far too serious. "This is your home."

Seregil shook his head with a soft laugh. "Home is wherever you are, talí. This is just someplace I used to live."

Alec's arms tightened. "Don't say that. I never had anyplace like this. It was just one inn or camp or tent after another, just my dad and me. You shouldn't take any of this for granted."

"Duly noted." Which was why they weren't going to be staying here long; not while they had Sebrahn with them.

When everyone was bathed and dressed in clean clothing, Seregil led them to the great hall at the center of the house, holding Sebrahn's hand on one side and Alec's on the other. Adzriel had made certain even the rhekaro had proper feasting clothes, and Alec had trimmed and braided Sebrahn's hair and his own.

"With his hair like that, you can really see the resemblance between you two," Micum noted.

"That's why I did it," Alec replied. "I want to see if it helps people accept Sebrahn more easily."

The feast was laid out, and Seregil found himself in his old place at table with his sisters and Akaien. Sebrahn knelt on a cushion on the chair between him and Alec and paid no attention to the courses as they came.

But Seregil did, recognizing many childhood favorites. There was spiced pear cider; venison roast with wine sauce; and a huge galantine pie thick with lamb, chukka, currants, and bog berries. There were beets with marrow, toasted hazelnuts, chestnut pudding, and turnips mashed with carrots, all served up with fragrant brown loaves of Aunt Alira's wheat bread and sweet butter still cold from the well room.

Ilina, who was quite taken with Sebrahn, eyed him with concern. "Why isn't the little one eating?"

"Alec fed him a little while ago," Seregil told her, which was true.

Just before the sweets course, Uncle Akaien looked down the table and waved to Seregil, motioning for him and Alec to join him. Micum had been given an honored place at his side.

"How does it feel to be home, nephew?" asked Akaien.

"Good, so far. It's been so long."

"I noticed that you weren't carrying the sword I sent to you at Sarikali."

Seregil gave him a rueful look. "I'm afraid I lost it—"

Akaien shook his head. "Another one!"

"It was in a good cause. It shattered while I was fighting a *dra'gorgos.* Not successfully, unfortunately. Alec lost his the same way. The ones we have now we stole in Plenimar."

"I see."

"I lost my bow, too," Alec added. He wasn't sure which had been the more grievous loss.

"Damn, and I wanted another match!" Kheeta said, overhearing, as he and several other young men and youths joined them.

"I'd hoped to see that Black Radly, too," said Akaien. "Kheeta's bragged up your prowess. But maybe we can find you another until you can replace it."

"Actually, the khirnari at Gedre gave me a new one," Alec told him.

"You'll have to start your *shatta* collection all over again, though," Kheeta pointed out. "It's too bad, too. You had a lot." Among the Aurënfaie, most of these match prizes were little figures or shapes carved from wood, bone, glazed clay beads, feathers, or coins with holes punched through, though some were made of precious stones or metals. "We'll have a match tomorrow."

"I'm in for that!" one of the young men exclaimed, and others joined in, crowding around to introduce themselves.

Seregil smiled, pleased to see Alec already making friends, as he always did, and so easily.

As soon as the meal was finished, the tables were carried away and musicians struck up dancing music.

Seregil felt the pull of it, but he was too tired to dance. Instead, he borrowed a harp and coaxed Alec into joining him for a few songs.

As the night wore on, people gradually drifted away to bed or other pastimes.

Akaien, who'd been talking swords with Micum, came over to Seregil and Alec. "I fancy a bit of fresh air, nephews," he said, with a meaningful look at Sebrahn, who was leaning back against Alec's leg.

A servant fetched their cloaks, and Akaien led the way out to a path by the lakeshore. Seregil inhaled the cold, fir-scented air gratefully, still trying to take in the fact that he was here, and walking with his uncle under the stars as he had so often, and with Alec, too.

"Adzriel told me a little before dinner," said Akaien, stopping to admire the view of the starlit islands. "Alec, she says you were given some sort of prophecy about a child at Sarikali. But this is no ordinary child."

Alec looked to Seregil, who nodded. "I trust him as I trust myself."

So Alec told him of the prophecy and the making, but not of Sebrahn's true powers. They'd agreed with Adzriel to keep that a secret. Sebrahn's appearance was enough of a hurdle.

Akaien listened in thoughtful silence, then held out his arms. "Will he come to me?"

Sebrahn allowed himself to be passed over. He sat calmly in Akaien's arms, gazing up at him, eyes shimmering in the darkness.

The older man smiled. "Such a dark birth for a child of light."

"How do you mean, Uncle?" asked Alec.

"He was made from you. And there's nothing evil in you or in 'faie blood. So how can there be evil in this little fellow?"

Only Adzriel's admonition kept Seregil from telling him the whole truth. Even he didn't think of Sebrahn as evil, but his innocent appearance was deceiving and he hated lying to his uncle. "There's more to him than meets the eye."

"I don't doubt that," Akaien said with a knowing look. "Otherwise, why would you be going to Tyrus? Would you like me to come with you? No, that's all right. I see the answer on your face, Haba."

"I'm sorry, Uncle."

Akaien looked at the three of them and smiled sadly. "Your sister hopes you've come home for good. That's not to be, is it? The Tír world has claimed you."

"I'm an exile, remember?" Seregil reminded him. "I'm not Bôkthersan anymore."

Akaien passed Sebrahn back to Alec and took Seregil by both shoulders. "You will *always* be a Bôkthersan, no matter what anyone says. Never forget that, Seregil. Perhaps—if I hadn't taken you with me all those times when you were so young—"

"No, Uncle," Seregil told him with a heartfelt smile. "You saved my life."

"That's good, then." He kept a hand on Seregil's shoulder and put the other on Alec's. "Let's walk some more before our feet freeze to the ground. Alec, you're a quiet one. Tell me more about yourself. I want to know the young man who put the light back in my nephew's eyes."

Later that night, as he lay in bed with Alec with the scents of the sea and night air still clinging to their skin, Seregil gazed around the familiar room and let out a long sigh of contentment, remembering Alec's admonishment earlier that day and his uncle's words. This was more than just somewhere he'd once lived. It was the first place he'd ever thought of as his *own*. And now? He laughed softly.

"What?" Alec mumbled, already half asleep.

"This is the first time I've ever had a lover in this bed. I feel a bit wicked."

Alec snorted softly. "Don't you always?"

CHAPTER 10

Snowbirds

To Alec's surprise, and Seregil's too, Seregil was summoned to Adzriel's chamber to meet with the clan elders the next morning. Adzriel had the authority to bring Sebrahn here, but she'd chosen to meet with the elders, as well, and fully apprise them of the situation. Seregil was part of the council. Alec and Sebrahn would be called in later.

Left to his own devices, Alec decided to do a bit of exploring, since Adzriel had kept her promise and not shut them up in their room; he fingered the bedroom key lying in his pocket like a talisman. Alec deeply appreciated the risk she was taking, both for herself and her clan, knowing what she did about Sebrahn's powers.

The clan house had seemed like a maze last night, and it was no different in daylight. Since he had no particular destination in mind, he just wandered around with Sebrahn, meeting a few people and finding a kitchen and several large halls. At last they found themselves on a long covered porch that overlooked the lake.

It had snowed again last night and the mountain air was biting cold, but it was a fine day. Too fine to stay indoors. Hoping he could find his way back, he hurried with Sebrahn back to his room. Mydri had found a warmer coat for him than the one he'd been given in Gedre, sheepskin with the fleece on the inside, and a hat to match. They were bulky but warm, like the garments he and his father had worn. She'd given him mittens, as well, knit in intricate patterns of green and white yarn. There was a fleece coat for Sebrahn, too, and mittens that he wouldn't keep on his hands any more than he would keep shoes on unless Alec tied them tightly, as he had today; no matter how Alec tried to explain the rhekaro's lack of needs, women were always fussing over him, and it wouldn't help anyone to accept Sebrahn's strangeness to see him walking barefoot in snow.

He did manage to find the porch again, though through a different door. Here, little bells tinkled overhead, hung from the eaves. Their clappers were tied to long cards that spun in the breeze, bearing prayers and wishes in elegant 'faie script. Seregil had put one up this morning. Its card read simply, WISDOM.

There were chairs here and there along the porch, and benches built into the wooden railings. It was easy to imagine a crowd out here on a summer's eve, enjoying the bells as they watched the sun set over the mountains, painting the lake with gold. The lake was silver-grey today, and frozen along the shoreline. Out in the middle wild geese and ducks bobbed among the whitecaps, diving for their breakfast.

He chose a chair and propped his feet up on the rail. Sebrahn immediately took his place on Alec's lap. A lone raven called from the forest, followed by the bright trill of a willow tit. Sparrows, doves, and a little green bird he'd forgotten the name of pecked at the crusts scattered on the ground for them. A few tiny brown dragons scuttled among them, too, and more scrambled and chirped for the red and yellow boiled millet and honeyed milk set out just for them. Several fluttered up to perch on Sebrahn and Alec's hands. Sebrahn patted them, and one curled up in the rhekaro's lap and went to sleep. Alec shook his head, smiling. Maybe Sebrahn was a "dragon friend," like the man Seregil had mentioned?

There were more dragonlings here in the mountains than at Sarikali, according to Kheeta, and it certainly appeared to be true. He spotted several in the rafters overhead, and more perched on the railings and chairs. It was for that reason that no one in Bôkthersa kept cats. He hadn't seen any in Sarikali, either, though cats were common enough in Gedre. Now that he thought about it, he'd never seen a dragon in Gedre.

The fingerlings didn't disappear during the winter, either, like a lizard or snake. The one he held at the moment was warm to the touch, perhaps from the fire in its belly. Or maybe they were like Sebrahn, and just didn't feel the cold at all? Or Sebrahn was like them.

Just then he heard laughter, and a gang of small children came running through the snow toward him. Stopping near the porch, they set about trying to make snowballs with the dry new snow. Grinning, Alec slogged out to help, with Sebrahn trailing along behind.

"You won't have much luck with this," he told them, scooping up a handful and letting it blow away on the breeze.

A little girl pouted up at him. "We wanted to make a family."

"Of snow people? It's just too dry. How about making snowbirds?"

"How do you do that?" a little boy demanded, wiping his runny nose on the back of an already crusty mitten.

By way of answer, Alec fell over onto his back and fanned his arms and legs, making the wings and tail as Illia and Beka had taught him during a winter visit to Watermead.

The children were delighted. Soon there was a large flock of snowbirds on the slope and everyone was dusted with snow.

Everyone except Sebrahn.

"How come your little boy doesn't play?" the girl, whose name was Silma, asked. Sebrahn was standing where Alec had left him, looking down at the first bird Alec had made.

"He doesn't know how," Alec replied. "Maybe you can show him?"

Silma and her friends gathered around the rhekaro, then fell back and flailed around, crying, "You, too! Like this!"

Sebrahn looked to Alec, who smiled and nodded. Sebrahn immediately fell on his back across one of Silma's birds and slowly imitated what the others were doing.

"He ruined mine!" Silma cried, offended.

"He didn't mean to." Alec pulled Sebrahn to his feet and

directed him to a patch of smooth snow. "There, do another one."

Sebrahn fell facedown this time, but made a passable bird.

"Very good!" Alec picked him up and dusted the snow from his coat and leggings, then helped the children make more up and down the hillside.

He'd assumed Sebrahn was doing the same, until Silma asked, "Why doesn't your little boy have any boots?"

Sure enough, Sebrahn had gotten them off when Alec wasn't looking. There they lay, up the slope, and there Sebrahn was, barefoot again.

"My mama would be angry if I went barefoot in the winter," another chimed in. "She says your toes can break off just like icicles. How come his mama didn't give him any boots?"

"He doesn't have a mama," Alec told her, and the words seemed to stick in his throat. Seeing Sebrahn among real children like this, he could no longer hold on to the fantasy that Sebrahn was anything natural. Sebrahn was something else entirely, and no more Alec's kin than the clouds in the sky.

He trudged up the slope to get Sebrahn's boots, blinking back sudden tears he didn't want the children to see.

He picked up the boots and knocked out the snow that had gotten inside them.

Sebrahn had followed him. He stared up at Alec, and then the boots. "Bad."

"No, they're not!" Alec growled. Sitting down heavily in the snow, he pulled Sebrahn into his lap and wrestled one boot back on, tying it tightly.

Sebrahn looked up at him and said again, "Baaad."

Alec understood this time and let out a soft, bitter laugh. "You're not bad. You're not anything, except . . . Except . . ."

"Are you crying?"

He forced a smile as he looked up at Silma. "No, I just had something in my eye."

He got Sebrahn's other boot on and quickly distracted the children by proposing a contest to see who could do the most somersaults to make the longest path in the snow.

Sebrahn copied them, and once he'd mastered the basic movement he was off, rolling like a wheel, blond braid flying. Faster than any natural child could go. The others looked slow and clumsy compared to him. The thought filled Alec with a mix of revulsion and guilt. What did he feel for Sebrahn, really? Was it love? Could you love such a creature? Or was it just neediness on his part? Pity? Duty?

Silma came back and squatted down beside him. "You're sad."

Alec wished the child wasn't quite so perceptive. "Maybe a little."

She reached out and took his hand in her snowy mittened one. "How come you and your little boy has yellow hair? Are you Tírfaie?"

"I'm half Tír. My mama was 'faie."

"Is she dead?"

Alec nodded.

"Did you cry when she died? Mynir cried and cried and *cried* when his mama died, and his father cried, too."

"Uh, yes." He'd cried after the vision of her death.

"What clan was she?"

Alec was spared answering when a woman in a shawl came hurrying down toward them. "Silma, you come in now."

"But I'm playing!" the girl whined, still holding Alec's hand.

The look her mother gave him made Alec gently free himself and stand up. "You'd better do what your mama says," he advised.

"Can we play with your little boy again?" asked Silma.

"That's enough of that, Silma," her mother said firmly. "The rest of you, come with me. There's hot honeyed milk for you in the kitchen, and apple tarts."

Sebrahn came up the hill with the rest of them and started to follow them to the house.

The woman cast a meaningful look over her shoulder at Alec, half frightened, half warning. Alec wondered what she'd heard, and how.

Alec sighed, sitting there in the midst of the birds and

paths the children had made with him. "Sebrahn, come here."

Sebrahn squatted down next to him.

"It's all right. We don't need any hot milk, do we?" But it would have been pleasant to join the others in a warm kitchen with women bustling around, fussing over them. He missed Kari Cavish, maybe even the way he would if he really were her son. He wished again, more strongly than before, that Sebrahn was really the sort of child who got invited into warm kitchens.

He was sitting there, just staring out at the waves on the lake, when he heard the crunch and squeak of boots on snow behind him. Looking over his shoulder, he saw Seregil coming toward them, bundled up to his chin and carrying a steaming mug in each hand.

Alec relieved him of one and took a careful sip. It was honeyed milk, with a generous lashing of rassos. He gave Seregil a grateful look. "Are you done with the elders?"

"Yes. They want to speak with you next." Seregil paused. "I saw what happened with the children. I thought you could use a little company first."

"You thought right." Alec held the cup in both hands, watching the reflections of clouds drift across the milky surface.

"Don't take it too hard, talí. People are protective of their children."

As I am of Sebrahn, he thought. *But if he's no child, then I'm no father.*

It made his head hurt. Taking another long sip, he asked, "So, what are the elders saying?"

"So far I've done most of the talking. Some of them aren't convinced there's no risk, having him here."

Alec's heart sank a little lower. He'd felt accepted by many of Seregil's kin last night, and thought he might make a few friends here, too. He was going shooting with Kheeta and some others later that afternoon. "I thought we were going to be welcome here."

"We are, for now. But some rumors are spreading already." He pointed at Sebrahn, who'd already worked his way out of one boot again. "We have to be more careful. The more ordinary we can make him seem, the easier it will be."

"Ordinary? He never will be that. Not ever. He'll always be exactly as he is."

Seregil gave him an odd look.

Alec set his cup in the snow and lashed the boot more securely onto Sebrahn's foot. The rhekaro didn't resist, but he began to pick at the laces as soon as Alec was done.

"No!" Alec told him sternly. "Just sit there." He retrieved his cup and downed the last of the milk, glad of the bite of the rassos burning his throat and belly. "What about Micum? He said he'd go home when we were somewhere safe."

Seregil took a swallow of his own drink and licked the lingering drops from his upper lip. "He hasn't said yet."

"It will be snowing in Skala before long. He'd better make up his mind."

"About what?" Micum asked, coming down the slope to join them. "I've been looking all over for you, Alec."

"We were just talking about you," Seregil told him, passing him the cup. "We're here. We're safe. You need to go home."

"Let me be the judge of that, eh? They're waiting for you three inside. Adzriel sent me out to fetch you."

Seregil stood up and pulled Alec to his feet. "Don't worry, talí. They just want to see him."

They shucked off their fleece coats in their bedchamber and Seregil led the way to a part of the house Alec hadn't seen. He braced himself as they entered a sunny room, expecting a stern gathering glaring at him from behind a long table. Instead he found himself in a pretty room with warm pine wainscoting, pale green velvet furniture, and polished tea tables. Two ancient-looking women and two equally ancient-looking men were reclining at ease with Adzriel and Säaban, sipping tea and talking quietly together. They all looked up as Alec and Sebrahn came in, and some of the smiles faded.

Adzriel stood and took Alec's hand. "I present my brother's talímenios, Alec í Amasa of Kerry, and of the Hâzadriëlfaie line. And Sebrahn, his rhekaro, foretold by prophecy at Sarikali."

"There's no need to be so formal," one of the women chided lightly. "Come here, Alec Two Lives. Don't make an old woman get up, there's a good boy." She extended her hand, and after a moment's hesitation Alec went to her and took it. "I am Zillina ä Sala, a great-aunt of the khirnari and her family. And this must be Sebrahn. May I touch him?"

Sebrahn was clinging to the edge of Alec's tunic, but he didn't flinch as Zillina stroked his hair and cheek.

"Well!" she said, sitting back and absently rubbing her hand. "I can see the dragon in him."

The other three did the same, with varying reactions. Trillius í Morin yanked his hand back as if he'd been stung; Ela ä Yhalina sniffed Sebrahn's hair and smiled; Onir í Thalir just shrugged.

"I see that he's made of flowers," Ela ä Yhalina told them. "Could you show us how it's done?"

Alec pricked Sebrahn's finger over a goblet of water and made one of the dark lotus blossoms. The rhekaro scooped it out at once and brought it to Ela, placing it on her knee.

It sank through the soft wool of her long tunic and trousers, and she let out a startled little cry as she flexed her leg. "By the Light, it's true. It's eased my rheumatism."

In the meantime Sebrahn had made a second and placed it on her other knee. She flexed both legs, then leaned forward and kissed Sebrahn on the top of his head. "Thank you, dragon child of flowers, for your lovely gift." She turned to the others. "There is power in him, and great danger, but there's a kindness there, as well. From what Seregil has told us, he even seeks out the ill to heal them."

"He does," Alec assured her.

"That may be so," Trillius í Morin said doubtfully, "but all I felt was death. And it's still blood magic."

"I felt nothing at all," Onir í Thalir said, shaking his head.

"Perhaps each feels what he or she needs to feel, or perhaps expects?" wondered Zillina ä Sala. "I see the dragon in his eyes, but I see the child in the dragon, too. I've never heard of such a being in any of the writings."

"Zillina is our greatest scholar," Adzriel explained. "She's studied at Sarikali and with the Khatme, as well."

"Do you know anything about the Hâzadriëlfaie?" Alec asked, then politely added, "Great-Aunt."

"Less than you, it would seem. The old story is that Hâzadriël had a vision and gathered only certain people from across the land to take away with her, never to be heard from again. As far as I know, they took their secret with them. But now, in this child of magic, I think I see their reason." She took Alec's hand in hers. Her skin was smooth and dry as vellum, but her eyes were warm. "What was done to create this child was evil, unnatural. This alchemy Seregil told us of sounds like some lesser type of necromancy. What happened to you, dear Alec Two Lives, was an abomination, and this rhekaro is an abomination—No, my dear, don't give me such a scowl. You know in your heart that it is true. Such beings, the homunculi, are not natural. They are not meant to exist."

It was true, and Alec knew it better than any of them. And yet he could not condemn Sebrahn as an abomination. It would be like cursing himself.

"Imagine if Hâzadriël's followers had remained," said Adzriel. "How many would have been taken and used to make these creatures for the benefit of their masters?"

"Or to be sold!" said Onir. "If these creatures can kill with a song and grant life to a corpse, then they are more valuable than gold or horses."

Ela sighed as she rubbed her knees. "If only it stopped at healing. Perhaps then—But to bring back the dead?" She shuddered. "I mean you no offense, Alec Two Lives, but such a thing isn't right, either. What was done to you goes against the flow of the world. What if some evil person had one of these creatures at his disposal, and would never die, but go on accruing power?"

"Are you saying I shouldn't be alive? That I'm an abomination?" Alec asked, feeling a cold lump forming in his belly.

"No, not at all," Ela replied, "but you have done something no one should do—come back through the gates of death."

Seregil put an arm around Alec's shoulders and a hand on

Sebrahn's. "No one asked Sebrahn to do that to Alec. Neither of us had any notion that his power could be that strong! Sebrahn just did it."

"And it almost killed him, too," said Alec. "If I hadn't been alive to feed him, he would have just wasted away."

"Ah yes, the feeding. It eats only blood?" asked Onir í Thalir.

"Only mine," Alec explained.

The old man considered this. "If that's the case, then I don't see how these alchemists could create herds of them to sell, since they cannot be parted from their progenitor. They must have been the property of a small elite."

"But there's also the matter of Alec's mixed blood," said Zillina. "He's not pure Hâzadriëlfaie. Who is to say that this rhekaro is exactly like one produced from a pureblood?"

"The alchemist did say that the two he made didn't turn out as he expected, according to some book," Alec explained. "They were supposed to have wings, and no voices. Sebrahn can't fly, but he can speak."

"Can he?" said Onir í Thalir. "Let us hear."

Alec picked up a cup and held it out to the rhekaro. "What is this?"

"Cuuuuup," Sebrahn rasped, barely loud enough to hear.

"And this?" Alec held out his dagger.

"Kniiiiiiiife."

"Who am I?" asked Alec.

"Ahek."

"And me?" asked Adzriel.

"Asreel."

"You see?" she said to the others. "He speaks. He learns. He's clearly very attached to Alec, and to Seregil, as well. And as far as we know, he is the only one of his kind. If he can be taught to use only his healing powers, then I say he will be an asset to this clan."

"That is a very large 'if,' honored Khirnari," mused Trillius í Morin. "I know what I felt, and it was death. He has killed before, and he will kill again."

"And yet he heals, too—Uncle. Isn't there balance in that?" asked Alec.

"The greater questions are what he is, and if someone can make more of them. If so, they must be stopped!" Onir insisted. "I think that only you two can find these answers, and you must!"

"You're right, of course, Great-Uncle," Seregil said. "We're going to visit Tyrus í Triel."

Zillina nodded approvingly. "That is a wise decision. Go quickly, and may Aura the Lightbringer protect you both."

"Thank you, Great-Aunt." Seregil bowed to her, then looked to Adzriel.

Adzriel nodded. "That is all, brothers."

Alec bowed low, and Sebrahn copied him, drawing a few chuckles from the onlookers.

Once outside, Alec let out a gasp of relief.

Seregil threw an arm over Alec's shoulders. "If they were going to throw us out, I'd have known it ahead of time. You did well."

Alec was relieved, and glad, too, but his earlier revelation about Sebrahn continued to haunt him. It had been so much easier, before. Shaking off the sadness that came with it, he asked, "Where is this dragon man?"

"'Dragon Friend,' Alec. It's a title of great honor. He's a hermit, and lives up in the mountains."

"Then let's go!"

"It's a day's ride in good weather. We'll go tomorrow, with an early start."

They started back to their room but were waylaid in the great hall by Kheeta and three young men Alec recognized from the feast. All were dressed for the outdoors and had bows and quivers decked with shattas. The tallest was carrying an axe.

"What's all this?" asked Seregil.

"It's time for our new cousin to prove his mettle," Kheeta announced, clearly meaning Alec.

"This fellow is Ethgil í Zoztrus," Kheeta told him, and the tall one with the axe nodded, smiling. Kheeta then ruffled the hair of the youngest. "This little one is Korit í Arin." That earned Kheeta a scowl.

Seregil's father had been named Korit. Alec wondered if this was another one of Seregil's kin.

"And I'm Stellin í Alia," the third youth told him. He was clearly a ya'shel like Alec, but his eyes were dark brown and he had curly black hair, like the Zengati slavers who'd taken him and Seregil to Riga.

"I'm glad to meet you all," Alec replied, bowing a little.

The others laughed at that.

"Go fetch your bow before the light goes on us," Kheeta ordered, clearly in charge of the younger ones, including Alec, it seemed.

"I'd like to see this," Seregil said, grinning.

They retrieved their winter clothing, and their new companions led them through another unknown part of the house, gathering a small crowd of onlookers along the way.

"Your reputation precedes you, cousin," Kheeta told Alec with a wink.

They left the house with their entourage and made their way out to a level stretch of land at the edge of the forest. There, Ethgil used his axe to cut an X into the bark of a large pine. "There. Let's see if you're as good as we've heard!"

Alec just smiled. He'd had plenty of time during their journey here to accustom himself to the lemonwood bow. He stood to one side, waxing his bowstring, while Korit paced out thirty yards from the target and drew a line in the snow with his heel.

Winking at Seregil, who stood with the little crowd with Sebrahn on his shoulders, Alec set his first arrow to the bowstring, then raised the bow as he pulled and let fly at the target. He'd been too cocky, and missed his mark, but still hit the tree. Frowning, he scooped up a small handful of snow and let it filter through his fingers, testing the direction of the breeze, then he nocked another arrow and took a bit more time. This one flew straight and hit the center of the X deadon, earning him some respectful whistles and murmurs of "Well done!"

"That's one, but can he do it again?" Stellin challenged.

"Let's see," said Alec.

His next shaft struck the upper left arm of the X.

"Oh, so close!" Korit exclaimed, as some of the others laughed.

Alec ignored them all and sent another shaft into the upper right arm of the X—then the lower left, and lower right. His fifth shaft found the center, shaving a bit of fletching from the arrow that was already there.

"How did you do that?" Stellin exclaimed.

Seregil grinned, "Didn't Kheeta tell you? He's good."

Alec shrugged nonchalantly.

"Stellin, you try!" Korit said, giving him a shove forward.

"Yes, defend Bôkthersa's honor!" Kheeta urged.

Korit retrieved Alec's arrows from the target and handed them back with a respectful nod.

"Thanks, cousin." Alec decided this wasn't a bad way to introduce himself. After all, it was what he was best at.

Dark Stellin took his place at the line and tried to match Alec's pattern, but aside from the center mark, three were only close and one missed the tree entirely.

"That wasn't too bad," said Alec as they waited for Korit to bring Stellin his arrows.

"But not good enough," the young man grumbled. "I bet you can't do that again."

Alec's blood was up now, and he gave him a cocky grin. "Let's see."

And he did, duplicating his earlier feat with ease.

After that, the challenges were inevitable. Kheeta had taken up a collection of shattas for Alec to pay his debts with when he had to, which turned out to be not all that often.

They used the X for a while, then set up wands in the snow and did clout shooting, firing arcing shots to come down on a handkerchief on the ground.

Alec's father had taught him to shoot this way, and he quickly began rebuilding his lost collection, to the point that the others began to grumble a bit.

"Are you a wizard?" asked tall Ethgil, who'd lost three good shattas to Alec. "Those arrows fly like magic!"

"I grew up with a bow in my hand," Alec told him, a little

insulted. "If I didn't shoot straight, I didn't eat. Hunger was the only magic I needed."

Kheeta smoothed it over, and they all stayed friends and went back to shooting. Alec thought fleetingly of aiming off the mark on purpose, but knew it would hurt their pride if they figured it out.

By the time the light failed and they headed back to the house with promises of hot tea in the kitchen, Alec felt almost at home. He liked his companions and they seemed to like him. Inwardly, though, he wondered what they thought when they looked at Sebrahn.

CHAPTER 11

Dragon's Friend

DAWN WAS just a hint of gold over the eastern peaks when Alec set off with Seregil and Micum through the bitter cold to take Sebrahn to Tyrus Dragon Friend.

With Seregil leading once again, they followed a road deep into the thick forest beyond the town, and up into the mountains. It had snowed in the night, and the towering firs were clad in white below a clear blue winter sky.

It's all so familiar! thought Alec again, breathing in the sweet, cold air as the way grew steeper.

"Except for the dragons, this place is a lot like the forests around Kerry," said Micum, echoing Alec's thought.

"And I always thought the forests around Kerry were a lot like here," Seregil replied with a smile.

"I can see how you would miss this place," Micum said, looking around. "And your clan."

"It is good to be back." He and Alec still hadn't discussed how long they would stay.

The forest was quiet, but not silent. Small birds sang among the branches, habas chattered as they scampered across the road with their bushy black tails curved over their backs, and hawks cried to one another as they circled against the sky. There were dragons here, too: dragonlings, and others as large as rabbits. Alec and the others gave those a wide berth and the creatures paid no attention to them, more intent on hunting for unlucky mice in their tunnels in the snow, and tiny dragonlings, too. Alec saw one of the larger ones gobble down two at once.

"They eat their own," Micum noted, surprised. They'd seen foxes and hawks, even ravens, devour a few, but never this.

"So will a pig," Seregil said. "I think that's why little dragons are so common and huge ones are so rare. You need a lot of young to start with, so at least a few survive. If all the little ones grew up, there'd be nothing but dragons left. They'd have eaten the rest of us."

Sebrahn pointed to the dragons constantly and tried to squirm out of Alec's arms, presumably to go to them.

It was midafternoon when they turned aside onto a trail, or what seemed to be a trail. The blanket of snow was smooth between the trees, but Alec soon spotted the hatch marks cut into tree trunks along the way. They were old, the bark long since healed around them. The snow was deep for a man, but the horses fared well enough. More than once, they saw larger dragons circling far above them.

"Are they likely to come down here?" asked Micum.

"You never know," Seregil told him. "Just keep an eye out for them."

But none did, and as the shadows lengthened across the trail Alec suddenly caught the scent of smoke—cooking smoke.

"Would that be from your Dragon Friend's chimney?" asked Micum.

Seregil nodded. "He's the only one up here. Well, the only person, anyway."

They came across horse tracks, and signs where a man had dismounted and gone into the trees. They were dusted over with snow—at least a day old, Alec judged. Very soon, however, they struck fresh tracks and came out in a clearing. The ground sloped down, and the large cabin that stood here was built into the hillside. It was crafted from large logs chinked with clay, and had a porch much like the ones at the clan house, except that this one was built on long posts, with what looked like a stable underneath. The smoke was coming from a large stone chimney on the far end of the building, carrying the aroma of grouse and onions.

The dragonlings were so thick here that Alec and the others had to dismount and lead their horses carefully to avoid trampling any in the failing daylight. Alec held Sebrahn tightly by the hand as the rhekaro tried to stop and pick them up. A few fluttered up to land on his shoulders.

Focused as he was on Sebrahn and not treading on any of the little creatures, he didn't notice the man who'd come out on the porch until he called out to them.

"Who comes to my house?" He held a lantern in one hand and a long sword in the other. A dragon the size of a cat crouched on his shoulder, its tail wrapped around the arm holding the lantern.

"Seregil í Korit," Seregil told him. "Is that any way to welcome an old friend, Tyrus?"

"Korit's boy?" Tyrus lowered his sword. "And you've brought friends."

"May we come in? It was a long ride."

"Of course. Take care of your horses and come up for supper." He started back into the cabin, but paused long enough to add, "Remember, boy, if you hear anything stirring in the shadows down there, or a hiss, back away slowly and come get me."

With these less-than-encouraging words, he disappeared inside.

They managed to get the horses settled and fed without incident. There were two others there—a white and a bay—and they nickered quietly to the newcomers.

Climbing back up to the porch, they stepped inside and found a table laid for supper and their host stirring a pot on the fire in the hearth.

The flowing hair beneath his faded green sen'gai was grey as iron. His eyes were a lighter shade, like Seregil's. Somehow Alec had half expected them to be gold, like a dragon's. Tyrus's hands were covered in lissik-stained dragon bite marks, some large enough to encompass his wrist. There were more on his neck, and a few small ones on his face.

"It's been a long time since you visited me, Seregil í Korit," Tyrus said, straightening up.

"Too long. I've missed you and your friend."

"He'll be glad to see you. And who have you brought me this time?" Tyrus asked, nodding at Alec.

"My talímenios, Alec í Amasa—"

"A talímenios at your age?" Tyrus shook his head, then looked Alec up and down. "And a ya'shel. Golden hair and blue eyes, but I see the 'faie in you, and that little bite on your ear shows a dragon's favor. Welcome, cousin."

"Thank you," Alec replied.

"And this is my friend Micum Cavish, a good and honorable man, accepted by the clan," Seregil told him.

"A Tír?" Tyrus's eyes narrowed a bit. "Not a Plenimaran, I hope?"

Micum grinned. "No, sir, I'm a northlander by birth and a Skalan by choice."

"Ah. That's all right, then."

Tyrus squatted down to look at Sebrahn, who only had eyes for the dragon on the man's shoulder. "Who's this little one?"

"This is Sebrahn," answered Alec.

"Silver eyes and yellow hair? Odd for one called 'moonlight.' What is he?"

"That's what we'd like to speak to your friend about, if we may," Seregil explained.

"Of course! But sit down and eat something first. You've had a long, cold ride."

Alec looked around curiously as he took his place. The long room was furnished in typical Bôkthersan style, with graceful furniture fashioned from light woods, and colorful hangings and carpets, and appeared to serve many purposes. The broad stone fireplace doubled as the kitchen; several pots were steaming on hooks and iron stands. The dining table was long enough to accommodate a dozen people. That was odd, thought Alec, for a hermit. Beyond it there were a few comfortable-looking chairs, and walls lined with books and scrolls. Broad glazed windows looked out over the valley below. Outside, the last of the daylight was fading.

The grouse and hard bread were tasty. There was no wine or turab, just mugs of cold springwater. Alec glanced around as he ate, expecting more dragons, but aside from the one that had fluttered from Tyrus's shoulder up to a perch in the rafters, there weren't any in sight.

When they were done with the meal, they moved to the chairs at the other end of the room.

"When are we—" Alec began, but Seregil caught his eye and shook his head slightly; apparently there was some sort of custom to this.

Tyrus lit lamps and closed the shutters, then took a long clay pipe and tobacco bag from a shelf. "Do any of you smoke?"

"I do, on occasion," said Seregil, although Alec had never seen him take more than a few puffs from Micum's pipe.

"As do I, sir," said Micum, producing his worn old pipe.

This seemed to please Tyrus, and he shared his tobacco with them.

The others smoked a moment in silence, while Alec tried to hide his growing impatience.

"You want to know if your Sebrahn is a dragon," the old man said at last. "Don't look so surprised, Alec. I see the dragon aura around him as clear as I see you." He went back to his smoking, staring at Sebrahn.

At last he took his pipe from his lips and pointed the stem at Sebrahn. "That is no dragon."

"But the aura?" asked Alec, though he was relieved.

"I didn't say he is no part of a dragon, only that he isn't one himself, any more than you are." He took a puff on his pipe and exhaled through his nose, looking a bit dragon-like himself. "Will he come to me?"

Alec put Sebrahn down, and the rhekaro immediately went to Tyrus and climbed into his lap. Once there, he pointed upward. "Drak-kon."

As if summoned, the dragon swooped across the room and landed on the arm of Tyrus's chair. Alec held his breath as Sebrahn reached to stroke its head and wings, but the dragon did not bite him.

"If he's not a dragon, then why do they come to him like that?" asked Seregil.

"Why do they come to me?" Tyrus said with a shrug. "Now, then, shall we go see him?"

Bundled once more against the cold, they followed Tyrus up a very steep but well-traveled path through the snow, moving steadily up the mountainside—Alec with Sebrahn in a sling on his back. A waxing moon balanced on the eastern peaks, and the stars were as sharp as glass.

The trees grew thinner and smaller as they went, and soon they were above the tree line, boots scraping on bare rock. The air was filled with the sound of wings, and now and then Alec saw a dragon silhouetted for an instant against the stars. Caught between fear and wonder, he stayed close to Tyrus.

He was glad of the sling; Sebrahn was as restless as a child going to a fair. Pointing frantically, he rasped out, "Drak-kon! Drak-kon!"

A little farther on Alec was suddenly aware of loud hissing, though he wasn't sure of the direction. It kept up and he couldn't tell if it was one dragon following them, which was unsettling, or if there were a lot of them about, which wasn't much comfort, either. Tyrus's presence must have been keeping them at bay.

We'd have been mauled and eaten by now, otherwise, thought Alec.

The way grew more level, and Tyrus finally stopped in the shadow of a high ridge. Alec could see dragons on the heights, perhaps dozens of them, some as large as bulls.

"Drak-kon!" Sebrahn said, more loudly than Alec had ever heard him speak.

"How large is your—friend?" Alec asked, wondering which dragon it was.

Tyrus chuckled. "Oh, he's a big one."

How large was large? The size of a horse, of a house? The ones in the murals and mosaics in Rhíminee were always portrayed as being as large as a city, but Alec doubted—

Suddenly the ridge moved and the ground shook so hard

that all of them went sprawling. Dragons of all sizes took wing around them, like bats streaming out of a cave at sunset.

What Alec had mistaken for a smaller, nearby ridge rose against the sky, the shape unmistakable. The horned head alone was half the size of the Stag and Otter; the curved, spine-ridged neck might be as long as Silvermoon Street. That large ridge was its back.

Laughing, Tyrus pulled Alec to his feet. "This is my friend. Friend, this one comes to you with questions."

The head descended, the one huge eye Alec could see glowing like molten gold. Then, in a voice like a softly spoken avalanche, it said, "Hello, little 'faie. You smell of far places."

Hot, reeking breath rolled over him—bitter, with a metallic tang like cold iron against the tongue. It reminded Alec of the tinctures Yhakobin had forced down his throat. Sebrahn had gone completely still.

"See? I promised I'd show you dragons one day," Seregil told him. "Go on, it's waiting."

"Uh—hello—Master Dragon." Alec bowed. "Forgive me, I don't know your name."

"My name?" The dragon raised its head and made an ear-shattering, incomprehensible sound. Then, lowering its head even with Alec again, it said, "You appreciate the difficulty. You may call me 'Friend.'"

"Thank you." He didn't know what else to say. He'd never addressed a living mountain before.

"Show me the little one," the dragon said.

With shaking hands, Alec freed the rhekaro from his sling. "This is Sebrahn."

"Drak-kon," Sebrahn said again.

The dragon brought its head within a few yards of them, and Alec could feel its heat and see himself and the others reflected in that huge eye.

Awed as he was, Alec reacted too slowly when Sebrahn ran straight to the dragon and grasped one of its spear-like chin barbs with both hands.

Alec started after him, but Seregil caught him by the arm. "It's all right."

Sebrahn was so tiny against that enormous head—smaller, in fact, than the fang Alec could see under the dragon's lip— but his voice was clear and loud as he began to sing a single drawn-out note so intense that it hurt the ears.

"By the Flame, what's he doing?" Micum shouted over it.

Was Sebrahn was trying to kill the dragon, perceiving it as a threat? "No, Sebrahn!" Alec yelled, trying to pull free from Seregil's grip. "Let me go! I have to—"

But then the dragon sang back, a different, deeper note, its voice no louder than Sebrahn's.

Everyone held their breath as they watched the strange pair continue their discordant duet. Sebrahn touched the dragon's face, stroking the long spines and scales as calmly as if he were petting a horse. At last, he pressed his cheek to the dragon's jaw and both fell silent.

"What was that about?" Micum whispered.

"A kinship song," the dragon told him.

"But Tyrus claims he's not a dragon," Alec said.

"He is not, but we still share kinship through the blood of the First Dragon. That is where this little one's power comes from, because it is made with your Hâzad blood."

"You mean Hâzadriël and her people really did—do have dragon blood?"

"All 'faie do, little friend. But some have more than others. That is the Hâzadriëlfaie's gift, and their burden."

"Then I—?" Alec's legs felt wobbly. It had been a terrific shock when Seregil had told him that he was part 'faie. But this?

"It does not make you a dragon, either," the great dragon told him with something like a chuckle.

It was too much. Turning his attention to the familiar, Alec knelt and examined Sebrahn. There were deep cuts on his hands where he'd caught them on the dragon's scales or spines. Alec pricked his finger with his knife and gave Sebrahn the blood he needed to heal.

"Ah, I see," the dragon rumbled. "You heal him, as he heals you. It is as it once was."

"You know about rhekaros?" asked Alec. It was disconcerting, talking to an eye, but the rest of the dragon was just too big to take in.

"I have heard of them by different names. But none that could kill."

"But how—?" Who was he to question a dragon? "It's because of my Tírfaie blood, isn't it? The man who made Sebrahn said it was tainted."

The dragon pulled back a little and sniffed them. The draft of its nostril sucked at their hair and clothing.

"You are not tainted, little friend. There is the smell of death on you, and your companions, but it comes from your actions, not your blood."

"Then why can Sebrahn kill and raise the dead? Why isn't he what the alchemist wanted?"

The dragon sniffed at them again. "You carry the memory of other Immortals in your Tírfaie blood, though you are of Hâzadriël's line as well. And perhaps this alchemist's own magic went awry. He did not understand fully what he was doing. Had he made such a creature before?"

"Only one that I know of, but he killed it. He needed me, since the Hâzad were gone."

"Yes. I remember Hâzadriël well—a sad woman, but a brave one. I watched her people pass, going to the north. Their gift was different than any other's."

"To be used for making rhekaros?" asked Alec. "What sort of gift is that?"

"Their making does not have to be evil, Alec Two Lives. Surely you realize this little one's worth, the worth of even a rhekaro that cannot raise the dead or kill, for they are not supposed to have that power."

"What if we take Sebrahn to the Hâzad?" asked Alec.

The dragon considered this, then raised its enormous head and turned its face to the moon.

They waited in silence. The moon was brighter now, and Alec could make out the jut of the great dragon's wing and spine-ridged back. Smaller dragons—though hardly small—crawled around up there, as if it were a mountainside rather than one of their own.

The great dragon lowered its head again. "The Light-bringer tells me that death lies in the north—your death. But you might not die if you return to the source of this creature. If you do go that way, then you must destroy the source, lest any more such creatures be made."

Alec's mouth went dry. "I—I am his source."

"No, you were only the means, Alec Two Lives. Words are the source of alchemy. Destroy the words and no more such creatures can be made."

"Words?" asked Micum.

"Books!" said Alec. "Yhakobin's workshop was full of books. And there was one on his worktable—a big red one, with a picture of a rhekaro in it. I never saw Yhakobin use a wand or an incantation, just his symbols and metals—and me. But there were always books open on his worktables, and he'd refer to them while he worked. But to destroy it—"

"We'd have to go get it," Seregil finished for him. "And if we don't?"

"Then you cannot destroy it," said the dragon.

Alec suspected it was unwise to be impatient with a dragon of any size. "But what will happen if we don't?" he asked as politely as he could.

"The future is not written, Alec Two Lives. The Lightbringer reveals only what can be, not what will be. Destroy it, or don't. The choice is yours."

"But if we do find it, whatever it is, will it tell us what Sebrahn really is?" Alec asked, frustrated now.

"That you know, little friend. He is unlike anything that has been or will be. The question is, what will *you* do with him?"

"But we came to ask you!" Alec cried.

The dragon did not answer. Raising its great head, it snapped up one of the dragons that had been resting on its back and swallowed it whole. Then, without another word, it stretched out in the position they'd found it in and heaved a great sigh that shook the ground again.

"He's finished, cousin," Tyrus told Alec. "It's time to go."

"But—"

"It's all right, Alec," said Seregil, setting off down the

steep trail with the others. Alec picked up Sebrahn and followed.

The rhekaro looked back over Alec's shoulder, pointing. "Drak-kon!"

"Yes," Alec said, feeling a little shaky now as the full import of what he'd just done set in. "It certainly is."

When they reached the cabin, Tyrus took up his pipe again. The small dragon flew down to curl up in his lap. Sebrahn stood beside his chair, stroking the little dragon as he had the giant one.

Alec sat with his chin in his hands, feeling dazed. "How can what the dragon said about me be true?"

Tyrus smiled. "Young Alec, do you know the origin story?"

"I think so. The sun pierced the Great Dragon with a spear and eleven drops of blood fell on Aurënen. The first Aurënfaie sprang up where the blood fell—the eleven major clans."

"That's right. And though it was the same blood for all, each drop fell on different soil, and that's how we came to differ."

"But how could the Hâzadriëlfaie be more—dragonish than any other clan?"

"That's the great question, isn't it, cousin? But then, even in the same clan, everyone does not have the same magic— or even any magic at all. For those who share the same type, though, it usually grows stronger when people of the same talents come together. It must have been like that with Hâzadriël's followers, bound by the blood that brought them together and drove them north. Those of the Hâzadriëlfaie blood must have more of the Dragon in them than most."

"You mean the origin story really is true?" asked Alec.

"There must be some truth to it, or we wouldn't have been telling it for thousands of years. Nothing appears out of nothing, as far as I know, and we are linked inextricably to the dragons."

"And Alec has more of that Great Dragon blood in his veins," Seregil noted, frowning.

"And Tír, and then there's the dragon kiss there on his ear," Tyrus pointed out. "You may be just as unique as your rhekaro, Alec. Your alchemist chose to ignore that."

"Then that's why Sebrahn didn't turn out the way he intended?"

"So it appears." Tyrus gazed down at Sebrahn and stroked his hair as Sebrahn continued to pat the dragon. "Do you understand that he is nothing like you, either, Alec? He's just magic with a form that resembles you."

"But he thinks. He has a mind. What *is* he?" asked Alec. "Your dragon didn't tell me that."

"He did," Tyrus replied. "Sebrahn is the first and last of his kind, unless another alchemist finds the means to use your blood again. To understand what Sebrahn is and what he can do, then you must understand what the man was trying to create, and how."

"Which means getting that book," Alec said.

"Well then, it's like my friend said. You'll have to find it, won't you?" said Tyrus.

Alec and Seregil exchanged a look and Seregil shrugged. "The dragon did say we *might* not die if we go in that direction."

They spent the night at the cabin and took their leave the following morning.

"So it's Plenimar now?" said Micum as they rode along the snowy trail. "How in Bilairy's name are two 'faie going to go back there without being captured or killed?"

"Well, we can't just walk into Riga," Alec admitted, riding along with Sebrahn. "We're obviously 'faie with no freedman's brand or collar."

"The collar is no problem. We can have those made," Seregil noted.

"Would your uncle make them for us?" asked Micum.

Seregil thought a moment. "He would, but he'd want to know why. I'd rather my family doesn't know where I'm headed. I want to spare them that, especially Adzriel, and I don't want to leave any trail behind if someone comes looking for us. Collars will be easy enough to find elsewhere."

"And the brands?"

"That may be a bit harder. Too bad we cut out the ones we had, eh, Alec?"

Alec grimaced. "I wish you'd thought of that at the time. But they were Yhakobin's mark, anyway. That has to be well known around the Riga slave markets, and anywhere between there and the estate. People would take us for runaways."

"Thero can probably do some sort of transformation—"

"No one would remark on a master and his own slaves passing by, though, would they?" asked Micum, grinning. "I speak Plenimaran as well as you do, Seregil. Alec's no good at it, but I'll do all the talking, anyway."

It was a good plan, Seregil had to admit, but still he replied, "No. Not this time. You're *not* going."

Micum gave him an exasperated look. "Not this again!"

"You'd never pass for a Plenimaran, any more than Alec or I could."

Micum ran a hand over his chin stubble. "I'll cut my hair, grow my beard, and let it be known I'm a northlander trader. I've met some who owned slaves."

"We can manage without you," Seregil said bluntly. Whatever they did, it was going to be damn dangerous. He didn't ever want another friend's blood on his hands.

"And Kari? She'll flay us alive the next time she sees us," Alec put in.

"She'll understand. She always has."

Seregil wondered if Micum had ever really understood the tension between his friend and his wife, back in their wandering days. As good as Kari had always been to him, and to Alec, Seregil always caught that same old flash of dread and resentment whenever they showed up unannounced.

"I'm going with you, and that's final," said Micum.

Seregil started to object again, then shrugged and pulled his cloak closer around him. "It's not like I can stop you, is it?"

Micum gave him a knowing look. "Swear it, Seregil. I don't want to wake up tomorrow and find nothing but a note again."

Fair enough, he thought, *given past history.* And it wasn't as if he hadn't already considered just slipping away. Leaning over in the saddle, Seregil clasped hands with Micum and gave him the pledge even he would never break. *"Rei phöril tös tókun meh brithir, vrí sh'ruit'ya."* Though you thrust your dagger at my eyes, I will not flinch. "There, are you satisfied?"

"I am. Now, what route?"

"It will be a hard trip to the coast this time of year. The road we took here will be impassable now. But if we stick to the main roads where there are way stations, we should be able to get through to Chillian in three weeks or so, and take a ship from there."

"To where?" Alec asked.

"Silver Bay?" suggested Micum. "It's a few days' ride north of Rhíminee. A lot of travelers go through there. I doubt anyone will pay us much mind. That way we can avoid the city altogether. There's not much out there but a few farms and inns. We can meet up with Thero somewhere. We'll need him to find Rhal for us, assuming the Plenimarans haven't captured him yet."

Alec and Seregil had been traveling in disguise when they'd first met Rhal, who'd been a Folçwine River captain then. Seregil was passing as a gentlewoman named Lady Gwethelyn, with Alec playing the role of her too-young protector. Seregil was very convincing as a woman, and had attracted the swarthy captain's unwanted attention, much to Alec's alarm and Seregil's amusement. Seregil had previous experience with that sort of thing, but the ship was a small one and Rhal had been quite persistent, to his own chagrin. Later, when Seregil had funded a privateering vessel for Rhal with a pair of emeralds, the man had the joke back on him, christening the ship the *Green Lady* and fitting her with a carved figurehead of a green-clad woman who bore a remarkable resemblance to Seregil. Out of pique over Rhal's joke, Seregil never spoke the ship's real name.

"It's not far to Watermead from Silver Bay. We can stop there for supplies," said Micum.

"Are you sure you want Sebrahn there?" asked Seregil.

"What safer place could there be, eh?"

"Safe for Sebrahn, maybe," Seregil reminded him.

"That may be so, but we won't stay long, and if we're really headed for Plenimar then I want a chance to see my family."

Seregil made a quick sign against ill luck. "Don't talk like that if you still want to go."

"I just meant we'd be away longer. Once we're properly equipped, we'll call for Rhal. He can meet us back at Silver Bay and take us across."

"You make it sound easy," Seregil said with wry grin. "It would be easier if either of us knew how to find Yhakobin's house. Neither Alec nor I was in any position to mark the way."

"There's that farm, where the tunnel from the workshop ends," Alec mused. "But I'm not sure I could find that again, either. We just sort of ran away and got lost."

"No, we'll have to start at Riga, and ask the way however we can," said Seregil.

"Could we use that tunnel you told me about to get back into the place?" asked Micum. Seregil could tell his old friend was enjoying this. Micum had always liked the planning stage of a job.

"I don't think we could lift the trapdoor from underneath," Alec told him. The door was hidden under a heavy anvil in Yhakobin's workshop. Pulling it up with leverage from above had been hard enough; trying to balance on a rickety wooden ladder and push up from below was probably impossible.

"We could get back out that way, though, if we have to," Seregil said. "I think we'll have to figure out the rest once we get there."

"And hope Illior's on our side," added Micum.

"What about Sebrahn?" asked Alec. "It's not like I can just leave him anywhere. And you're *not* going without me!"

"No, it's probably going to be a two-man job, at least," said Seregil. "And here we are, at the crux of the Sebrahn problem."

"Yhakobin is dead. As far as we know, he was the only

one in Plenimar who knew what Sebrahn is, right?" Alec pointed out.

Seregil shook his head, frowning. "We're definitely going to need to talk to Thero about this. Let's see what he can do for us and proceed from there."

CHAPTER 12

Family

SEREGIL went alone to tell his sister they would be departing soon. He found her in her sitting room.

"Leaving?" She sank into a chair by the window. "But you only just got here!"

Seregil knelt and took her hands in his. "I know, but Tyrus told us things that have decided our path."

"Where will you go?"

Seregil hesitated. "I'm sorry, sister, but I can't tell you that."

She looked down at him with sadness in her eyes. "Even here, you don't feel safe?"

"It's not that. We have work to do."

"About Sebrahn?"

"Yes."

Tears welled in her eyes. "When will you leave?"

"We have to prepare for the journey, and there are a few things I need to do. The new moon festival is a week away. We'll leave sometime after that."

"A few weeks. After all these years?"

"It's not what I want, either, Adzriel. But we have to go."

She sighed and wiped her eyes. "I see. Well, I'll provide anything you need for your journey, but promise me that you'll hunt with me at least once?"

Seregil smiled as he rose to his feet. "I won't leave until we do."

Seregil kept his word. By day he, Micum, and Alec went hunting, dancing, ice fishing, and on sleigh rides—whatever

Seregil's sisters asked. Alec and his newfour ¹ friends spent hours at their shooting and his quiver was already heavy with shattas, some made of silver and one of gold he'd won cleaving a birch wand at twenty paces. Kheeta still teased him about using magic, but it was only in jest.

The night found them at Akaien's forge in the village, where Seregil painstakingly set about making two sets of lock picks and other small instruments they needed for nightrunning.

Stripped to their trousers under leather aprons, Seregil and his uncle heated thin steel rods while Alec or Micum pumped the bellows. The lean muscles in Seregil's bare arms stood out as he brought the small hammer down on the anvil, sparks spraying off the red-hot steel, shaping it to his needs. Some of the picks were straight; others had angled tips for more complex locks. Some were slender and supple as a branch tip—just the thing for a Rhíminee triple crow lock; a few were half as thick as an arrow shaft for the large locks that secured prisons, the gates of fine villas, the grate locks in the Rhíminee sewers, and other interesting places.

Akaien looked on with interest, taking a break from his own work. "So this is what all my training with you came to? Little hairpins?" But he laughed as he said it, and Alec saw the pride in the man's eyes.

Alec, meanwhile, tried his hand at carving the special ones out of long goat leg bones. These they used on the tiny locks of jewel cases and locked books. The bone was strong enough to turn the lock, but less likely to leave telltale scratches.

It took four nights to make everything they needed. On the third, Alec found himself alone with Akaien, waiting for the others. Alec liked the man a great deal—there was something of Seregil about him.

Perhaps that was what prompted him to ask a few questions. "From the way Seregil speaks of his father, you two must not have been much alike."

Akaien was quiet for a moment. "Well, Korit was the elder son, and more serious by nature. That's probably why he ended up being khirnari. He was a good one, too. He had real vision and a way with people."

"Except with his son?"

"Perhaps if Korit had lived, and Seregil had grown up with him, they might have come to understand each other."

"Seregil told me you're like a father to him."

Akaien smiled at that. "Things might have gone differently for him if he had been mine. Korit was the serious, responsible one; I took after our father, and liked my fun too well. It was our mother Korit took after. She groomed him for khirnari, and he was elected when he was still a young man. But you were asking about Seregil. His mother, Illia, was the light of my brother's life. She was a lovely woman, with a laugh that made everyone who heard it join in. Seregil took after her in more than looks. If he hadn't had the life he has, I think he'd be more like her."

"It's sad, losing his mother before he even knew her," Alec murmured. *Another thing we have in common.*

"The time for childbearing is short for Aurënfaie women compared with their long lives," Akaien explained. "She was too old when she carried Seregil, and died giving birth to the son they both wanted so badly, after having four girls already. Korit never forgave himself."

"But if that's true, why didn't he love Seregil for being like her?"

"Seregil thinks his father blamed him for his mother's death. Korit didn't, but that didn't bring her back, and his heart never really healed. Seregil would be no different if he lost you. I could see that the minute I laid eyes on you two."

Just then they heard Seregil's voice, and Micum laughing at whatever he'd said.

"Thank you, Uncle," Alec said, emboldened by the confidences Akaien had shared, "I love Seregil more than I can say. I promise you, I'll always take care of him."

Akaien gave him a grin much like Seregil's. "I know that."

When the tools were finished, Seregil turned tailor, sewing the canvas rolls with thin pockets to carry the tools in a small, compact bundle.

Alone in their room, Seregil rolled and tied one set and tossed it to Alec. "Now we're ready for anything."

The following afternoon Mydri sent word that she wanted to speak with Alec—alone.

She had a small house of her own on the south side of the clan compound. With Sebrahn at his side, Alec knocked softly at her door.

She apparently had no use for servants, for she opened it herself. "Don't stand there gawking on the mat. Come in," she ordered brusquely, although she was smiling.

The front room was given over to cots for the sick, bundles of herbs, and other accoutrements of her art. She led him through to a pleasant room overlooking the valley. He caught a glimpse of a tidy kitchen through an open door and smelled something sweet baking there.

"May I look at the wounds you received in Plenimar?" she asked.

Alec pulled down the neck of his tunic, showing her the faint scars on his chest and throat where the slave takers' arrows had struck.

She ran her fingers over them, feeling carefully through his skin to the vessels and throat beyond. "You have no trouble swallowing or talking?"

"No."

"Weakness in your limbs?"

"No, I'm fine, really!"

"I'm glad to hear it."

"So, what do—"

"Not so fast, little brother. This is a civilized house. Tea first." Leaving him, she went to the kitchen.

Alec sat down in a rocking chair. Sebrahn went to the window overlooking a snowy herb garden and gazed out. Mydri returned a few moments later with a tray loaded with a steaming pot, mugs, a cream pitcher, and a plate of round spice cookies, still warm from the oven.

She set the tray on a little table between his rocker and a sagging armchair and poured for them both, adding cream without asking. Alec sipped his tea and was glad of the slaking; she brewed it even stronger than her brother did.

She popped a cookie in her mouth. "Go on," she urged when Alec shyly kept to his tea. "They're not poison."

Alec took one, wondering why he was always so nervous around the women. The cookie was delicious, laced with anise and honey, and he took a second more eagerly.

"That's better. Now, I want to talk to you about Sebrahn, and I want you to listen closely."

"Of course, older sister." He still felt awkward using the title, but knew it pleased her.

"I use magic in my healing," she told him, running a finger over the lines under her right eye. "But I also rely on my simples and tinctures, and a hot knife when necessary. It's a skill, healing, not a trick."

"Sebrahn's healings aren't a trick."

"Of course not. But you must understand that they are nothing but magic, and sometimes magic doesn't last. Why do you think I keep checking your wounds, and Seregil's?"

That had never occurred to him. He thought of the first person Sebrahn had healed, revealing his power. What if that girl's leg had gotten worse again, after they left? What if the gash high up on the inside of Seregil's thigh opened up? And what about his own wounds? "So do you understand now, Alec Two Lives?"

"You think the healing will wear off, and I'll drop dead?"

"We don't know that it won't."

She set her cup back on the tray, then reached into a basket beside her and took out some knitting—a half-finished mitten like the green-and-white pair she'd given him, but blue this time. She set to work, wooden needles clicking swiftly. How could she just sit there and calmly knit after that?

"I think you're wrong," he managed at last.

"And why is that?"

"If his magic doesn't last, then why would the alchemist go to such trouble to make one? Yhakobin didn't know Sebrahn could kill, but he knew their bodies and blood could be used to make some elixir. And maybe he knew Sebrahn had the power to give life, as well."

"And wouldn't that be worth any risk to recover Sebrahn and you? And all the more reason to think that whoever is left in Plenimar who knows the secret of his existence will not let you go so easily."

"That's not going to happen again," he vowed, meeting her gaze without wavering this time. "I'll die first. And this time for good."

She looked up from her knitting. "Don't say that lightly, little brother, in case one of your gods is listening."

Mydri's words haunted him, and he kept them to himself, even when Seregil asked why he looked so serious that night at supper.

Over the next few days he managed to fill his time with other things, which wasn't that hard to do. He'd never had so many people treat him as kin. Micum's family had been the first, but now that feeling was multiplied by dozens. He especially enjoyed the young friends he'd made, and it saddened him to wonder when—or if—he'd see them again.

CHAPTER 13

Making Use of the Useless

ULAN Í SATHIL'S SPIES sent word that Seregil and the other had indeed gone to ground in Bôkthersa, and that there was a child with them, one with yellow hair and silver eyes—one never seen to eat. To kidnap them from there would be far too difficult, not to mention an unforgivable breach of honor. If caught at it, the consequences were too dire to contemplate. Having lived this long, Ulan had no intention of dying by the two bowls—not when he was so close to his goal. However, his prey had youth on their side; he could only afford to wait so long. Perhaps spring would bring them out.

In the meantime, he fought against the disease in his lungs as best he could, and between fits amused himself by nursing Ilar back to life and winning his trust. It was too dangerous to call him by his true name, lest someone remember him. Instead he went by his slave name—Khenir. He'd borne it for so long, he seemed more at ease with it.

It also became clear that Ilar had been genuinely devoted to his alchemist master, whom he still called "Ilban" and spoke of as if the man were still alive. He often rubbed the lighter skin at his throat, too, as if he missed the collar being there. What he felt for the others was less clear. He seemed to hate Alec, but sometimes rambled about pleasant moments spent together at the villa before their escape. And Seregil? In some twisted, angry way, he seemed to want to possess him, and spoke at times as if he had at some point.

It finally came out that Seregil had been his slave for a brief time—something that Ulan had a hard time imagining.

For the first weeks Ulan had feared that the man's mind might remain unhinged. Ilar could not bear to be touched, would not leave his room, and kept his scars carefully hidden, unaware that his host had observed him many times through the peephole in his room. Ilar had been a proud young man, and that had worked to his detriment as a slave, as his many stripes and scars attested.

Ulan visited him each morning and evening, listening for any new detail. Ilar had wept a great deal in the early days, and when he did talk, he went round and round in his mind, recalling scattered details of their escape and dwelling on the fact that Seregil was still alive. Ulan couldn't tell if what Ilar felt for Seregil was love or hatred, and he began to think that Ilar himself didn't know. Nonetheless it was clearly still a strong attachment. And who knew? That might prove useful.

As Ilar's body healed and gained strength, so did his mind. He grew increasingly lucid and paid more attention to his surroundings, but the fear and the longing remained. Questions about the rhekaros and their making remained unanswered.

At last Ilar—now Khenir to the household—allowed Ulan to lead him out of his room for short walks inside the clan house. After a few days Ulan was able to draw him out into the snowy garden for some fresh air. The color had returned to Ilar's face, and some of his beauty, as well. As long as he remained clothed, he looked like nothing more than a young man recovering from a long illness.

With this promising turn of events, Ulan began to ask more probing questions.

"Why was he so frustrated with the first one?" he asked one day as they sat together on the long balcony overlooking the harbor after one of Ulan's coughing fits. "Why would he go to such lengths and then destroy it?"

Ilar stared out at the boats for a while, pain clear in his eyes, and Ulan worried that he'd overstepped. But at last the young man sighed and said, "He was trying to distill an elixir of some sort from its blood."

"Yes, I know, but how was the rhekaro made?"

"I don't know, exactly. I only assisted him when required, but he used Alec's flesh, blood, spit, tears . . . Ilban combined it with other things he called 'elements.' Still, it wasn't enough. He had more hope for the second one, and seemed pleased with it, even though it didn't have wings. He hadn't yet found how to unlock the secrets of its blood, either. But it could do little tasks around the workshop. I think he meant to keep it as a pet."

"And Alec—" Another cough tore at his chest and Ulan tasted blood. Ilar patted him awkwardly on the back until the fit was over. Ulan fell back in his chair, wiping his lips. "He kept Alec to make more rhekaros. What of Seregil?"

"He was given to me. If only—" Ilar broke off and would say no more. He looked thoroughly miserable.

"I see. Well, perhaps you will see him, in time."

Ilar's eyes widened. "But how?"

"Time will tell. In the meantime, would you like to live here permanently, under my protection?"

"Yes, Khirnari." Ilar sank to his knees before Ulan and kissed his hand.

"Now, now, dear boy. No need for such dramatics. We'll bide our time, and my spies will keep an eye on things. I doubt Seregil and Alec will go anywhere before spring, if they move at all. "

"Spring?" Ilar said, disappointed. "Will I see him then?"

"Perhaps, and you'll be that much stronger by then. Now, I would like to hear more about the rhekaros and how they are made. Where did your Ilban's knowledge come from?"

Ilar actually looked around, as if he was still afraid of being overheard. "Books," he whispered. "He has three great thick books that he keeps in the little tent. He pored over them for years before Alec came. You told me about the boy—the Hâzadriëlfaie boy—and I told Ilban. I've never seen him so excited! That's when he promised Seregil to me."

"Ah, I see. But the books?"

Ilar subsided and the light went from his eyes. "In the little tent."

"And where is this little tent?"

"It's at the far end of the workroom, opposite the forge. I wasn't allowed to look in there, but I often saw him take out the books."

"And did you see what was in them?"

Ilar shifted uneasily, looking guilty now. "Sometimes I looked, when Ilban went back to the house for something. I couldn't read the writing. Most of his books are like that. Ilban says that alchemists keep their secrets by writing in code."

"In code? The book he showed me was not."

"Then perhaps he didn't show you the real ones. In the one I looked at, the words made no sense, but I saw a fine engraving of winged beings. Ilban was disappointed that neither of the ones he made had wings. They were larger in the drawings, too: the size of a man, at least in the pictures I saw."

Ulan knew that much already. He'd corresponded regularly with Charis Yhakobin, anxious for news of success that never came. No, what caught his interest and made his pulse quicken was this talk of books. Codes could be broken. And then?

And then I could unlock the secrets of the use of a rhekaro, perhaps even make one for myself! Of course that would mean possessing young Alec, as well.

"Do you think the books are still there?"

"Ilban never allows anyone to touch them. I think his servant Ahmol and I are the only ones who know about them."

Ulan sat there for some time after Ilar went back to his room, pondering deeply. Ilar was the only one who knew what the books looked like. If they had been moved, only he could identify them. It seemed Ilar might be of use after all.

He'd had no word from Elisir in weeks and had to assume that Seregil and Alec, and therefore the rhekaro, were still safely in Bôkthersa.

"Patience," he whispered as he gazed out over his beloved

city and the harbor below. No, he was not ready to give up all this.

But patience had its limits.

Returning to his library, he settled at the desk there and began a letter to his nephew. Alchemists were not the only ones to use code.

Moonlight and Snow

IN SKALA, the last night of Cinrin—the longest in the calendar—was celebrated with Mourning Night, when the Immortal, Sakor, died, to be reborn the next day. Here in Aurënen, it was a celebration of the first moonrise of the new year. Bôkthersa everyone gathered in rooftop colos to watch the full moon come up over the mountains.

Bonfires were lit a few hours before sunset and people gathered around them to drink cold tea and a special sweet soup, served by the older children. Adzriel gave everyone gifts of jewelry made out of silver, many of which had been fashioned by Akaien. In addition to two torques set with polished garnets, Adzriel presented Alec with a fine cloak pin and Seregil with a small traveler's harp inlaid with shell pearl.

"Think of your people whenever you play it, Haba," she told him. "And I'll expect you to play at the dance tonight."

Later, Alec and Micum stood in silence with Seregil and his family in the central colos of the clan house and watched the first pale glimmer of moon glow appear over the eastern peaks. He truly felt like he belonged here now; that he was really part of this clan, this family, even though they were leaving soon. Sebrahn stood between him and Seregil, holding their mittened hands and looking up at the night sky. Alec had explained the event to him, hoping he'd understand at least some of it.

The glow over the mountains slowly brightened, expanding into a gauzy nimbus so bright Alec could even make out the trees on the peaks.

As the edge of the moon appeared over the mountain, everyone began to sing.

> *Blessings of Aura descend in the moon's glow.*
> *People of Aura, bathe in the light.*
> *Blood of the Dragon runs in our veins,*
> *Shed on our land in the long-ago night.*
> *Blessings of Aura, reborn in our sight*
> *Blessings of Aura, the Lightbearer's gift.*

The verse was repeated over and over, and echoed among the peaks, doubling and trebling, almost harmonizing with the voices.

Blood of the Dragon runs in our veins—A chill ran up Alec's spine. He was *not* a dragon! The dragon had said so.

"Alec, look," Seregil whispered, jarring him out of his dark thoughts.

Something dark moving against the stars.

"Drak-kon," said Sebrahn, his eyes like silver coins in the moonlight. Raising his arms, he sang a single clear note, the same one he'd sung to Tyrus's great dragon. Startled looks came their way, and Alec wondered uneasily if Sebrahn was calling the dragons down from the sky.

Little dragonlings fluttered into the colos to light on Sebrahn's shoulders, and Alec's, but the ones overhead remained in the sky, a huge one surrounded by countless others of all sizes.

"Is that Tyrus's dragon?" Alec asked, amazed and delighted. This must be the surprise Seregil had spoken of.

"It is," Seregil replied, smiling. "I wanted to watch this with you. And you, too, of course, Micum."

Micum just laughed.

The dragons swooped and dove against the night sky, like fish playing in a stream, and the great dragon sang back to Sebrahn, his roar softened by the distance.

Watching them, Alec's heart swelled a little. Maybe it

wasn't such a bad thing, sharing a connection with something so wondrous.

This went on until the moon was high above the peaks. Then the great beasts disappeared as quickly as they'd come.

Adzriel turned and kissed him. "Come now, my brothers, it's time for the dancing!"

Everyone went home to dress for the dances and parties that followed. As Alec descended the stairs from the roof with Sebrahn in his arms, he could hear the musicians tuning up in the great hall. The sound always stirred his blood, ever since Micum's daughters had taught him how to dance, but the feeling was mingled with sudden misgivings.

This was the night they would finally try leaving Sebrahn alone. His misgivings grew as they reached their room.

"Seregil, I don't know if this is a good idea," he began, setting Sebrahn down and pulling off his mittens.

"Oh come on, talí," Seregil gave him a comically imploring look. "If we were in Rhíminee tonight, we'd be drunk off our assess by now. And you can't very well dance with me lugging Sebrahn on your back. He'll be fine here, and it's not so far to the hall that we can't look in on him as often as you like. As soon as we've danced ourselves out a little, we'll fetch him to the party, I promise."

Alec cast a worried look at Sebrahn, who was staring back just as intently from his place on the bed, as if he knew exactly what was going on. Alec had trimmed and braided the rhekaro's hair, and dressed him in the little tunic embroidered with flowers that Kheeta's mother had made for him. There had to be some moment when Alec allowed himself to be parted from Sebrahn; it was inevitable. But did it have to be now? All the other children in the house would be there. Sebrahn hadn't exactly made friends with anyone. However, he did seem interested in how they played, and would mimic them now and then.

Yet Alec didn't need the pull of their bond to see that behind Seregil's inveigling smile was a genuine plea. Seregil pulled him close, sighed heavily for good effect, then danced him around the room. "Please, talí? Just this one time? He couldn't be anywhere safer." Letting Alec go, Seregil made a show of barring the shutters, then held up the iron key that they hadn't used since their arrival.

Alec wavered; he hadn't danced in months, and now he could hear a reel beginning. "Well, I guess he'd be all right for a little while. Maybe . . ."

"Then it's settled! I'll tell you what; as soon as we meet with Micum, I'll have him look in on him for us, too."

"Well . . ."

Seregil sensed his weakening resolve and grinned. "Good."

Alec sat down with Sebrahn and tried to explain. "Seregil and I are going out." He pointed to the door, then the bed. "And you stay here, understand? Right here."

It was difficult to tell what Sebrahn thought of that. Alec found one of the little dolls Mydri had given him in Gedre, as if that would keep him company.

"Come on, Alec. Listen—they've started without us. The musicians are already playing," Seregil urged gently, slipping a hand under his arm.

Alec glanced back over his shoulder as they went out. Sebrahn sat in the middle of the bed, holding the doll upside down in one hand.

As soon as they were in the corridor Alec locked the door. More music floated down from the hall, enticing him.

Maybe this is a good thing. Just get it over with.

He'd just turned the key when a piercing shriek split the air.

"Bilairy's Balls!" Seregil yelped, clapping his hands over his ears.

Then came a loud thud from inside the room as Sebrahn threw himself against the door, shrieking again at a pitch that made the hair on Alec's arms stand up and his heart pound.

"For hell's sake, open the door!"

"I'm trying!" The sound was like a knife grating against bone. Alec's hands were shaking so badly that he had to use both to get the key back into the lock. When he finally got the door open Sebrahn flew at him, wrapping his arms and legs around him with shocking strength and still shrieking.

Seregil dragged them both back into the bedchamber, then wrested the key from Alec's clenched fingers and locked the door from the inside.

"Stop!" Alec shouted, shaking Sebrahn. The painful shriek tapered off, but Sebrahn didn't loosen his grip.

"It's all right," Alec whispered, hugging Sebrahn tight. "I'm sorry. We didn't mean to scare you."

"Scare *him*?" Seregil gasped, running a shaky hand back through his hair. "Bilairy's *Balls,* Alec!"

"He didn't know what he was doing!"

"Even worse—" Seregil broke off suddenly, staring at Sebrahn. "Don't move, Alec," he whispered. "You're bleeding."

"What?"

"Your nose is bleeding, and Sebrahn's eyes are completely black. Tell him not to hurt me."

"He wouldn't—" Alec could taste blood on his lips now, and remembered how Sebrahn had hissed at Seregil in Gedre. He got a hand under the rhekaro's chin and raised his face. Sure enough, Sebrahn's pupils were dilated like a cat's in the dark, with only a thin rim of silver showing around them. "It's all right now," he soothed, not really believing that as he stroked Sebrahn's hair. "If you hurt anyone, I'll be sad. Do you understand? You will make me very sad. Tell me if you understand, Sebrahn."

Bit by bit, Sebrahn loosened his painful grip and slid down to the floor. His eyes weren't quite so black now, but more than Alec liked.

He knelt and took Sebrahn by the shoulders, heart hammering against his ribs now as the shock of it all rolled over him. What if—? "Don't *ever* do that again!"

Sebrahn reached out and touched Alec's upper lip. His finger came away bloody. He licked at it with his little grey tongue and reached out for more.

Seregil's hand closed over Alec's shoulder and pulled him back. "No, Sebrahn! That's bad. Making Alec bleed is very, *very* bad."

The rhekaro's gaze flickered between the two of them, as if he was trying to make sense of all this. "Baaaad."

Alec nodded. "Bad. You hurt me. You could have hurt Seregil, too, and our friends. Never do that again!"

"Bad," Sebrahn whispered again. He clenched both fists against his chest and sank into a squat at Alec's feet. His braid had come loose somehow, and his hair cascaded around his face and shoulders.

"Sebrahn?" Alec knelt down by him.

From behind that curtain of hair a tear fell to the floor, spattering on the polished wood, and then another. One mingled with a stray drop of Alec's blood and formed a tiny white blossom.

"He's crying," Alec whispered, amazed. He reached out to Sebrahn, but Seregil pulled him back again.

"These are what Sebrahn saved you with. There's no telling what these will do to a living person."

Alec shrugged his hand off and took Sebrahn in his arms, pressing his bloodied nose to Sebrahn's cheek. Blood and tears mingled and fragrant white blossoms tumbled into Alec's lap.

Nothing else happened.

Seregil picked up a flower and held it in his cupped hand. "That's different."

Alec tasted more blood on his lip as he looked up at Seregil. "Maybe these white ones only work on the dead?"

"I hope we don't need to test that anytime soon."

"What in Bilairy's name are you up to?" Micum demanded, rattling the door handle. "Everybody's at the dance."

Seregil let him in and closed the door again. Micum took in the situation at a glance. "Everyone's asking for you."

"Did you see anyone else on your way here?" asked Seregil.

"No, I think the whole household is at the dance."

"Come on, Micum. We'll check all the unlocked rooms within earshot," said Seregil.

"You think he's killed someone?"

"I hope he hasn't."

But they returned with good news. "I couldn't find a soul,

alive or otherwise. And if anyone at the dance had heard, they'd have come running," Seregil told him.

"The music must have drowned it out," Alec said, relieved.

Seregil sat down on the bed. "That doesn't change what happened, though. We were just lucky. You know what this means?"

Just then they heard someone coming.

Seregil pulled out a handkerchief and quickly wiped the blood from Alec's face, finishing up with a spit-slicked thumb. "That will have to do. Try not to bleed for a minute."

"What do we do with all these?" The flowers were still there, scattered around Alec. Together they scooped them up and threw them under the bed.

"What's keeping you, brothers?" Adzriel called.

"Nothing. Just a little—upset." Seregil gave Alec a worried look, then let her in. Mydri was with her.

"It turns out that Sebrahn is frightened of being left alone," Seregil explained.

"He's not used to it, that's all." Alec pulled Sebrahn close to his side, hoping they didn't notice that he was still shaking. "This is the first time we ever tried to leave him on his own. He's fine now—" He stopped, tasting blood and feeling it trickling down his lip.

Mydri pulled out a lacy handkerchief and gave it to him to stanch the flow. "Press under your nose. What happened?"

"Sebrahn was struggling."

"He does still look frightened, poor thing." Adzriel paused and looked at Alec and the others. "You three look rather shaken, yourselves."

"We were just surprised," Alec said quickly.

"Ah, well. Do come along as soon as you can!"

Mydri gave them a look over her shoulder as she followed her sister out.

When she was gone, Micum sat down in her place and held out his hands to Sebrahn. "Well now, little sprout, you've caused some trouble tonight." He looked up at the others, face grave. "You were both white as milk when I came in. So Sebrahn sang again, did he?"

"Well, it was actually more of a screech," Seregil pointed

out, attempting to make light of it. "Just one that made my head feel like it was going to burst."

"Don't forget that I've seen the results of the power of his voice," Micum replied, not amused.

"He couldn't have meant to hurt us, though," Seregil said, studying Sebrahn, who was still clinging to Alec, looking very much like a scared little boy. "At least not Alec. I think he lost control of himself. And that's a frightening prospect."

Alec looked down at the rhekaro. "Sebrahn, you won't make that hurting noise again, right?"

"Baaad."

"That's right, bad. So, now what do we do?"

Seregil rested his head in his hands. "Either we don't go to the dance, which will break Adzriel's heart and raise questions, or we take him with us and risk him finding another reason to sing."

"That wasn't a killing song," Alec pointed out.

"We don't know that. He doesn't hurt those he trusts—luckily he trusts Micum! Maybe no one else was close enough to be affected. And you *were* hurt, all the same."

"Why not you?" wondered Micum.

"You know me and magic," replied Seregil. "But I do have a nasty headache."

"I'll go tell them you're both indisposed," said Micum.

"Tell Adzriel not to spoil her own fun on our account, and that I'll talk to her later, when I'm feeling better. Try to keep her from coming back, if you can."

Micum grinned. "You know how persuasive I am with the ladies. But what if Mydri wants to come heal you?"

"Damn. Tell her we're napping."

"I'll do my best and come back when I won't be missed."

"Thank you."

When he was gone, Alec flopped down on the bed beside Seregil. "So, we start packing?"

Seregil closed his eyes and nodded. "If we needed a sign, that was it."

Sebrahn climbed in between them and sat looking from one to another, hair loose around his shoulders.

Frowning, Alec reached up and lifted a strand of hair near his face. "Seregil, look at this." Thero's magic had turned Sebrahn's hair the same blond as Alec's, and given color to his skin. But now there was a thin streak of silver in his hair, and, when Alec pushed his sleeves back, a patch of white skin showing through, too. Alec combed through Sebrahn's hair and found more silvery streaks. They were small enough to mingle with the blond so as not to be especially noticeable, but there were a lot of them. While he was looking, Alec found another blotch of white on the nape of Sebrahn's neck.

"Thero did say the magic might not last on him," Seregil reminded him. "The hair's not so bad, but we don't want people thinking he's a leper."

Alec found another white patch on Sebrahn's right calf. "Maybe it's another sign."

Adzriel was still flushed with dancing when she tapped at their door again a few hours later. "Oh, brothers! To miss Alec's first—" She stopped in the doorway, looking at the packs lying on the bed. "What's this? Oh. Did Sebrahn do something?"

Seregil took her hand and drew her into the room. "Nothing serious. All the same, we have to go before something worse happens."

Adzriel sank into a chair, all traces of merriment fled.

"I warned you in Gedre that something like this could happen," Seregil pointed out.

"Yes, you did. I'd just hoped it wouldn't."

"At least we got to talk to Tyrus," he said with a sad smile.

"I'm so sorry, Khirnari." Alec said the title with the deep respect that he truly felt for her.

Seregil held out a hand to his sister. "We'll stay in this room tonight and leave tomorrow. Everything's ready."

Adzriel stared at them in silence, and Alec was certain he saw a fight between her roles as sister and khirnari in those clear grey eyes. "I thought perhaps—You seemed so happy here."

"I told you'd we'd have to go, sister."

"Very well. But you must make your farewells before you go, and not sneak away like thieves in the night." She looked sadly at Sebrahn. "He's been so good, all this time."

Seregil made his sister a deep bow. "I give you my word, Khirnari. You'll have no more trouble from us."

"If you have no objections, I'd like to stay with them," said Micum.

"Of course." She glanced at the packs again. "You will promise me you'll stay here until tomorrow?"

"Of course, older sister." He kissed her on the cheek. "And we were sorry to miss the dancing."

"Oh, Haba. You always were the one to get into trouble." She stood to go. "Good night, all of you. May it be a peaceful one."

Micum followed her out. "I'm going to go find us some supper. We can enjoy that much, anyway. I won't be long."

When they were alone, Seregil rummaged in his pack and pulled out a worn pack of cards. "I don't think we'll be sleeping much tonight, do you?"

Micum came back with a large plate of cold meats and a jug of turab. They sat on the floor to eat, then passed the jug around.

Micum lit his pipe and took a long puff as Alec shuffled and dealt the cards for a game of Blue Goose.

"Well, I guess we'd better let Thero know we're heading back." Going to his pack again, Seregil took out one of the painted message sticks the wizard had given them and snapped it in half. A tiny message sphere appeared in front of him. "Thero," Seregil said quietly. "We're leaving Bôkthersa for Skala. I'm not sure how long it will take to get there, so I will send another message when we make landfall. When you come, please bring us some Skalan clothing and our horses. They're at the Wheel Street house." He touched the little orb with a fingertip, and it sped away. A moment later another appeared. Seregil touched it.

"I understand," they heard Thero's voice say. "Magyana and I haven't found anything of use, I'm afraid. Do try to stay out of trouble, won't you?"

The light winked out, and Seregil gave the others a rueful look. "I'm glad he wasn't here tonight."

Mydri came to fetch them early the following morning. "Everything is ready. Adzriel insists you two make use of the baths and take breakfast with her. Come to the morning room when you're ready."

Seregil would rather not have prolonged the process, but he could tell Mydri was heartbroken to see him go.

Breakfast was a quiet affair, just Adzriel, Akaien, Mydri, and Säaban. Seregil was glad; they didn't need any great send-off. Adzriel graciously put Alec on her left, but Seregil saw how she kept an eye on Sebrahn, crouched on a chair between Alec and Micum.

"I have something for you," Akaien said as they were finishing. Going to the sideboard, he lifted a long bundle wrapped in a tapestry and unrolled it to reveal two swords in plain leather scabbards. "I hadn't intended for these to be a farewell gift."

Seregil recognized one at once; it was a twin to the one he'd lost. The tapered quillons were curved just enough to catch an opponent's blade; the round pommel was set with a round disk of green Sarikali stone.

The other was similar to the one Seregil had bought for Alec soon after they met. The curved bronze quillons ended in finials shaped like tightly coiled fern heads. The detailing was exquisite; each tiny leaflet peeking out from the coiled heads cast in sharp relief. The blade was longer, too; Akaien had taken account of Alec's growth.

Alec stared at his in amazement. "But—how on earth did you know?"

Akaien smiled, obviously pleased with his reaction. "Weapons came up in conversation one day when Thero was still with us, and he mentioned yours. He greatly admired the design, and I sketched it to his description. Micum helped with the final details. I hope it pleases you."

"Oh, yes! Thank you! But I have nothing to give in return, Uncle."

Akaien smiled and patted his shoulder. "No need for that among family, my new nephew."

"By the Light, Uncle, thank you!" Seregil said, stepping away from the table to draw his. The steel was polished so fine he could see himself reflected. And like the last, it had a grooved fuller down the center of the blade, making it both strong and light. Alec's was the same. He felt a lump in his throat, holding it and feeling the perfect balance. Akaien had made his very first sword for him, too.

When they went out to their horses, they found Kheeta and his mother, as well as Alec's three friends waiting for them.

"You didn't think you'd get away without saying good-bye, did you?" Korit chided. "Here, take this to remember me by." He handed Alec an agate shatta.

"We'll miss you, but at least some of us will have a chance of winning again," said Stellin, giving him one made from a white stone with a hole through it.

"And we'll have a chance to win them back when you return," added Ethgil, gifting him with a shatta made of bone carved in the shape of a dragon's head.

Alec's voice was a little hoarse as he thanked them.

Kheeta clasped hands with him. "I'm beginning to think the only way to see you is to go with you."

"Another time, maybe," Seregil replied, pulling him into a hug. Aunt Alira was in tears beside them.

A tear spilled down Adzriel's cheek, and her voice trembled as she bade them farewell. Seregil went to her and embraced her. "Don't cry, sister."

Adzriel wiped her cheek on the front of his tunic. "You're always having to go away."

"I know."

"When will we see you again?"

"I can't make you any promises," he whispered against her hair, fighting back tears of his own.

Stepping back, he motioned to Micum and Alec, who were finishing their own good-byes. "Time to go."

Alec mounted his shaggy horse. Micum passed Sebrahn up to him, then climbed into the saddle and fixed the long rein of the three packhorses to his saddle. Seregil allowed himself a backward look as they rode slowly out of the courtyard. Adzriel was weeping in her husband's arms, and Mydri was already heading back into the house. Akaien waved. Seregil's vision blurred for a moment, and he wiped away the tears before they could freeze.

CHAPTER 15

Closing In

As THEY moved farther south and the map grew more vague, Rieser found himself relying increasingly on Turmay and his moon goddess. But if the oo'lu visions were true, then their quarry were unexpectedly coming their way like charmed rabbits, almost as if the witch was luring the tayan'gil ever closer.

In Nanta, Rieser's gold had bought them and their horses passage on a large ship bound for the place on the map that Rieser had shown the master of the ship.

"You want to go to Cirna?" the stupid Tír had asked, speaking slowly and tapping the map as if Rieser were an idiot child. "Cirna?"

Rieser gave him a narrow-eyed scowl. "If that is what that place is called, then that is where we want to go."

The crossing was more difficult than the trip down the river had been. Great waves buffeted the ship and threw water onto the deck like rain. Young Rane and Morai fell sick the first day, but the master of the ship just laughed and called it "seasick." Apparently it was nothing to worry about. By the second day the others were well again, if a bit pale. Once again, Turmay could not play for them, and Rieser prayed to Aura and the spirit of Hâzadriël that their prey would not slip away in the meantime.

They reached their destination after a few miserable days, and Rieser was surprised to discover that—if this was indeed where they'd been meant to go—this Skala land was no island. A land bridge connected it to the mainland. Cirna lay at the bottom of a huge cliff that extended as far as the eye could see on either side. At the head of the bay was a great dark channel called Canal, flanked by soaring columns carved into the rock, with huge watch fires burning at the top. The captain claimed it had been made by a wizard called Orska, if Rieser had understood him correctly. He doubted the story; what man could have such power?

The city itself climbed all the way to the heights above.

They put in at the large harbor. There were more warships here, and the waterfront was teeming with soldiers, many of whom appeared to be drunk.

The captain directed them to a precariously steep road that led up to the larger part of the city. Reaching it at last, even Rieser let out a whistle of amazement. The city that spread out in every direction was larger than Wolde or Nanta, and it straddled the Canal. A long bridge wide enough for several wagons to pass crossed over it to the other side. Rane and Thiren walked out a little way on it, until Nowen noticed and shouted for them to come back. Both boys were pale but grinning. Rieser went to see for himself; the bottom of it was lost in darkness, but he could hear voices and the creak of ropes echoing up from the depths as some ship passed through.

Yet even with such a wonder, Cirna was still nothing more than another filthy Tír city. The crowded streets were strewn with garbage, and dirty children, roving dogs, and pigs ran wild through the midst of it all. Vendors carrying ring-shaped bread, hats, painted bladders, or bunches of ribbon on tall poles moved among them, crying their wares. Rieser had never been surrounded by so many Tír at one time and it was making him nervous, especially with half his riders gawking at everything like children. As always, Hâzadriën was a calm, silent presence at his side. The glamour still held, and no one gave the tayan'gil a second glance.

He caught sight of a few Aurënfaie among the throng as they rode south through the city. They looked just like his own people in their long coats and sen'gai, but the head cloths were all different colors and patterns. They even wrapped them differently, in complicated ways unlike the simple wrap and knot of his clan. He counted four different clan patterns as they continued on.

He was sorely tempted to stop and speak with some of them, but when he overheard them talking and could barely make out what they were saying, he held back. He couldn't reveal what clan he was, even to his own kind. It was strictly forbidden.

So they continued on through wealthy streets, and then impoverished ones at the edge of the city, overrun with dirty people on every corner and around each public fountain. Sly-looking beggars called out unintelligibly to them as they rode by, some of them even holding out bowls, as if they expected Rieser to feed them. It was disgusting. Any 'faie would kill himself if he were brought so low.

Safely outside the city that night, Turmay played again, then shook his head. "They won't come to this place."

"I thought you said they were coming right toward us," said Nowen.

The witch shrugged. "This is a big land. Bigger than I expected from the marks on your map. But I do see them. They are on a boat coming to this land."

"Can you narrow it down at all?" asked Rieser.

Turmay played again for a few minutes, mingling owl sounds and catamount cries into the booming drone. When he was done, he lowered the oo'lu and pointed. "They will be that way."

"That way" was south, and the witch was right about this being a large place. From here, the land stretched to the horizon, much of it mountains. How in Aura's name were they going to find one ya'shel and something the size of a child out there?

The journey thus far, he realized, had been a general following of a direction. Turmay had been a good guide, assuming he was leading them the right way, but the map had become less trustworthy the farther south they went, perhaps because Hâzadriël and her followers had not come this way during the long trek north.

They made camp on a windswept plain above the sea. Looking around at his riders shivering in their cloaks, Rieser felt great pride. None of them had complained or shown doubt through all the long weeks it had taken to get this far, not even the young ones. Rane and his brother Thiren were joking with Sorengil about something, and Kalien and Allia had their heads together. Love might be budding there, he thought disapprovingly. That would be a needless complication. Nowen, Sona, and Morai had been with him longer and were old enough to know better, as was Taegil. Rieser was not bothered by such feelings any more than Hâzadriën; not when he was on the hunt.

Turmay played while they ate around the fire, then said, "Yes, this is the way."

Rieser was secretly growing a little uneasy about their dependence on the witch, and this city had unnerved him. The khirnari's seer had seen the tayan'gil and its keepers going to Aurënen, not here. Now Turmay said otherwise.

He looked up to find that the dark tracery of witch marks had appeared on Turmay's hands and face, which was all he could see of him. "You doubt me?" the witch demanded quietly.

An unpleasant chill ran up Rieser's back. "You didn't tell me you could read thoughts."

Turmay held up his oo'lu and looked around the circle of suddenly distrustful faces. "I can't. I don't need this, or any other magic, to read faces, Rieser, and yours is full of doubt. I see clearly when I play. I promise you, we are very close now. A few days at most."

Rieser sensed no duplicity in the witch; from the start he hadn't, and it occurred to him now how odd that was. He was not a trusting man when it came to outsiders. Had some of Turmay's "songs" been responsible for that?

Still, he gave Turmay a grudging nod. "I meant no offense. It's been a long journey, and an uncertain one. I'm grateful that you have led us in safety this far." It was true. They hadn't encountered so much as a bandit along the way, and the closer they had come to this land, the less any attention was paid to their 'faie looks.

A few days. He held on to that. Once they were that close, he could rely on his own skills and Hâzadriën's once more.

"They're coming on a boat," Turmay said again. "If we ride south, I will know the way to find them. The Mother will not fail us."

Rieser sighed inwardly. "Well, it's a start."

CHAPTER 16

Old Friends

THE BÔKTHERSAN SHIP glided safely into Silver Bay as twilight painted the western clouds gold and pink. A tidy little town spread out around the harbor, with rolling hills beyond. Firelight glowed warmly from a hundred windows, gleaming across the water and making Alec feel a bit homesick for Rhíminee, less than a day's sail away.

Seregil used one of the remaining message sticks to alert Thero to their arrival, and tell him to meet them at an inn called the Bell and Bridle in a few days. It was on the highroad north of Rhíminee. Magyana knew the place and could direct him.

"It's been a while since we passed this way," Micum noted.

Seregil nodded. "Ten years? Twelve?"

"Something like that."

"I could do with a clean room and a decent bath," Alec put in hopefully. "It's too late to keep going, anyway."

"I'm of the same mind," said Micum, glancing up at the first stars of the night. "Where shall we put up? The Codfish?"

Seregil thought a moment, then shook his head. "That will do for our trusty sailors. I'd rather take leave of them here and stay with Madlen, if she's still around. Sorry, Alec, the bath will have to wait."

Micum laughed. "I never thought I'd hear *you* say that!"

They said their farewells to the captain, carried their packs down the gangway to the torchlit wharf, and set off through the dark streets.

"Who is Madlen?" asked Alec.

Seregil held up his hand and made the Watcher sign—left thumb curled over his forefinger. For centuries Watcher members had been scattered all over Skala and Mycena, and some in the northlands beyond, too: wizards, merchants, innkeepers, even drysians, all of whom were well paid through various channels to keep their secrets from all but their leader, and some of them had no idea who that was. Since Nysander's death, it was Thero. In spite of Phoria's orders, the organization was still in place. The queen had no idea of the breadth of it, assuming it was just Seregil and a few others in Rhíminee.

Seregil paused in a tiny market and looked around. "I don't remember this being here."

Micum scratched at the thick, greying stubble on his cheek, looking thoughtful again. "I hate to think we've lived long enough to forget our way."

After some casting about, Seregil got his bearings again and led the way down several muddy streets to a little back lane near the forest's edge. There were only a few houses here, and they continued on to the last one, which stood apart from the others. Alec was heartened to see firelight through its two windows. As they approached, two huge hounds emerged from the shadows, growling with their heads lowered and hackles up.

Seregil held out his left hand and did the dog trick. As usual, the hounds went from growling menace to happy tail wagging in an instant. Seregil gave them both a good scratching behind their ears, then moved to the door and tapped out a pattern. A moment later a muffled voice demanded, "Who is it?"

"Luck in the shadows," Seregil whispered.

They heard the bar lifted inside. The door swung open to reveal a plump old woman in a nightgown and shawl. "And in the Light!" she whispered back. "I should have known when the dogs went quiet! It's been years, and you look just the same, you shameless bastard. What brings you here after all this time? And Micum! By the Maker, but you've aged."

Micum laughed and kissed her on the cheek.

"And who's this pretty young thing?" she demanded, looking Alec up and down.

Seregil fought back a grin. "This pretty young thing is our friend Alec. He's one of us, so you can speak your mind in front of him."

Madlen gave Alec the Watcher sign. When he returned it, she seemed satisfied.

"Well, I'm glad to meet you, Alec." Then she caught sight of Sebrahn as he peeked out from behind Alec's legs. His hood had fallen back, and his eyes and the wide silvery streaks in his hair shone like metal in the firelight. The white patch on his cheek looked pink.

"And a little one!" Madlen exclaimed before Alec could muffle him up again, not seeming the least put off by Sebrahn's odd appearance. "Dear me, what have you boys been up to?"

"Not what you think," chuckled Micum.

She gave him a playful slap on the shoulder. "You may be a bit greyer, but you haven't lost that sparkle in your eye."

Seregil gave Alec the nod to unwrap the rhekaro. Madlen's eyes widened for an instant at the sight of him; then she scooped him up against her ample bosom before Alec could stop her and carried him over to the hearth.

Seregil caught his breath, exchanging a worried look with Alec, but Sebrahn just settled in her arms and looked back at Alec.

"The poor little thing is cold as ice!" she scolded. In the firelight, Sebrahn's eyes didn't look so unnatural. "Just feel his poor little hands. Whose child is this, if he isn't yours, and what are you doing with him?"

"The less said, the better," Micum told her.

"We didn't kidnap him," said Alec. "He's mine."

Madlen pulled back to look at Sebrahn's face. "Of course. He favors you. But how did a young one like you come to have a child this old?"

"As Micum said," Seregil told her, "the less you know, the better. Can you give us a safe place for the night?"

"You know you're always welcome here, though if you stay away this long again, I'll be in my grave next time you come by. And now, since I have such strong men here, I'm going to take advantage. Can you fetch me in some firewood from the byre?" She pointed to the empty wood box near the hearth. "I've got some nice fish chowder I can heat up for you, if it hasn't curdled."

"We'll do it for the joy of your company," Micum replied. "But your chowder is always much appreciated."

It took several trips, and some explaining as to why Sebrahn had to help, but when they came with the last load of wood, stamping snow from their boots, they found supper laid out for them on Madlen's polished wood table. Seregil's mouth watered painfully as he took in the steaming bowls of milky chowder with bits of fried salt pork floating on top, accompanied by mustard pickles, brown bread, and butter.

Alec used some quick sleight of hand to make it appear that he was feeding Sebrahn bits of bread, then ate a spoonful of chowder with a chunk of fish in it and groaned with pleasure. "We've been living on ship's fare. This is the best thing I've ever tasted!"

Madlen grinned and gave his braid a playful little tug. "Compliments like that will earn you seconds. Now, don't let your little one go hungry."

Seconds led to thirds and Seregil was feeling content and dozy by the time he pushed back his bowl. It was damn good to be back on land and under a friendly roof again.

Once Madlen was satisfied that none of them could eat another mouthful, she eyed their stained Aurënfaie tunics. "You'll be needing proper clothes. I'll go see what I have."

She came back a few minutes later with an armload of tunics, coats, and trousers. They sorted through them and found some that fit—even a tunic and a cloak Sebrahn's size.

"What news of the war?" Seregil asked.

The old woman threw up her hands. "According to the heralds, Queen Phoria has the upper hand for now. It's stretched on far too long, if you ask me. Shortages of everything. The sutlers have bought up meat, flour, sugar, horses, leather, even candle wax! All carried across the sea for the soldiers. From what I've heard, the jewelers in Rhíminee can't find gold to work with anymore, or silver. I don't imagine the nobles are too happy about that. But the worst of it is the conscription. There isn't a young man left in the village here, and some of the young women, too—all gone off to war."

Micum shook his head. "My oldest daughter, too. This war's already cost us a good queen. If Phoria's killed, there's only that green niece of hers, unless one of the others steps in."

"It ought to be Princess Klia," said Madlen. "First a barren queen, and then a child heir? Mark my words, if—Lightbringer forefend—the queen is killed, there will be some unrest."

"That might not be a bad thing," said Seregil.

They talked a bit longer about the war, then Madlen bid them good night and retired to a bed behind a curtain at the far end of the room. Seregil and the others climbed up a ladder to the loft and settled in among the cobwebs and mice.

"That was a nice bit of fooling you did down there," Micum noted as Alec shook little pellets of bread from his sleeve and shared them around.

"I had a good teacher." When he was done, Alec pricked his finger and gave Sebrahn a proper feeding.

"My heart about stopped when Madlen grabbed him up like that," whispered Micum.

"So did mine," said Seregil. "He seems to have a good sense of who is a friend and who isn't. Most of the time, anyway."

"It's good to hear that Phoria's winning," said Alec.

"It may be too soon to say that," warned Micum. "She may have the upper hand, but once fighting starts up again soon, it could go either way."

"A stalemate," Seregil said, shaking his head. "Both sides will come to ruin if this goes on much longer."

Micum nodded, looking grim. "And Beka right in the middle of it."

Putting their trust in Madlen's hounds, they all slept the night through, and woke late.

"Lazy creatures," she scolded as they climbed down the ladder. "I've had your breakfast ready since sunup, and have already been into town to find you some horses."

Seregil gave her a kiss on the cheek and sat down to his cold porridge. "I don't have enough to pay you for the horses."

"No matter. I've plenty put by. We can settle up when you come through again."

They all knew that it might be never.

Fortunately for Alec, the old woman went out to feed her pigs and chickens, sparing him the need of pretending with Sebrahn. Seregil smiled to himself, imagining Alec trying to hide porridge up his sleeve.

Madlen had found them three sound geldings, with saddles and tack, too.

Seregil raised an eyebrow at the old woman. "You're very generous."

"No more than you've been to me, in the past. Pass them along to someone who needs them." She smoothed her chapped hands over the front of her apron. "It's good to know you two are still about. I'd begun to wonder."

Micum hugged her. "We're lucky bastards, don't you know?"

"You're courting trouble from the Four, bragging like that. Better bite your tongue."

Micum laughed and caught his tongue between his front teeth for her to see. "There now. Safe again."

It was only a joking exchange, but Seregil suddenly felt a superstitious chill run up his spine. "Come on. We've a long ride ahead of us."

They set out with hot roasted yams warming their pockets that would serve as a midday meal later on, when they were cold. Alec was glad of the warmth, as the morning was bitter.

The sky was clear when they set off, but by noon the clouds began to gather, and by the time they reached an inn called the Drover's Head that evening, most of the stars were blotted out.

"I don't like the look of that," Alec said, studying the sky. "It will be hard riding tomorrow."

"We could just stay put," Micum suggested. "Thero

doesn't know what day to expect us, if he's even there by now himself."

"We'll see," said Seregil. "I'd rather keep moving."

The Drover's Head was a ramshackle establishment, with poor ale and worse food. The only good thing about that was that there were only a few other patrons, and none who stayed the night.

The dispirited innkeeper gave them a room at the back, off the kitchen, which turned out to be more of a shed, with a few lumpy pallets thrown about on the warped floorboards.

"Hold on," Seregil warned as Alec went to toss his bedroll on one of them. He nudged the one closest to him with his boot, then slapped at his pant leg. As he'd feared, these poor excuses for beds they had paid a full sester for were jumping with fleas. And where there were fleas, there were probably lice, too.

"No," he said, regarding the room in disgust.

"No," Micum agreed.

"Definitely not," Alec said with a grimace.

Gathering their things, they moved into the dirt-floored kitchen and spread their blankets in front of the broad hearth, where the banked coals were still giving off a nice warmth. Their innkeeper and his servants evidently slept elsewhere; the room was empty.

Taking advantage of that fact, Seregil took a turn around the kitchen and came up with some hard black bread and a jug of sour cider. They sat on their blankets and passed the food around, gnawing a bit of the bread off and taking a swig of the cider to soften it up.

"Another day to the Bell and Bridle, and another two to Watermead," Micum calculated.

"Do you think Beka and Nyal will still be there?" asked Alec.

"I imagine so," said Micum.

"How is it, having an Aurënfaie as your daughter's husband?" asked Seregil.

"He's a good man." Micum stared into the fire. "They say they don't mind the fact that he'll see her grow old and die, but they're both young yet."

"He'll have their ya'shel children, though," said Alec.

"That's true, but it's not the same as having your wife. It's not the way things are supposed to be. You two are damn lucky to have found each other when you did."

In every sense of the word, Seregil thought.

CHAPTER 17

🙠

Snow and Blood

ALEC WAS the last one on watch and woke the others just before dawn. Seregil left the innkeeper a few coppers for the bread and moldy cheese they took for a saddle breakfast.

The weather had turned damp and bitter, and dark clouds sealed the sky around the horizon like pastry on a pie.

"What do you make of that?" asked Seregil.

Micum eyed the clouds. "Snow before the morning's gone. Probably heavy."

"Then we'd better make good time while we can, if we want to reach the inn before nightfall," Seregil said. The cold affected him more than the others, and Alec knew he wouldn't be happy spending the night around a fire in the open.

Micum's assessment of the weather was, unfortunately, correct. The first flakes began to fall soon after they started out. By midday it was snowing so hard Seregil could barely make out the road ahead, much less what lay to either side. It was a wet, heavy snow that stuck to their clothes and the horses' shaggy coats and manes. It was already deep enough to obscure the terrain, and they took turns leading on foot, tramping along trying to tell frozen road from frozen grass. It was open country, but no wind stirred the heavy curtains of snow that surrounded them.

"How long to the inn, Micum?" Seregil asked, shaking off the snow that had collected in the folds of his cloak and Sebrahn's hair.

"At this rate? We'll be lucky to make it by nightfall."

By afternoon it was falling even more heavily, blotting out both sky and the surrounding landscape.

Alec, in the lead on foot, suddenly held up a hand to signal a stop. "Do you hear that?"

Micum reined in. "Hear what?"

"That strange sound."

They sat listening. After a moment, Seregil thought he did hear something in the distance—a deep, dull sound with a pulsing rhythm.

"What is it?" asked Alec.

"Damned if I know."

"I don't hear anything," said Micum.

"Well, whatever it is, it's too far away to be our problem," Seregil said, setting off again.

He couldn't hear it now, and soon it was the least of their worries as the snow came down harder than ever and the whole world went white—so white and blank that it hurt the eyes. Sound took on an eerie, muffled quality, as if his ears were just a little numb or lightly packed with wool, everything deadened by the soft hiss of snow on snow. The hair on the back of his neck started to prickle, the way it did in a dark room when he was certain there was someone hiding just behind him.

The rhekaro stirred restlessly, looking around as if he felt it, too.

Seregil tightened his arm around Sebrahn's waist and called out, "Wait!"

Alec turned and called back, "What's wrong?"

"I don't know. Something doesn't feel right. Sebrahn, keep still!" The rhekaro was pushing at Seregil's arm now.

"That's the way he acts where there's someone who needs healing nearby."

"We don't have time to—" Micum began, then reined in with a grunt of surprise.

No one heard them coming, not even Seregil. The white-cloaked figures on white horses were suddenly just there in the road ahead of them, no more than twenty paces from where Alec stood. Their wolfskin hoods were up, and a mask of some sort covered the upper parts of their faces. Seregil couldn't see how many there were, just the hint of other shapes moving among the curtains of snow.

"Alec!"

"I see them!" There was no time to get to his bow, tied on behind his saddle. Mounting his horse, he drew his sword.

Sharp whistles came from all sides, which meant their would-be attackers were signaling to each other.

They were being surrounded.

Tightening his one-armed hold on Sebrahn, who was fighting to get away now, he gestured toward the men blocking their way, signaling *break for it!*

They kicked their horses into a gallop and ran straight at them. As Seregil closed with one, he saw that the mask was shaped like the face of a red bird, with black painted eyes surrounding narrow horizontal slits. The man who swung his sword at Seregil's head had a mask like a wolf.

With his arms full of rhekaro, he barely managed to duck the blade and keep his one-handed grip on the reins.

They must have caught their attackers by surprise, because they were able to get through. With Micum in the lead now, they kicked their horses into a hard gallop, hoping to lose them in the snow before any of the horses broke a leg in a hidden ditch or rabbit hole.

"Bandits?" Alec said, looking back over his shoulder. He was riding so close that Seregil could have reached out and touched him, but his voice was so muffled Seregil could barely make out what he said. That eerie quiet had settled over them again, making the hair on the back of his neck prickle again.

As they pelted along, trying to keep Micum in sight, Seregil caught motion from the corner of his eye, but when he turned to look there was nothing there.

It happened again to his right, just past Alec, and this time he saw one of the masked riders pacing them. This one wore a fox mask. His horse's hooves didn't make a sound, but Seregil heard his whistle, and the answering ones behind them. Micum reined his horse away from the ones they could see, and Seregil and Alec followed hard on his horse's heels.

We're going to break our damn necks, Seregil thought. And Sebrahn was still struggling!

The whistles started up again, all around them, sounding so close Seregil wondered why he couldn't see any of them.

Suddenly Alec lurched forward in the saddle, an arrow protruding from his left shoulder. Micum slowed and grabbed the fallen reins.

"Damn!" Seregil reined in beside them, intending to make a stand. Before he could dismount, however, Sebrahn opened his mouth and sang.

The burst of power that emanated from that thin little body nearly threw Seregil from the saddle. It was like being struck in the chest by lightning and being on fire, all at once. The high-pitched cry drove a spike of pain between his eyes, blinding him for a moment.

Clinging on with his thighs and one hand, he managed to stay in the saddle and follow the others as they dashed away, hoping to take advantage of whatever Sebrahn had just done. He was relieved to see Alec upright again and riding hard, even with the arrow wagging up and down in his shoulder.

They drove their horses until the beasts were exhausted and they had no choice but to stop. The snow had ceased somewhere along the way, and the wind had come up. Looking back, all Seregil saw was a triple line of hoof marks slowly being scoured away. He reined his gelding around, looking for their pursuers. He hadn't seen or heard any sign of pursuit since Sebrahn had sung, and he didn't see them now across the snowswept plain. The masked bastards were probably lying in the snow, dead, just like those slave takers who'd killed Alec in Plenimar. He hoped so, anyway, though he was curious about who they were. They'd been better organized than most bandits he'd encountered. As much as he'd have liked to inspect the bodies, they'd have to back-track for miles. Without their own trail to follow, they'd end up casting around while it got dark.

Just then Alec slid awkwardly from the saddle and collapsed in a heap, gripping his wounded shoulder with his good hand.

Seregil dismounted and shoved Sebrahn into Micum's arms. "How bad is it?" he asked, pulling off his gloves.

"Shit! Hurts like hell!" Alec hissed between gritted teeth. "Don't think it went all the way through, though."

"Can you move your arm?" asked Micum.

Alec lifted his left arm and swore again.

Seregil knelt beside him. "Steady, now. Let me take a look."

The arrow had gone in at an angle. Seregil grasped the shaft and gave it the slightest tug. It moved a little and he felt it grate against bone, probably Alec's shoulder blade.

"Brace yourself," he said calmly. "I'll do this as quickly as I can." Grasping the shaft in both hands this time, he snapped it off close to the back of Alec's coat.

Alec didn't make a sound, just fumbled one-handed at the bone buttons on the front of his thick coat.

"Let me do it."

When he had the coat open, Seregil reached down the back of Alec's shirt until his fingers found the arrow shaft and the hot blood soaking the fleece lining and the wool of Alec's tunic. Bracketing the broken shaft with two fingers, he lifted the coat free of it, then gently pulled Alec's arm from the sleeve. Most of the blood had soaked into the thick fleece at the collar. If it had been summer, he'd have left a blood trail for their pursuers to follow—if they were still alive. That doubt was going to haunt him.

Micum handed him his belt knife and Seregil carefully cut the fabric away from the wound. The arrowhead was lodged in the muscle between Alec's shoulder and neck. A few inches to the right and it would have hit his spine. It was a painful wound, but not a serious one.

It meant pulling or cutting it out, though, depending on the type of arrowhead and how barbed it was. "You'd better lie down. I can get a better purchase on it that way and get it over with."

Alec stretched out on his belly in the snow and rested his face in the crook of his right arm. "Just do it!"

Micum held down Alec's left arm and Seregil straddled Alec's waist. The bloody stump of the arrow was long enough to get a good grip on, but slippery. He grasped it and pulled as Alec stifled a growl against his sleeve. To everyone's relief, it pulled out clean. Instead of being barbed and triangular, the head had the long leaf shape meant to pierce a stag, or a man, deep into the organs.

He packed a handful of snow against the wound and showed Alec the arrow. "You were lucky. Your coat must have helped stop it. Micum, would you bring some water and a cup? Sebrahn—" He paused, looking around. A trail of small footsteps in the snow led back the way they'd come. Sebrahn hadn't gotten far, but he was going as fast as he could through the snow.

Seregil sprinted after the rhekaro and grabbed him around the waist, swinging him off his feet. Sebrahn didn't struggle as Seregil lugged him back, but he kept staring off in the direction they'd come from.

"Where in Bilairy's name were you headed?" Seregil snapped, puzzled and annoyed in equal measure. Sebrahn just pointed in the direction he'd been trying to go.

"No, Alec's over here and he's hurt! How can you not know that?"

A cup of water stood ready in the snow, and Micum had wiped the knife clean. Alec was still bleeding, and covered in gooseflesh.

"Hurry now," Seregil urged, putting Sebrahn down beside him.

The rhekaro cut his finger and made half a dozen healing flowers, pressing each to Alec's wound. It slowly stopped bleeding and closed up, leaving an angry pink circle of flesh.

"That's better," Alec said, still breathing a little fast as he flexed his left arm. Sitting up, he gathered in Sebrahn with his good arm and hugged him. "Where were you off to?"

Sebrahn just looked over Alec's shoulder at his own footsteps in the snow.

Seregil frowned down at him. "What I want to know is what could be more important to him than healing you? He knew you were wounded. That's why he sang."

"Did it sound the same to you as his killing song?" asked Alec as he pulled his bloody clothing back on.

Seregil shrugged. "I don't remember, but the power of it damn near knocked me off my horse. It's a wonder *I'm* not dead."

Alec pushed the tangled hair back from Sebrahn's face. "Where were you going?"

Sebrahn pointed again.

"Yes, but why? Who were you going to?"

Sebrahn said nothing, just pointed again.

"Is someone hurt?"

Sebrahn knew yes and no pretty reliably, but again he just pointed.

"It doesn't matter now. We've got other problems." Micum picked up the broken arrow and wiped the head clean in the snow. "This is interesting."

"What is?" asked Alec.

"The shape of this arrowhead, and the way the edges are serrated. It's a damn lucky thing that you had a thick coat and were nearly out of range. I've never seen one like this in Skala, or anywhere else."

"I have," said Seregil, frowning. "Some of the southern clans use arrowheads like that."

"You think someone followed us all the way from Aurënen?" asked Alec.

"I don't know, but that's where that arrow came from." He picked up the other part of the broken shaft. "See, it's fletched with four vanes, rather than three. I've seen that among the Goliníl clan members."

"But they aren't a southern clan," Alec pointed out.

Seregil twirled the broken arrow between his fingers. "No, they're not. So we have a southern arrowhead on a Goliníl shaft."

"I'd say someone is trying to look like they're Aurënfaie, but didn't get their methods straight," said Micum.

"Maybe. Then there's the question of the masks."

"They spooked me a little," Alec admitted.

Micum pocketed the arrowhead. "That's why they wear them, I'm sure, besides hiding their cowardly faces."

"Actually, I think I've seen something like them, too," said Seregil. "Not with the animal motifs, but the Khatme who live up in the highest valleys wear some sort of slotted visor to protect them from going snow blind. It cuts down on the glare."

Alec stood up and flexed his shoulder. "That makes three clans."

"So who in Bilairy's name are they?" growled Micum.

"Aurënfaie, or someone pretending to be them," Seregil said with a shrug. "Which makes me think that it wasn't just happenstance that we ran across them."

"Ulan?"

Seregil shrugged. "I don't know how long his reach is, here in Skala."

Micum grasped his stick and pushed himself up to his feet. "We're not going to be able to answer that unless we go back and search the bodies."

Seregil considered that. "Assuming they're dead. None of us knows one of Sebrahn's songs from another, but that didn't sound the way I remember the killing one. Whatever the case, either they're dead, and no problem, or alive and we don't know how many of them there are, except they outnumber us. I say we head for the inn for now, and reconsider in daylight. Alec, can you ride?"

"I'm fine. Come on, before they catch up with us."

"Then I'd better find the road," Micum said as he climbed up into the saddle using his good leg.

Seregil stood, holding his horse's reins. "Micum?"

"What?"

"I don't think we should go to Watermead. You don't want us leading trouble to your doorstep. Not after all these years of being so careful."

"I know," Micum said, regret clear on his face. "Let's find the damn inn before it gets dark, and see if Thero has any news for us."

They cast around for nearly an hour before they found the road again, and Seregil was glad to find it well traveled. The frozen mud and trampled snow were marked with hundreds of other hoof prints; even Micum would have trouble tracking them here. Hopefully if their pursuers had survived, they'd have given up on them by now. Somehow, though,

Seregil couldn't shake off the feeling that someone was right behind them, even when a look over his shoulder across the flat terrain showed that there was no one there.

Rieser came to slowly, aware at first of nothing but the stabbing pain in his head, snow on his face, and the taste of blood at the back of his throat. Someone was shaking him and that only made everything worse. He grabbed for the hand and opened his eyes. Hâzadriën was leaning over him, and the sky beyond was full of sunset color. It had been afternoon when they'd found their prey. And lost them.

"Stop it, my friend. I'm alive." He sat up and felt blood run down over his lips from his nose. Hâzadriën reached back for something and presented him with a yellow healing flower.

Rieser pressed it to his face gratefully and the bleeding stopped, but the pain in his head did not. Using the tayan'gil's shoulder to steady himself, he climbed to his feet and looked around for the others.

They lay where they'd fallen, covered with a thin layer of fresh snow. Turmay lay next to him in a crumpled heap, his oo'lu trapped awkwardly under his left shoulder. Two horses remained, pawing in the snow for grass; the others were nowhere to be seen.

Nowen sat up, holding her head in both hands. "What in the name of Aura was that?"

"I don't know," Rieser told her. "Help me check the others."

She appeared to be in as bad shape as Rieser, and they moved like invalids as they slowly went from one to another, shaking them awake.

All of them were hurt to some degree. Rieser came last to young Thiren lying facedown in the snow. When he didn't stir, Rieser rolled him over and found the boy's eyes fixed and his face dark with settled blood. His bow lay broken beside him.

Nowen came to Rieser and rested a hand on his shoulder. Her voice was thick with grief and pain as she whispered hoarsely, "Why didn't the witch know, if his 'Mother' is so—"

"Mind your tongue," Rieser cautioned, covering her mittened hand with his own.

Rane staggered over and sank to his knees beside his dead brother, blood trickling from both ears, and began the death keen.

"Not here, Rane," Rieser said, wrapping an arm around the boy's shaking shoulders. "There'll be time later to mourn, when we've found some safe place for the night."

Rane wiped the tears from his face with his sleeve.

Rieser found his eyes stinging, too. He had lost riders before, but Thiren was his mentor's son. He was glad Syall í Konthus wasn't alive to know this.

Turmay was on his feet now, white and unsteady. He hands shook as he tried to warm himself in his frozen clothing.

"You didn't know that one of them was a wizard?" Rieser demanded.

"Because none of them are," Turmay replied, sinking down beside him, looking very green and ill. "I—I would have seen such a one. That was not magic; it was—power. This must have come from their tayan'gil."

"That's impossible. They don't kill."

Turmay gestured weakly back at the dead boy, and at the other riders staggering around holding heads and stomachs. Several were vomiting into the snow. "This one can. And your own tayan'gil was the only one of us not stricken by its power."

"A lucky thing for us," said Rieser, watching Hâzadriën minister to the others. "Sona, Taegil, go look for the other horses. Turmay, you come with me. Nowen and Hâzadriën, you take care of the others here."

Mounted on the two remaining horses, he and the witch set off to see what direction the ya'shel and his tayan'gil had gone. Three distinct lines of shallow hoof marks dimpled the fresh snow, heading southeast. The horses had been running at a gallop. They were probably miles away by now, but he kept going.

"What was that sound?" Rieser asked as they rode along, not really expecting an answer.

"I think that must be the power of the tayan'gil."

"I still say they don't have such an ability."

Turmay frowned at him from the depths of his fur-lined hood. "Even so, I tell you this one does. Remember that it was made from a half-breed's blood. Who knows what that would do?"

Rieser snorted softly. "That should make it weaker, not stronger. One of the others must be a wizard. They exist among the Tír in the north, so why not here?"

Turmay shrugged. "Then perhaps it was that."

They followed the trail for nearly a mile before it ended; the snow was less deep on the ground here. The wind had swept away all trace of them.

With a muttered curse, Rieser turned back and kicked his horse into a gallop, retracing his steps with Turmay beside him. The chase would have to wait for as long as it took for his riders to recover.

And what then, he could not say.

C H A P T E R 18
A Wizard's Touch

SEREGIL and the others were relieved to finally see the glow of firelight through windows in the distance. They urged their tired horses into one last gallop and reached the inn a few minutes later.

He and Micum knew the Bell and Bridle well; they'd sometimes stayed here when they were out working for Nysander, and Seregil had sung for their supper by the broad hearth a time or two. It was a large, friendly establishment frequented by traders and travelers of all sorts, with a comfortable, smoky taproom on the ground floor and rooms of passable cleanliness above.

There was a sizable crowd tonight, mostly traders and drovers, with a handful of soldiers mixed in. Few of them gave the newcomers a second look, focused as they were on the pretty young woman plucking a harp by the fire. That suited Seregil just fine, together with the fact that he didn't recognize the woman giving orders from behind the polished bar. Better not to leave a trail of acquaintances if someone might be tracking you.

He looked around for Thero as he made his way through the crowd to the bar, but didn't see any sign of him. "Have you any rooms for the night, Mistress?"

She gave him a pretty smile. "Have you the silver to pay for it, sir?"

Knowing he didn't look much like a sir, much less Lord Seregil of Rhíminee after so many weeks on the road, he gave her a wink and slid two silver sesters across the bar. "Will that do for a private room and a hot bath?"

She scooped up the coin. "Just right. You can have the small room at the top of the house. The bathhouse is behind the kitchen. I'll have the cook put some cans of water by the fire while you carry up your gear."

Their room looked out over a chicken yard in the back but had a broad, clean, vermin-free bed and no holes in the roof, which was about all Seregil required of a place like this. An oil lamp stood on a small table. A washstand and a single chair stood by the window.

"Much better than last night, aside from the smell of the chickens," Alec said.

Micum sat down on the edge of the bed to test the mattress. "I'll take that over fleas any day."

They stowed their gear and went back downstairs to take turns in the cramped wooden tub, then sat down to a piping-hot rabbit pie, thick with onions and turnips.

"This was worth the ride," Alec said around a mouthful, digging in with his spoon for another bite. With his bangs cut long over his eyes, Sebrahn attracted little attention.

Seregil nodded absently, glancing around at the crowd. There was still no sign of Thero, upstairs or down.

They stayed, listening to the harper until she stopped for the night, then returned to their room.

"Now if you don't mind, I'm going to get some sleep," Micum said, stretching out on the bed with a happy groan. "Seregil, you can have the first watch, and don't the two of you get up to any mischief."

"That could be taken several ways," Seregil noted.

"And I meant all of them." With that, he threw an arm over his eyes. A few minutes later he was snoring loudly.

They waited for two days, passing their time as they could. Alec remained upstairs with Sebrahn while Seregil and Micum went out hunting with the innkeeper's daughters in the early morning. They added considerably to the house larder, for which they got much praise at supper. In the afternoon Seregil played his harp and made a bit of silver, which he parleyed up in the evening as he and Micum gambled with the other guests. They won more than they lost, but not so much that anyone would remember them for it. The second night Seregil had no luck at all, but his looks and charm had made him the darling of the tables. Everyone gave him a bit of their earnings at the end of the night, little guessing that a few miles away in Rhíminee, Seregil was a rich man.

Thero arrived at sunset on the third day as Seregil sat plucking his harp by the fireside. The young wizard was dressed in ordinary riding clothes and could have easily passed as one of the traders Micum was currently drinking with. His dark, curly hair was pulled back in a black ribbon, and a few days' worth of stubble darkened his thin cheeks. He caught sight of Seregil and pushed his way through the crowd to clap him on the shoulder. "Greetings, friend! I hope I haven't kept you waiting too long."

"Not at all, friend. I have a room for us. Come. I'll show you."

"Hold on. You can help me first."

Thero led the way out to the stable, where Seregil and Alec's horses were tethered. Cynril nickered contentedly as Seregil leaned over the side of the stall to rub the tall black mare's nose. Alec's brown mare Patch and chestnut stallion, Windrunner, were in the next two stalls. Alec would be glad to have Patch back, preferring the scrubby brown mare to Windrunner, even if she did try to eat every bit of leather within reach, including belts and purses, not to mention tack left hanging unwisely in her stall. Seregil crossed to the other stalls and stroked his grey gelding Star's neck. "Hello there, boy. Ready for a proper journey after all that lazing around?"

Several heavy packs lay in a heap on the clean straw of another. "I didn't know what you wanted," said Thero, "so your man Runcer packed a bit of everything, including this." He handed Seregil a heavy money purse, then wrinkled his nose at the tunic Seregil had been wearing since they'd left Madlen's house.

"The innkeeper doesn't do laundry," Seregil said ruefully.

Even though he'd bathed again last night, his clothes were getting rather ripe.

"Your hair has grown quite a lot since I last saw you," Thero remarked as they hefted the bags and carried them inside.

Seregil grinned and ran his fingers back through his dark hair; it was a bit past his shoulders now and not so ragged as it had been, thanks to Alec's careful trimmings. Between that and the daily attention to Sebrahn's ever-growing hair, Alec could probably set up shop as a barber when they got back to Rhíminee. Assuming they did.

Micum met them and insisted on taking one of the small bags as he stumped up the two steep flights behind them.

Alec was on the bed with Sebrahn, pitching cards at the washbasin and looking very bored. He brightened up at the sight of Thero. "You made it! Any news?"

As Thero bent to set his packs down under the window, however, he caught sight of Alec's bloodstained coat, thrown into a corner and forgotten. He looked around at the rest of them in surprise. "Who's wounded?"

Seregil held a finger up to his lips and waited until Micum closed the door.

Thero cast a ward on it to keep out prying ears. "What happened? Who's hurt?"

Alec pulled down the back of his shirt to show Thero his latest scar. It hardly showed, after Sebrahn's healing. "We were ambushed and one of their archers hit me in the back, but I'm fine."

"When did this happen?"

"A few days ago," Seregil told him. "There were a dozen or so and they caught us by surprise."

"Bandits?"

"I don't think so," said Micum. "The arrow that struck Alec was of Aurënfaie make."

"Why wait until then to ambush you? And why would 'faie attack you, anyway?"

"We aren't sure about any of that."

"They wore animal masks," Alec told him. "Ever hear of anything like that?"

Thero shook his head. "Not that I recall. Where did you get the Skalan clothing, by the way? Steal it from some poor cottager's clothesline?"

"We spent a night at Madlen's."

"Ah, good. I hope you found her well?"

"Same as ever."

"I'm glad to hear it."

Thero opened one of the packs and took out a leather tobacco pouch wrapped in string. "I thought you might need this." Grinning, he tossed it over to Micum.

Micum pulled the string loose and lifted the flap to sniff the contents. "Oh, that's good! Many thanks, Thero. That was kind of you."

"Nothing for me?" asked Alec.

Thero took out a small cloth drawstring bag and handed it to him. "Hundred Year Plums. I guessed you hadn't had any for a long time."

Alec eagerly opened the bag and offered the sweets to Seregil, who declined. They were made in Rhíminee, where a particular small, tart plum grew. Once harvested, they were pitted, stuffed with ground pepper, then packed in salt for months, until they were wizened and black, and looked as if they were a hundred years old. The combination of salt, tart, and hot wasn't to Seregil's taste, but Alec loved them.

Thero sat down on the bed next to Sebrahn. "So you saved Alec again, did you? You're a useful little fellow."

"But a conspicuous one," said Seregil. "Your transformation is wearing off."

"So I see," said Thero, taking in Sebrahn's piebald appearance.

Seregil turned Sebrahn's face to the light, then pushed up his sleeves, showing the wizard the patches of blotchy white showing through the tan skin. There was more silver than blond in his hair now, too.

Thero passed his hands over Sebrahn's hair and shoulders. "It's as if it's worn off, like paint. I'm afraid all I can do is reset the spell and hope it lasts as long as the previous one. So, what will you do now? I assume you're still going to avoid Rhíminee?"

Seregil exchanged a look with Alec, then said, "We're going to Plenimar."

Thero stared at him in disbelief. "You can't be serious. Why?"

"We have reason to believe that Yhakobin had books on how the rhekaros are made. If we can get those, it will not only tell us more about Sebrahn and how to handle him, but also keep any more from being made." It had sounded better when they'd come up with the plan.

"I don't suppose I can talk sense into any of you?"

"No," said Alec.

"Well then, how do you mean to go about it?"

"I know a good man with a good ship, who happens to be at my beck and call."

Alec grinned. "Captain Rhal. I hope he still has that sighting charm nailed to the mast."

"He does," the wizard told him. "I dined with him a month ago, aboard the *Lady*, and he had me make certain the magic was still in place on it."

"So tell me, Thero, where is that ship of mine?" asked Seregil.

Micum and Alec shared an amused look. Seregil knew it was at his expense.

Thero climbed onto the bed and sat cross-legged in the middle of it. "Give me a moment." He closed his eyes and pressed his palms together, pointing away from him. After only a moment he opened his eyes. "He's in Nanta harbor."

"Damn," muttered Seregil. "It will take him a month or more to get here, this time of year."

"Indeed." Thero paused a moment. "There is another route you could take, though it's not an easy one. Do you know of Tamír's Road?"

"I know the queen's name, but I didn't know she had her own road."

"It goes through the central mountains of Skala from near Rhíminee to Ero," the wizard explained. "It's said to be the route Tamír the Great and her army took to outflank her usurper cousin for their final battle. Rhíminee was built on that same battlefield."

"And it still exists?" asked Micum.

"It's actually more of a trail than a road," Thero explained. "The mouth of it is hidden, but I can show you. I've been down it with Magyana."

"And it comes out at Ero?" asked Alec. "I thought that city was destroyed back in ancient times."

"The city was," Seregil told him. "All that remains of it are some ruins up on a hill, and bits of the city wall. There's still a little village down at the harbor, though, called Beggar's Bridge. I've been there a time or two. Rhal can meet us there."

"Is the trail even passable this time of year?" asked Alec.

"It should be. The passes aren't that high," Thero explained.

"I've heard that some strange folk live up in the mountains," said Micum.

"Yes, though you're not likely to see any along the road. They avoid travelers."

"How long will it take us, do you think?" asked Micum.

Thero thought a moment. "Ten days—maybe two weeks to Beggar's Bridge, if the weather doesn't slow you down."

"All right then. Tamír's Road it is!" said Seregil. "Send word to Rhal to meet us there."

Thero cast a message spell and a little point of light sprang to life in front of him. "Captain Rhal, Lord Seregil sends word that's it's time to honor your bargain again. Please be at Ero Harbor by the first day of Klesin." He looked up at Seregil. "Anything to add?"

"Wait for us there and have someone we know keep watch for us at Sea Horse Tavern."

Thero nodded and sent the light speeding off to the east. It disappeared through the window and was gone. "That gets you to Plenimar, but how can you take Sebrahn there? You three might be able to blend in, but he won't."

Seregil nodded. "I haven't worked that out yet. Do you have any suggestions?"

"Not that I can think of. And what about you, Alec?" the wizard asked, reaching out to tug the end of Alec's braid. "This hair of yours is like a beacon."

"Do it."

"Red or brown?"

"What? Oh—brown."

Seregil gave Thero a strand of his hair and Thero performed the transformation spell, leaving Alec's the same dark brown, then did the same to Sebrahn's and used the pouch of brown powder to restore the color of his skin. "There. It makes you both look almost full 'faie. I only hope it holds long enough this time for you to do what you need to do."

Alec held up his braid. "Changing the color may not be enough. I think it's time to cut it."

"I'm afraid so," Seregil said with a pained look. "I'll ask the innkeeper for a pair of shears."

Thero shook his head. "I don't know why I'm helping you. It's pure madness."

"There's no help for it. Aside from Ravensfell—where we would most assuredly be killed—where else are we going to find out how to manage Sebrahn?" asked Seregil. "I assumed you'd be the most interested in such knowledge."

"I assume you know where to look once you get there?"

"Well, I know what it looks like," Alec told him. "Yhakobin had all sorts of books lying around in a workshop."

Thero shook his head. "And you're assuming that the one you want is still there, with its owner dead?"

"If it isn't, then we'll find out who took it," Seregil said with a shrug, though the more he tried to convince the wizard, the worse it all sounded, even to him.

"Assuming we don't all get killed," Thero noted dryly.

Seregil arched an eyebrow at that. "Who said anything about 'we'? You're not going."

"And who are you to tell me that?"

Micum laughed at that.

"It's going to be dangerous enough for 'faie to go in with a magical creature like no other in tow," Seregil explained as patiently as he could. "Your wizard blood and magic as strong as yours is? They would make you shine like a torch to any necromancer we encounter. Maybe alchemists and Plenimaran wizards, too. You'd be more liability than help."

"Liability?" Thero looked like he was about to launch into a lengthy retort, but he stopped instead and nodded. "That's probably true. But I'll take you as far as the beginning of the road and show you where it is."

"I didn't mean to insult you about the rest of it, Thero," Seregil told him. "I never doubt your skills, or your bravery."

Thero raised a dubious eyebrow. "Thank you."

"Now, about that slave mark?" said Micum.

"Slave mark?"

"The slavers branded us on the arm and leg. Every slave bears the marks," Seregil explained.

Alec took out a small bit of parchment and showed Thero the design he'd created. "Yhakobin's mark was round, but I saw some square ones like this, too. This is the size."

"And I'm to be their new master." Micum said, grinning at Seregil. "I'm rather looking forward to it, too."

Thero sat down by the room's single lamp and held the design to the light. "Yes, I think I can do that in a way that won't leave any traces of the spell. Who wants to go first?"

Seregil pulled his right sleeve back. "Right here, on the underside of the forearm."

Thero pressed his hands together under his chin, chanting softly, and Seregil felt the air around them begin to crackle and warm. He clenched his teeth against the sudden pain as Thero closed his right hand over Seregil's arm and gripped it tightly. The pain only lasted a moment, but it felt like a hot iron had been pressed to his skin again.

When Thero took his hand away, the others leaned in to see the square outline of the slave mark just where the old one had been. It was slightly raised and had a faded look, pale against Seregil's fair skin.

"Will that do?"

"It's perfect!" Seregil smiled as he ran a thumb over it. "I take it this doesn't have any magic clinging to it, either?"

"No, it's just a transformation spell, like Sebrahn's hair. I altered your skin. I'll change it back when you're done with it."

"Did it hurt?" asked Alec.

"Yes, it did." Seregil gave him a crooked grin as he pulled off his left boot. "But it was still much nicer than the way the slavers do it. I need one on the back of my left calf, as well."

Thero invoked the spell again and laid a hand on the back of Seregil's calf. The fleeting pain took hold and the mark appeared. Thero made the brands on Alec's arm and leg, then turned to Sebrahn. "What about him?"

"Why not let him be my son?" Micum suggested. "He won't be much use as a slave."

Alec shook his head. "Sooner or later we might end up having to stay in someone's slave quarters, away from you and Sebrahn. And you know what happened last time we tried that."

"What happened?" asked Thero.

Seregil described Sebrahn's "tantrum" and its aftereffects. "It will be hard enough to keep him from seeing every Plenimaran as an enemy."

"Are you certain that a necromancer won't sense him?" asked Alec.

"Certain? No, but we don't have much choice at this point. Thero, will you try that spell on Sebrahn?"

Thero approached the rhekaro again with obvious trepidation.

Alec pulled Sebrahn into his lap and held the rhekaro's right arm out to the wizard. "This will hurt a little, but it's all right."

"Hurrrrrt."

"Go ahead, Thero."

The wizard carefully laid his hand on Sebrahn's arm, and to everyone's relief the spell took effect without incident. The faded-looking brand stood out against his brown skin. Thero placed the last one on his leg, and it was over.

"I suppose you'll need slave collars, as well."

"We'll just have to find a blacksmith who won't ask any questions," said Micum. "I know a man over in Riverton who could do the job, and he's only three days from here. It's a bit out of our way, but he's got the craft and the sense to keep his mouth shut if anyone comes asking."

"I don't like it," said Seregil. "What more obvious crumb could we leave in our trail than having someone make Plenimaran slave collars all the way over here?" He turned to Thero again. "Nysander was pretty handy with metal. Do you know any of that magic?"

"He did teach me some, as one type of the transformations. I only mastered it on gold, silver, and iron, though."

Seregil weighed his purse in one hand. "Not enough gold or silver, and Micum probably doesn't look rich enough to have slaves of that quality."

"Rather you don't look like you're good enough quality," Micum shot back with a grin.

"Indeed," Thero said with a dry smile. "As for the collars, if I'm to work metal, I'll need some rest first. You lot are very demanding!"

Seregil chuckled at that, then disappeared downstairs, returning a few minutes later with a pair of kitchen shears. With a resigned sigh, he cut Alec's braid off just below the nape of his neck, then trimmed up the ragged ends. "It's shorter than mine now. But you're right, it would have gotten you noticed." He paused and yawned. "You three get some sleep. I'll take the first watch. I have some thinking to do."

He wrapped himself in his cloak and made his way downstairs to the mostly deserted taproom. Sitting by the hearth nursing an ale, he waited until the servants and the few lingering rum pots had gone to bed, then pulled a chair over to the west-facing window. Snow was falling again, and clouds covered the moon, making it too dark to see much. He kept watch, anyway, as his thoughts turned again to the strange masked riders and that arrowhead.

I hope we did kill you, you bastards, whoever you are!

CHAPTER 19

❧
Useful Magic

THERO WOKE at dawn to find the others already awake. A sooty fire poker and a rusty crowbar lay on the bed beside him.

Seregil was sitting near the window with his bare feet propped on the sill and his fingers laced around a steaming mug, looking pleased with himself. "These were the best I could find, unless you can work with a sack of horseshoe nails."

"I could do with some tea first," Thero grumbled, sitting up and combing his fingers back through his disheveled curls.

Micum handed him a mug and Thero gratefully inhaled the steam, which smelled of a passable quality leaf. "So, can you tell me exactly what you want them to look like?"

Seregil smoothed a square of stained blotting paper out on the bed. On it were drawn two fairly detailed collars, each open on one side, with flattened ends and rivet holes, presumably where the thing would be fastened around the unfortunate slave's neck. Seregil was a more than passable artist, and Thero could make out the simple patterns he'd decorated them with. "I didn't know they could be so fancy."

"The type of collar speaks to the owner's means and taste," Seregil explained. "A rich man's favorite could have a gold or silver collar, decorated quite nicely. You almost forget it's not just jewelry."

Setting his mug aside, Thero picked up the poker and ran his hands over it, familiarizing himself with the metal. Iron was less malleable than gold or silver, but not as resistant to magic as silver. He continued stroking the poker as he closed his eyes and began to visualize what he wanted. He imagined it becoming a long roll of beeswax, and felt the heat under his fingers as the iron responded, beginning to bend. He pulled back a little, not wanting to melt it. Checking the drawing again, he broke off a usable length of it and gently curved it around into an open circle.

Seregil let out an impressed whistle. "I didn't think it would be that easy!"

"It's not," Thero muttered, concentrating to keep the metal workable. It was a small matter to pinch the ends flat and fashion a hole through them large enough for a rivet. With that done, he ran his hand over it again, smoothing the surface, and laying down a vine-like pattern as if it had been incised by some talented artist—which, as it happened, he was. Finished, he passed it to Seregil for inspection.

"Very nice. Do you have it in you to make the other two, or do you need to rest?"

"No, let's proceed." There was enough of the poker left to make a little collar for Sebrahn, but he had to work with the crowbar to make the third. This iron had been more crudely refined and took more concentration, but the others were quietly cheering him on and it was surprising how much that helped. Even Sebrahn seemed mildly interested.

The third collar was heavier than the others, with a double line of arrowhead designs. When he was done, Seregil took it and weighed it against the first. "It's not as fine."

"It's the best I can do with the quality of that metal," Thero told him, at the end of his strength for the moment.

"I'll wear it," Alec offered. "After all, I'm a little bigger than you are, Seregil."

"Stop bragging," said Seregil, with what might have been a hint of pique. "It's only an inch of height, and you still have that baby's face of yours."

Alec smoothed two fingers over the barely discernible fuzz on his upper lip. "You won't say that when I'm shaving."

"I hate to disappoint you, talí, but you're no more likely to sprout a beard than I am."

"Are we leaving, or are you two going to stand around preening yourselves all morning?" asked Micum, who was sporting a respectable scruff on his chin and cheeks this morning, in addition to his bushy moustache. Seregil made a rude gesture in his friend's direction.

Thero watched with amusement and, if he was honest with himself, a bit of affection, as well.

Micum stowed the collars away in a pack while Seregil and Alec dressed in clothing Thero brought from the Wheel Street house. The surcoats they chose were plain but stylishly cut, and the breeches of soft doeskin were just loose enough to ride in. He'd forgotten about boots, which would have been unwieldy to conceal, but those they'd worn from Aurënen were close enough in cut not to be remarked on, especially since the men who wore them were unmistakably Aurënfaie themselves. Thero studied Alec's face in the morning light; his dark blue eyes gave away his mixed blood, but he still retained the heightened features that had resulted from whatever strange magic the alchemist had put Alec through to purify the strain of Hâzadriëlfaie blood in his veins. At this point Thero was quite sure the change was permanent. He hoped the people who knew him as Lord Alec in Rhíminee would put the change down simply to him growing toward manhood.

"Come on then!" Seregil said, slinging a pack over his shoulder. He'd buckled on his sword, and Thero could see the slight bulge on the outside of Seregil's right boot, where he always carried the wickedly sharp poniard. Alec had somehow come out of Plenimar with his black-and-silver-handled dagger, too, and wore it in his belt, in a new sheath worked with a 'faie design.

They had breakfast in the tavern, paid their bill, and set off in good spirits, leaving Madlen's horses with the innkeeper with instructions to sell them and hold the money for their return. Both Seregil and Alec were as delighted to be reunited with their own horses as if they were long lost friends. Thero even caught Alec letting Patch gnaw on a leather wrist guard when they stopped to water them at a roadside spring. But he also saw how watchful Seregil and the others were, constantly checking behind for their masked pursuers. The weather was clear and the terrain flat, allowing them to see for some miles, but still they looked.

"Let me see that arrowhead," he said at last.

Micum reached into his belt purse and handed it to him. The bloodstains on the broken bit of shaft still attached to it had turned black.

Thero clasped it in his left hand and looked over at Seregil. "This should work."

"Good. I'm getting a stiff neck looking over my shoulder so much."

Thero looped the reins over the saddlebow, pressed the arrowhead between his hands, and closed his eyes. The first thing he saw was Alec, thanks to the blood, which he was adept at reading. Things would be much simpler if some of the original archer's blood was on it, but no such luck. Instead he had a brief, vague impression of a tall man on a tall white horse, traveling across a snowy field. Thero set free the wizard eye and experienced a moment of dizziness as his perception changed to that of a bird, flying high above the surrounding terrain. He saw the inn behind them, and the muddy roads. Moving west, he scanned left and right for signs of riders, but the only ones he found were clearly Skalans abroad on business.

"Nothing, I'm afraid. No sign of pursuit," he told them, massaging his forehead with two fingers to ease the dull ache there. "They could have given up, or you killed them."

"Or they're holed up somewhere, licking their wounds," Seregil murmured, looking back over his shoulder again as they set off again.

The Ebrados had found refuge in an abandoned cottage. Rane and Morai were still ill and Hâzadriën tended them as best he could, but the magic that had struck them down didn't leave wounds on skin or bone.

Turmay had been very quiet since it happened, not speaking or offering to play the oo'lu, but Rieser often caught the witch with a distant look in his eyes, as if he could see far, far beyond this miserable redoubt. Still, for four days he said nothing at all.

Then, on the morning of the fifth day, Turmay suddenly stood up and went to the door, oo'lu over one shoulder and his little bundle over the other.

"What is it?" Rieser demanded, looking past the little man for signs of trouble.

But the witch just glanced back at him and said, "Time to follow them," as if they'd been talking about it all morning.

As they set off, Turmay was suddenly talkative again. "This tayan'gil you seek? It is not like this one with you. Yours has a different feel, less powerful magic than the little one. The other tayan'gils your clan guards are the same as this one, mute and harmless. But this other?"

"You mean he's not a real tayan'gil?"

"I don't say that, only that he's not the same as Hâzadriën or his brothers. He is something different."

"Either he is or he isn't!"

Turmay looked up at him, black eyes suddenly bottomless. "No. And you must catch him."

"Of course! That's why we're here, leagues from our valley, with a man dead," Rieser snapped. "This is no time to talk in riddles!"

Rieser waited impatiently for the witch to explain himself, but Turmay lapsed back into his frustrating silence for the rest of the day and refused to answer any questions.

Alec had seen Skala's long mountainous spine many times, but only from a distance. Now he felt a thrill of anticipation as they neared the head of the trail named for the famous queen. He'd seen her statue in the Cirna Canal—a grim and determined figure in gown and breastplate, sword raised in protection of the ships passing before her. He tried to imagine Tamír as she must have looked going to war, and no older than he'd been when he first met Seregil. The thought of seeing her ancient capital made his heart beat faster, even if the place was nothing but a ruin. But it wasn't only that. Riding along with his friends, on their way to new places and new dangers—he lived for this. All those desultory months knocking around Rhíminee, he'd longed for this kind of freedom. Of course all he'd gotten was a stint in slavery, but at least they'd gotten out of the house.

It took a day and a half of uneventful riding to reach the foothills where Tamír's Road began, and it was a distinct relief not to have to keep Sebrahn hidden anymore. Thanks to Thero's reinforced magic, he looked even more like a skinny little boy—or girl, for that matter, with all that hair. In his weaker moments Alec could almost imagine taking him back to Wheel Street or the Stag and Otter, thinking how they might explain the sudden appearance of a child. But then Sebrahn would look up at him with those empty silver eyes and the daydream ended in thoughts of Queen Phoria and what she would do to obtain such a weapon as this.

Following a faint trail, they rode up through an ancient forest of towering, snow-covered fir trees. The way grew steeper and the forest more dense as the day went on, but Thero led the way without hesitation.

"Here it is," he said at last.

This part of the forest looked pretty much like what they'd been riding through all afternoon, until Thero pointed out the faint carving of a handprint on one of the trees. Alec could tell it had been made a long time ago by the way the bark had grown in around the edges, obscuring the thumb. He brushed his fingers across the mark, then pressed his hand to it. It was made by a smaller hand than his.

"Is that an Orëska mark?" he asked.

"No. It's something to do with those hill folk," Thero told him. "Nysander said that they lived down here, before we Skalans came."

"And took their lands," Seregil added.

"Unfortunately, yes. These marks lead to the head of the trail."

The handprint carvings, few and far between, led to the bank of a small, rushing river, and then upstream into the mountains. The snow was old here, icy and dirty. Spring was not far off.

"This is the start of it," Thero told them. "Just follow the stream to the trail. It goes between some cliffs for a while, so there's no missing it."

"Then I guess it's time we say our farewells," Seregil said.

"All right, then. But let me cast another wizard eye for you, to look for trouble ahead." Closing his eyes, Thero murmured the spell and sat very still for a moment. "There are people up in the hills, but they live there and they're well back from the trail. When Magyana and I passed through, we never saw any."

"Thank you." Seregil clasped hands with him. "For all you've done for us."

"Don't make it sound so final! Just be sure to bring that book to me. I'll keep it safe and secret."

"A Guardian," said Alec.

"I suppose so. Good luck to you all. Luck in the shadows."

"And in the Light, my friend," Seregil returned.

Alec missed Thero immediately, but there was an added sense of urgency with his departure that he couldn't quite explain, as if the parting marked the passing of some boundary.

The way grew narrower as they went on, threading between steep rock faces that barely left enough room along the ice-edged riverbank to pass. In places they were forced to ford through uncertain waters, and all the while the sun was sinking behind the trees. There was fresh snow here, but it was not deep. It leveled out to a windswept span of rock and dead grass. There were a few conies nibbling there and Alec took two with his bow, shooting from the saddle.

Stars were showing overhead when they reached a little pocket valley between steep, snow-clad peaks.

"I've had enough, and so have the horses," said Micum, stroking his mount's neck. "This is as good a place as any."

There was no sign of habitation, so they made camp in a copse of young firs. Dead grass and weeds stuck up through the snow, and they left the horses to forage while they scraped out a fire pit. There was plenty of wood to roast the rabbits, and they'd sleep warm that night, bundled close together around the fire.

Alec was just about to settle down for the night when Sebrahn suddenly jumped to his feet and ran across the clearing, pointing up at something. Micum and Seregil had already drawn their swords, but Alec saw what Sebrahn was excited about and waved them off.

A large white owl sat blinking down at them from a bough.

Sebrahn held his arms up to it and rasped out, "Drak-kon!"

"Now, why would he think that?" said Micum.

"Owls are as much Aura's creatures as dragons are," Seregil explained. "And since there aren't any dragons around here, maybe he's making do with what he has."

"You're not suggesting that owls are really dragons, too, are you?" Micum asked, skeptical.

"No, just that they both belong to Aura."

Suddenly Sebrahn began to sing, as he had with the great dragon, but this song was softer. The bird swiveled its round head to look down at the rhekaro, then shook its wings, sending a few tufts of fluff drifting down onto Sebrahn's upturned face. When Sebrahn kept singing, it gave a loud hoot and fluttered down to perch on his shoulder. The bird was too big and ended up clinging to his arm, digging its talons in hard enough to draw white blood. Tiny dark blue flowers formed where drops fell like jewels against the snow.

Sebrahn stroked its snow-white breast. The owl hooted again, and a third time before taking wing into the darkness.

"Drak-kon!" Sebrahn called after it.

"Look, Alec," Seregil said quietly, pointing up at the trees. Four other white owls perched there, their gold coin eyes fixed on Sebrahn.

"They're solitary hunters," Micum murmured. "Did he call them here?"

"Maybe," said Seregil. "I didn't notice them before."

Alec knelt by Sebrahn and pointed up at the birds. "Owls. Not dragons. Owls."

"Drak-kon."

"No. Owls."

Sebrahn looked confused. "Aaaaals?"

"Yes. Ow-els."

"Aaaaaals."

Seregil chuckled. "Close enough."

"Drak-kon!" Sebrahn pointed up to the birds again.

"It's not a dragon. It's an owl," Alec explained again.

Sebrahn sounded almost sulky as he whispered, "Aaaaaal."

They traveled like that for the next two days through stony divides, winding stretches of open, ice-slick rock, and small valleys where herds of elk wintered. Eagles and sharp-winged hawks soared against the clear blue sky and dazzling peaks by day; at night owls hooted as they hunted on the night air and came to visit Sebrahn in answer to his song.

Alec was carefully turning a spitted rabbit over the fire that night when he heard a high-pitched, familiar call. A tiny saw-whet owl sat on a branch almost over his head. It was a lucky sign; of all their kind, these little buff-and-white birds, no longer than his hand, were considered the Lightbearer's most sacred emissary, and seeing one always brought good luck.

Sebrahn held up his hand. Even without a song to draw it down, the bird fluttered down to perch on his hand, preening. "Drak-kon aaaaaaaal."

Seregil put down the armload of firewood he'd gathered and gave the bird a respectful nod. "Whatever he wants to call it, we'll need all the luck we can get before we come back this way."

"You think we're being followed again?" asked Micum, looking up from the rabbit he was gutting.

"I just have a—"

"Wait." Alec's hand stilled on the spit as he caught sight of movement from the corner of his eye. Something or some-one was there between the trees, just beyond the reach of the firelight. "To the left," he whispered.

"And behind you," Micum whispered back, reaching for his sword. Seregil tossed Alec his bow and quiver and pulled Sebrahn to his feet. Together, they all backed slowly out of the circle of light that made them an easy target. Keeping the rhekaro shielded among them, they waited.

As Alec's eyes adjusted to the darkness, he saw more movement. Whatever it was, it didn't make any noise. It felt like a hundred eyes were staring at him from all directions.

"What do you think?" Micum murmured.

"They could have surprised us if they'd wanted to attack," Seregil pointed out.

"Maybe," said Micum. "I don't see anything now. You, Alec?"

"No."

They stood like that for some time, but nothing happened.

"I think they're gone," Micum said at last.

With Seregil in the lead and Alec holding Sebrahn by one hand and his bow in the other, they made a circuit of the copse and beyond, finding half a dozen odd trails in the snow.

"Looks like they used a brush tail," Micum said, inspecting one of the marks. Their visitors had brought boughs with them, dragging them behind themselves to cover their footprints. There was no telling how many of them there were, if they'd walked in lines.

"How could we not have heard them?" Alec whispered, wondering how far their visitors had retreated, and if they could still see him and the others.

"Do you think it was our friends in the masks?" Micum whispered.

Seregil stared down at the brush marks. "If it was, then why didn't they attack? It's a lonely place, and they got close enough to shoot at us before we even knew they were there."

"Sebrahn didn't react, either," Alec pointed out.

"It was someone who knows how to move around up here, and how to cover their tracks. They were on foot, too." Seregil rubbed absently at his chin. "Which means that they're probably from around here somewhere."

"There hasn't been so much as a woodcutter's shack since we started up here. Where would they have come from?"

Seregil exchanged a look with Micum. "Hill folk?"

"Damn!" Micum looked sharply around. "If so, then this might be exactly what they wanted us to do. I'll go back to see if we still have horses."

Seregil and Alec circled the copse again, trying to discover where the tracks came together and which way they led, but each one snaked away into the darkness in a different direction. They cast out farther, but there was no sign of convergence.

They gave up at last and returned to find their campsite untouched and the horses still tethered.

"I think someone was just having a look at us," said Seregil.

"You're probably right. They didn't leave any sign in camp," said Micum.

Alec knelt down in front of Sebrahn. "You don't feel anything like those riders who hurt me?"

Sebrahn cocked his head slightly. "Aaaaal drak-kon."

"Another owl dragon." Seregil ran a hand back through his hair as he looked up at the little saw-whet on a branch over his head. "Well, if that's the only thing he's concerned about, maybe we're safe, after all."

The owl stayed with them, but no one slept again that night.

Tense and bleary, they set off again at dawn in a light snowfall. Everyone kept an eye out for pursuers, but there was no sign of them, just a few game tracks and the broom-straw marks of sparrows and crows.

Even after Rieser's people were fit to ride again, it took several more days to pick up the trail. Once they had it, however, it wasn't hard to follow: One of the men rode a horse with a crooked nail in its right front shoe.

Turmay played that morning, and took longer at it than usual. When he was done, he looked puzzled.

"Can you see them?" Rieser asked.

"They want to go farther east, across the sea to the other great island on your map."

Rieser's eyes widened. "Plenimar?" He pulled out the map and Turmay looked at it.

"Yes, he said, pointing to Plenimar. "That is where they are going."

Every Hâzad knew that Plenimar was where the dark witches of old came from—the ones who'd enslaved Hâzadriël and others to make the first tayan'gils. The name was like a curse on their people. The ya'shel had already been used once, perhaps there; were his companions forcing him back there to be used again?

Hâzadriën, too, seemed to sense something, as he had when they'd caught up with them in that disastrous ambush. When Turmay hesitated, or Rieser lost the track, the tayan'gil silently reined his horse in a certain direction and Rieser trusted him. He soon led them through wooded hills to the mouth of a track partially hidden in a small pass. Without Hâzadriën in the lead, they'd probably never have found it.

As they followed it, Turmay suddenly reined in his horse and ran to the nearest tree. "What is it?" asked Sona, who was closest to the witch.

"Look!" he said, pressing his hand to the trunk.

Rieser dismounted and walked back to see what had excited the witch. Turmay took his hand away from the tree trunk, showing them a carved, partially overgrown shape: a handprint. Rieser had seen such marks dozens of times, up in the peaks where the Retha'noi lived. "I don't understand. What is this doing here?"

Turmay pressed his hand to the design again. "Your people aren't the only ones who had to leave their rightful homeland."

"Retha'noi lived here?"

"Maybe. It's a very old mark." Turmay touched it again, looking thoughtful. "Perhaps my own ancestors traveled this way when the lowlanders drove them out."

"I thought your people had always lived in our valley."

"My people have lived many places," Turmay said as he went back to his horse. "We've been driven out of many places. Maybe someday your people will drive us out of our villages, too."

"There's always been peace between us. That will never happen," said Rieser, puzzled by this revelation.

Turmay only shrugged.

CHAPTER 20

The Bait

THE FICKLE WEATHER had turned mild in Virésse. The moist air eased Ulan í Sathil's lungs a little, but the disease was slowly taking its toll. It was time to take action.

He was in the garden with Ilar when he broached the subject.

Sitting beside him on the arbor bench, Ilar tilted his face up to the afternoon sun and closed his eyes, enjoying the warmth of it.

"I have a favor to ask you," said Ulan, taking Ilar's hand to get his attention. Ilar was much better than he had been, but Ulan doubted he would ever fully recover. He was still thin, and shy of other people. He suffered from nightmares, and his mind wandered easily when he was awake. Still, he knew enough to be useful.

"Listen to me, dear boy," he coaxed, and waited until he was sure he had Ilar's full attention. "You're happy here, aren't you?"

"You've been so kind to me. I don't know how I can ever repay you."

"Indeed. Now I need you to do something very important for me."

"Anything!" Ilar exclaimed. "I will do anything for you, Khirnari."

"I hope you truly mean that, Khenir." He was always careful to call Ilar by his false name, especially when they were in a place where they might be overheard. Several gardeners had come into the courtyard. Ilar regarded them uneasily.

Ulan leaned closer and spoke softly. "What I require, Khenir, is for you to come with me to Riga."

Ilar went ashen and his hazel eyes filled with fear, but he did not refuse.

Pleased, he patted Ilar's hand. "You shall go with me. I mean to visit Charis Yhakobin's widow. I've already written Lady Meran, saying I have business affairs to set in order, and that I wish to pay my respects to her on the loss of her husband. I received her answer today." He showed Ilar a letter written in purple ink on fine vellum, with a pale green wax seal. "An invitation, though I daresay the lady was surprised, given that there was not any particular warmth between her husband and me. I did bring the children little gifts, however, and she seems to think well enough of me to allow me to visit. You shall go with me."

Ilar was shaking badly now, and his voice quavered as he whispered, "But she'll recognize me. I'll be sold again, tortured!"

"Ah, but you will be wearing the slave veil and Skalan clothing. We shall cut your hair short and say that you are simply another Virésse slave I've ransomed, one who is mute, so your voice doesn't give you away."

"But—but *why?*"

"Because I must have the books, Khenir."

Ilar went blank. "The books?"

"Your Ilban's books in the little tent," Ulan patiently reminded him. For a moment he feared that Ilar did not remember, or that the books had only been a figment of his ramblings. But then Ilar's eyes seemed to focus and he nodded. "Those books. Yes."

"I shall need you to identify them for me."

"But I can't! What would Ilban say? He'll have me flogged again and—"

"Calm down, dear boy." Fear had unhinged that fragile mind again. "Your master is dead, remember? You saw him lying dead on that plain."

"Oh—Oh, yes. But still, it's forbidden!"

"You said you would do anything for—" The cough came on again, the first time today. Ilar patted his back nervously as Ulan doubled over, wheezing into his handkerchief. Today there was no blood. "Thank you, dear boy. I'm fine now," he managed, when he'd regained his breath enough to speak. "As I was saying, you've told me more than once that you would do anything for me."

Ilar wilted and returned to his fawning manner. "Of course. Yes. Even if it costs me my life."

"It won't come to that, I'm sure. First, you will look to see if the books are still there. If they are, then you will take them just before we leave. By the time their loss is discovered, we shall be long gone and quite safe."

"When will we go?"

"Soon, now that the weather is better. And you know, there is a chance that we might see your friend Seregil again, as well, since I must have Alec, too."

Ilar's demeanor changed in the blink of an eye, as it always did when Seregil was mentioned. Fear was replaced by hope, and perhaps a bit of greed.

That was a reassuring sign, thought Ulan. Sore joints aside, living long had its advantages. Most people were so transparent, it was easy to read their motives. As long as he could dangle that hope in front of Ilar, the man would do whatever he asked.

Alone in his room that night, Ilar could not sleep. They *would* find Seregil. He *would* see him again! And with hope came desire. This wasn't the first time he'd imagined capturing and enslaving him, as he had before, possessing him at last. He dreamed of it so often, but each one ended in disappointment, with Seregil always just beyond his reach. In those dreams he chased futilely after him, calling out, trying to convince him . . . But of what he wasn't sure. His regret? His aching compulsion to see him, touch him again? Sometimes he was overwhelmed by a simple, sincere desire to befriend him—honestly this time.

Awake, he dared not hope.

Noises in the Night

No one spoke of the feeling of being watched they'd all had since yesterday. They hadn't had any visitors last night, but Alec could swear he'd caught sight of someone on the high ground to their left, just after they'd set out. There was still no sign of habitation, but the feeling persisted.

The weather was fair here, but dark clouds and mist hung heavy over the pass they were approaching, promising icy footing.

"We could wait for it to clear," Seregil suggested.

Micum studied the sky. "Let's see how far we can get. I'll be happier once we're on the other side."

"Wait. Look at this," Alec said, holding up a lock of Sebrahn's hair. The color was fading from it in streaks again, leaving it a mix of dirty grey and silver. "It's happening again, and sooner this time."

Seregil leaned over and lifted the rhekaro's hair away from his neck. "There's white showing through here, too. Damn!"

"What do we do now?" asked Micum. "We could contact Thero with one of those message sticks Magyana gave you."

"To what end?" asked Seregil. "It would take him days to get here, if he could get through at all. It was a long shot at best."

"What are we going to do?" asked Alec.

"What we were going to do before Thero stuck his nose in. Think of some plausible explanation and keep going."

The Ebrados rode hard, trying to make up for lost time, pushing their horses and themselves to close the distance to the ones they sought. Once they were on the mountain trail, it was harder going, but easy enough to follow, and there hadn't been any discernible side paths. Wherever this trail led, it appeared there was only one way to get there. Rieser's scouts brought back word that there was no sign of anyone living up here, though they had found the ruins of a small village not far from the trail. Even in the small valleys, they saw no houses, flocks, or fields.

The occasional sign of a hoofprint with the crooked nail assured him that they were closing on their prey.

The second night in the pass Nowen found where the others had camped for the night. The marks of footprints and bedrolls were clear enough to read in the snow. The ashes in the blackened fire pit were only a day or two old.

Casting around, Rieser found the area they'd used as a toilet, and another spot where they'd thrown out the skin and guts of a few rabbits.

"The half-breed and his bow are keeping them fed, eh?" asked Rane, squatting down to count the skulls. "At least he's good for something else than breeding tayan'gil."

"And maybe something else, besides," Taegil said with a snicker. "I saw where they spread their bedrolls. One slept alone and two slept together. And come look at this." He led them back to a line of footprints in the snow where one of the three had gone off by himself, perhaps for wood. "The heaviest one—the Tírfaie—from the depth of the prints. And the one who slept alone I think."

"That's good to know, if it comes to a fight," said Rieser.

"Look what I found!" Rane exclaimed as they returned to the fire pit. Stooping down, he picked up a long white feather with a few grey lines. "The feather of a white owl, like the one I saw last night."

Rieser glanced down at it. "It might make a good pen, if you cut the shaft right."

"That's the Mother's bird," Turmay told the boy. "Keep it safe and it will bring you good luck."

"What about this?" asked Sona, squatting beside the fire

pit. She held up a lock of hair. It was brown, and singed at the ends.

"So they cut their hair," said Nowen. "What of it?"

"No, smell it, Captain."

Rieser took the lock and sniffed at it. It smelled faintly sweet, like a flower, with an underlying taint of some magic Rieser did not recognize. There were a few silvery strands among the dark, too. "They're trying to hide it, and not very well."

As darkness fell they built a large fire and stood around it eating the last of the fresh venison Nowen had provided for them with her strong bow, and munching on slices of turnips stolen from a farm a few days ago.

When he had eaten, Turmay settled on his bedroll by the fire and began to play. The others had gotten used to the strange music; Rieser had even come to look forward to it, wondering what strange sounds the witch would weave next.

Perhaps it was that distraction that left him unprepared when half a dozen small men stepped into the circle of firelight. Rieser's first thought was that they appeared to be unarmed; the second was that one of them carried an oo'lu very much like Turmay's, and had similar witch marks on his face and hands. They were dressed in loose leather tunics decorated with animal teeth, and their black hair was longer than Turmay's, and wilder.

Turmay looked almost as surprised as he stood and bowed to the man with the oo'lu.

The other man bowed back and said something in a language that sounded very much like Retha'noi. And it must have been, because Turmay smiled and replied in the same difficult accent. They spoke for some time and examined each other's oo'lus before Turmay began to translate.

"These are Retha'noi people!" he said, grinning broadly. "Their ancestors stayed here in the mountains, after they were driven away from the sea. And Naba here, their witch man, knew that I would come."

The other witch held up his oo'lu for Rieser to see. Like

Turmay's, it was decorated with rings of painted designs and carvings, and the same black handprint, too, though at a different place on the oo'lu.

"The way the handprint falls across the rings foretells what a witch will do," Turmay explained. "Mine said I would make a long journey. Naba's says that he will meet with a stranger who is not a stranger. He says that is me, one of his own blood from far away."

"What do they want with us?" asked Rieser, still suspicious despite Turmay's obvious delight.

"They heard me playing and came down to find me. They have no concern for the rest of you, except for your tayan'gil. He's the second one they've seen."

"They saw the others?"

"He says three riders came this way, with a white child, though it has been disguised by some sort of magic as yours is. Hâzadriën is 'white man' to them."

He spoke with Naba again, then turned back to Rieser. "He says that the white child is a thing of evil. Naba is a very powerful witch, but even he did not dare approach it. He says he can smell blood on all of them, and the little one, too. He says our tayan'gil does not smell of killing, and he is glad of that, since I'm with you, too. If he smelled that on me, he would have attacked."

"Well, that's a lucky thing, then." Rieser had often wondered if Retha'noi witches could kill with their magic; there were stories of that kind of power. He glanced around the clearing, looking for more of them. Who knew how many other witches were hiding out there in the dark? "Ask him how long ago he saw them."

Turmay spoke to Naba again. "One day."

"Give him my thanks. And ask if he and his men would share our meal with us."

The offer was accepted and the Retha'noi offered pouches of food in return. The 'faie knew from experience that it was a serious insult to refuse a gift from a Retha'noi, so they chewed their unexpected guests' tough berries and nibbled some of the rancid jerky as best they could.

When the shared meal was through, Turmay and Naba played their oo'lus together. The throbbing, hooting, buzzing drone echoed from the peaks, filling the little valley with eerie reverberations.

"What if those we are chasing hear?" asked Kalien. "Sound carries a long way in the mountains."

Rieser gazed off into the darkness, then gave him a rare, thin-lipped smile. "Let them hear."

Rane sat next to him, twirling the owl feather between his fingers. "I wonder why they haven't cracked?"

"What hasn't cracked?" asked Rieser.

"Their horns. Belan the Ya'shel is my aunt. She told me that when a witch man has done whatever his destiny is with that horn—the thing that black handprint marks—then it cracks. Naba's hasn't, even though he met Turmay. Listen. There's nothing wrong with it."

Rieser looked with more than his usual casual interest at the oo'lus. "There are a lot of rings touched by those marks. It's probably more than one thing they have to accomplish."

"Oh. That's probably right. I'll ask her when we get back."

"Why not ask Turmay?" asked Nowen.

The witch man paused in his playing. "Rieser is correct. Destiny is made up of many threads." And with that, he went back to his strange song.

Alec looked up from feeding Sebrahn. "What in Bilairy's name is *that*?"

"I have no idea," Seregil replied, pausing as he spread their bedroll on the bare stone of the summit. The faint sound in the distance was like nothing he'd ever heard.

They'd reached the top of the pass at sundown and had to make a fireless camp when a chill mist closed in around them. The rising moon turned it to silver and gave enough light to see a few yards to either side.

The damp was worse than the cold, chilling them through their woolen clothing and leaving any exposed skin clammy. Seregil's teeth were chattering, and he'd been about to coax Alec under the blankets to share what warmth they could when the weird sound wafted up to them on the night breeze. Discomfort forgotten, he listened to the rise and fall of it, baffled.

"No animal makes that sound," said Micum. "Could it be a dragon?"

"They don't sound like that." Seregil glanced back at Sebrahn, who was squatting next to Alec, apparently unfazed by the sound. "And he'd have gotten excited like he did that day in Aurënen."

"At least it sounds far away."

Micum listened for a moment. "It's hard to judge sound in the mountains."

"I wish to hell we could see something!" Seregil muttered.

The strange sounds continued, rising and falling on the breeze coming up from the pass.

"It doesn't sound like it's moving," said Alec.

"That's probably a good thing, if the sound of it carries this far," said Micum. "You two get some sleep. I'll take first watch."

"Thanks." Seregil unbuckled his sword, but kept it close to hand and his boots on as he curled up under the damp woolen blankets. A little warmer now, he stared up at the sky. Or would have had it been visible. There was nothing to see but more mist and the faint blur of the moon.

And the moon-white streaks in Sebrahn's dark hair.

Turmay lowered his oo'lu for a moment. He and Naba had exchanged the knowing song and formed an alliance that did not include the Hâzadriëlfaie. Naba was concerned to find him in the company of the tayan'gil. Turmay had needed to play an entire telling song to put the images of the good the tayan'gil could do in the other man's mind; the Mother tolerated this sort. If she had not, the Retha'noi and Hâzad could not have coexisted this long. The small tayan'gil, though? That was another matter, and Naba already understood that.

He played on, weaving a prayer into the song. *Thank you, Great Mother, for showing me the way so far, and bringing*

*me to these distant Retha'noi. I think I see your design now.
Let me play out the next threads to your will.*

The first sounds of a new and powerful song were already
taking form in his mind, a song the Mother meant for him to
share.

CHAPTER 22

Turnabout

SEREGIL woke cold and confused. He'd been dreaming of snow, and wasn't sure if he was really awake or not; he could still feel snowflakes melting on his face. He sat up and shook the snow from his hair and the blankets. He was most certainly awake and it most certainly was snowing. Alec sat beside him, wrapped in a blanket with Sebrahn. Micum sat on a stone just beyond.

Micum looked at him, bemused. "Looks like winter isn't done with us just yet." He had his hood up; it was capped with white. "You kept muttering in your sleep. Bad night?"

Seregil just shrugged. He didn't remember any details.

It was a windless day and the snow was falling silent and heavy, making it hard to see for more than a few dozen yards in any direction. The solid cover of big-bellied clouds promised a long day of it.

They broke their fast with cold rabbit and water, then set off again, beginning the long descent.

It was midafternoon when Sebrahn suddenly grew restless in Alec's arms.

"What is it? Another owl?" Seregil wondered, looking around.

"Or someone who needs healing. There could be a village on this side, or a traveler," said Micum, almost lost from sight in the dull glare of the snow. "Bilairy's Balls, I wish I could see farther than I can piss!"

Suddenly they were startled by a strange, distant thrumming

sound that made the hair on the back of Seregil's neck stand up.

"It's the same as last night!" Alec exclaimed, reining in. "And a lot closer."

Half snow blind and distracted by the sound, Seregil didn't hear Micum fall and nearly rode him down as his friend struggled to get to his feet. Cynril, who was usually a steady, reasonable beast, bucked wildly, throwing him off, and galloped away, pulling Star away on the lead rein.

Alec was close behind, and reined in so sharply that Patch reared and Windrunner whinnied in alarm. Hampered by Sebrahn, he couldn't keep purchase on the saddle and they both tumbled off, Alec somehow managing to land on his back with Sebrahn still clutched to his chest. Micum was already on his feet, but Seregil could tell he was favoring his bad leg. In spite of Sebrahn's healing, he still needed his stick now and then, and carried it tied behind his saddle. He had his sword, though, and he drew it, casting around for a glimpse of the enemy.

Alec already had his bow in hand. He held it low, left hand tight around the leather grip, right hand holding an arrow to the string. Seregil knew how quickly he could raise and shoot.

"Are you all right?" Seregil asked.

"Did you see them?" Micum growled, staring around at the falling snow.

"See who—"

And there they were again, those white-clad figures, drifting in and out of sight all around them in the falling snow. As before, it was impossible to tell how many there were. That strange sound was louder now, and it was giving Seregil a headache. This time it was familiar; he'd heard something like it the last time these bastards had caught up with them in the snow.

He closed ranks with the others as they backed up to shield Sebrahn. No sooner had they done that, however, than the rhekaro suddenly darted away, heading back the way they'd come. Seregil barely managed to catch him by the arm and drag him back. Sebrahn hissed and struggled, but his eyes hadn't gone black. Seregil kept a tight grip on his thin arm, all the while staring so intently into the falling snow that black spots danced before his eyes.

"He did that last time this lot showed up," muttered Micum.

Sebrahn tried to pull away again, but Seregil yanked him back.

"Who are you?" Alec called out. "What do you want?"

By way of answer, a masked rider surged into view, swinging a heavy cudgel at Micum. He ducked a blow that would have taken his head off, but was knocked off his feet anyway.

Alec loosed an arrow but missed his mark. Their attacker disappeared back into the shifting veil of snow. Alec sent another arrow after him.

"You don't get us that easily," Alec taunted.

The strange sound began again. It swelled and the sudden pain behind Seregil's eyes felt like a hammer pounding on the inside of his skull.

This is magic! Illior only knew what kind, or how his traitorous body would react to it. All he knew was that if it didn't stop soon, blood would probably start running out of his ears.

Even through the pain, he somehow kept his grip on the struggling rhekaro and reached for his sword.

"Something's happening to Sebrahn!" Alec warned. "His eyes are black again!"

Seregil didn't have time to let go. Even through his thick clothing, he felt the sudden rush of power that flowed out from Sebrahn as he opened his mouth and sang. The power exploded around them, throwing Seregil to the ground.

Bilairy's Balls, I'm going to be sick . . .

A man called out in odd, thickly accented Aurënfaie, "And you do not get us that easily, either, ya'shel."

Seregil exchanged a stunned look with Alec; how in Bilairy's name had anyone survived that?

"I guess we should have gone back to check on them that day," Seregil muttered. At least the magic had stopped. He grabbed a handful of snow and filled his mouth with it as he struggled up to his feet. Somehow he'd managed to keep a grasp on Sebrahn, if not his sword. Right now Sebrahn was the more important of the two.

"If your tayan'gil makes that noise again we will kill you all," the man called back to them.

Noise? Seregil thought. *If that wasn't his killing song, then what in Bilairy's name was it?* Something about the man's accent caught Seregil's attention again, but he couldn't put his finger on it.

The same voice called out, "Put down your weapons."

Alec drew his bow and let fly in that direction. It was made clear once again that their attackers could see somehow; an answering shaft narrowly missed his head.

Alec ducked, then yelled, "You're a poor archer, you cowardly bastard!"

"You would do well not to offend those who hold your lives in their hands, ya'shel."

"What Aurënfaie ambushes another, except ones without honor?" Seregil called back hoarsely. "What kind of man hides behind magic rather than face his enemy?" That was said tongue-in-cheek, of course. He attacked from cover any chance he got. But the taunt had the desired effect.

A rider came forward on a white horse, keeping his distance. Seregil recognized him by the wolf-face mask he wore under his fur-lined hood. "So you didn't die, that day."

There hadn't been time during their last meeting to get a good look at him. Seregil now saw that he sat tall in the saddle and held a long sword in his right hand, pointed at the ground for now.

The man ignored him, looking instead at Alec. "Yes, I can see that you are the one, Ireya's bastard child."

"What did you say?" Alec's voice was low and dangerous.

"Bilairy's Balls!" Seregil murmured, putting all the pieces together, including the archaic way the man spoke. "They're Hâzadriëlfaie."

Other riders appeared on their white mounts, surrounding them. Seregil counted only six, but he thought he saw more through the shifting snow. "What do you want with us?" he demanded. He couldn't see anyone's face; they all wore those masks with the slotted eyes, but each of a different animal or bird.

"Put your weapons down," Wolf Face ordered again.

"Why should we?" Alec retorted angrily. "You'll kill us either way."

The man said nothing, but two archers appeared beside him on foot. One wore the fox mask Seregil had seen last time, and the other was wearing a lynx mask. Both had arrows set to their bowstrings.

"Can I at least have your name, friend?" asked Seregil. "I always like to know who's trying to kill me."

Wolf Face turned his way. "I am not your friend. You are nothing to me. Neither is your Tírfaie companion. No man who willingly keeps such low company matters to us."

"I think he just insulted both of us," Micum muttered.

"This Tír is my friend," Alec shot back. "And this Aurënfaie is my talímenios. If you're so superior, why are you afraid to show me your face? Where's your honor?"

The tall man didn't take off the wolf mask, but he pushed back his hood. His long dark hair was streaked with grey.

"How do you know my mother's name?" Alec demanded.

"I knew your mother well, before she betrayed her people," Wolf Face told him.

"Are you the ones who hunted her down?"

"Her own kin took care of that. I hunted your father, and you. It seems to be my destiny. And now I hunt your tayan'gil."

"Tayan'gil?"

"That little one."

Seregil had heard something like that before. *Tayan* was a word the old grandmothers sometimes used. It meant "white" or "silver"—he couldn't remember which. And *gil*? He knew that one as well as he did his own name; it meant "blood." White blood? Silver blood?

The leader pointed to Sebrahn. "The Tír magic can't hide him from us. But you must realize that, now that it's wearing off."

There was no running now, and even if they could, it would mean leaving Micum behind. That pretty much narrowed their options down to one.

He held up his free hand, hoping Alec wouldn't shoot him next. "If we give you the tayan'gil, will you let us go?"

He could tell from the corner of his eye that Alec had turned to him, and for once he was thankful he couldn't see the expression on his talí's face.

Wolf Face didn't answer, just waved a hand to someone Seregil couldn't see through the snow. The strange sound was very loud this time. It was like hornets buzzing and an owl's hoot combined.

"Oh shit!" Seregil mumbled as his stomach turned over and the world went sideways . . .

Alec woke suddenly, aware first of a stinging pain on his left cheek and the fact that his hands were bound.

Oh, not again!

He opened his eyes to find the man in the wolf mask on one knee in front of him. He had his hand raised to slap Alec again, but stopped when he saw that his eyes were open.

Night had fallen, but someone stood to one side, holding a torch. Below the mask the man who'd struck Alec had a long face, with deep lines on either side of a thin, unfriendly mouth. The hank of dark hair hanging over one shoulder beneath a blue-and-white-striped sen'gai was streaked with iron grey. His wolfskin coat and pants were grimy, and his boots were worn.

Hâzadriëlfaie? Alec took all that in at a glance, and next that he was propped against a stone wall, with his feet bound as well; a short length of rope secured them to his hands so he couldn't get up. From what little he could see past the man, they were in the remains of a round stone hut. It was still snowing a little, and it was cold. He could see his breath and the other man's freezing on the air and feel it seeping up through his clothing.

His tongue and throat felt a little numb as he rasped out, "Where are my friends?"

The man moved aside enough for him to see Seregil and Micum trussed up the same way against the far wall. Neither was awake.

"Are they—"

"They are alive. For the moment."

He looked around again as his head cleared. "Where is Sebrahn?"

The man cocked his head slightly, making him look more wolf-like. "Sebrahn?"

"The—" He searched his muddled brain for the word the man had used. "My tayan'gil."

It was impossible to read the man's eyes through the slotted openings, but he sounded surprisingly nonthreatening when he replied, "You named him well. Sebrahn is safe. How did you change his appearance like that?"

"I want to see him."

Alec had judged him too soon. The man slapped him again and Alec tasted blood on his lower lip. "You are in no position to make demands, ya'shel. What magic was used?"

"Orëska."

"Never heard of it. What name do you have?"

Alec glared at him.

The man's thin lips curled in a way that made Alec distinctly uncomfortable as he drew a very large knife from his boot. Instead of threatening Alec, however, he went to Seregil and pressed the edge of it against the unconscious man's cheek. "I will only ask you once more."

"My name is Alec."

"Alec. A Tír name." The way the man said it sounded like an insult.

Alec was in no position to object; instead he asked, "Your sen'gai—I've never seen that pattern. Are you really a Hâzadriëlfaie?"

"Yes."

"From Ravensfell?"

"Where else would we be from?"

"And you actually came looking for me?" Alec almost felt like laughing. "How in Bilairy's name did you *find* us?"

The man just smiled that unpleasant smile.

"Now that you've found me—us—what are you going to do?"

"I have questions for you, but first I want you to see something." He stepped out through the ruined doorway and returned with several people. Alec ignored all of them except for one thin man in a red bird mask, and he only noticed him because the man was holding Sebrahn in his arms. The rhekaro clung to him like a little porie, head on his shoulder, looking perfectly at ease.

The man in the wolf mask said something to the other man, who took off his mask. He was young and unremarkable as 'faie went, except that his back seemed slightly hunched and his face showed no more expression than Sebrahn's. The man in the wolf mask took Sebrahn from him and said something else softly as he waved a hand in front of the other's face.

Alec stared up in amazement as the young man's appearance changed completely. He had the same white skin and silver hair and eyes as Sebrahn. As Alec watched, he put Sebrahn down, pulled off his tunic, and unfolded—wings! Pale, leathery ones like a dragon's; not large enough to actually fly with, maybe, but wings all the same. They extended an arm span to either side, opaque as new vellum. He stretched them as if it felt good to have them free of confinement. It probably did, too. "He's a rhekaro!"

The man in the wolf mask was clearly amused now. "My magic is better than this Orëska's for hiding them."

The tall rhekaro didn't resemble Sebrahn in his features, yet he had the same ethereal look.

Wolf face made no move to stop Sebrahn as he wiggled free and went to Alec. Kneeling beside him, brown and silver hair spread around him like a striped cloak, Sebrahn touched a cold finger to Alec's lip, then licked the blood from it. A woman in a lynx mask placed a wooden cup of water and a small knife on the floor beside Sebrahn. He made a healing flower and pressed it to Alec's lip. Alec's nostrils filled with the familiar sweet smell. He ran his tongue over the healed place and waited for the others' reactions.

The man in the wolf mask knelt beside Sebrahn and gently took his hand to let another drop fall into the cup. "I've never seen one this color," he said, inspecting the new flower. "But the effect is the same. I looked at your fingers.

You feed him too much. That's why his hair is so long. They don't need to eat except when they've used their magic, or are badly injured."

Alec thought of how depleted Sebrahn had been in Plenimar, and how it had taken days of careful feeding to bring him back to what passed for health. Clearly this man, this companion of a man-sized rhekaro, knew more than Alec did about them. "What do you want with Sebrahn? You have one of your own."

"I'm more interested in what you want with it, ya'shel. How did you learn to create it?"

"I didn't. It was made from me without my consent."

"If that's true, then why are you taking it to Plenimar?"

"We're not."

"I know that you are. Are you in league with the dark witches of that land?"

"That particular dark witch is dead," said Seregil, and Alec wondered how long he'd been awake listening.

The man turned to him. "How do you know this?"

"Because I killed him."

"Really? What proof do you have of that?"

Seregil struggled to sit up against the wall, hampered by his bound hands and feet. He was pale and had a familiar sickly look to him; whatever magic had been used on them wasn't agreeing with him at all. Even so, he still managed to look a little cocky as he said, "We have the tayan'gil. You can see who he was made from just by looking at him, can't you? He was made in Plenimar and we escaped with him."

"Then why would you go back?"

"So we can keep any more tayan'gils from being made."

"That's a good tale."

"I swear by Aura, it's the truth. But I am rather curious as to why *you* have one."

"That's no concern of yours, Aurënfaie." With that, the man and the one in the fox mask went outside, leaving Sebrahn with them, and the woman in the lynx mask to guard them. Alec caught a glimpse of other masked figures moving around outside Sebrahn nestled in beside him and rested his head on Alec's shoulder. Their guard had grey in her hair, too.

"I'm glad you're alive!" Alec whispered to Seregil.

Seregil laughed softly. "So am I, talí."

"And Micum?"

"He's breathing."

"What happened?"

"Damned if I know," said Seregil, bracing his elbow against Micum's hip to sit up a little more. "Can't say I like the flavor of their magic."

Micum grunted and sat up. "So far I don't put much stock in Hâzadriëlfaie hospitality, either," he said in Skalan, glancing over at their guard. "They could do with some lessons from their southern cousins."

"So you heard?"

"About the dark witches? Yes. He must mean alchemists. And where do you suppose he got his rhekaro? Do 'faie have alchemists?"

"Not that I know of."

"Maybe that's why they want Sebrahn, if they can't make them for themselves."

"That's enough," the woman growled in that thick 'faie. "Speak in our language or don't speak at all."

They sat in silence for a while, listening to their captors moving around outside. A large fire was burning, and the smells of cooking and tea drifted in with the smoke. Someone was speaking loudly and angrily now, something about revenge.

At last the woman went out, taking the torch with her, and a much smaller man with a wild mop of curly black hair came in to stare at them. Enough light came in through the doorway to see that he wore a jacket stitched with animal teeth and held an ornate staff over one shoulder. Alec had never seen anyone like him.

Half obscured by shadows now, Seregil spoke to him in a language Alec had never heard him use before.

The man shook his head and said in passable 'faie, "I do not understand you. That is not my language."

"You're not Dravnian?" Seregil sounded surprised.

The little man hunkered down just out of arm's reach. "I do not know 'Dravnian.' Who are they?"

"They're a people from my land who look very much like you."

"Do they have oo'lu?" The man held out his staff, and Alec saw that it was actually hollow.

"No," Seregil replied.

The man laughed. "Then I am certainly not a Dravnian!"

"Who are your people, if you don't mind me asking?"

"I am Turmay, witch man of the Retha'noi of the far valley."

"Retha'noi? You live in the mountains?"

"Where else would a Retha'noi live?" Turmay replied with a shrug.

"Here in Skala, in these mountains?"

Turmay shook his head and pointed out the door. "No, many, many days that way, to the north." With that he turned his attention to Alec.

Alec held his breath at the rank smell of him as the little man grasped him by the chin and turned Alec's face this way and that, looking intently at him. He made a thoughtful noise deep in his throat, then moved away and set one end of the hollow, painted staff to his lips. Alec saw the beeswax mouthpiece and realized that it must be some sort of musical instrument even before he began to play—if you could call it that.

The witch settled his mouth inside the wax ring, puffed out his cheeks, and proceeded to make a series of noises that were nothing like music, but exactly like what they'd heard in the pass. It throbbed and buzzed and squealed. The sound of it made Alec lightheaded, and his eyes fluttered shut. Images began to dance behind his closed lids: hanging face-down in that cage in the cellar of Yhakobin's workshop with his blood dripping into the dirt below; Ilar's face; the flight from the slave takers; the moment he faced down the archers who'd killed him . . .

The witch abruptly stopped playing and looked at him for a long time. Finally he nodded as if satisfied about something and went outside.

"That's what we heard that night, up in the pass, wasn't it?" Micum whispered in Skalan.

"I think you're right. How are you, Alec?" asked Seregil, looking him over with concern. Even being on the edge of this latest magic had made him a little queasy.

"Fine." Alec paused, blinking. "I think he read my mind, though."

"We'll do well not to underestimate this witch. He's probably the one who knocked us off our horses, and put us to sleep, too."

"I remember hearing a strange noise," said Micum.

"Yes. They must have gotten close to us, for him to do that." Seregil gave them a wry grin. "If they weren't probably going to try and kill us, I'd have to admire them. However . . ."

He held up his right hand, showing them it was free. He'd worked it loose before the man in the wolf mask had come in, then kept it in his lap, feigning sleep. He hadn't even had to dislocate his thumb this time, a fact he was very thankful for. He'd done it often enough over the years that the joint ached in cold weather, as it did now. Instead he'd simply folded his hand in on itself enough to work it out of the bonds.

"Now we start playing by our rules."

Rieser stood by the fire with Naba, waiting patiently for Turmay as they sipped their tea. A whole pan of it sat hot by the fire, sending up a sweet aroma. They'd run out weeks ago, but their captives had several pouches of it in their packs. It was good, too, strong on the tongue. A bit of milk would have been nice, but he wasn't complaining. One of the captives carried tobacco and a pipe, which Allia and Taegil were presently attempting to smoke. The stuff smelled vile, and they already looked a bit green.

"Stop that!" he ordered. "It's a filthy Tír vice. Have some tea."

Allia tossed the pipe away down the hill, and the pouch after it, then went to join the others, who were examining their captives' weapons and the rest of the contents of their packs. Judging by their clothing and boots, these were men of substance, even the Tír. And the man's sword had seen much use, Rieser acknowledged grudgingly. The other two swords were new, finely made by some expert smith but with little sign of use. *The Tírfaie is probably their protector,* he thought with a sneer.

Rane was still pacing angrily, saying nothing to anyone since his outburst. He would have to wait to avenge his brother until Rieser was satisfied he'd gotten all the information from these strangers that he could.

Naba had found them a good site for the night; a few of the stone huts of this deserted village still offered some shelter. Naba's people had once lived close to the trail; it had been theirs. Then the Skalan Tír came, and at some point the Retha'noi people had moved farther up into the mountains to avoid them.

Turmay came out of the ruined hut at last.

"What is it? Did you learn something from them?"

"The boy," Turmay said slowly. "I sensed something strange about him, and now I know. He died, and now he is alive again." He turned and said something to Naba, who took up his own oo'lu and went in to the captives.

"How is that possible?" asked Rieser as Naba began to play.

"It should not be. The Mother gives life and the Mother takes it away," Turmay said, rubbing a hand over his oo'lu. "It must be the tayan'gil's doing."

Naba emerged a moment later, looking perplexed as he spoke with Turmay.

"My brother says the same," Turmay told Rieser. "This is a great evil!"

"Are you saying their tayan'gil somehow restored him to life?" asked Nowen in disbelief.

"I don't know how, but that is what we saw in this Alec."

"The small tayan'gil can take life. Why not the reverse?" said Rieser.

"Is the boy an unnatural creature now?" asked Sorengil, making a sign against evil.

The witch nodded as he dipped up a cup of tea. "He is alive when he should be dead."

"So this little tayan'gil kills and gives life," Rieser murmured, astonished. "Thank you. I'll deal with them."

When he reached the darkened hut, however, he found it empty except for three hanks of rope lying where his captives had been.

"They've gotten loose!" he snarled, striding back out to the others. "Find them. Now!"

Whoever had tied Seregil up had been either considerate or careless enough not to tie his hands too tightly. He'd almost gotten caught undoing his other hand when the second witch came in and played his horn at them, but fortunately the man had been focused on Alec, rather than the two of them sitting across the hut in the shadows. As soon as the witch was gone, Seregil had gone back to work on the ropes. Once he had both hands loose, it was a simple matter to get himself and the others untied. Alec picked up Sebrahn as Seregil carefully peered over a low place in the broken wall at the back of the hut.

Just as he'd expected, there was a masked guard posted there. The man's sword was in its scabbard and he was chaffing his arms against the cold. Seregil bent down and felt along the ground inside the wall until he found a couple of palm-sized stones. He was a better shot with a rock than with a bow; Alec often joked about making him throw arrows rather than shoot them. Even in the dark, he hit the guard in the head on the first try. The man dropped without a cry.

Seregil led the way over the broken wall and caught Sebrahn as Alec passed him over. Micum came next, then Alec.

They could hear the Hâzadriëlfaie on the other side of the hut, talking and moving about. Keeping just inside the edge of the forest that ringed the ruined village, they hurried down to the picketed horses and found only one man on guard. Their horses were tethered among the others. That was good. Seregil had owned Cynril for years, and Alec would be heartbroken to lose Patch or Windrunner, who'd been a gift from Micum's family.

Stripped of his sword and knife, Seregil made do with another rock. Sneaking up behind the guard, he gave him a good knock on the head. The man went down with a pained grunt. Praying none of the horses would shy, Seregil and the others untied the whole string and led them away into the trees, moving downhill, hoping the trail was that way. They had no weapons, no food or water, and no way of making a fire, but at least they were free.

They struck the trail at last and untied the horses, leaving the Hâzadriëlfaie's to wander off on their own. Seregil held Sebrahn while Alec mounted Patch and handed him up to him, then jumped lightly up on Cynril's back and set off after Micum with Star trailing after him on a lead rein. He could hear shouting from the camp now.

"Go!" he hissed to the others, and they kicked their mounts into a gallop.

The ya'shel and his companions had been clever enough to steal all the horses. It took some time to whistle in enough of them to give chase.

The moon was on the rise by the time they did. The snow was sparse on the ground and the mud was frozen, but Rieser managed to determine which way they'd gone after a little casting around. He cursed himself for a fool for leaving the small tayan'gil with them. There was more to these strangers than he'd given them credit for. Either the crippled Tír was craftier than he looked, or the other ones weren't quite as helpless as their shiny new swords suggested.

Seregil and the others rode hard through the remains of the night, expecting at any moment to get an arrow in the back. They left the trail when they could to confuse the chase, wending up wooded hillsides and riding down ice-rimmed streams, spelling the horses as long as they dared, which wasn't long. The way grew steadily steeper, forcing them back to the open trail. They stopped to change horses when the moon set.

"Do you hear that?" asked Alec, looking back over his shoulder.

Then they all heard it, the distant sound of the horn the witch had called an oo'lu. But this time it was more than just one, and seemed to be coming from different directions.

The sound of them sent a nasty shiver up Seregil's spine. "Come on, let's go."

He took Sebrahn to give Alec's arm a rest and they set off again. As they rode, Seregil hoped it was just a trick of the wind that made it seem like the oo'lu sound was coming from in front of them now.

Just before dawn, they entered a narrow divide—only to find their way blocked by several huge trees across the trail.

"They didn't just fall," said Micum, reining his horse in close to the nearest. "They've been cut down with an axe." He reached down to touch one of them. "The sap is still running."

Behind them they could hear the sound of hooves on stone, and the jingle of harness as their pursuers came on at a gallop.

"If they're behind us, then who the hell did this?" Alec wondered.

"Most likely whoever was playing those horns," Seregil muttered, looking around frantically.

There was no question of riding around the obstruction; steep stone faces penned them in on both sides.

When Seregil dismounted to look for a way over, an arrow whistled close to his ear and embedded itself in one of the massive trunks. It was short and crudely fletched; not 'faie work, that was certain. Taking cover behind Star, he stared up into the shadows above them and thought he could see someone moving about at the top of the rock face. The sound of the horns was getting louder, too.

"Here they come," Micum said, looking grim.

Unarmed and trapped, there was nothing they could do but wait under the brightening sky.

The man in the wolf mask was in the lead. As soon as he saw Seregil and the others, he signaled a halt and dismounted, holding his hands wide to show that he wasn't armed. Behind him, however, Seregil saw several archers with arrows ready.

"You're not going any farther, no matter what you do," the man shouted to them.

"You know what will happen if you attack us," Seregil retorted, jerking a thumb at Sebrahn, who was now peering out from behind Alec. Or that's where he thought he was. Instead, Sebrahn had darted out in front of him and was hurrying back toward their pursuers.

"Sebrahn, no! Come here," Alec shouted. Micum caught him by the arm as he started after him. The strange rhekaro came out to meet Sebrahn and hoisted him up in his arms.

"No!" Alec cried. He pulled loose from Micum, only to be grabbed and held by Seregil.

"You see?" the man in the wolf mask called to them. "The call of his own kind is too strong. So long as we don't directly attack you, we are as safe with him as you are."

"That leaves us at a bit of a stalemate," Seregil shouted back. The sun was coming up, and now he could clearly make out a number of people on the rocks above them. At least one had a long horn. Turmay and the other witch were with the masked riders, both with oo'lus in hand.

"Bilairy's Balls," he muttered, then, to the man in the mask, "What now? Are you going to stay there until we starve?"

"That was not my plan. Give us the ya'shel and you and the other ones can go."

Seregil tightened his grip on Alec's arm. "You know we're not going to do that."

"And we can't let you go, Aurënfaie. Not with him."

Seregil folded his arms and gave the man a crooked grin. "Then I guess we all stand here and starve."

The masked man turned to the archers and said something. They lowered their bows. "That won't suit any of us. Will you parley?"

Seregil looked at the others. "Anyone have a better idea?"

"We've got no weapons and no food, and someone up there is taking aim at us where we stand," said Micum.

"I just want Sebrahn back!" whispered Alec, his dark eyes burning with anger and betrayal. "Why did he go to them like that?"

Seregil squeezed his arm apologetically. "I'm sorry, Alec. I think he's been trying to all along. Stay here."

"No! He's my—"

"I said stay!" Seregil ordered, then, more softly, "I don't want you within arm's reach of any of them. If they get you, then Micum and I are as good as dead."

Alec quickly stepped back.

"Thank you. Stay close to Micum." With that, Seregil walked halfway up the trail toward the others and stood waiting.

After a moment the man in the wolf mask came to meet him. Drawing his sword, he leveled it at Seregil's heart.

"If we're going to talk, then we should probably exchange names," said Seregil. "Mine is Seregil í Korit Solun Meringil."

"I am Rieser í Stellen Andus Orgil. You wear no sen'gai."

"And I don't recognize yours. Blue and white?"

"We are the North Star people. Do you have a clan?"

"Bôkthersa."

"My grandmother was a Bôkthersan."

Seregil grinned. "That makes us kin. Can't kill me now, can you?"

"Don't presume too much."

"I won't, I assure you. So, what do we do now?"

"Do you know why we've tracked you down, Bôkthersa?"

Seregil pointed to the two rhekaro, watching placidly from a small distance. "I assume it has something to do with them."

"And with your talímenios. If you have a tayan'gil, then you must understand already."

"That it takes Hâzadriëlfaie blood to make them? Yes, and I've also heard it said that your people hunt down half-breeds and kill them. I'm afraid I just can't allow that. Look, could you take off that mask now? I feel ridiculous talking to a wolf."

Rieser gave him a humorless smirk and lifted the mask from his face. It was a grim visage, to be sure, but now that Seregil could look him properly in the eye, Rieser struck him as a man who might be reasoned with. "So, what shall we do?"

"You say you are going to stop more tayan'gils from being made. How do you intend to do that?"

Seregil saw no point in lying. "The dark witch who made Sebrahn used a book, some sort of alchemy magic text."

"You mean to destroy this book?"

"Certainly." It was one option, though probably not the one Thero would prefer.

"How will you get it?"

"The usual way you get something someone else doesn't want you to have."

"Steal it?"

"Yes."

"You are thieves?"

Seregil grinned. "Something like that, and we're very good at it."

"As you are at escaping. Two of my riders are nursing sore heads."

"I could just as easily have killed them," Seregil replied, and he could tell the man believed him.

"Why didn't you?"

"You may be strangers, and damn troublesome ones, too, but you're still 'faie. Is that why my friends and I are still alive?"

"No."

"Let me ask you something, then, before you try to kill me again. Why aren't you all dead? Our rhekaro—tayan'gil, that is—sang. People usually die when he does that."

"Sang? Is that what you call it? One of my young riders did die, so you have that blood on your hands. It made me and the others very sick, but we share the same blood as the tayan'gil, so it does not affect us the way it would the Tír or other 'faie."

"You got off easy, then." He masked his concern as he looked back at Sebrahn in the other rhekaro's arms. He looked perfectly content, the little traitor!

"They're like that," said Rieser. "Yours is different than the others, but alike enough to feel the bond."

Seregil raised an eyebrow in surprise. "Others? How many others?"

"That's no concern of yours, Bôkthersa."

"So you make them, too? How are you any better than the 'dark witches'?"

"We don't make them! We gather in those that are made and keep them safe. This little one can never be safe in your world. You must know that by now."

Seregil nodded slightly, glad Alec wasn't hearing all this. "They can kill and heal."

"Tayan'gil do not kill, or sing, for that matter. They have no voice at all. Except for this one of yours. I think it must be because of the tainted blood it was made with."

Seregil let the insult pass, thinking back to what Tyrus and his dragon had told them; somehow, Alec's blood had made a stronger rhekaro, the only one of its kind—unless another alchemist got hold of Alec and the book. "But it also heals people, and very well, too. I imagine that makes some people rather greedy to own one. We've been trying to protect him, too. Alec—the ya'shel—considers him his child. He had a prophecy about a 'child of no woman' and Sebrahn appears to be just that."

"It is no child," warned Rieser. "The witch says that this one of yours can raise the dead. Is this true?"

"Why would he think that?" Seregil didn't like where this was heading.

"He sees what he sees, more deeply than you or I. He told me that your ya'shel has two lives."

"Really?" Seregil returned dryly, sidestepping the question of Alec's death. "So, here we are. You can't attack us, and we can't get away. What shall we do?"

Rieser considered this for a moment, then lowered his sword slightly. "I will make you a bargain."

"I'm listening."

"I will let you all live if you will give me the book, the tayan'gil, and the ya'shel."

"We don't have the book, Alec will have something to say about you taking Sebrahn away, and you can't have Alec."

"As long as the ya'shel walks in this world, he is a danger."

"As I said, the dark witch—who is actually called an alchemist, by the way—who made Sebrahn is dead. He won't be making any more tayan'gil out of anyone, and if I can get those books, neither will anyone else. You're welcome to them. Take them off to your valley and guard them all you like. But Alec stays with me. That's not on the table. And if you kill him, then you'd better make certain I'm dead, too. Otherwise I'll hunt you to the ends of the earth and leave your meat for the crows. Then again, Sebrahn will probably do the job for me. You may have survived wounding Alec, but if you kill him, the results will be dire."

Rieser considered this for a moment, then shrugged. "It's madness to take the ya'shel into Plenimar, and unthinkable to take the tayan'gil. Your 'alchemist' may be dead, but there could be others who know what Sebrahn is, and seek to own him."

"Well, we can't really leave him just anywhere. He won't be parted from—" Seregil paused, struck by a sudden realization. Sebrahn hadn't been with them when they'd awakened in that ruined hut. And he'd tried to get free and find the other rhekaro—or tayan'gil—every time they got close to the masked bastards. Which meant—

"As you see, you can leave Sebrahn with Hâzadriën," Rieser said with a knowing look.

"Really?" A guilty hope sprang up in Seregil's heart, one he quickly quashed. "Even if that's so, why would we leave Sebrahn here? What's to stop you from taking him away the minute we're out of sight?"

"Because I will go with you to Plenimar. My people will not go home without me."

Seregil stared at him in surprise. "And how is that any less insane than taking a half-breed? You're the pure article."

"I can take care of myself, Bôkthersa. I will leave you and your talímenios alive if—"

"And Micum."

"And the Tírfaie, if you will give me the books once you have them."

"Just like that?"

"Yes. If what you say is true, then without the book, they

cannot be made. That is the mission of the Ebrados, to keep that from happening."

"Ebrados?" He'd never heard that word before, but the parts were as archaic as *tayan*. "'White road riders'?"

"Yes."

"What does that mean?"

"It means a number of things, none of which are any concern of yours. Now, do you accept my bargain or not?"

"I'll have to speak to the others. And assuming that we do get the book and make it back, what about Sebrahn?"

Rieser regarded him impassively.

"Right." Seregil stole a look back at Alec, who stood with Micum, watching them intently. "Alec will never agree."

"We will see, when the time comes. But I stand by my pledge for your safety if you keep your part of the bargain. You have my word."

"And what is that worth, when you give it to a stranger?"

The older man's mouth twitched in what was in no way a smile. "You don't want 'faie blood on your hands. Neither do I."

"I need to speak with my friends."

"Be sure to make it clear that your only other option is to stay where you are and die of cold and thirst. We can outwait you and we will not weep for any of you."

"I'll keep that in mind." Without thinking, he made Rieser a slight bow, and was amply repaid by the surprise on the other man's face as he returned it.

He turned over all the things Rieser had said as he walked the short distance back to the others, all the while thinking of how peaceful Sebrahn looked in the arms of the rhekaro called Hâzadriën—

Hâzadriën? Seregil looked back over his shoulder at the tall rhekaro. Rieser spoke of it as "he," but was it just his imagination that the face could just as easily be that of a woman? No, it wasn't possible.

"Why do they still have Sebrahn?" Alec asked.

"The only reason we're still alive is that we still have you, and that's not a very strong guarantee, seeing as how they came all the way down here to finish the job they started the day your mother died." Alec's stricken look made Seregil hate himself, but there was no time for coddling now. "They have us in a narrow place, literally. Look around. Even if we could get past them, or over these trees without them catching us, how far are we going to get with no horses, no weapons, no food—"

"What else are we supposed to do?"

"He's offered us a trade. He goes with us to steal Yhakobin's book, and we leave Sebrahn here as a ransom while we're gone."

Alec's eyes narrowed dangerously. "You're not serious?"

"It will make our task considerably easier, Alec. Look at him." There was more silver showing in Sebrahn's hair this morning. "Do you really want to risk having him fall into the hands of another alchemist?"

"No—" Alec gazed up the trail at Sebrahn, frowning at dark memories. "But even if we wanted to, how could we leave him? He'll have another of his fits."

"They flock to their own kind. He's happy with Hâzadriën. Didn't you notice that he wasn't there after we were captured?"

"But he'll starve!"

"If Rieser is telling us the truth, he doesn't need to eat that often."

Alec's blue eyes were accusing now. "You *want* to leave him, don't you? You want to be rid of him!"

Seregil had made a vow long ago never to lie to Alec, and he'd never broken it. For that reason, he said nothing, knowing his silence would be damning enough. Alec turned away, but Seregil could read the set of his shoulders as well as if he could see his face.

All I care about is you, talí! And Micum. If Sebrahn is the price of your lives . . .

"And this man will go with us, just like that?" asked Micum, looking skeptical. "What's to keep us from slitting his throat a mile down the road and circling back for Sebrahn?"

Seregil shrugged. "Atui, Micum. But if he breaks it first, then that's exactly what we'll do."

"What is your answer, Bôkthersa?" Rieser called.

"A moment, please!"

Seregil went to Alec. Standing shoulder-to-shoulder, he looked sidelong at the younger man and whispered, "I don't see another way right now, but it's up to you."

"You want this?"

"I want to get us out of here alive. I want to get in and out of Plenimar without attracting attention or having you and Sebrahn fall into the hands of another alchemist, or worse. Leaving Sebrahn here makes sense on both accounts."

"Do you really believe that his people won't just leave?"

"I don't know, but we have time between here and Ero to figure that out. Right now, I don't see that we have much choice except to go along with him."

Alec rubbed at his eyes and took a deep breath. "All right. But if I decide I don't trust him, then we go back to our original plan."

"Agreed. Micum?"

The other man shrugged. "I'm just a Tír along for the ride. But I don't think his precious honor holds him to keeping his word to the likes of me."

"I have his assurance on that, too. So, we're all agreed?"

The others nodded. Together they walked back up the trail to where Rieser was waiting.

"Trust me, talí," Seregil whispered to Alec, but the younger man said nothing, keeping his gaze fixed on Sebrahn.

"What have you decided?" asked Rieser.

"We need a show of good faith," said Seregil.

"Do you?" The grim-faced bastard sounded amused.

"We want our weapons and gear back."

"And our own horses," added Micum.

"Gear and horses for now. We'll see about the weapons later."

"And Sebrahn rides with me," said Alec.

"No."

"We're supposed to trust you, but you don't trust us?" Alec shouted. "Sebrahn rides with me, or you can all go to the crows!"

"You can carry him, and walk," Rieser countered.

"Fine!"

"I'll take turns with you, and so will Seregil," said Micum.

"Then it's settled." Seregil extended a hand to Rieser. The man clasped it grudgingly, and the deal was struck.

So it was that Alec and the others came to be sitting around a morning campfire with Rieser, the two rhekaros, the witch Turmay, and half a dozen Ebrados, sharing a tense, silent breakfast while Naba and the rest were at work on the trail below, dragging the fallen trees aside. Alec's dried venison and bread were like leather and ashes in his mouth as he thought of leaving Sebrahn with strangers, even if the rhekaro didn't care. That hurt a bit, too. More than a bit.

It took considerable effort to turn his initial anger at Seregil onto Rieser instead, though Alec knew in his heart that Seregil had done the best he could. As he grew calmer, he regretted that he hadn't answered Seregil's plea for trust as they'd walked back to surrender. The look in Seregil's eyes then had made Alec's heart turn over in his chest, but there was nothing he could do about that right now except to keep his guard up and his eyes open.

From where he sat, it was a short sprint to where his bow and sword were, strapped to the back of a white packhorse. Windrunner and Cynril were tethered nearby; Patch, Star, and Micum's horses were gone, put to work hauling trees.

"So how did you get ahead of us on the trail?" Seregil asked Rieser, seemingly at ease now and playing as if he didn't already know that answer.

Rieser spared him a brief glance, then turned back to minding the fire.

"My oo'lu has a long voice," the witch told him, grinning.

"You signaled someone?" asked Seregil, showing the witch more respect than he did his master. "Who?"

"I have—"

"That's enough," growled Rieser.

"As you like, friend. As you like," the little man chuckled, but Alec was almost certain he saw a flash of something less friendly in the witch's black eyes. Small and dirty as he was, Alec could feel a power in him, and felt a gut level mix of respect and dread when he saw the way the dark tracery on the witch's face and hands seemed to move on its own with his moods. Micum was watching him closely, too, and gave Alec the slightest hint of a nod as their eyes met.

Seregil was not oblivious, he knew, but was playing his own game—one he was very good at.

Pointing over at Sebrahn, who was still with Hâzadriën, Alec asked, "So, why are they drawn to each other like that?"

Rieser looked annoyed. "It's the blood."

"You mentioned others last night. Do they all look like yours?"

"More than yours does."

"Do they all favor the one they are made from?" asked Seregil. "Sebrahn certainly looks like Alec, and nothing at all like Hâzadriën."

"They do," a young man replied. He had the same dark hair and long face as Rieser, but appeared to be half his age and twice as friendly. "Or at least that's what I've been told. Except for the coloring, they all are a little different in the face."

"Is that why this one has a woman's face but a man's name?"

"They have no sex," Rieser snapped. "Shut up and eat. We ride as soon as the way is clear." He turned to one of the older men. "Sorengil, you're in charge. If any of the captives give you trouble, bind and gag them. Turmay, come with me." Tossing his last crust into the fire, Rieser stalked away down the hill to oversee the work.

With weapons, Alec and the others probably could have taken the half dozen men and the woman left, but Alec had no idea what the witch would do and Seregil seemed content to play the toss as thrown for now.

Sorengil looked to be the same age and temperament as Rieser, while the one who'd answered Seregil appeared to be friendlier.

"What's your name?" Alec asked him, sensing a weak point on the enemy's side.

"Kalien í Rothis. And you?"

"Alec í—"

"Bastards don't name their fathers," one of the young ones sneered, tossing the bit of stick he'd been whittling into the fire just close enough to stir up sparks in Alec's direction. This one was maybe even younger than Alec in pure 'faie years.

"That's enough, Rane," warned Sorengil.

"I'll speak to him if I want! Who has more right than I do?" Rane snapped back.

"Let him speak," the youngish woman with dark eyes said, sparing Alec a none-too-friendly look.

Alec looked around and found the others watching him like a pack of wolves, looking for his weaknesses. "What do you mean by that?" he asked, meeting the younger man's glare with one of his own.

"I mean, you whore's get, that you've cost me a father and a brother already, and I'll be more than happy to stick the knife in you when the time comes!"

"Rane, I said stop it," Sorengil ordered.

"I don't mind him," Alec shot back. "If my tayan'gil's song killed your kin, then you've got no one but yourself to blame. We didn't skulk after you through a snowstorm, now, did we?"

The boy launched himself across the fire at Alec, drawing a belt knife before any of the others could react.

Rane was fast, but Alec was faster. He jerked out of the way and caught him by the wrist, using the boy's own momentum to flip him on his back and wrench the weapon away. Grabbing up the fallen blade, Alec straddled his chest and had the blade to Rane's throat before the other Hâzad pulled him off. The seemingly friendly one nearly broke Alec's fingers taking the knife away. Only then did Alec see that Seregil and Micum were on their feet now, too, and that Seregil was holding a struggling Sebrahn around the waist, a hand clamped over the rhekaro's mouth as he whispered frantically into Sebrahn's ear.

Kalien got an arm around Rane's neck and restrained him. "Sit down, ya'shel, and your friends, too, or this will end badly for all of us."

"I had a father," Rane wheezed, struggling to get loose. "His name was Syall í Konthus, and he died hunting the filthy cur of a Tírfaie that rutted you into your mother's belly! And your cursed tayan'gil killed my brother."

"My father was a good man!" Alec yelled, lunging against the arms that held him back. "*Your* people killed my mother!"

"Let them fight," some of the others urged, forming a loose circle around them. "No knives, just fists!"

Alec glanced back at Sebrahn, who was clawing at Seregil's hands now, and then at Seregil, who was regarding him steadily.

If I let Sebrahn go, you know what will happen, that look said, clear as a hand sign. *Is that what you want me to do?*

As tempting as it was, Alec couldn't do it. Not against an angry boy who'd lost his father, even if it wasn't Alec's fault.

He dropped his arms to his sides. "I've eaten your food. I won't dishonor myself and my talímenios," he shot back. But he couldn't resist adding, "Or my parents' memory."

"What about you, Rane?" Sorengil demanded. "Does the ya'shel have more atui than you?"

The boy pulled away. "Where's Rieser's atui? The honor of the Ebrados? Why are these bastards still alive?" he snarled, and strode off into the trees.

A young woman spat in Alec's direction. "You honor your parents little, backing down from a blood feud."

"I'll have a blood feud with your kin, Allia, if you don't watch your tongue," snapped Sorengil.

Alec pulled away from the men holding him and smoothed down his coat. "My father was a good man, not a kin killer."

"If your mother had let us have you and your father, she might be alive now, though her shame would have followed her to the grave," Sorengil told him.

"Alec, maybe you should calm Sebrahn," Seregil suggested with a look that said *let it go for now.*

No one tried to hold Alec back as he lifted Sebrahn in his arms. "It's all right, Sebrahn. Don't hurt anyone, understand?"

"Huuurt," the rhekaro whispered, eyes still dangerously dark.

Kalien and the others stared at them. Even the tall rhekaro seemed to take notice.

"It talks?" one of the riders gasped.

"He's not like yours," Alec growled, "and you'll do well to remember that. The next time you lay a hand on me or any of my friends, I won't hold him back."

The threat didn't win him any sign of respect, but no one taunted him after that.

It took four horses to drag away the huge firs that the Retha'noi had felled for them. Rieser could see several more of the small hill folk watching from their heights. Not knowing how many more there might be made him uneasy.

When the sections of the great trees were finally moved to the side of the trail, Rieser sat down on a log and wiped his forehead on his sleeve. He'd taken off his wolfskin coat, but even so he'd worked up a sweat. Nowen did the same as she sat down beside him.

"The others asked me to speak for them," she said without preamble. Nowen was always direct. "We don't like you going off with these men."

"Do you think you could convince the ya'shel to come with us and bring his tayan'gil?"

"No."

"And what do you think that tayan'gil will do, if we try to take them by force? Do you want another taste of its power?"

"Of course not."

"Then what would you have me do?"

"They will kill you, the first chance they get."

"That would mean abandoning their tayan'gil. The ya'shel will never do that. He still mistakes it for a child, one that can feel and love."

"Perhaps it can. It's so different from Hâzadriën."

"It is, which makes it all the more imperative to bring it back to the valley."

"Yes," said Turmay, who'd been eavesdropping. "You must take it back. You must! Perhaps you could let your people take it away when you and the ya'shel are gone? You could find your way back, yes? I could wait with you and guide you."

"That would leave the ya'shel behind."

"Once you're away from his tayan'gil, you can kill him."

Rieser mopped his brow again. "I've thought of that, but you said yourself that he is something new, too. He died and came back to life. I believe our khirnari would rather have him brought back than killed. Besides, there's always the chance that this Sebrahn is connected to the one he was made from, as Hâzadriën and the others were to their 'faie. If I kill Alec, then Sebrahn might know and attack you. From a distance he killed one of us. What do you think will happen if he's in your midst?"

"So you're going to trust them?" asked Nowen.

"No, but I will go with them. If they attack me, I can defend myself. But they won't."

"You believe the Bôkthersan?"

"I do."

"But why? For all you know, they are going back for the book so that they can make tayan'gils for themselves!"

"I watch Seregil as he watches the little one. He won't make any more. And he would not do that to his talímenios."

Nowen gave him a frustrated look. "I have followed you all these years, and never known you to be a fool. I pray to Aura this isn't the first time."

Rieser chuckled. "So do I. I will keep my word to them and you will stay here. When the time comes, we will find a way to bring them both back."

"I think that would mean killing the other two."

"We'll see. We owe nothing to the Tír. The other is a problem."

"I wonder what Khirnari Seneth ä Matriel would make of that, bringing a stranger into the valley?"

Rieser pondered that for a moment. "We can deal with him, once we have him there."

Unwelcome Companions

RIESER kept his word. When the road was clear, he gave them back their horses. Seregil had, with some difficulty, managed to convince Alec to let Sebrahn ride with Hâzadriën rather than try to carry him on foot for a day's march. If a chance to escape presented itself, Seregil wanted Micum and Alec both mounted and ready. Their weapons were bundled away on one of the packhorses; if they made a break for it again, they'd do it unarmed, but that might still be their best hope.

Someone had masked Hâzadriën's true appearance again. Seregil hadn't seen the witches do it, or heard them play the oo'lu horns, which meant that there must be a proper wizard among the company, as well as the witch. Even with normal coloring, though, Hâzadriën was hard not to notice, the way his face remained expressionless. He might as well have been still wearing one of those animal masks.

Their captors were not a friendly bunch. They talked and laughed among themselves, but ignored Seregil and the others, except to keep an eye on them. Micum might as well have been air for all the attention anyone paid him. The youngster named Rane looked like he'd go after Alec again without much provocation, but Alec kept to himself and rode beside Hâzadriën, more at ease with the tall rhekaro than any of its companions.

What will you do when the time comes to part from Sebrahn? Seregil wondered. His own doubts were exacerbated by guilt; if it had been up to him, he'd have been very tempted to tell Rieser to take Sebrahn and go. He was not proud of that, but knew it would probably be better for everyone concerned, including Sebrahn. If it was true that the Hâzadriëlfaie kept tayan'gil safe, then it was the best place for him. If Hâzadriën was anything to go by, then the tayan'gils were treated with respect. The others sometimes spoke to him and it was clear that they considered him their equal.

The witch named Naba had left them after breakfast, but Seregil caught the occasional glimpse of other Retha'noi on the heights. Rieser and his people were keeping a watchful eye in that direction, too.

"Think they're going to drop another tree on us?" Micum asked in a low voice.

"It would open up certain possibilities if they did, but I suspect they're just making certain we keep going out of their lands."

"You see them?" asked Turmay, coming up beside them. "Those are Retha'noi people, too."

"The ones who blocked the road?" asked Seregil, though he had no doubt of it.

"Yes."

"That's what you meant by your oo'lu having a long voice, then." The painted horn slung across Turmay's back apparently had many uses, including putting one to sleep at the most inopportune moments, as demonstrated yesterday. "You signaled ahead. Or was it magic?"

The witch just smiled.

"Why did they help you? Because you are of the same people?"

"I'm no kin of theirs. They helped me because they want you to go away."

"Are they frightened of Sebrahn?"

Turmay shrugged. "They want all of you to go away. They don't like strangers in their mountains."

"Tell me, Turmay, are you frightened of our tayan'gil?"

"It is not a tayan'gil," the witch said softly. "It is a monster."

They rested their horses by a stream at midday, then set off again as the way sloped down more steeply before them.

The snow was fast disappearing and the meltwater turned the trail into a muddy stream in places.

The forest grew denser, closing in around them and blocking out the sky. As they rode along in the pine-scented twilight, Seregil nudged Star up beside Rieser's tall white horse.

"That's a fine-looking animal you've got there, Captain."

Rieser spared him a brief glance.

"Do you really mean to go into Plenimar with us?"

"I said so."

"You do realize that you're going to have to pretend that Micum is your master?"

That got the man's attention. "What?"

Micum overheard. "You didn't think three 'faie could waltz into the Riga slave markets and tell them you're only passing through, did you?"

Rieser scowled at Seregil. "And you will allow this? To play the slave to this Tír?"

Seregil gave him the crooked grin. "You'd be surprised, some of the roles I've played. And I might point out that the risk to Micum is just as great. Those caught with wayward slaves aren't treated well, either."

"And you think you can fool these Plenimarans?"

"Certainly. When you searched our baggage, you must have seen the metal slave collars. Those are one sign." Seregil pushed back his sleeve and showed him the fake brand. "And this. More Orëska magic. Too bad our wizard isn't with us, to fix you up properly. That's going to be a problem."

Rieser snorted softly, then pushed his own sleeve back and passed his left hand over his forearm. An identical mark appeared on the underside. "I have no need of your magic. I have my own."

Ah ha! Got you. That explains who is maintaining Hâzadriën's disguise. This man might actually prove useful in a pinch. "No amount of magic is going to hide us from a necromancer or slaver's wizard. Sometimes a bit of lying works better. So with Micum as our master, we should go unnoticed."

"And then what?"

"Then I steal that book for you, we all come back, and you let us go."

Rieser just gave him a smug look and kicked his horse into a trot.

"Now I trust him even less," Micum muttered in Skalan.

"Me, too, but he knows if he double-crosses us and tries to hurt Alec, Sebrahn will sing again. Maybe Sebrahn could kill a few more of them, in close proximity."

"Then all we have to do is get Alec to pick a fight with that surly young fellow Rane and we're home free."

Seregil had been thinking the same thing, but for later, not now. It had been madness to think that they could take Sebrahn back into Plenimar without someone noticing him. Thero's disguise was fading away more rapidly now. In the morning light Sebrahn's skin was blotchy and his hair was more silver than brown. If the Hâzad wanted to look after him while they were gone, he couldn't think of better caretakers—if Sebrahn let Alec leave. He glanced at Sebrahn ahead of them, riding contentedly on Hâzadriën's saddlebow. "Maybe he won't be so quick to defend Alec anymore, now that he's found another of his own kind."

"Don't let Alec hear you say that. I think he's heartbroken already."

Seregil sighed. "Bilairy's Balls! Why does he have to love the damn thing so much?"

"Wouldn't you if it had your face?"

"No, I would not!" Seregil whispered.

"Can you love Sebrahn, who has Alec's face?"

"I wish I could. I care for Sebrahn, but keeping him is simply impossible for so many reasons. Alec knows that as well as I do. He just can't admit it to himself yet."

"He's softer hearted than you."

"Soft headed, more like it," Seregil muttered. It wasn't the best trait in a nightrunner, but Seregil had to admit it was one of the things he admired about Alec. Still, it wasn't going to make things any easier when they came back with the book and had to face the inevitable.

That night they camped beside a small waterfall. As Alec scavenged for firewood, he noticed that there were handprints carved into the trees here, as there had been at the western end of the trail.

"This must mark the end of Tamír's Road," Seregil said.

Alec's heart sank lower; this meant they were that much closer to parting from Sebrahn. He knew Seregil was right about the risk of taking him, and the thought of Sebrahn being torn apart by another alchemist made him sick.

But what about when we have the book and come back? Of course Seregil would barter Sebrahn for him; Alec even felt the pricking of guilt. He'd had to choose between the two of them once before; he'd chosen Seregil. He believed he would again, but hoped to hell he didn't have to.

They reached the edge of the forest early the following morning. Rolling foothills fell away to a plain, and Alec could just make out the thin blue line of ocean on the horizon.

"We'll reach Beggar's Bridge by tomorrow," Seregil told them.

"It's a Tírfaie town?" asked Rieser.

"That's right."

"Then my people will go back to the waterfall and make camp there."

"We'll be needing our weapons back," said Seregil.

Nowen and Rieser exchanged a look, and the captain nodded.

Their weapons were returned. Alec smoothed a hand along his bow's smooth limbs, checking for damage. It was sound, as were the arrows, thank the Light.

Alec stole a glance in Seregil's direction, looking for any sign that they were going to fight their way out of this or make a break for it. He'd stayed close to Hâzadriën and figured out half a dozen ways to get Sebrahn away from him when the time came.

Instead, Seregil turned in the saddle and offered Rieser his hand.

"Will you keep our bargain now, Bôkthersa?" asked Rieser, ignoring it.

"We will if you will," Seregil replied.

"The tayan'gil will be kept safe, and my people will be here when we return. I swear it by Aura, and so do they."

Seregil turned to Alec. "Well?"

It was tempting to refuse. He even thought of letting Seregil and Micum go without him, but he couldn't bring himself to do that, either.

"Alec?" Seregil gave him an apologetic look.

There didn't seem to be any way out. Dread settled in the pit of Alec's stomach. "But if they aren't here, if Sebrahn is gone, then I'll kill you, Rieser í Stellen, and I'll track down the others, too. I swear *that* by Aura."

Rieser smiled, almost as if he approved. "I know you would, Alec í Amasa."

"You should take off your sen'gai here," Seregil advised. "Aurënen ships often put in at Beggar's Bridge. Your pattern isn't one anyone will have seen before. And if you're caught with it in Plenimar, there's bound to be trouble."

The man unwound the long length of blue-and-white cloth and handed it to the woman named Nowen, who carefully tucked it away in her saddlebag.

Seregil gave Alec a look that said clear as words, *There's no help for it, talí. We'll take this one step at a time.*

But there was still the matter of what Sebrahn would do now.

"At least let me say good-bye." Alec dismounted and went to Hâzadriën's horse. Sebrahn came willingly into his arms. Alec hugged him close for a moment, his heart like a stone in his chest, then he set the rhekaro on his feet and knelt in front of him.

"I'm leaving, Sebrahn." His throat went tight and he had to clear it before he could go on. "Seregil and Micum and I, we're going away for a little while."

Please, throw a fit. Sing this away!

But Sebrahn just looked up at him with those wide silver eyes. "Leeeeaving."

"Yes, leaving. You're staying. Staying? With Hâzadriën."

Sebrahn looked at him for a moment, then turned and held his arms up to the tall rhekaro.

"It's time to go," Seregil said quietly. "Come on."

Alec's heart ached as he lifted Sebrahn back up into Hâzadriën's arms. "Take good care of him."

The tall rhekaro said nothing, and his expression did not change as he shifted Sebrahn in his lap.

Going back to Windrunner, Alec swung up into the saddle and looped Patch's lead rein over his pommel. Looking back over his shoulder, Alec saw Hâzadriën and the other 'faie ride off without a backward glance.

Sebrahn did nothing.

And Alec's heart broke a little more.

Rieser braced for an attack as soon as they were out of sight of the other Ebrados, but his traveling companions appeared to be ready to keep their word, at least for now. If they slipped away from him, he would hunt them down. If they murdered him, Turmay would know and there would be nothing to stop his riders from heading home with the small tayan'gil. Either way, he would have accomplished his mission.

All the same, he couldn't help noticing how Alec bit his lip and looked away as they went on.

"Sebrahn will be safe. I've given you my word."

Alec spared him a black look and rode to the head of the line.

Seregil admired Rieser as they rode away from his people. The man might not trust them, but he trusted in their honor. It was astonishing, really, and so ill-founded.

"We have a day or two of riding ahead of us," Seregil told him as they set off down through the foothills toward the coast. "We might as well pass the time pleasantly. Why don't you tell us about this 'white road'?"

"Haven't you guessed?"

"*Tayan'gil* means 'white blood.' The white road leads to them?"

"Yes, and the white road we followed when we left Aurënen. But the tayan'gils themselves are sometimes called 'white roads.' It is their blood that heals us, and the same blood that made us exiles."

"I see. And am I correct in assuming that Hâzadriën was made from your ancestor, Hâzadriël?"

"Yes."

"That was more than four generations ago. He's really that old?"

"That's correct. She is dead, but he still exists. No one knows if they ever die."

"How do you feed him, if the person he was made from is dead?" asked Alec, breaking his silence at last.

"Any Hâzadriëlfaie can feed a tayan'gil. We all share the same blood. Think what you like of us, but my people will not let Sebrahn go hungry or be harmed."

"Anyone?" Alec looked positively dismayed at that.

Seregil's heart went out to him. First the little rhekaro's disregard for their departure, and now this. *Perhaps this will help him accept the truth, and what has to happen when we get back.*

Turning to Rieser, he asked, "How did Hâzadriël and her people come to be in that valley?"

"How much do you know of her?"

"Only that she had some sort of vision, gathered up some followers, and headed north."

"That's the end of the story, but not the beginning. She was captured by the Plenimarans, and was used by a—What did you call them?"

"Alchemist."

"Yes, by an alchemist to make Hâzadriën. Somehow she escaped, and brought four other 'faie back with her, and five tayan'gils, including Hâzadriën. They were the only ones to return. What she saw in Plenimar—" Rieser paused and made some sort of sign with his right hand, probably one of reverence, or warding. "It was only then that it was revealed to her that her blood and those of the people she saw treated in the same manner was different, special."

"Dragon's blood," Alec murmured.

Rieser gave him a surprised look. "Yes, we are blessed with the Great Dragon's favor. It is our gift and our burden."

"Do they all have the power to heal?" asked Micum.

Rieser acted as if he hadn't heard him.

"Do they?" asked Seregil.

"Yes. They are a treasure to our people. Some even count them as a gift of Aura, but the white blood was a curse when we lived within the grasp of the Tír. They tortured and enslaved us to make tayan'gils, and bled us to make dark magic."

"Not my people," Micum replied.

Rieser smiled darkly. "Oh, yes. Tayan'gils have been found in all the Tír lands over the years, so it isn't only the Plenimarans who know the secret of their making. That's why we withdrew so far. There were no Tír near the valley you call Ravensfell when she led her people there. Now that there are, we have to guard ourselves all the more carefully."

"I'm from Kerry," Alec told him. "Most people up there don't even believe in you anymore. I always thought the 'faie were just some tales the bards told."

"Your father knew better," Rieser pointed out. "Did he lie to you, his only child?"

"To protect him," Seregil cut in. "To keep him from going off to look for his mother's people, or seek revenge. Alec's father knew what would happen to him if he got anywhere near you."

"How did your father meet her in the first place, Alec, if you don't mind me asking?" said Micum.

"He never told me anything about her, except that she died when I was born. Whenever I asked more questions, he'd go silent. Sometimes he looked sad." Alec paused, gazing off into the distance as if he could see his past there. "He had no people, so it was just him and me, all those years, always moving around. We never went near the pass." He turned to Rieser. "It was because he knew about the Ebrados, wasn't it? You came hunting us."

"Of course. Until the day our captain's horse came back with blood on the saddle. We always assumed that he'd found you, and that your father had killed him."

"No. I would have known." Alec paused. "He did leave me with an innkeeper sometimes, when I was little. Maybe he knew that the Ebrados were close by."

"He was a brave, good man," said Micum.

Alec swallowed hard. "I never knew. He was just—my father. He didn't even carry a sword."

"If he was half the archer you are, he wouldn't have needed one."

"A good man wouldn't have left the mother of his son to die alone," said Rieser.

"He didn't!" growled Alec. "I saw what happened, in a vision at Sarikali. He was trying to save her when she died. Your people killed her before he could, but he saved me."

"He didn't know what he was doing," Rieser replied solemnly.

"So that's what you Ebrados do? Kill innocent people?"

"The ones we kill are not innocent. Men came looking for us and we killed them to protect ourselves. Others caught some of us who unwisely ventured out of the valley, and carried them away to make more tayan'gils. The Ebrados hunted every one of them down, and brought back the Hâzad, if they still lived, and the tayan'gils. We take care of our own."

"Just how many tayan'gils do you have?" asked Seregil.

"Nineteen. They are gentle, silent creatures like Hâzadriën, and great healers." He turned to Alec again. "They are treated with the highest respect."

Alec frowned and looked away.

"But you're willing to risk Hâzadriën, to bring him along as your healer?" asked Seregil.

"It was Hâzadriël's will, when she led the Ebrados. And it's not only that. He can sense others of his kind. He helped Turmay find you, and now you see how he cares for Sebrahn. When the time comes, Sebrahn will come with him willingly."

"But he's not harmless like the others," said Alec, still frowning. "What will you do with him?"

"That is up to our khirnari, but I know he will come to no harm, as long as he causes none."

"How did alchemists find out about the white blood in the first place?" wondered Seregil. "You don't look any different than any other 'faie. How did Hâzadriël know, for that matter?"

Rieser shrugged. "Aura guided Hâzadriël to find others with the same special blood. The annals say that she was guided by visions. She did not go north until the Lightbringer revealed the way to her."

"You weren't a people then, were you?"

"No. We were scattered among all the clans. Some 'faie have magic. Some have music or the hand for art. We had the white blood of the Dragon."

"How could no one else in Aurënen ever have known?" Seregil wondered.

"They knew at Sarikali. That is where she went with the first rhekaros, and that is where she was given her first vision that sent her to find the people of the blood."

"She must have been a very strong woman," said Micum.

Rieser finally spared him a glance. "She was. We strive to be worthy of her legacy, and that of all our forebears."

A proud people, thought Seregil. That would make them all the more dangerous.

"We should have gone to Sarikali when we had the chance," said Alec. "If she could take a rhekaro there, then we could have, too!"

"Other rhekaros can't kill," Seregil reminded him.

"We could have found a way."

Seregil sighed inwardly. He didn't blame Alec for being angry right now, and probably feeling helpless into the bargain. All Seregil could do was trust that he wouldn't do anything stupid and impulsive. Alec was too smart for that.

Even so, Seregil was still all too aware of the pain his talímenios was in, and how much he hated their unwanted companion. He had no doubt that if Rieser tried anything, he wouldn't get more than a bowshot away.

They came in sight of Ero early the following afternoon. The ruins of the citadel were visible for miles, and Alec forgot his simmering worries for a moment at the sight of them.

The remains of towering walls and ruined castles stood stark against the blue sky on a high promontory. As they drew closer, he could make out the broken outline of the wall that had encircled the city from harbor front to the citadel. It hadn't been as large a place as Rhíminee, but still worthy of a royal capital.

"Someday when we have time, I'll take you up there," Seregil told him. "It was called the Palatine, and all the nobles in Ero had palaces and villas there."

"What happened to this city?" asked Rieser.

"The Plenimarans burned most of it when they raided it in Queen Tamír's day."

"How long ago?" asked Rieser.

"Five centuries. Later on the rest of it burned again. I think they just gave up on it in the end. Some even say it bears a curse, from the days when Tamír's kinsmen seized control. Plague was a problem, too, though that was more likely a problem with the swamps or drains than a curse. It must have been a beautiful place in its day, though. You can still find traces of murals inside some of the old villas and palaces, and a bit of statuary. They were a very prosperous people. The original royal crypt is up there, too, or what's left of it. Queen Tamír had the remains of her kin moved to Rhíminee when she built her new city."

Alec resisted an urge to snap at Seregil. When he fell into his storytelling ways, he could go on for a long time. Rieser didn't need to know all this. Deep down, however, he realized that what he really resented was the familiar way Seregil was speaking with the Hâzad, almost as if they were comrades by choice.

Play every role to the hilt, Alec. He knew that this was what Seregil was doing, but with rather more relish than Alec was feeling right now.

"The Skalans must be a powerful people," said Rieser, shading his eyes as he stared out at the ruins. "I've never seen cities as large as they have here."

"They are a good people, overall," Seregil told him.

Rieser snorted at that.

They reached the outskirts of the old wall and followed it past scattered farmsteads and pastures to Beggar's Bridge, which lay just south of the old city. There really was an ancient stone bridge there; a large one, with traces of the ornate carvings that had once decorated it.

"That's a pretty fancy bit of work, to be called Beggar's Bridge, don't you think, Alec?" Micum remarked.

"I suppose so."

"Seregil?"

"I don't know. Maybe it was a popular place for people to beg."

Beggar's Bridge was small but didn't seem particularly impoverished. In fact it was no different from any of the little ports Alec had seen. There were a number of small vessels moored close to shore, and several larger ones farther out. Even from here he recognized the *Lady*. She was sleeker than the high-prowed trading carracks, and was the only ship there with battle platforms.

It was getting dark as they entered the town through a simple gate.

"Don't speak unless you have no choice. Your accent is too thick," Seregil warned Rieser.

"Who would I speak to here?" the man replied, wrinkling his nose at the stench from the gutters.

The one small square had a shrine to Astellus, the patron deity of sailors, fishermen, and women in labor. The lintel was carved with the traditional wave pattern, and there were dozens of little wax votives shaped like boats and fish scattered in front of it.

The Sea Horse Tavern was a respectable one-story establishment near the waterfront. It had a low thatched roof, and its whitewashed walls were painted with the same wave design in blue.

"Remember, don't start any conversations," Seregil murmured as they dismounted in front of the stable. Leaving their horses in the care of the stable hand, they shouldered their packs and went inside.

The front room was crowded, but Seregil quickly spotted Rhal's cabin boy, Dani, standing by a window overlooking the harbor. As soon as the boy caught sight of them, he pushed through the crowd and began to bow to them. Seregil caught him by the shoulder in time, not wanting to draw attention.

"It's good to see you again, my l—"

"No names here, Dani," Seregil ordered, keeping his voice down.

"Well, welcome anyway, sir. And you, sirs!" He nodded to Alec and Micum, then gave Rieser a curious look. The Hâzad turned away with a grunt and glared around at the crowd, clearly uncomfortable being in such close quarters with so many Tírfaie.

"How's your captain?" Seregil asked the boy.

"He's fine, sir. He sends his regards. I'll row you out now, if you like."

"Is Tarmin still doing the cooking?" asked Micum.

"Aye, sir."

"Then I say we take our chances here."

Seregil chuckled at that. "Not a bad idea."

The house's jellied eel pie was not a disappointment, and a far cry from what Alec recalled of the bland fare favored by Rhal and his largely Mycenian crew. When they were done, they left the stable boy with enough silver to ensure that their horses would be well cared for until they returned. Giving the horses a few last apples and some affectionate scratching, they set out along the dark street with their packs and saddlebags slung over their shoulders.

Beggar's Bridge had no piers or jetties, just a line of dinghies upended on the beach. Dani and Alec dragged their boat down to the water's edge.

"What has the *Lady* been up to since we last saw you?"

Dani gave him a gap-toothed grin. "We took thirteen car-racks this winter, and one of them was loaded with north country gold baps. Another had Aurënfaie wine and silks and all sorts of lady's things. There were even some slaves, and we carried them all the way home to Aurënen. We lost two, though. They threw themselves overboard. Damned if I know why."

"The Lightbearer will bless you all with luck for your kindness to those who made it home," said Seregil.

Dani manned the oars and they were soon skimming along

past the fishing boats and out toward the broad mouth of what had been Ero Harbor.

The *Green Lady*'s two masts cast writhing double lines of black across the water; Alec could just make out the shape of her figurehead. The "green lady" pressed one hand to her ample bosom, the other to her rounded belly. The flowing folds of her dark hair and gown shone silver and black in the moonlight.

Lanterns glowed fore and aft, and the windows of the cabins at the stern were lit up. Dani put his fingers to his lips and let out a shrill whistle as they approached. With a crew of forty men one step up from being pirates, it was better not to surprise anyone.

The boy's whistle was answered with another and was followed by the rattle and splash of the rope ladder being let down for them.

Rhal—together with his helmsman, Skywake, and Nettles, the first mate—was there to meet them as they climbed aboard. "Welcome, my lords. And Micum Cavish, too! Well met, sir. It's been a while. How's the leg?"

"I manage," Micum laughed, clasping hands with Rhal.

The captain was dark and stocky, and going a bit bald, but still rakish enough to attract women in any port. He was northern-born, like Micum and Alec, and with his black beard he could pass for a Plenimaran. On occasion, he had. He greeted Seregil and Alec warmly, then turned to Rieser and extended his hand. "I haven't had the pleasure, sir."

Rieser ignored the hand. "I am Rieser í Stellen."

"I can't place your accent."

"No need to," Seregil told him.

"Fair enough." Rhal was used to secrets. "It's been a long time since you've called for me."

"We had a bit of trouble."

"You have a 'bit of trouble' more often than not," Rhal noted as he led them belowdecks to the small guest cabin. "What was it this time? Angry wizards? Plots against the queen? An outraged wife? Or did you get caught in the wrong house with your fingers in the jewel box?"

"Slavery, actually," Alec told him.

Rhal shook his head. "Well, that's a new one."

"You are lords and thieves?" asked Rieser.

"Depends on the company," Seregil replied.

Their cabin was more luxurious than Alec recalled. The wide bunk was fitted out with a red velvet coverlet with silver fringe, and an ornate lantern on the hook overhead cast fretwork shadows across the small polished table, the velvet tufted chairs, and the silver cups and crystal decanter in a fancy leather box on the narrow sideboard.

"What happened here?" asked Seregil. "It looks like a Street of Lights whorehouse."

"We've had good fishing," Rhal replied with a wink as he poured them cups of fine Zengati brandy.

"So Dani said. Have you given the queen her share?"

"Of course, but that doesn't mean I can't keep the best back for myself. And you, of course, as our patron. I've sent your share in coin to your man in Wheel Street."

"Thank you."

Alec knew that Seregil never asked for an accounting; he had more gold than he knew what to do with in various Rhíminee money houses, under various names. He did the same with clothing and traveling gear; he had caches all over the city in sewer tunnels and abandoned houses, always ready for a quick change or escape.

Rhal and Rieser remained standing as the others found places on the room's two chairs and the bed. "So, where are we bound this time?"

"Riga," Alec told him.

Rhal raised an eyebrow. "That's a tall order. The Overlord has half his navy anchored there, and most of the ships are full of marines."

"You can put us ashore outside the city where you'll draw less attention," said Seregil.

"It still means changing the sails. We'll have to put in at one of the Strait Isles for at least a day." He'd captured a set of striped Plenimaran sails soon after the *Lady* first sailed and often used them to slip into enemy waters. "I can have you across in a week, if the winds cooperate. In the meantime, if the shape in that bag of yours is what I think it is, perhaps you and Lord Alec can provide us with some entertainment during the crossing."

Seregil reached into the bag at his feet and took out the harp Adzriel had given him. He plucked a few notes and grimaced. "After a bit of tuning."

Alec reached into his own bag and took out one of the iron collars. "We need another of these, too."

"I've got a collection of them, taken off the poor bastards we found on some of the ships we've taken," said Rhal. "Now, for accommodations. There isn't room for all of you in here."

"I'll berth with the crew, if they have an extra hammock," said Micum.

"There's no need for that. Take the third cabin, next to mine."

"I will sleep on the deck," Rieser told him.

"You don't know ships," said Micum. "You'd be lucky not to get washed overboard if a storm comes up. You take the cabin. I'll stay with the crew."

Alec couldn't tell if Rieser was more surprised by Micum or himself as he nodded slightly and muttered, "Thank you."

Morthage had a been a crew member on the *Lady* for over a year now, and liked his captain and the work. So he felt a bit guilty as he slipped below to his billet and took out one of the bespelled message sticks his other employer supplied him with. Breaking it, he whispered, "Lord Seregil and Alec have returned to the ship—"

When he was done, a little ball of magic light sped away through the thick planking of the hull.

❧
Return to a Dead Man's House

THE SHIP'S lantern swung on its hook as Ilar clung to the heavy bench fixed to the floor beside the little table in Ulan's cabin. The *White Seal* was a large merchant ship, broad in the beam and built to cross stormy seas, but the rolling of the floor under his feet was still alarming. The rains had come their second day out from Virésse—and the swells that had kept Ilar bent over the rail for most of that day, until he grew accustomed to the rocking of the ship. But even that did not match the torture of being trapped on this vessel with so many strangers—men who seemed to look right through him to the shame and weakness he carried in his heart. Without the khirnari to protect him, he wouldn't have dared venture out of the cabin they shared. Ulan was coughing more, too.

They were already under way when word had come from Ulan's spy that Lord Seregil's privateering vessel, the *Green Lady,* had docked at Beggar's Bridge, and that Seregil was aboard, together with Alec—who'd shorn his hair and dyed it brown—a Tír named Cavish, and a 'faie with the odd name of Rieser. There was no mention of the rhekaro, or the Tír wizard who'd been with them in Gedre.

"That is troubling, yet fortune has smiled on us all the same, Ilar," Ulan had told him. "If they have gone all the way to Beggar's Bridge, then they may well be going back to Riga on the same errand as ours. Do you think Alec knows about the books?"

"He could have seen them, as I did."

"Assuming that he does, then we've still stolen a march on them. We'll have the books, and perhaps Alec, as well. And if so, we shall learn what has become of the rhekaro."

"What if they aren't going there?" asked Ilar.

"One step at a time, dear fellow," Ulan had said with a smile.

Ilar gripped the bench until his fingers ached, trying to rein in the hope and excitement that overwhelmed him again. *Please, Aura, let them come to us in Plenimar!*

"Come now, dear boy, and pay attention," Ulan chided gently, tapping the drawing spread between them on the table.

"What? Oh, yes."

At the khirnari's request, Ilar had drawn the outline of each floor of his former master's workshop, and marked out the contents of each room as well as he could remember.

"You are certain this is where the book your master showed me is kept?" Ulan asked, tapping a finger on the X Ilar had labeled for him.

"Yes, in the little painted tent."

"And if it is not there?"

Panic tightened Ilar's chest. "There are other books. Shelves of them, Khirnari. He might have hidden the books I saw among them. I'm sure I can find them!"

Ilar didn't dare ask what would happen if he failed, knowing how close they would be to the slave markets of Riga. Why would this great man keep him if Ilar proved himself worthless? He had nightmares every night: the horrors of the slave markets, the cruel masters he'd survived before Ilban Yhakobin had taken pity on him, and always the terrible night that Ilban had him whipped and said he was going back to the markets . . .

Those dreams had not gone away, but now he also dreamed of those days abandoned in the wilderness after the slave takers had caught up with them. He didn't know how long he'd spent lost in the cold rain with no shelter, no food, and no water but what he could suck from a depression in a stone or a muddy rill. He didn't know how many days he'd wandered, shaking with hunger and certain every moment that the slave takers would find him. How could they not, with their dogs?

Instead, Ulan's men had found him dying in a ditch. He still carried that coldness, that fear, deep in the core of his soul, and nothing could ever take it away. Except, perhaps, to find Seregil and beg for . . . He still could not decide what it was he wanted, but the hunger was eating away at his mind. The thought of being alone in the world again froze him with terror.

The *White Seal* made port at Riga in fair weather, but Ilar felt sick. Hiding in the cabin, he peered out the porthole as the cargo was unloaded at one of the many quays. A land breeze brought him the scent of the city—the smoke and reek of it—and he thought he could even smell the sweat and despair of the slave markets. It was something he knew all too well. Only when Ulan came looking for him was he able to leave the cabin. Ilar was dressed in Aurënfaie style, and a Virésse sen'gai covered his cropped hair, but he also wore a lace-edged slave veil tied securely to hide all of his face below his eyes.

Emerging into the sunlight, trying to ignore the stares of the crew and other passengers, he took the old man's arm as if to steady him, but in truth it was the only way he could walk down the gangplank without his own legs giving way under him. He had no brand, no collar! What if someone discovered that?

Ulan gave him an understanding smile and patted his hand. "Steady now, dear fellow, there's nothing to fear. No one will dare touch me in this city, or trouble anyone wearing the sen'gai of my clan—at least not in daylight. You are a freedman under my protection here."

His words were little comfort as they set off into the city in a hired carriage. An armed escort rode behind them, led by a hard-eyed captain named Urien. Even wearing the colors of Virésse, Ulan practiced caution, not trusting the Plenimarans, despite the trade agreement that allowed him and his ships to come into Plenimaran harbors.

"I have a small but very secure house down that way,"

Ulan told him, pointing down a street that ran along the harbor's edge. "I daresay we shall end up there shortly. I doubt the good lady will tolerate our presence for long."

At the slave market, an auction was in progress on the very platform where Ilar had once been sold, and it was being overseen by the same lean, hatchet-faced dealer who'd sold him. Everywhere he looked, he saw misery and the dealers in flesh.

Ulan took his hand again and murmured, "Never again, my friend."

Ilar had some respite from fear when they left the city, but terror began anew as they finally neared the outskirts of Yhakobin's estate. By the time they drove down the tree-lined lane and through the gates, he was trembling uncontrollably and blinking back tears. If *Ilbana* recognized him, even Ulan would not be able to save him.

"Calm yourself," Ulan said sternly.

When the carriage came to a halt, it took all his tattered will to get out. He'd never imagined being here again, walking up these white marble steps between the tall red pillars that flanked the ornate double doors of the entrance.

Servants Ilar recognized met them and escorted them into the black-and-white paved courtyard. One of them was Ahmol, who had been Ilban's assistant. Ilar nearly fainted when the man gave him a sharp look, but Ahmol showed no sign that he recognized him.

The front courtyard looked just the same—the long fountain pool surrounded with statues, the shaded portico, and, at the far end, the archway through which lay his dead master's workshop. Ilbana Meran and her two young children—little master Osri and his younger sister, Amela—met them there, and Ilar was introduced as a newly ransomed slave. To Ilar's relief, she hardly spared him a glance. Master Osri stared at him for a moment, though, and Ilar's heart turned over in his breast; the child was spoiled and spiteful, and had always treated Ilar with contempt. If *he* discovered who Ilar really was, he would surely tell.

Ilbana did not offer the khirnari her hand, and greeted him with a somewhat questioning look. As Ulan had told him, relations had not been warm between them. "Ulan í Sathil, welcome back to my home, though I fear you will find it empty without my husband to entertain you." Her tone was not as welcoming as her words.

"That's quite all right," Ulan assured her. "I am grateful for your hospitality."

"Of course. I've had rooms prepared in the east wing for you and your people."

The one with the windows overlooking the workshop yard, Ilar thought with a shudder, wondering if the whipping post was still there.

Suddenly Ilbana turned and looked straight at him. "And this one? It's not safe to let him walk around without you, even if he is a freedman. We had several slaves escape this past winter. You remember Khenir, I'm sure. He was one of them. The other two were new. I never knew their names, but I believe they are the ones who murdered my husband. My guards are very protective of the children and me. It wouldn't do for this veiled one to wander about unescorted, especially at night."

"I understand. I prefer to keep him by me in any event. He is quite invaluable as a servant, no doubt due to his training as a slave. He was only a boy when he was brought here from Virésse." The khirnari spoke lightly, though the kidnapping and enslavement of his clan members would have been a blood feud offense on Aurënen soil.

"Why does he still wear the veil, if he's free?" the boy demanded rudely.

"He is too frightened not to, in this land," Ulan replied calmly, smiling as if Osri had addressed him with proper respect.

"What is your name?" little Amela lisped, staring up at him now with wide brown eyes.

Ilar's mouth went dry and he nearly blurted it before Ulan spoke for him.

"He is called Nira, and he is a mute," he told the girl, then, to her mother, "Another reason to keep him by me. He's quite timid."

"Ah, I see. Just as well, I suppose. At least he has attractive eyes."

Much to Ilar's relief, she then appeared to dismiss him from her mind altogether. Like any slave, he might as well be empty air unless she had some use for him.

Ulan waited several days before broaching the subject of Ilban's workshop. He really did have business to attend to, including a shipment of ransomed slaves Yhakobin had assembled for him. Some were still at the barns—Ulan had kindly left Ilar under guard in the carriage when they went there—while others had been sold, and so had to be tracked down all over again.

The khirnari also dined with the family, and seemed intent on becoming their friend. He played with the children in the garden beyond the workshop, watching them play ball and helping to feed the precious fish in the fountain basin. Ulan had brought them clever Aurënfaie toys, too, and soon even Osri began to warm to him, even though the khirnari was "only a 'faie."

Ilar felt lightheaded the first time they walked through the archway to the courtyard that had been Ilban's. The workshop loomed at the back of it, by the tinkling wall fountain and the herb beds. It had been one of Ilar's tasks to gather and dry the herbs. A few green sprouts were pushing up through the compost—mints, chives, mugwort, and the nightshades and dragon tongue vines he'd worn gloves to handle. The whipping post was still there, too, with a hank of frayed rope dangling from the iron ring at the top.

Finally, over breakfast on the fourth day, Ulan said to Ilbana, "I do miss your husband. Would you mind if I visited his workshop?"

She looked up in surprise. "I wasn't aware he had ever taken you there."

"But he spoke of it often. I've always been curious, and since there are no experiments to interrupt—"

"Well, I suppose so." She dabbed sudden tears from her eyes with her napkin. "I've kept everything just as it was."

"Most admirable. I'm sure he would want it so, my dear."

She gestured to Ahmol, who was in attendance that morning. "Unlock the workshop for the khirnari and show him whatever he wants to see."

Ilar glanced nervously at his protector, but Ulan merely smiled, apparently unconcerned that they would have a witness.

When the meal was done, they followed the servant through the fountain court and down the stairs to the workshop. Ahmol took out the big iron key and opened the door, then stood back to allow Ulan to enter. Ilar followed on his heels, keeping his face down and hoping Ahmol didn't look too closely at him.

Ahmol pulled on the ropes that operated the skylights and bright morning sunshine filled the large room. The cold air was dusty and stale with the mingled scents of the dead coals on the forge, and the herbs and roots filling the simples chest and hanging from the rafters in their faded cloth bags among the dried carcasses of frogs and lizards and dragonlings.

To Ilar's considerable relief, the little painted pavilion still stood at the far end of the room. The flap was tied down with black ribbon, as always. If Ahmol hadn't been there watching them, he'd have gone to it immediately. Instead, he looked around the workshop, feeling empty and sad inside. Until that last terrible night, Ilban had treated him kindly, and made him feel valued and useful as Ilar crushed bits of ore for him, or tended the cylindrical brick furnace that dominated the center of the room. The small windows near the top that had looked like glowing golden eyes when it was stoked were just black circles now.

The tall bookcases and cabinets looked just the same, too, orderly and carefully arranged. Calipers and tongs lay forgotten on the forge; the worktables were littered with instruments, stacks of precious metals, and books left open next to stained crucibles, as if Ilban had only just stepped out for a turn in the garden. The glass distillation vessels sat gathering dust on their iron stands, the largest coated inside with the dregs of the rhekaro blood concoction Ilban had been working on when he died. The thin copper tubes sticking out of the pear-shaped retort were already going green with tarnish.

Chains that had once bound Alec to the large anvil near the forge lay where they had last fallen, still attached to the big iron ring on its base. The leather funnel they had used to force the purifying tinctures down Alec's throat had rolled into a corner to gather dust. Ilar wondered if Ahmol or Ilbana knew of the secret tunnel hidden under the trapdoor to which the anvil was bolted. He hadn't even told Ulan about that. Now he wondered why.

Ahmol led Ulan downstairs, past the holding room at the landing, and on to the small, dirt-floored cellar under the far end of the workshop where the rhekaros had been made. The flat metal cage hung from the ceiling joists, and the hole in the earth that the last rhekaro had been birthed from had not been filled in. It was damp here, and smelled faintly of blood and metal.

Under the watchful eye of the servant, Ulan looked his fill, then thanked the man and left.

That night at supper he spoke enthusiastically of what he'd seen, in particular praising Ilban's library.

"If it would not be asking too much, dear lady, might I go there and read tonight? There are so many fascinating titles, and I must soon leave you."

She hesitated, then nodded graciously. "I ask only that you put them back exactly as they were when you are done."

"But of course!"

After that it was a simple enough matter to request the key and a pot of tea. Ahmol escorted them, as before, but took his leave when he was finished lighting the lamps. They'd worn cloaks against the chill, since Ilbana had asked that they not build a fire.

As soon as the door closed behind him, Ulan went to the pavilion. "Come, now. You must open it for me. My knees are too painful to bend that much today."

Poor Ulan, thought Ilar as he pulled the black ribbons loose and threw back the flap. The villa did not have the elaborate bathing chamber that Ulan enjoyed at home, and the old man had missed his daily soaks.

Inside he found a few leather pouches, a golden cup he'd seen Ilban use a few times for special concoctions, and a large brass-bound casket.

"This must hold the books," he said, dragging it out. He tried the lid, but it was locked.

Ulan bent and touched a fingertip to the brass faceplate of the large lock, and Ilar heard the click of the tumblers falling. Ulan smiled as he opened the lid and had Ilar lift out the three large tomes it held.

"Now, are these the one you saw?"

"Yes. This one with the red leather cover is the one he used most often." Ilar opened it and they saw that it was indeed written with normal letters, but arranged in such as fashion as to be total gibberish without the key to the code.

Ilar carried the books over to the chair under the lamp, and Ulan sat and paged through the red one to the picture of the rhekaro. In fact, there were several in what appeared to be a chapter devoted to their making. Other sections were illustrated with other creatures and objects, and intricate designs that Ilar could make no sense of.

"Well done, my dear fellow," Ulan exclaimed softly. "And now, for the others." He opened the slimmest of the three and nodded. "Ah yes. This is the one he showed me, when I last was here. It must be the least important, as it is written in plain Plenimaran. It speaks of the powers of the elixirs to be made from the rhekaro's essences, but no doubt it does not say how they are made. All the same, it should be most useful."

The last book appeared to be a journal. It, too, was written in code, but the script was haphazard and strayed across the pages at odd angles in places, interspersed with drawings of equipment and more of the incomprehensible designs.

"Now what?" Ilar looked nervously toward the door. What if Ahmol returned? Or Ilbana herself?

"We shall spend some hours here, enjoying the library while we wait for the house to settle," Ulan explained. "Then we shall hide these books beneath our cloaks and hope the guards do not decide to search us. Tomorrow we will take our leave and retire for a few days in my house by the sea."

"But what about Seregil?"

Ulan smiled. "I'm sure he can find me there." He patted the books. "And these shall be the bait for our trap."

"And then?"

"He was your prize once before. He will be again. Now, why don't you pour us some tea before it gets cold?"

Heart ablaze with hope, Ilar did not notice the old man regarding him with a mix of pity and disgust.

Mixed Emotions

THE SUMPTUOUSLY DECORATED ship's cabin was the best accommodation Alec had seen since they'd left Bôkthersa. Seregil, who had a taste for luxuries of any sort, sprawled across the bed at all hours like a big contented cat, and for the first time in a very long time it was just the two of them at night. No Sebrahn. No Rieser, who looked vaguely uncomfortable whenever they so much as clasped hands. Seregil was like a man dying of thirst, and Alec was the spring. After the tension of the past weeks, lovemaking was as much relief as pleasure for both of them.

On their second morning at sea, Rhal took one look at them over breakfast and burst out laughing, as did Nettles, who was eating with them in the captain's cabin. Alec had been amused to see that this one was decorated even more garishly than their own, but he wasn't amused now, sensing that the laughter was at his expense.

Seregil looked up from the runny grey porridge Tarmin had served up. "What's funny?"

"Look in the mirror, both of you," Rhal told him. "You've got matching love bruises on your necks."

"And you've been so quiet, too," said Micum. "We could hardly hear you in the forecastle."

Alec's face went hot to the roots of his hair as he pulled up the collar of his coat. That just made the others laugh harder, of course, all of them except Rieser, who kept his attention on his breakfast, expression carefully neutral. Seregil was clearly controlling himself with an effort; he couldn't care less what anyone thought, but he also knew how Alec hated it when things like this happened. Not that Alec was ashamed of their relationship—far from it—but his father had been a modest man, and their lonely wandering life had left Alec ill at ease in personal matters around other people. He kept hoping he'd at least grow out of blushing, but so far he hadn't been that lucky.

As much as he valued having Seregil to himself again, though, Alec missed Sebrahn badly. He'd grown used to the little rhekaro's constant presence, even if Seregil hadn't, and felt bereft without him. More than once he caught himself looking around for him, purely out of habit. Sebrahn crept into his dreams, always being carried out of reach by the Ebrados and their tall rhekaro. But he kept all that to himself, and busied himself helping Seregil prepare for the task ahead.

Seregil and the other "slaves" were leaving most of their gear behind, but he and Alec kept their tool rolls, in spite of the danger of being caught with them. For now they were stored at the bottom of their small traveling packs, but Seregil and Alec both had a medium-sized lock pick sewn into a seam of their tunics. Weapons presented another challenge, and they had a heated discussion about that with Rieser behind closed doors in their cabin.

"Even if you're only presenting yourself as a horse trader, wouldn't you have armed men to protect the string?" Rieser demanded.

"You have to play every role to the last detail," Seregil explained. "Slaves caught carrying weapons will get their master into some serious trouble, not to mention what would happen to them. If we get backed into a corner, we'll either steal some or use whatever comes to hand."

"Or run very fast," added Alec.

"It's usually better to avoid a fight altogether," said Micum.

Rieser raised an eyebrow at that. "You're afraid to fight?"

"No," said Seregil, "but fighting attracts attention, and that's something we want to avoid at all costs. Still, we won't go in without any protection. Micum has his sword, and no one will question him carrying Alec's bow. If he can't get it to Alec in time, Micum's a very good archer. Does that satisfy you? Or are you afraid?"

"I fear nothing, but dying won't accomplish our purpose."

"None of us plans to die. Just follow our lead when the time comes. This is what we're good at."

"I caught you easily enough," Rieser reminded them.

"And we escaped just as easily."

"The first time."

"That's enough!" said Micum. "It's settled: no swords or knives. We each play our role. That should be protection enough."

For clothing, the ship's sailmaker was able to alter some of their clothing and some loose trousers traded from the crew into outfits befitting a well-to-do northlander's slaves. They would wear shirts under the usual sleeveless tunic, but with sleeves loose enough to readily display the slave brands. Seregil sewed plain veils for each of them out of some of the ribbon and fine lady's handkerchiefs Rhal had plundered from a Plenimaran ship.

When it was all fixed, Alec modeled it for them.

Seregil frowned. "It's not perfect."

"It's good enough for a foreigner's slaves," said Micum. "The brands and collars should be enough to convince anyone."

That night Seregil and Alec sat down to map out all that they recalled of the alchemist's villa. Alec had seen only a bit of the cellar under the house where his cell had been, and the way from there to the workshop with its two gardens. Seregil had been kept in an upper room overlooking the inner garden, and then in the same cell that Alec had been in, but he had been unconscious for the transitions. The night he'd escaped with the Khatme nurse, it had been dark and she'd been in the lead, but he had some sense of the direction she'd taken, leading him down through the dining room into the central courtyard. The workshop garden lay just beyond. He'd also spent a night in an attic overlooking that same garden.

Alec knew the workshop best, and sketched it, marking

the forge and athanor, tables and other structures, including a small ornate tent at the far end. "And here's where the tunnel begins, under the anvil nearest the door," Alec said, showing Rieser.

"And you can't just go in that way?"

"I considered that, but I don't think we could lift the trapdoor with that anvil bolted on top of it," Seregil explained. "I almost killed myself getting it closed last time."

"Perhaps with my help—" Rieser began.

"You won't be there."

"You are not going to get the book without me."

"Oh, yes, we are. We know what we're doing and don't need you there, bumping around and knocking things over in the dark. If you want the book, then you damn well better leave it to us."

"He's right," Micum told Rieser. "You and I will have our own task."

"And I'll find out what that is later, I suppose?"

"The night I got out and hid in that attic, I overheard the guards talking about a gully behind the workshop's garden wall," Seregil told them. "That might be a good route in, if the workshop backs up to it."

"What about the tunnel?"

"Repeating ourselves would be dangerous. Unless something better presents itself, I think a straightforward burglary by way of the gully is the best plan for now. If all else fails, then we can use the tunnel, but I'd rather not."

"You seem to be leaving a lot to chance," Rieser noted.

Seregil grinned. "We don't know how else to operate."

They reached a small wooded island on the afternoon of the third day out. Alec and the others went ashore while the sails were changed for the black-and-white-striped ones and the figurehead was removed and stowed away. The sails were a bit of a risk, since meeting a Skalan ship was a very real possibility in these waters.

"I've done this before," Rhal had assured them. "And I haven't encountered the warship, Skalan or Plenimaran, that my *Lady* can't outrun."

It was peaceful here. No one lived on the island. There was only the sound of the waves, the wind, and the cries of gulls and ospreys. Alec drank it all in, knowing this was likely to be their last respite for a long time.

Seregil picked up a flat stone from the beach and sent it skipping across the surface of the cove toward the *Lady* with a practiced snap of his wrist.

"How much longer until we reach Plenimar?" asked Rieser, watching the progress with the sails.

"Three or four more days, according to Captain Rhal." Micum sent a stone skimming after Seregil's. It went a few skips farther.

Alec watched the two of them compete, but his thoughts were elsewhere. The Skalan coast had dropped below the horizon yesterday. He was feeling very far from home—and from that waterfall where Rieser's Ebrados were supposedly waiting for them. "Sebrahn could be halfway to Cirna by now."

"I gave you my word," Rieser replied calmly. "My riders will not disobey my orders, if that's what you're thinking."

And to Alec's surprise, the man picked up a flat stone half the size of his palm and sent it skipping farther than any of the others.

The striped sails went up quickly, and they were under way again before sundown.

Alec stood by himself at the rail as the coast of Plenimar came into view on the horizon, distracted by old memories. Gazing north, he pulled absently at the collar he now wore and wondered how far they were from that distant stretch of ledges where they'd battled Duke Mardus for possession of the Helm. His eyes stung a little as he said a silent prayer for Nysander.

Micum joined him and must have read his thoughts on his face, for he rested a hand on Alec's shoulder and said, "Seems like it wasn't that long ago, doesn't it?"

"Sometimes. I haven't dreamed about it for a while, but Seregil still does."

"I doubt he'll ever quite get over it. How could he?"

Alec sighed and went back to studying the distant shore. It was open country here, similar to what they had trekked through after their escape from Yhakobin. At least it wasn't raining this time.

Rhal put in at a deserted inlet south of Riga, and Alec and the others readied to disembark.

"I figure it will take us at least four days to find the book and get back here, if all goes well," Seregil estimated.

"I'll sail back in then. But what if you're not there?"

Seregil thought a moment. "Come back again in two days, and then again until we either show up or a few weeks go by."

They changed into their slave clothing and stout sandals, and let the carpenter fix the collars around their necks with lead rivets that could be cut with a knife if necessary. Rieser's collar was made of bronze; the slaves Rhal had liberated had belonged to wealthier men than Micum.

Rhal chuckled as he looked the four of them over. "Well, you certainly look the part, from what I've seen of such things. And you've got all you need?"

"I think so," said Seregil, ticking items off on his fingers. "Rope, grappling hook, lightstones, our tools, veils, food . . . Yes, I think that's everything."

"What about the documents?"

"What documents?"

"The warrants of ownership," Rhal explained, surprised. "One of the Plenimaran merchants we captured tried to sell me his slaves and showed me the documents for them. I figured you knew about that."

"No, damn it! I never had any occasion to. Alec, did you see anything like that change hands when Yhakobin bought us?"

"No, I was busy looking for you."

"Shit! Rhal, can you describe them?"

Rhal gave him a wink. "I can do better than that. I saved them as a curiosity. I'd say it's all the more important for

Micum to have something like them, being a foreigner, wouldn't you?"

"It's a good thing you mentioned it," said Micum. "It might have been a short adventure if you hadn't."

They followed Rhal below to his cabin and waited impatiently while he rummaged through several cabinets. At last he pulled out a leather packet containing several sheets of parchment folded in thirds. "Here they are."

Seregil opened one and studied it for a moment. "Let's see. This translates as 'To all who meet this man Rhasha Ishandi of Vostir, know by this letter of ownership that this slave, Arengil by name, is his rightful property, as shown . . .' Hmm. Yes . . . yes . . ." He tapped his lower lip with one long forefinger. "And here's a description of the poor wretch, right down to a birthmark on his chest, whip scars, and a missing front tooth. Very detailed, but easily copied. I suspect forgers are well employed in Plenimar, if this is all it takes to claim a slave. Look here, Alec. This design at the bottom must be the owner's mark. I'll need you to draw that out when I'm done."

It took several hours to complete the three letters of ownership, and they ended up spending the night aboard the ship. Although he and Seregil took advantage of what might be their last night of privacy for some time, Alec had trouble sleeping afterward, and he drifted in and out of nightmares that he couldn't remember, except that they had to do with getting captured again. A few hours before dawn he gave up and went above.

A cold fog hung over the water, masking the shore. He heard a loud splash, followed by the harsh croak of a heron.

He wasn't scared—risk and danger were as much a part of his life as eating—but the stakes were very high. There might well be another alchemist who could use him as a magical winepress. His hand stole to the center of his chest, where the scar of the blood tap would have been if not for Sebrahn's healing.

He didn't hear Seregil until he was right beside him.

"Are you well, talí?" Seregil looked a little hollow-eyed himself.

"I'm fine. I just didn't sleep very well."

"Me, either." He gave Alec that crooked grin of his and rubbed his hands together happily. "It's going to be very nice, going back in there like this, instead of bound. And not half killed with their stinking slaver magic, either."

Alec grinned back, dreams discarded and the old spark of excitement in his belly. "Yes, it will."

They lingered there as the crew began to appear, and it wasn't long before the smell of porridge and salt fish drifted out from the galley. Micum and Rieser came up to join them and they ate on the deck, watching the mist swirl away with the morning breeze.

At last there was nothing left to do but say farewell.

Rhal clasped hands with all of them, even a startled Rieser, as they stood at the head of the ladder and the sailors lowered their gear to the longboat below. "Good luck to you. The striped sails should keep us safe enough if anyone happens by."

"Just show them the guest cabin," Seregil said with a grin. "Only a Plenimaran would decorate like that."

"Micum, are you sure you can walk all the way to Riga?" Seregil asked as they were being rowed ashore, noticing how Micum was absently rubbing his thigh.

"I may have to rest a bit now and then, but I'll make it. Sebrahn did a pretty good job on my leg."

"We'll buy horses as soon as we find some."

"Buy?" Micum raised an eyebrow at that. "You?"

Seregil grinned. "We have plenty of money, and it will attract less attention. I didn't come all this way to be hanged for a horse thief."

Rhal's coffers had provided them with as much gold and silver as a successful trader was likely to get caught with, all in Plenimaran coin. Each of them had a money purse hidden away in his pack.

They reached shore safely and pulled the boat up onto the rocky shingle to unload their meager belongings, then shook hands with the boatman and waved him off.

"Well, it's time to complete our disguise." Seregil took the linen veils from his pocket and showed Rieser how to tie his over his face, just under his eyes.

"I feel ridiculous," the Hâzad muttered. "And what about him?" he asked, looking at Alec. "Even with his hair dark, it's obvious to anyone with eyes that he's a ya'shel."

"Slavers aren't that particular," Alec said. "Ya'shel are common, though they're not as valuable. Yhakobin didn't own any, except for me, and that was just for my blood."

"If anyone asks about you, I'll just tell them I got you cheap," said Micum with a wink.

Seregil chuckled. "See, Alec? I told you he was going to enjoy this. Come on, let's go."

"Wait." Alec dug in his pack for a moment, at last producing the little pouch with his flint and steel, and a handful of striped owl feathers. "I brought them from the mountains. I think we can use all the luck we can get."

Turning his back to the breeze, he kindled a little fire with twigs and dry bits of driftwood. When the flames licked up strongly enough, he carefully laid the feathers on. Smoke rose at once, and each of them quickly bathed his hands and face in it.

"Aura Elustri málreil," Rieser said, solemnly invoking the Lightbringer's protection for them all.

"Even me, Hâzad?" Micum asked dryly, recognizing the prayer.

"I assume you have some Immortal of your own to look after you," Rieser replied, and walked away.

Micum laughed, refusing to be insulted. "Come on, you lazy lot. We're wasting daylight."

They shouldered packs and started up the rocky beach.

Rieser scanned the empty countryside ahead. "I still think it was a mistake to come unarmed."

"All we have to do is play our parts and stay out of trouble," said Seregil.

"That's right," said Micum, carrying Alec's bow in his free hand. "So behave while we find some horses. I got my fill of being chased by your lot, Rieser. I say we try for a nice, easy journey this time."

They walked to the head of the beach and headed inland

until they struck a forked road: the left fork was a rutted dirt track that led down to the water; the right, a proper high-road heading north toward Riga. One lonely cottage stood on the seaward side, but it looked deserted.

With nothing to hide, they took the highroad. Spring was more advanced here and the day soon grew too warm for cloaks, but they kept them ready in case they met anyone on the road.

"This is a dry land," Rieser observed. Dust rose around their shoes with every step.

"It's said it was forested here before the Plenimarans came. It still is in parts of the north," Seregil told him. "But they've been here a good long time and cut it all down for their ships."

"They have to trade in the north for mast timber now," Micum added. "Even where they have forests, there aren't enough old trees large enough to make a mast."

Rieser shook his head. "It's a large, strange world you live in. I miss my valley already."

"What's it like?" asked Alec.

Seregil listened with half an ear as the Hâzad extolled the beauties of his mountain fai'thast. It sounded a lot like Bôkthersa. He was more interested in the interplay between the two. Alec had been hostile to Rieser in the beginning, and with good reason. But that had been somewhat tempered during the time they'd spent in each other's company.

For his part, Seregil had considerable respect for the tall, grim man. He was made of stern stuff, and brave to a fault. How else could he have offered to go with them like this, strangers sailing to the most dangerous place a Hâzadriëlfaie could possibly go?

Rhal waited until Seregil and the others were gone from sight, then set sail for open water. They'd left the coastline far behind when Nettles emerged from below, dragging Morthage by the arm.

"What's this?" asked Rhal.

"I found a traitor, Captain," Nettles told him as more of the crew gathered around. He held out his free hand, showing them a painted stick that had been broken in two. Rhal had seen enough message sticks since he'd met Seregil to know what this was.

"And just who are you sending word to?" he demanded.

Morthage was pale and trembling, but said nothing.

"Caught the last of what he said," the mate told him. "He said, 'to Riga, my lord.'"

"A lord, eh? A Plenimaran?" Rhal growled.

"No! I swear!" Morthage cried, finding his voice.

"Who then?"

Morthage went down on one knee. "Please, Captain. It's only the Virésse lord, Ulan í Sathil! I meant no harm."

"Bilairy's Balls, you didn't. By the Old Sailor, man, what were you thinking? Don't I pay you well enough? And it's Lord Seregil's money!"

The knave was thoroughly cowed now. "I—I beg your forgiveness, Captain."

Rhal wasn't in any mood to forgive, and hanged the blackguard with the full approval of the crew, but it was already too late to get word to Seregil. He and the others were long gone.

Just beyond the beach Seregil and the others struck a rutted road and followed it. They soon reached a crossroads, with a marker that told them they were twenty miles out from Riga and only six from a town called Rizard.

"I hope they have a horse market there," Micum said, sitting down heavily on a large stone.

Seregil knew Micum would ask for help if he really needed it, and that pride would keep him from need as long as possible. Despite the grey in his hair, Micum was still tough as an oak bole.

Not long after that they came upon a prosperous-looking farm with a corral full of fine-looking horses.

"Even better," said Micum. "It will be easier convincing people that I'm a horse trader if I have some horses."

They approached the house cautiously, but there were no dogs about, though they could hear barking from one of the outbuildings.

Micum went to the door and knocked.

A servant girl answered and looked him up and down. "What do you want here, sir?"

"I want to buy some good horses. Will your master sell a few, do you think?"

She left them there and went to inquire. The master of the house, a plump clean-shaven man, soon appeared.

"Good morning, sir," said Micum. "My name is Lornis of Nanta."

"And I'm Digus Orthan. So you like my horses, do you?" the man replied, smiling as he clasped hands with him.

"That's a nice-looking herd you have. Would you part with any of them? I can pay you a good price."

"That's my trade, sir. Let's go have a look, though you flatter my stock. The best have all been taken by the army."

The man spoke the truth, but the horses he had left were good enough. In short order Micum picked out a spirited piebald mare for himself, a pair of chestnut geldings, and three cheaper mounts for the slaves. He paid in silver.

"You'll be needing a saddle, too," Digus noted. "I have one that might do for you, if you don't mind it being used."

"Not at all. Do you have just the one, though?"

"You put your slaves on horseback?" Digus asked, surprised.

"I'm a trader myself, sir, and travel long distances. These three are good, loyal slaves and I work them hard. They need steady beasts for that."

"Well, I don't have any saddles for them, but I can spare a few blankets and bridles."

The bargain was struck, and Micum parted on good terms with the man.

"Always good to make a friend here and there," Seregil told Rieser as they rode on. "You never know when they'll prove useful."

At the next crossroads, they overtook a drayman with a load of turnips, heading in the same direction they were going.

Seregil and the others pulled up the hoods of their cloaks. Between that and the veils, only their eyes were visible. The sharp, dangerous look in Rieser's was enough to warn Seregil that the Hâzad might find the role of slave harder to play than he'd bargained for.

"Lower your eyes!" Seregil whispered in Aurënfaie. "And stop looking like you're about to kill him."

They rode forward until Micum came abreast of the man.

"Where are you headed, friend?" Micum asked as the farmer reined in his dray horse.

"Rizard market, if it's any of your business," the man replied.

"Why, so am I!" Micum exclaimed. "I don't suppose you'd mind us riding along with you?"

The man scowled up at him, taking in the long sword at Micum's hip. "I might, or I might not. You speak my tongue well enough, but with that red beard I don't think you're a countryman."

"No, but I've been a trader here nigh onto twenty years now."

The man turned to look at Seregil and the others. "Are you heading in to sell these?"

"Are you looking to buy?"

Seregil was glad that Rieser didn't speak the language.

"They any good for field work? I got no use for any fancy house slaves."

"Ah, you're right. You'd be throwing your money away on this lot for field work," he scoffed good-naturedly. "But Sakor's Flame, I wish I had three more just like 'em. They're loyal as hounds. I hardly ever have to beat them."

The farmer was still sizing Micum up. "What is it you do?"

"I trade in horses, friend. I've sold most of my string, as you can see. I'm here for more, and then sailing north. Can you recommend an honest trader?"

"There's a man in Rizard, but his stock is nothing to speak of. You'll have better luck among the rogues in Riga, if you want better."

"Riga it is, then."

"So, you've been up north? What news of the war?"

Seregil rode behind the wagon with the others, leaving

Micum to trade lies for gossip with the drayman. In no time they were laughing together like old friends.

"He's good at this," Seregil whispered to Rieser.

"So I see. A useful skill."

They were nearly to Rizard when they were met by half a dozen riders in brown coats, all carrying whips and cudgels as well as long swords.

"The damn slave takers!" the farmer muttered under his breath. "They'll be stopping us on your account. I want to be off the road before sundown."

"Halt in the name of the Overlord!" their leader ordered. "What's a dirt farmer like you doing with slaves?"

Meanwhile his riders had surrounded Seregil and the others.

"They're nothing to do with me," the drayman told them. "This red-bearded fellow's the one you want for that."

"Lornis of Nanta," Micum replied, extending his hand.

The slave taker ignored it. Turning instead to Seregil and the others, he ordered sharply, "Take off those hoods, all of you."

When they quickly complied, the one closest to Alec grabbed him by the hair. "Look at that, will you? Soft as a girl's! You a girl?"

"He's pretty enough. Look at those eyes!"

"What does it matter what he is?" another said with a crude laugh. "'When whores are few, a boy will do,' right, Zarmas?"

Alec kept his gaze averted, but his hands were curled into fists on the reins. He might not understand much Plenimaran, but he clearly got the gist of it and none of his experiences with Plenimarans had been good ones. If nothing else, he wouldn't like strangers manhandling him.

Rieser's eyes gave nothing away, but Seregil suspected he understood well enough, too.

"You're a northlander, aren't you?" their captain asked Micum. "We don't see many of you this far south these days."

"I'm a horse trader, and these three slaves are mine," Micum replied, relaxed and friendly. "I have their warrants."

"I need to see them."

Micum took the packet of documents from inside his coat and gave it to him. As the man read through them, Micum turned and locked eyes with Seregil for an instant. He was ready for trouble if it came.

But the captain just handed the documents back. "Sorry to trouble you. We've had a lot of runaways this past winter and I've got my hands full trying to find them. There was one slave in particular, a blue-eyed one like this one of yours, but he was a blond."

"Can't be this boy," Micum said. "I've owned him since he was just a little thing. The dates are there in the warrant."

"So I see. I'll just check their brands and you can be on your way."

"Show him," Micum ordered. Seregil was the only one who understood the words, but Rieser and Alec both pushed back their sleeves as he did and showed the fake brands. This satisfied the captain. He waved them on and continued on his way.

When they were gone, Micum heaved a deep sigh of relief. "That always takes a few months off my life, getting stopped like that!" he told the drayman. "Sorry if I've caused you any trouble."

"No trouble for me, friend. This happens all the time. Sakor help the man who forgets to carry his warrants. The markets are full of seized slaves these days."

"More than usual?"

"So I hear. Seems some escaped from a nobleman in Riga, and when he went after them they killed him. The widow has offered a good bounty for them, but it will be the Riga Master Slaver who gets them in the end."

"I almost pity the ones who end up like that." Micum was fishing for information.

"I don't, sir. Slaves who kill their masters deserve to be tortured to death in the market square."

"I've never seen it myself."

"Oh, I have! Their hands and feet are cut off, and their guts are pulled out and burned in front of them while they're still attached. And then their eyes are gouged out and their head cut off. But even that's too good for murdering slaves, if you ask me."

Seregil was very glad Alec and Rieser didn't understand any of that. He and Micum and Alec had courted grisly deaths before, but not one like this.

They reached Riga late that afternoon and were stopped and searched again at the city gate. Once again, Seregil's forgeries stood up under scrutiny.

The harbor was thick with warships sporting the striped sails. There were Virésse vessels moored there, as well.

Seregil shaded his eyes, brow furrowed above his veil. "I suppose that's not unusual, given the trade agreements. Still—Oh, no."

"What?" asked Rieser.

"See that Virésse ship flying the red-and-black pennant? That little flag isn't flown unless the khirnari is aboard."

"Ulan í Sathil is here?" Alec exclaimed softly. "He might know about the book, too, if he was in league with Yhakobin."

"Who is Ulan í Sathil?" asked Rieser.

"The khirnari of that clan," Seregil replied.

"A khirnari that treats with makers of tayan'gils?" The man looked truly shocked.

"We don't know that for certain," Seregil admitted. "But it's possible."

"What now?" asked Micum.

"I guess we'd better go see if the book is gone or not."

"Even if it is, it doesn't necessarily mean Ulan has it."

"No," Seregil replied, "but it gives us a place to start."

"I can ask around the docks and see what he's been up to," said Micum.

But Seregil shook his head. "No, we'd better not do anything to get you remembered just yet. We know where he is, and if he leaves we know where he'll go."

The horse market was several streets on. The pickings were slim; the war was taking its toll here, too.

The others hung back respectfully again while Micum

bargained for four horses and some used saddles, telling the trader he'd sold his slaves' saddles during a slack time.

"Buying saddles for your slaves?" the man asked as he sat down at a small table to write out the bill of sale.

"I have a long way to go and I expect them to work. They can't do that sliding around on nothing but a blanket," Micum explained.

"Ah, well then. Where are you headed?"

"I mean to make my way to Nanta, and then up the river from there to the outposts to sell my horses."

"What about the fighting?"

Micum laid a finger to the side of his nose. "I've got my routes, friend. No one bothers me. And it's still winter up there where I'm heading. Skala's whore queen is probably still snug in her palace for now." He spat on the ground. "This will be her last year, I say. Death to Skala!"

"Death to Skala, friend!" The trader slapped Micum on the shoulder.

"Say, can you tell me if there are any rich nobles around here, who might have special stock to sell? Some with a bit of 'faie blood in 'em? Not that your beasts are inferior." He stroked the neck of the ordinary bay he'd just purchased. "Fine animals! But if I should meet up with some officers along the way in Mycena, it's 'faie beasts they want. It'd help me along, if I could put a bit more gold in my pocket going north."

"Well . . ."

"And I'll put some gold in yours, too," Micum assured him. "Steer me right and I'll give you a gold sester for every horse I find." With that he spit in his palm and held it out to the trader. The man did the same, and they clasped on it.

Leaning at ease against the corral, the trader rattled off half a dozen names, none of them Yhakobin's. "They might have a few horses left. But you'd better have a lot of gold in your pocket, if you mean to trade with them. The richer they are, the tighter the purse strings."

"Isn't that the truth! Any widows among them? They're likely to not deal so sharp."

"That would be the Lady Meran. You'll want to keep your slaves on a short tether, though, if you go near her."

"Why's that?"

"Because her husband was killed by escaped slaves a few months back. It was the scandal of the city."

"I'll keep that in mind, friend." Micum dropped another coin in the man's hand. "And where would I find this grieving lady?"

"You want the east high road. You'll find yourself on it if you go to the second slavers' square and take a right turn at the barn with the sun and moon sign above the door. You can't miss seeing it. From there you ride out to the second crossroad and turn right again. By and by you'll strike a lane lined with tall trees. That's the way to the estate."

"Thank you, friend. One last thing, though. Can you tell me the name of the dead husband?"

"You could ask anyone in Riga that and get the answer. He was Charis Yhakobin, alchemist to the Overlord himself and the richest man in the duchy—even richer than the duke himself."

"Does the duke have horses to sell?" Micum asked.

"No, but if you find any 'faie ones, he's likely to be a good customer for you."

Micum clasped hands with him again. "You've been a great help, my friend. Give me your name and I'll come to you first with northern stock, and make you a special price for whichever ones you want."

"Ashrail Urati. And yours?"

"Lornis of Nanta. Look for me in the fall."

Ashrail glanced up at the sun. "You won't get to that house before nightfall and she'd not likely to welcome you then. My house is just in the next street over. Be my guest tonight and take supper with me, why don't you? I've a slave cupboard in my stable, so you needn't worry about them."

"Very kind of you. I believe I will!"

Ashrail left the market with them and took them to a large house in a respectable street. Micum was ushered in the front door, while Seregil and his fellow slaves ended up barred in a cramped, windowless room hardly bigger than the aforementioned cupboard, with one small flyspecked lantern for light. It reeked of stable muck, and there was no source of heat except for the lamp and their blankets and cloaks.

"This reminds me of our last visit to Plenimar," Alec said in Skalan, whispering in case of any prying ears outside. "Cold all the time. At least we can take these damn things off, though." Alec pulled his veil off and tucked it inside his coat.

"At least it's not raining."

Sometime later they were given a hot supper of stew and bread and let out once to use a stinking privy, for which they had to put on their veils.

"We might as well be horses!" Rieser muttered when they were barred in again.

"I think the horses get better treatment," said Alec, running a finger along the inside of his slave collar.

Rieser pulled at his. "And this is what you escaped?"

"What we escaped was worse," Seregil told him.

"And yet you come back here. You're either very brave or just plain mad."

"Bit of both," Seregil said with a grin that was hidden.

"And all for the sake of the tayan'gil?"

Alec nodded. "We don't want more of them made, any more than you do. And whatever is in that book may help us understand him better."

"To what end?"

"To make sure he doesn't hurt anyone else."

"That won't be a problem, among my people."

"You're not taking him," growled Alec.

"You can't stop us."

"Hush, both of you, before someone hears," hissed Seregil. "Nobody is to mention any of that again until we're well away from all this!"

✖

CHAPTER 26

Scouting the Ground

ONE OF THE horse trader's servants roused them early the next morning and brought them into the kitchen for a hot breakfast. Alec rubbed the sleep from his eyes as they entered the warm, steamy room to find bread trenchers already set out for them on a side table. The kitchen girl even gave them a smile as she brought them a platter of crisp turnip cakes fried in bacon grease and a pitcher of fresh milk. Micum must have made a good impression on his host.

Micum and the horse trader came in and ate with them, talking and laughing like old friends. When they were done, Micum kissed the serving girl to make her giggle, then the four of them set off toward the slave market.

"I wish there was another direction to go," Alec said when they were away from the house.

"Actually, I'd like to see it this time," Seregil replied.

"So would I," Rieser murmured, eyes hard above his veil.

The markets were as Alec remembered, but he had more time to look around than he'd had before. Slave barns, money houses, taverns, and inns surrounded a series of squares. Each barn had a raised platform out in front, and already a few slaves were on display to small clusters of bidders. At this hour it was mostly children; the poor things were half naked, with heavy chains attached to their little collars.

The sights and smells brought back bad memories and made Alec's stomach hurt, but he didn't recognize anything until they reached one of the larger squares, where he caught sight of the maimed slaves chained along a wall with filthy bandages where limbs had been.

"By the Light!" Rieser gasped softly behind his veil. "What happened to them?"

"Punishment." Alec made himself look back at them again. "Run away and lose a foot. Be rude to your master and they cut out your tongue. Steal and—"

"I understand," Rieser replied. Even whispering, his outrage was obvious.

"Quiet, you lot!" Micum ordered sharply, giving them a meaningful look over one shoulder.

Alec obeyed, then turned to find Seregil looking up at a handsome young Aurënfaie man on one of the platforms. He was naked, hands shackled behind his back so that he couldn't cover himself. Pale with cold, he stared out over the crowd, eyes devoid of hope.

Seregil turned to Alec, telling him with narrowed eyes that this place should be burned to the ground with every slaver locked in their own barn.

They came at last to the barn with a moon and sun sign done in gilt work hanging over the door, and the street they were seeking. Turning right, they left the market and continued up a busy thoroughfare, following it to the east gate.

Alec had been made to kneel in Yhakobin's carriage and hadn't been able to see anything more than the tops of houses and trees out the open window. It wasn't much help to them now; they left the city behind and rode through rolling farmland, following the horse trader's directions.

It was greener here than on the coast, and they rode past horse pastures and fields of winter wheat and turnips that had been left in the ground through the cold season. At last Alec spotted a sprawling villa on a wooded hilltop half a mile or so in the distance.

"That's the place," he told the others.

"Are you sure?" asked Seregil.

"Yes. It's the right shape and I recognize the tree line behind it, with the dead oak."

"You don't know the place?" Rieser asked Seregil.

"I was kept inside more than Alec, and it was dark when we escaped."

"And we're going there now?"

"Not yet."

They reached the tree-lined lane the trader had told them of, but continued past it. The road was less traveled here, and the farms spaced farther apart.

They stopped at last in a copse of trees at the edge of a field.

"Micum, you and Rieser can wait for us here. The farm should be within a mile of here." He looked up at the sun; it was coming to midafternoon now. "I think we have time to find it, just in case we end up having to use the tunnel. Alec?"

"I think it was—" He scanned the horizon. "Northish."

"Northish?" Rieser looked less than impressed.

"Don't worry. He has a fine sense of direction," said Seregil, but as soon as Rieser looked away Seregil raised a brow at Alec. *Northish?*

They continued up the road, blending their horses' tracks with those of all the riders who'd been along this way since the last rain. As always, Alec's sense of direction stood them well. Within the hour he spotted a little horse farm with an apple orchard and an onion field. "That's it."

"Smoke is coming out of the chimney. Someone's home," noted Micum.

"Last time we were here, there weren't any dogs," said Alec.

"Well, just in case." Seregil held out his left hand to Rieser, the fingers curled against his palm except for the first and last. "I know you have a bit of magic, at least. Do you know how to do the dog charm?"

Rieser mimicked the hand gesture. "*Soora thasáli,* you mean? Of course. What do we do now?"

Micum gazed off at the house. "I'd say we should have a look while we have the chance, just to see what's what."

The farmstead was just as Seregil and Alec remembered— a small, well-kept place with a large corral, a barn, and a good-sized stable.

Micum approached first, with the others well behind him, but this time a snarling dog appeared from the open barn door and ran at him. Micum had to rein in his piebald before she could buck.

"Hello in the house," he called out over the barking.

A man in a leather apron came from the barn, wiping his hands on a grimy cloth. "Brute, come!" The dog retreated grudgingly, still growling as he went to sit by his master's feet. "What do you want?"

"Water for our horses, and to see if you have any you'd part with," Micum replied. "Do you have any to sell?"

The man brightened at that. "I do, sir, if you've got gold to pay for them."

"I do."

"Well, then. Have your slaves water your mounts while we look over the herd. Are they safe to leave on their own?"

"Oh, yes. No worries there." Micum turned to the others and curtly ordered them to see to the horses.

Seregil and the others bowed and led the string over to a long trough beside the corral. They stayed there, hooded and silent, while Micum and the man headed up into the meadow beyond the house.

"Yhakobin's widow must be selling off her herd for capital," murmured Seregil.

"I don't understand. Why are you doing this in broad daylight?" Rieser asked.

"Micum is finding out how many people live here, so we know what to expect if we come back tonight. This place is part of Yhakobin's estate."

"Where is the tunnel?"

Seregil pointed to the stable. "It comes up in there."

Micum and farmer returned and went into the house together. Micum came out again after a time, smiling and smelling of beer and sausage. He'd brought them some of the latter in a napkin. A woman and a young girl with dark braids stood by the open doorway, smiling as they watched the men go back to the stable.

"Oh hell, a child!" Seregil muttered under his breath.

Micum? Alec signed.

Seregil gave him a slight nod. The girl looked to be the same age as Micum's youngest daughter, Illia.

"If the time comes, I will kill them," Rieser whispered.

"Because they're only Tír?" hissed Alec.

"We're not killing anyone unless it's absolutely necessary, and leave out the girl and the woman," Seregil told him. "We're not murderers."

"And yet you kill?"

"Only when necessary. This lot shouldn't be any problem. I haven't seen anyone else around."

"There was a drunken stable hand the night we escaped," Alec reminded him.

"Let's hope he hasn't improved his habits."

Micum struck a deal for three fine Aurënfaie horses and parted on the best of terms with the master of the house. Alec tied the new ones into the string they already had, and they set off the way they'd come.

"Well?" asked Seregil when they were out of sight of the house.

"It's just the family you saw, a hired man, and a stable boy," Micum told them. "There's a front room as you go in, with a kitchen on the left and the bedchamber at the back. I assume the hired man sleeps in the front room or the barn."

"Good to know. Hopefully it won't come to needing it, though," Alec said.

They reached the thick stand of trees and took their horse string to the heart of it, tethering them there. Then they waited for night to fall, watching the bow of a waxing moon sinking in the west. Seregil took a spare shirt from his pack and cut it into strips with Micum's knife, then wrapped them around the iron hooks of the grapple, to deaden the sound of it when he used it on the wall.

"I guess it's time," he said when it was full dark. He tied the neck of his cloak more tightly to cover his collar. "We should be back by sunrise if everything goes according to plan. If we're not and you don't find us between here and the farm, ride into the city and see if they're burning our entrails and gouging out our eyes."

"You shouldn't joke about such things," warned Rieser.

"He jokes about everything," Alec explained.

"It's better than worrying," said Seregil. "Micum, if we're not captured, go to an inn by the south gate and we'll find you. Come on, Alec. We've got risks to face and books to steal."

❧

CHAPTER 27

Nightrunning

SEREGIL and Alec were doubly careful as they rode back toward the villa, keeping well away from the road. It was a clear night, and the stars cast enough light for them to be seen. If they were caught now, with no master and no papers—not to mention the bag containing the grappling hook and the rope slung from Seregil's saddlebow—then they would find themselves back in the slave market pretty damn quick.

But Illior's luck was with them; they reached the villa lane without encountering anyone. Avoiding that, too, they flanked the hill. It took some searching, but they found the mouth of the gully that ran behind the villa. It lay at the end of a farm road, and the mouth of it was choked with rubbish. From here they could see a bit of the villa and torches burning there.

Picking their way over discarded crockery, broken tool handles, furniture, and a few rotting bed ticks, they led their horses as far in as they could, then left them tethered when it grew too narrow. As hoped, the gully brought them in back of the house directly behind the workshop. They stayed there, watching the stars wheel an hour's time and talking in signs. Sounds came to them on the still night air—the banging of pots being washed in the kitchen, guards talking in the courtyard above their heads, the flittering of bats and yipping of foxes on the hunt.

Seregil wondered who was tending the children now. Their nursemaid, Rhania, had killed herself while helping him escape, and he still felt the loss. He'd known her for such a short time, but she was a brave woman who'd deserved better than dying with a collar around her neck.

A little after midnight, Seregil climbed the side of the gully and pitched the muffled grapple up with practiced ease. It caught on the first try with only a small scratching sound. He and Alec grasped the rope together and put their weight on it to be sure. It held.

"Here we go, then," Seregil whispered, then caught Alec by the back of the neck and gave him a kiss.

"Just in case?"

A chill ran up Seregil's spine. "No, talí. For luck. Wait for my signal."

"Luck in the shadows," Alec whispered after him as he started up the wall.

"And in the Light," Seregil whispered back, though he hoped light wasn't going to be a factor.

He made it easily to the top of the wall; from there it was a short jump to the low-pitched roof of the workshop. Fortunately, one of the shuttered skylights was on this side of the ridgeline. If he could get it open without alerting the entire household, it was a safer way in than climbing down to the front door.

Lowering himself onto the roof tiles, he climbed up to the ridge to scan the courtyard. There was no one there that he could see but a sleeping watchman.

He crawled back to the skylight. The shutter was six feet high and about half that across. Fortunately it was lifted by means of a pair of pulleys mounted on a post on the hinge side. The thick rope that operated it passed through an opening in the roof, and there was enough space around the rope for Seregil to see that no light was coming up from below.

He went back to the wall and hissed softly for Alec, who climbed nimbly up. Seregil signaled silently and together they hauled on the shutter rope. It opened smoothly on well-oiled hinges. The workshop below was pitch-dark, so he took a lightstone from his tool roll and dropped it in. It bounced off something and rolled under something else, but they could still see the glow of it. As far as they could tell, the place was deserted.

Alec pulled up their rope and reset the grapple so they could climb down into the shop. Seregil slid down first and retrieved the stone. Going to the cellar door, he opened it enough to see that there was no light there, either.

Alec came down and took out a light of his own. "Look," Seregil whispered.

There were footprints in the dust around the bookcases and a chair beside a lamp stand. A few others showed that people had walked around the room and gone to the small tent at the far end. It was painted with rings of what were most likely alchemical symbols of some sort. The dust was disturbed in front of it, showing where someone had knelt down, presumably to investigate its contents.

Curious, Seregil went to the tent and pulled back the flap while Alec began searching the bookcases. In addition to a few leather bags and a gold chalice, there was a locked casket that looked large enough to hold a book like the one Alec had described.

The lock was a large one. These were often the most dangerous, being large enough to hide a nasty surprise, like a poison needle on a spring. After a close inspection, however, Seregil slid a pair of slender picks from his roll and went to work. A moment later he heard the click of several tumblers. He grinned as he raised the heavy lid, but the casket was empty.

"I don't see it in the bookcase," Alec whispered, joining him. "It's not on any of the tables, either."

Seregil showed him the empty box. "Would it have fit in here?"

"Yes."

"Damn!"

They spent some time searching the room, but it was no use. Nothing like the book Alec recalled was to be found.

"Bilairy's Balls," Seregil hissed.

"Maybe some other alchemist took it." Alec looked around. "Then again, everything else is just as I remember it. Nothing appears to have been moved."

"Except books." Seregil went back to the cluster of footprints in front of the bookcases. There were no empty spaces between the volumes. "Whoever it was knew what they were looking for, to the exclusion of all else. They paid no attention to anything else here, except books and that tent. You're certain the book you saw would fit in that casket?"

"Yes." Alec stared around into the shadows. "Wait. What about the cellar? And that locked room they kept me in down there?"

But once again, there was nothing like a book anywhere; everything was just as Alec remembered.

"Ulan?" whispered Alec.

"We'll see. Come on."

Seregil went up the rope first. As his head cleared the roof, however, he heard an outcry in the distance. It was coming from the direction of the gully. From what he could make out, someone had found their horses and raised an alarm.

"There, in the workshop!"

Seregil looked around to find a man balanced on a ladder placed against the garden wall to his left. He must have gone up to see what the fuss was about.

"Guards! The workshop," the man shouted, disappearing down the ladder. "Fetch the key, someone!"

Seregil quickly climbed down the rope and found Alec already struggling with the heavy anvil. He hurried to help and they heaved the trapdoor up. People were at the door now, and someone was not waiting for the key. The door shook on its hinges as someone tried to break it down.

"Go get the lower door open," Seregil whispered.

Alec disappeared down the rickety wooden ladder bolted to the side of the narrow shaft.

Seregil took a deep breath and grasped the ring on the underside of the trapdoor. It was tricky, pulling the heavy door in such a way as to not get brained by it. The only way was to throw all his strength into it, then hang on tight to the ring as the whole thing crashed back into place. If the ring came loose, it was a long way down.

But it didn't, and he found the ladder with one foot and clambered down after Alec.

Alec was at work on the large iron lock with two of his heaviest picks and had it open as Seregil's feet touched ground. Dashing into the tunnel beyond, they closed the door. Alec jammed one of the picks into the workings of the lock, then bent the long end flush with the door. "That should slow them down a bit!"

They set off down the dank passageway at a run. By the time they reached the ladder at the far end of the tunnel, they were both winded. Seregil climbed, gasping, up the ladder and pushed the trapdoor up just enough to peek out into the stable. He barely noticed the horseshit that fell down around him, though he heard a muffled curse from Alec below.

All was dark and quiet, except for the sound of snoring coming from a stall near the door. They couldn't count on the stable boy being drunk, but at least he was asleep. Seregil levered himself out of the shaft, heedless of the fresh horseshit covering the floor. At least it deadened sounds well.

There was no time to find saddles. As soon as Alec was up, they closed the trap, kicked some shit over it, then each took a horse and led it out by the bridle. The useless stable boy never stirred as they passed. Once outside, they hurried away on foot, away from the farm and away from the road. They'd just reached the apple orchard behind the barn when they caught the sound of horses in the distance, coming on at a gallop.

There was no time for subtlety. Springing onto their horses' backs, they gathered the reins and kicked their mounts into a gallop, heading north and hoping the riders wouldn't hear them over the sound of their own horses.

After several miles, they reined in and listened. There was no sound of pursuit.

"I think we got away," Alec said, still scanning the starlit landscape behind them.

"Only just."

They circled back and reached the copse just before dawn. Micum and Rieser were both awake and waiting for them in the cold campsite.

"There you are!" Micum exclaimed, clearly relieved. "I was just about ready to go looking for you."

"Did you find it?" asked Rieser.

"No," Seregil told him, sliding off his lathered horse. "Someone's taken it. We saw plenty of footprints in the dust, so someone's been in there since Yhakobin's death."

"Or maybe the wife knew about it and moved it—or sold it," said Alec as he dismounted. "Or it was Ulan. I say we start there."

"Rather than go back and search the house?" Rieser asked.

"It's going to be a bit tougher to get back in there now," Alec told him.

"You raised the house, did you?" asked Micum. "Did anyone get a good look at you?"

"No," said Seregil. "At least I don't think so. I saw one man, but it was dark enough that I couldn't make him out, so hopefully he couldn't see me any better. And it was only for an instant."

"What does this khirnari have to do with the book?" asked Rieser.

"The alchemist told me himself that he did business of some sort with Ulan," Alec explained.

"And our wizard friend Thero and I tracked down a slaver in a Virésse port who claimed Ulan ransoms slaves back from Plenimar, presumably with Yhakobin's help," Micum explained.

"Not to mention the fact that Ulan knows of Alec's mixed blood," Seregil added. "Since he's involved with the slavers that Micum and Thero spoke with, it's not a great stretch to think that he knows something of the rhekaro—perhaps was even having Yhakobin make one for him. Add that to the fact that he's here himself, and as far as I'm concerned that's a pretty strong set of coincidences pointing to the possibility that he knows about the book, too."

"Then we must go back to the city?" asked Rieser.

"Looks that way. But at least we have a few new horses to trade."

"The two you stole aren't on the bill of sale, though," Micum pointed out.

"We'll have to lead them away a bit and let them go," Alec said, stroking his stolen mare's sweaty neck. "That should throw off any trackers, if we can get into the city before anyone catches up with us."

Micum tapped the heel of his boot against the ground. "Still frozen hard. You couldn't have left much of a trail, and not one easy to follow in the dark. We'd better go now, though, just in case."

"We'll use the north gate this time, I think," Seregil said.

"You don't want anyone who saw us today wondering why we're back so soon," Rieser observed.

Seregil gave him a crooked grin. "You're catching on."

"So what are we going to do now?"

"Find Ulan and see if he has the book," Seregil told him. "That's most likely going to involve the sort of work we did tonight."

"How do you break into a ship?"

"The same way you do a house, only wetter."

CHAPTER 28

Taking in the Sights

NO ONE seemed to take undue notice of Alec and his companions when they entered the city again with their string of horses. From there they made their way through a busy merchants' quarter toward the waterfront. Micum's "slaves" were veiled and hooded; if they inadvertently ran into Ulan, he would not recognize them, and he didn't know Micum.

They were nearly there when something startled Seregil's horse and she jerked around in the opposite direction. Seregil quickly controlled her and took a moment to stroke her neck and murmur some reassurance before turning her back to follow Micum.

"Please, Master," Seregil said as they reached a market square at the edge of the waterfront. "Can we buy some food? I'm very hungry."

"So am I," said Alec. It had been hours since their cold breakfast.

"Very well," Micum snapped, still playing the role.

There were food vendors along the northern side of the square. Micum chose one selling hot grilled sausages.

"Go buy for us," Micum ordered Alec, reaching for his purse.

"Please, Master, let me," Seregil said.

Micum raised an eyebrow, then gave him a few coins. "You—" He turned is attention to Alec. "There's a woman selling cider down there. Fetch us some."

Something's going on, Alec thought as he headed for the cider booth. Seregil was up to something.

They ate standing by the public well. The sausages were full of hot spices, and Alec was glad of the cider.

"I think we're being followed," Seregil said quietly around a mouthful. "There's a young beggar behind me, over there by the ribbon seller. He's wearing a white kerchief around his neck. I'm sure I saw him by the gate."

"I see him," Micum said, glancing past Seregil. "Plenimaran?"

"Looks like it."

Alec turned his head slightly until he could see the ribbon merchant from the corner of his eye. The ragged fellow Seregil was talking about was leaning at ease against the side of the booth, laughing with another wastrel. "You think the men who chased us last night have followed us here?"

"Maybe," Seregil replied, but he sounded doubtful.

"If they did track us, why wait until now to come after us? It would have been easier out on the road," Rieser murmured.

"Exactly," Seregil replied.

They finished their food and made their way down to the harbor.

Some of the Virésse vessels they'd seen yesterday had sailed, and two others had come in.

"Is he still with us?" asked Micum.

Seregil's unruly horse turned again, tossing her head and snorting.

"He is," Seregil whispered as he brought the mare under control again.

Ulan's ship was still riding at anchor, but the pennant was gone.

"What does that mean?" asked Rieser.

"That the khirnari isn't aboard," Seregil replied.

A group of idle sailors had gathered at the end of a nearby quay, sitting on crates and passing a flask. Dismounting, Micum strolled over to them and was soon laughing and talking between pulls from the bottle.

"He seems so at ease," murmured Rieser, sounding impressed in spite of himself. "Just like with the horse dealer."

"Micum can talk to just about anyone," Alec told him.

Soon Micum was pointing, apparently asking about some of the ships. The sailors appeared to be happy to answer. When Micum finally parted from them and walked back to the others, he was grinning.

"What—" Rieser began.

"Hold your tongue, slave," Micum ordered curtly, and loudly enough to be overheard. Mounting again, he led the way along the waterfront toward the far side of the city. Along the way they came to a smaller horse market, and Micum stopped to sell off their string and be free of it.

While he and the others waited, Alec managed to position himself so he could look back the way they'd come. Sure enough, the beggar was there, sitting against a wall with several others of his kind, hand out, imploring the passing crowd for alms. What he lacked in subtlety he made up for in persistence.

"I made a tidy profit, enough to afford a decent inn for the night," Micum said when he returned.

Alec knew he was speaking for the benefit of anyone listening to them; they all had money in their packs, more than enough for the best inn in the city. "The trader tells me there's a good one in the next street—the Two Hens Inn," Micum went on. "And they have a decent slave pen, too."

They made their way to a large, prosperous-looking inn with a friendly innkeeper who obliged Micum with a back room, away from the noise of the street. The room's single window overlooked a cheerless yard with sheets drying on a line stretched between the back of the inn and the sturdy shed that served as a slave pen. Beyond that, a low wall blocked what appeared to be an alleyway.

"What about these?" the man asked, jerking a thumb at Alec and the others. "I can take them out to the pen for you, if you like, and see that they get a decent meal."

"In a bit," Micum replied. "I need them for a few things first."

"Ulan has a house near the waterfront," Micum told them as soon as the man was gone.

"Then it's time to get rid of our unwelcome follower,"

Seregil said. He leaned out the window for a moment, then turned back to the rest of them. "There's no one around right now."

Slinging on their packs, the four of them went out the window and over the wall. Micum grunted as Alec gave him a leg up.

"I miss the days when I didn't need the help," he muttered. Fortunately the wall was low enough for him to drop down on the other side without assistance.

The alley was littered with rotting fruits and vegetables that stuck to their shoes and sent up a sour stink. At the far end was a marketplace full of farmers' carts and booths. They scuffed their shoes clean against the cobbles, then doubled back to the waterfront and the street Micum's idlers had pointed him to. There was no sign of the man who'd followed them.

"Who do you suppose set him on us?" Micum wondered, still keeping his voice low and a sharp eye out. "No one knows we're here. Even if that man at the alchemist's house got a good look at you, there's no way he'd know you in that getup."

Seregil's grey eyes were serious above the veil. "I don't know, and I don't like it."

"If he did, he'd probably have set the slave takers on us, rather than following us," said Alec. "How are we going to get the horses back?"

"They're safe for now," Micum replied. "Once it's dark, we'll go back and claim them."

With Micum in the lead, they strolled down the quays to a street that ran along the harbor's edge. The houses here were like the walled villas of Wheel Street, except that the dressed stone walls were much higher, hiding the houses inside completely. Two guards wearing the sen'gai of Virésse flanked the gate of a house midway down, on the water side. Ulan's pennant fluttered on a short pole set into the stonework.

"So there you are, you old fox," muttered Seregil.

"He must be held in high esteem, to be safe staying here so close to the slave markets," Rieser whispered back.

"Virésse trades with Plenimar. Always has. I didn't expect him to have a house here, though."

Ulan was in the library, recovering from a particularly bad coughing fit, when Ilar came in without knocking and closed the door behind him. Ulan quickly balled up his bloodied handkerchief and kept it hidden in one hand.

A hectic flush colored Ilar's cheeks as he stood shaking with barely contained excitement. Closing the door, he hugged himself and whispered, "They are here, Khirnari! Your man at the north gate saw them come in this afternoon."

"Do they have the rhekaro with them?" Not even the pain still lingering in his chest could spoil this heartening news. It was the first news he'd had of them since his spy aboard the *Lady* had gone silent.

"No, but Alec is there, with Seregil and the red-haired Tír. The other 'faie is still with them, too. The spy is certain it's them."

"What did he say?"

"There's no mistaking them. Alec's hair is brown now, but the eyes are the same—a most distinct dark shade of blue. The spy got a good look at him and the red-haired Tír when the guards searched them. The Tír is playing the master."

"Clever boys. How long ago did they arrive?"

"No more than two hours. Your man followed them to the waterfront and heard them asking about you. Some men told the Tír about this house. They didn't come this way, though. He followed them to an inn in a street called Irsan. He waited to see if they came out again, but they didn't, so he came back."

"No matter. We know that they're coming," Ulan said with a smile of satisfaction. "Ilar, I must ask you to be my watchman. There is no one else whom I can trust with the task. No one else must know of the books."

"I understand, Khirnari, but what if they see me?" Ilar replied, eyes widening with fear.

"You shall be perfectly safe, keeping watch from there." A

curtained alcove at the back of the room between two book-cases was the best he could do for a hiding place for Ilar.

Several large volumes lay on the table at the back of the room, books the same size and color as the ones they'd taken from Yhakobin's house. "There is our bait. When our mice come into our trap, you're to wait until they've gone, then come to me. I shall raise an outcry and we'll have them as escaped slaves and common thieves."

"As you wish, Khirnari." Ilar was pale now, and trembling.

Ulan nearly changed his mind; one of his escort could just as well be stationed here under some pretext, but his secret was too valuable to risk. It would not do for his people to learn that their khirnari had played the thief himself, or the nature of what he was trying to protect. The making of a rhekaro stank of necromancy, no matter what Yhakobin had said about his so-called art. There was no question of taking Alec and the books to Virésse city, of course; he already had made preparations at a mountain hunting lodge far from there. He would keep Alec there. The boy would not be mis-treated, either. Perhaps in time, he could even be made to understand his own importance.

This is for the good of the clan, he reminded himself, steeling his resolve. It was the duty of the khirnari to sacri-fice for his people, even his life.

But my honor?

That was even more precious, but he had no choice but to press on with his plan. He was too close to success to lose his nerve now.

That night Ulan waited until the household servants had gone to bed, then had Ilar blow out the lamps in the library, leaving only the fire on the hearth for light.

"At last," he murmured, smoothing his hand over the cover of the topmost book. The real ones were safely hidden away. He held out his own silver-handled dagger. "Take this, dear boy, just in case."

Ilar looked at the knife as if it were a serpent. "I could never win against them!"

"So long as you keep quiet, there'll be no need. I shall feel better if you're armed. You must be careful and silent, Ilar."

"Like they are," the younger man whispered, taking the knife with shaking hands.

Ulan gathered the trembling man in a fatherly embrace. "How many times have you wished to repay my kindness? Do this for me, Ilar, for the love you bear me. Just be quiet, and things should go as planned."

Ilar nodded, though he still looked terrified. "I won't fail you."

✣

CHAPTER 29

Paths Cross

SEREGIL and the others spent that day and the next exploring the seaside district, taking note of potential hiding places in abandoned buildings and accessible cellars, and the layout of the streets. The new inn where Micum had taken a room was just two streets way from Ulan's villa, and had a spacious slave pen in the back, the door held by nothing but a stout bar; Micum was no hand at picking locks. For the time being, Seregil, Alec, and Rieser were the only ones there. There was no heat, but the straw was deep and clean and Micum saw to it that they had blankets and passable food.

Leaving his slaves behind, Micum went out to taverns each night, seeking information about Ulan's habits. He'd done this sort of nightrunning innumerable times over the years. He enjoyed the challenge of finding the right tosspot to coax information from. Most folks he talked to here didn't pay the Virésse any mind, though some allowed that Ulan was a fine man to trade with, except for being Aurënfaie. There was one well-dressed fellow, a cloth merchant, who confirmed what Micum had learned at Virésse: that Ulan í Sathil bought back slaves taken from the Virésse and the Goliníl fai'thasts, and that he had bought the majority of them from Charis Yhakobin before the alchemist's murder. A few more men gathered around them when they overheard the name.

"That was the first slave killing in years," one of the old ones told him. "It's made a lot of masters take sterner measures with their own slaves, especially the males. And in the markets there's more call now for little ones that you can train up right. The slavers can hardly keep up with the demand."

Micum also learned that the Virésse 'faie kept carefully to themselves here in Riga, never ventured out unless in an armed group, and even then seldom at night and never to anywhere like a tavern. Not everyone respected the treaty between Plenimar and Virésse. As several of Micum's drinking companions were glad to tell him, once you got their head rags off and got a brand and collar on, who could tell one 'faie from another? And who was going to take the word of a slave if they tried to tell? A mile or two inland no one gave a damn about Virésse; a slave was a slave and they all lied.

He returned the second night to find Seregil and Alec in the midst of an argument made up of hand signs and whispers.

"What's going on?" Micum asked.

"He says I'm not going in!" Alec whispered, and it was clear it was an effort to keep his voice down.

"Why?"

"We were nearly caught last time," Seregil told him. "If he gets you and the book?" He gave Alec a meaningful look that was half order, half plea. "It's too risky."

In the end Alec gave in, but he wasn't happy about it.

One more day and Rhal should be there to meet them. That night, Micum waited until the house was asleep, then took up a pack and stole out to the slave pen. He lifted the bar as quietly as he could and let the other three out. Behind them, Micum could just make out two bodies prone on the thick straw that covered the floor. Another man with slaves had come to the inn that afternoon.

"Quick, the rope!" Seregil hissed. Micum pulled it from the pack and Seregil cut four short lengths of it. He and Alec quickly tied up the unconscious slaves. That done, they gagged them both with rags.

"I hate to do that to them," Alec murmured as they stole away from the inn. "They have a hard enough life as it is."

"There's no help for it," Seregil said.

The groom in the stable woke while they were saddling their horses, but a quiet word from Micum and a coin or two was enough to make him think they were getting an early start on a long ride.

They made their way to a small side street behind Ulan's villa. There they tethered their horses in front of an abandoned house just up the street and moved silently back to the wall. All was dark up and down the street. There were no trees to climb, or sturdy vines, and the stonework didn't offer much purchase, either. They'd have to chance the muffled grapple again.

Seregil scanned the top of the wall for torches and sentries, but saw neither. "That's odd."

"The man must feel safe behind his high walls," whispered Rieser.

"Just because there isn't light doesn't mean there aren't any guards," whispered Alec.

"I hope this isn't a fool's errand," muttered Micum.

"So do I."

Seregil spun the grapple on the rope and sent it flying up to the top of the wall. It missed and nearly brained Rieser when it fell. The second try was successful, but the hooks of the grapple grated against stone as they found purchase. They pressed up against the wall, waiting for an outcry, but nothing happened. Micum would almost have been happier if there had been. At least they'd know where the guards were.

Seregil checked that his tool roll and Micum's knife were tucked securely in his belt under his shirt, then slung the loose cotton bag over one shoulder. With a kiss for luck from Alec tingling on his lips, Seregil quickly scaled the wall, his bare feet making hardly a whisper against the rough stone.

Pausing just under the top of the wall, he listened carefully, but heard nothing except the faint tinkling of bells. He chanced a look over, and found there was no parapet. A

formal garden filled the space between the wall and the back
of the house, a white crushed-shell path bright between the
dark clipped hedges and flower beds. The sound of bells
must be wind chimes hung somewhere in the garden.

Dark windows like accusing eyes lined both the lower and
upper stories, and torches burned on either side of a central
door framed with two imposing pillars that seemed too big
for the plain façade. It wasn't Aurënfaie architecture, and he
couldn't be certain it was similar to a Skalan villa, either,
which meant he'd have to be doubly careful, and probably
take more time finding what he wanted. At least in Skala the
houses usually followed a somewhat similar plan.

From here he could also see that the sides of the house
stood apart from the surrounding wall—just the sort of place
to find a side door.

There were no watchmen or dogs in sight. Pulling the rope
up, he reset the grapple and slowly paid the rope down into
the shadows below. Seating the grapple more firmly on top
of the wall, he climbed down into the garden. He debated
taking the rope with him, but that meant carrying the heavy
grapple, too, and he suspected the night's job was going to
need more finesse than that would allow. It was dark here;
perhaps no one would see the rope, even if they happened by.

Clipped turf gave softly under his feet as he moved
silently toward the right side of the house. The torchlight
reached nearly to that corner, and he had to make a dash to
the safety of the shadows beyond.

The lack of watchmen, not to mention dogs, was making
him nervous.

There was no door on this side of the house, or windows,
since there was no view, he supposed. Skirting back the way
he'd come, he approached the left side of the house. A low
wall separated the main gardens from a smaller courtyard,
with a well, kitchen garden, and wood stack. This at least
was familiar ground; where there was a kitchen garden, the
kitchen was usually not far away.

Sure enough, there was a promising door near the back of
the house. It was flanked on either side with rain butts fed by
sturdy wooden downspouts that offered a way upstairs if he

needed it. As it turned out, he did. The kitchen door was barred from the inside, so there was no lock to pick.

Seregil pressed his ear to the door, but either there was no one stirring or the door was too thick for him to hear anything. He stepped back and scanned the upper story of the house. There was a window close enough to the downspout; he hoped Ulan didn't lock up his windows as tightly as he did his kitchen.

Gripping the drainpipe in both hands, he gave it a shake. It held solid and felt sturdy enough. He took several small picks and a wooden shim from his tool roll and stuck them in the corner of his mouth.

The wooden pipe held. Holding tight to it with one hand, he leaned over as far as he could and slipped the shim between the two leaded glass panels of the window, then slowly moved it up and down until he found the latch and unhooked it.

Swinging the far panel open, he stretched over and got his footing on the bottom of the deep casement. He crouched there for a moment, letting his eyes adjust to the deeper darkness of the room. Gradually he could make out enough to know that this was a sitting room or ladies' day room. He lowered himself to the floor, which was partially covered by a round rug.

This is as good a place to start as any, he thought, although it was unlikely that Ulan would leave the book lying around in plain sight.

There were a few books on a side table near the hearth, but they were much smaller than the one Alec had described. Chancing the lightstone, he quickly paged through them anyway, but they were common romances, nothing more. He crossed to the door and inched it open. Beyond it lay a short hallway. Two small night lamps in sconces lit it well enough to see several doors on each side of the corridor and where it took a turn at the far end. A pair of expensive shoes sat next to one of the doors near the corner, set out for some servant to clean. Just as he was about to head down the hall to begin his search, he heard footsteps from the far end. A man wearing a Virésse sen'gai and a short sword at his hip came around the corner and started in Seregil's direction.

Seregil quickly dropped the lightstone down the neck of his shirt and waited, weighing his options and keeping watch through the crack of the door. He could knife the man as he passed, but once again the thought of spilling 'faie blood kept his hand from his knife. No, he'd much rather knock him out or choke him unconscious and leave him here alive.

But the man seemed satisfied with his search halfway down the corridor. Turning back, he disappeared the way he'd come.

Seregil waited until he was certain he was gone, then inched the door open and listened. Yes, there were more men beyond that corner.

He crept silently down the hallway and chanced a quick peek around the corner. A short stairway led down to an open door, and from here he could make out enough of the murmured conversation to know that they were expecting a burglary.

But why are they down there? Why only one man making a cursory search up here?

Because it's a trap, of course.

Keeping a sharp ear out, he quickly began his search, inching each door open a little and listening intently for breathing before chancing the lightstone. The first two were unoccupied bedchambers; there was no sign of books of any size. He even lifted the rugs and felt under the beds for some secret hiding place under the floorboards, but there was nothing to be found.

Moving on, he opened the door across from the occupied bedchamber, well aware, as he slipped inside, that any sound he made here was likely to be heard.

This room overlooked the garden. The torches below cast enough light for him to see that it was a library, with a few half-filled bookcases against the walls, several armchairs, and a long table with unlit lamps on either end and several orderly stacks of books between them. Large books.

Too easy, he thought again, expecting any moment for armed guards to burst in. Going to the window, he unlatched it and peered down. Fancy carved stonework looked like it offered enough purchase to climb down low enough to jump if he had to. With that settled, he turned his attention to the books.

Ilar bit his knuckle to keep silent as he left the low divan and cautiously peered out between the heavy velvet curtains. It *was* Seregil. It must be. Certainty came when the shadowy figure drew a lightstone on a stick and held it between his teeth as he looked around the room. The sight of that illuminated face made the breath catch in Ilar's throat and his heart pound. Seregil was dressed only in loose trousers and a shirt, with a slave collar around his neck. Had he been caught and enslaved again by some other master? And if so, what was he doing here like this? Ilar couldn't think straight in his excitement. None of that mattered, anyway. Seregil was *here*!

Seregil was examining the books Ulan had set out, quickly paging through each one and setting it aside. There was no sound but the soft ruffle of the paper. Apparently not satisfied with what he found, he began searching the bookshelves, taking down only the larger books. This brought him closer and closer to the alcove, and Ilar began to feel lightheaded. All the old yearning came over him in full force and before he knew what he was doing, he parted the curtains and stepped out, revealing himself when Seregil was hardly more than arm's length away. Seregil quickly backed away, shoving the lightstone under his shirt and drawing a knife in its place. Ilar knew he should raise the alarm, even at the risk of his life, but they both stood frozen, staring at each other in the faint light from outside. Then, before he gathered anything like coherent thought, Ilar sank to his knees, shaking with excitement and guilt, unable to make a sound.

Seregil stared down at him, face lost in shadow now, though the knife blade still caught the light from the window. "What are you doing here?" he hissed.

"I—" Ilar struggled to find his voice. "I am under the khirnari's protection now. This—" he gestured weakly around the library. "It's a trap. For you. And Alec."

Seregil looked around quickly again, but Ilar reached out
a hand to him. "No, not unless I call out. And I won't, I
swear! Ulan has the books about the rhekaros and he
needs—"

"I *know* what he needs. Wait, did you say 'books'? You
mean there's more than one?"

"Yes. Three. And he was certain you would come looking
for them, once he knew that you'd come back to Riga."

"He—? Never mind. Where are they?"

"Take me with you!"

"You said Ulan has offered you his protection."

"Please!" Ilar didn't even know what he was pleading for,
except that he wanted to be near this man, to somehow . . .

"If only you'd forgive me!" he whispered, voice quavering
as the tears came.

Seregil's manner softened a little. "Tell me where the
books are, Ilar, and I'll consider it. You already helped us
once, and I haven't forgotten that. But I need those books.
They're not here, are they?"

"I'll tell you, but only if you take me with you!"

"How am I supposed to do that? You could no more get
out the way I got in than fly!"

"I know a way," Ilar told him, desperate.

"Another tunnel?"

"No, a postern door with only one guard."

"And that's where the trap really springs, is it?"

"No! I swear by Aura," Ilar exclaimed, forgetting himself.

Seregil clapped a hand over Ilar's mouth, then dragged
him bodily back into the dark alcove, leaving just enough
space between the curtains to see the door. An instant later
Ulan's man Tariel burst noisily in with sword drawn.

Seregil still had an arm around him, and put his lips so
close to Ilar's ear that it sent a shiver through him. "Get rid
of him!" The arm fell away and a hand pressed firmly
between Ilar's shoulder blades.

Quaking with fear, Ilar emerged from the alcove, careful
not to leave any gap in the curtains.

"What are *you* doing in here?" Tariel asked in surprise.

"I—I was just—" He took a shaky breath. "I fell asleep while I was reading. I must have cried out in a dream."

The man raised an eyebrow. "Reading with no lamp?"

"I was sleepy, so I lay down in the alcove . . . It must have gone out."

Tariel shook his head. "You should go back to your room before you take a chill."

"I'm not tired, and I want to read some more," Ilar told him, gathering a little courage now that his ruse had worked.

"Suit yourself, then," the man said, sheathing his sword. "But see you don't rouse the house with your dreams."

As soon as he was gone, Seregil pulled him back into the alcove and put his lips to Ilar's ear again. "You did well. How did you know that I was coming?"

Ilar nearly blurted out the truth, but suddenly he didn't want to confirm what Seregil had no doubt already discerned for himself. Torn between his loyalty to the khirnari who'd saved him and the man he dreamed of every night, he couldn't get any words out at all.

But Seregil read his silence. "That was Ulan's footpad the other day, wasn't it? So the khirnari guessed I was coming at some point, and put you here to watch for me. But why you?"

"No one else knows about them," Ilar told him. "The books."

"So he's protecting his dirty little secret. It wouldn't do for his people to learn of things like rhekaros, and how they're made, would it?"

Ilar shook his head.

Seregil suddenly reached out in the dark and cupped Ilar's cheek with one hand—as close to a tender gesture as Ilar had had from him since they'd met again in Yhakobin's house. "But you saved me instead—again," he said gently. "Tell me where the books are, and we'll go."

Ilar's heart leapt. "They're in the khirnari's room."

"Bilairy's Balls!" Seregil muttered, taking his hand away. "Of course they are."

Ilar caught it and pressed it back to his cheek. "I won't run away this time. I won't be any trouble!"

"All right, but you have to tell me where in his room."

Ilar's heart swelled with hope. "Locked behind a hidden panel in the casework at the head of the bed. I can show you!"

Seregil was glad the darkness hid his pitying smile as he placed his left hand on Ilar's shoulder. "Thank you. I won't forget this. And I'm sorry."

"Sorry? For—"

Seregil struck him a controlled blow to the chin, then caught him as Ilar went limp and held him a moment, shocked at how thin the man was, and how pathetic; nothing like the vindictive creature who'd tormented Seregil in the alchemist's house. He felt nothing for Ilar now except pity, and perhaps a touch of guilt for playing him so dirty this time—especially after he'd kept Seregil secret from the guard just now.

The second time you've risked yourself to help me, damn it! What in Bilairy's name do you want from me?

Forgive me! Ilar's voice whispered in his mind.

Standing there in the darkness, Seregil weighed all the help Ilar had been—tonight and when they'd escaped from Yhakobin's house—against the sight of Alec hanging face-down in the alchemist's cage. By Ilar's own admission, he'd put Alec there.

"Forgive?" Seregil whispered. "No."

Placing the unconscious man on the divan at the back of the alcove, he quickly bound him with the drapery cords and gagged him with a clean handkerchief he found in Ilar's sleeve. Seregil left him there with the heavy draperies drawn shut and moved silently across to the door. The guard had obligingly left it slightly ajar and he was able to open it just enough to see that the corridor was once again empty. The sounds of a dice game came up the stairway.

The street wasn't as deserted as Alec had hoped. A few drunken revelers happened by, but they were too blind with liquor to notice them. Not so with the night watchman who came by a few minutes later. He said something to Micum, sounding suspicious, but Micum reassured him somehow.

"Come on, you lazy lot," he growled at Alec and Rieser. "It's time we found our inn."

They went up the street a little way, giving the watchman time to move on, then led the horses into an alley and left Rieser there to guard them while he and Micum kept watch for Seregil. It was cloudy tonight; Alec couldn't see the stars to judge how long Seregil had been gone, but it felt too long now.

Seregil paused in the hallway just long enough to snuff out the nearest night lamp. Then, bracing himself for a sudden dash, he carefully opened Ulan's chamber door and slipped inside.

There was no night lamp, a fact Seregil was instantly grateful for when he heard the rustle of bedclothes and an old man's whispered, "Who's there? Urien?"

"No, Khirnari, just Ilar," Seregil whispered back, trying to match Ilar's slightly tremulous timbre.

"What is it, dear fellow? Why aren't you on watch?"

Seregil took a cautious step forward, following the sound of the man's voice. "I thought I heard something."

There was more rustling and the creak of the bed ropes as Ulan sat up. "Why didn't you alert Captain Urien?"

"I thought the sound came from your room, Khirnari. I just wanted to see if you were safe." Seregil could tell he was nearly within arm's reach of the man. There was an unhealthy smell in the room; Ulan was sick.

And needs a rhekaro to heal him. It must be something serious for him to take such risks.

"Ah, well then, I'm fine. Go back to the library, Ilar."

Seregil reached out and grasped the old man's thin hair. Placing the edge of his knife to Ulan's throat, he brought their faces close together and hissed, "I have other plans, Khirnari."

"Seregil?" Ulan sounded less surprised than Seregil would have liked. "So I suppose you've killed Ilar and now you mean to kill me?"

At this distance, the sickly sweet smell of his illness was strong—something in the lungs, perhaps.

"I'd rather not," Seregil replied. "All I want are the books."

"What do you need with them? You have the rhekaro."

"You know why, Khirnari."

"It would be comforting to think you meant to use them as I do, but that isn't so, is it? You want to destroy them, and all the knowledge they contain."

Seregil wrinkled his nose at the sickly smell on the man's breath. "You're dying."

"By inches. I don't have long. Not without the rhekaro's elixir."

Elixir? thought Seregil. *Does he really know so little about them, even with the books?* "I know the books are in here, and I know where. I'm going to ask you to keep very quiet while I take them, otherwise I will slit your throat."

"It seems I underestimate you, even now," Ulan whispered.

"Let's just say I'm here to collect a debt on behalf of my talímenios. One it would not do for your people to hear about, eh?"

"Or yours."

Seregil wished he could see the man's face now, not liking his tone.

"You know what would happen if your sister learned of my actions toward you and Alec," Ulan went on.

"You're actually willing to risk a war to save your own life?"

"Not my life, my clan! Give me the rhekaro and you can have the books. I swear by Aura, I will never trouble you or your talímenios again."

"I don't know what your word is worth these days, old man. Not that it matters. We don't have the rhekaro anymore."

For the first time Ulan's voice betrayed a hint of alarm. "Where is it?"

"Far from your grasp. I swear by Aura, too, so give up any hope of that. How long do you have? A handful of months?"

"Less than that. Weeks perhaps."

"Do you really think that's long enough to find someone else to work that filthy magic for you?"

"With the books, I can work it myself. Alchemy isn't our sort of magic; it's simply joining the right elements in the right manner."

"The most important of those elements being Alec's blood. No, Ulan. Give it up."

A cold hand closed around Seregil's wrist. "You may keep the brown and the blue books, and Alec; I'm willing to accept the rhekaro and the red book."

"No. The rhekaro is a living creature. He feels pain, and Alec told me what Yhakobin did to him. But it's a moot point anyway. I told you, we don't have him."

"You're lying."

"I'm assuming you've had us watched. Did any of your spies see a child with us?"

"You've hidden him!" Just then a violent coughing fit seized the old man, and he dug his fingers into Seregil's wrist until it passed. It was brief, but when he wiped his lips on the edge of the white linen sheet, the cloth came away spotted dark. "I am dying," Ulan told him, wheezing a little. "And I cannot let that happen. Not while Gedre fai'thast remains an open port, draining away our trade. That was never meant to be part of the bargain. The Skalan queen regularly sends emissaries there, and I have reason to believe that she and the Gedre khirnari mean to renege on the pact and keep the port open to Tír trade even when her war is finished."

"Surely there's enough trade for both of you?"

"Now, perhaps, but when the war and their need for Aurënfaie horses and steel is past, what then? No! We were betrayed and I will not die before my clan is made secure and prosperous again. Charis Yhakobin made that rhekaro for me, and I mean to have it, or another in its place. Or you can kill me now to stop me. The choice is yours."

"I may be an outcast, teth'brimash, but I will not spill a khirnari's blood," Seregil told him between clenched teeth. "Not even yours. And do you even know what a rhekaro really is? A distillation of the blood of the Great Dragon that made us, carried in the veins of a chosen few, the ones who call themselves the Hâzadriëlfaie. *That* is what you sold into the hands of someone like Yhakobin."

"One does what one must for the clan."

Resisting the urge to shake the old man, Seregil took out the lightstone and tossed it on the bed, then cut the cords of the bed curtains. Ulan's bones felt brittle as wheat straw as he bound him.

Ulan's sharp old gaze never left Seregil's face as he worked. It was a little unnerving. "You're a fool, Seregil í Korit. With the rhekaro that is already made, I would have all I need to save my people. No one would have to suffer."

"Except the rhekaro." Who knew what was in those books, what it took to make these elixirs? Seregil suppressed a shudder, thinking of all Alec had told him of what had been done to Sebrahn and his predecessor. He thought of Sebrahn playing with the dragons, fidgeting off his shoes, climbing into his lap like a real child . . .

"A small price to pay!" hissed Ulan.

"You have it backwards, old man. You should be spending these last days grooming your successor, not torturing those weaker than yourself. Everyone dies."

And Alec? Seregil pushed that thought away. That had been Sebrahn's doing, not his.

"You will never leave these shores, Seregil. Not alive."

Seregil gave him a crooked grin as he gagged him with a blood-spotted handkerchief. "I'm not a man you want to gamble against, Khirnari." Once Ulan was secured, Seregil went to work finding the books, aware every moment of Ulan's hate-filled gaze upon him, and his ineffectual pulling at his bonds.

The bed was built of polished casework, and there were three panels in the headboard. It took only a moment to find the secret latch in the narrow space between two of them and lift it with the point of the knife. The center panel came loose, revealing three books stacked neatly in the dusty space behind. They were large and heavy, and strained the sides of the bag Seregil had brought with him; he had been expecting only one.

Taking up his lightstone again, he looked down at Ulan for a moment, almost reveling in the fury of the glare directed back at him. "I don't expect this to be the end of things between us, Khirnari. But I won't be so merciful next time, if you come after us."

Tucking the lightstone back in his tool roll, he went to the door and listened for a moment. "Good-bye, Ulan í Sathil. Pray to Aura our paths never cross again."

Alec heaved an inward sign of relief when he saw a dark form slide down the rope. Leaving Micum in the shadows, he stole out to meet Seregil.

Found it? he signed, noting the heavy bag swinging against Seregil's side.

Seregil nodded and held up three fingers, then signed back, *Go, hurry!*

He followed them up the street to the alley where Rieser waited for them with the horses.

"Success?" asked Micum, also noting the bag.

"Yes. Ulan saw me and it probably won't be long before we have company."

"We should leave the horses and steal more when we can," said Rieser. "That is what I would do. Horses will be too loud and noticeable this time of the night."

"So they will," said Seregil, heading for the narrow passageway at the far end of the alley.

When the door opened again so soon Ulan thought perhaps the young Bôkthersan had come back to kill him after all. But it was Ilar, holding a night lamp from the hallway. His face was ashen, and a sizable bruise was darkening along his jaw.

"Oh Aura! Khirnari! Forgive me!" Hurrying to the bed, he removed the gag and began to pull at the cords that bound Ulan's hands.

"He overpowered you, too?"

"Yes." Ilar was concentrating on the rope binding Ulan's ankles.

Captain Urien burst in with several of his men. "Khirnari! By the Light, I've failed you!"

"Indeed you have, Captain," Ulan said with a sigh as Ilar helped him sit up. "Thieves have broken in and stolen three of my rarest and most valuable books. Large ones—you won't mistake them. Rouse our Plenimaran hounds and send four of them to the harbor and the gates with word that they are looking for the same red-haired northerner and his three slaves. It seems they've followed me to the city. As soon as you have word back, go after them as quickly as you can. Take all your men. I must have those books back, and the blue-eyed slave. I want that one alive!"

Urien hurried out with his men, already shouting orders.

Ilar stayed behind, fidgeting with the hem of one sleeve as he hesitated by the door. He was trembling.

Ulan fixed him with his sharp gaze. "Tell me, Ilar. How did Seregil know where the books were?"

The younger man fell to his knees, covering his face with his hands, and remained like that in damning silence.

"I see. Very well, then. You will go with Urien to make certain of the books. I wouldn't put it past Seregil to substitute false ones and hide the others."

Ilar looked up with mingled anguish and gratitude. "I will, Khirnari. Can you ever forgive my weakness?"

Ulan regarded him a moment longer, until the man began to wilt again. "Come back with the books, Ilar, or don't come back at all."

Their days of reconnoitering had not been in vain. Seregil led the way through the dark streets, moving steadily in the direction of the waterfront.

But it was well guarded at night, and there were no small boats moored in close enough to steal. Guards of one sort or another were posted on every quay.

Seregil, Alec, and Rieser tied on their veils and put up their hoods in the shadow of a chandler's shop.

"We could book honest passage," Rieser suggested.

"Always a last resort, but I suppose we could try," Seregil said.

"You three stay here," said Micum. "I'll go see what I can find."

The others watched from their hiding spot as Micum spoke to the guard on one jetty, and then another. He was heading for the third when a mounted man suddenly clattered into view, holding up a lantern.

"Oy, you lot!" he cried out, voice echoing down the waterfront. "I'm looking for four fugitives—a big northerner and three slaves. They're thieves and there's a good bounty on their heads." He wasn't 'faie, but the spy who'd followed them that first day in Riga hadn't been, either. Ulan's money had bought him a few Plenimarans, it seemed.

"Shit!" Seregil muttered. "Well, that's the end of that."

"And now Micum's been seen!" whispered Alec.

If Micum had run for it then, or even turned from his task, it would probably have raised suspicions, but he coolly continued on his way, and Seregil saw money change hands on the fifth jetty. Micum waved to the guards and walked calmly back into the maze of streets at the head of the harbor.

Seregil saw Rieser shake his head and guessed he was more impressed than he'd willingly let on. What they'd just witnessed took a level head and steady nerves that few possessed—traits that made Micum a fine Watcher.

Seregil and the others remained where they were, and Micum soon appeared from the shadows behind them.

"What did you tell them?" asked Alec.

"That I would be back at dawn with my wife and children. The fare wasn't cheap but it's bought us some time."

Ghosting away, they made for the south gate, hoping word of them hadn't spread that far.

It hadn't. Micum showed their documents, and the other three submitted to the inspection of their collars and brands.

It wasn't until one of the guards turned to him that Seregil registered the weight of the tool roll and dagger against his belly under his shirt. Making a show of fumbling with the strings of his bundle and the bag holding the books, he got the knife free and hid it under the bags as he set them down beside Micum. The bored guard glanced at the marks on his arm and leg, matching them against those on the document, then waved them on. Seregil gathered the bags, using his cloak to mask his movements as he tried to kick the knife out of sight between two nearby barrels stacked against a wall, but it had landed point-out and he nearly skewered his foot. One of the curved guards caught between the barrels, leaving most of the thing in plain sight.

"Come on, you!" Micum ordered roughly, cuffing Seregil on the ear. Seregil scuttled quickly under his arm to join the others on the far side of the gate. They were out, free and—

"Hold on there!" one of the guards called after them. "You, trader."

Micum shot Seregil a tense look, then settled his features into a look of mild impatience as he turned back. "Yes, what is it?"

The guard waved them back, and Seregil's heart sank as the man held out the knife. "Is this yours?"

"It is!" Micum exclaimed without missing a beat as he felt at his belt in surprise. "Sakor's Flame!"

The guard glanced back at his companions. "Told you the slave was up to something." Then, to Micum, "You were too hasty with your dog, there. He was trying to fetch it for you."

Micum looked at Seregil. "Is that so?"

Seregil bowed his head and nodded mutely.

Micum patted his head roughly, as if he were a dog, then pushed him off toward the others again. "Thank you, Sergeant. That was a gift from my late wife. I'd have been sorry to lose it."

"Glad to help, trader. Good journey to you! Take care on the road. Say, where are you headed at this early hour?"

Can't you just let us go? Seregil thought furiously.

"Oh, I've got a friend up the road with a warm bed waiting. I meant to be off earlier, but luck was with me at a gaming table," Micum told him with a chuckle. He threw back his cloak, showing off his sword and Alec's bow. "And I fear no man on the road, or off it."

The guard grinned and waved him on. "Good luck to you then."

The four of them walked on in silence for some time, until Rieser finally broke the silence. "You are an accomplished liar, Micum Cavish."

Micum grinned. "Many thanks."

There was no time for complacency, though, knowing that word of them was likely to spread fast, given the bounty. They walked on, passing by houses and hamlets, and then farmsteads. It was dangerously close to dawn now; the houses were dark, but farm householders were notoriously early risers. Coming across one at last with horses in a corral, Seregil went in first to deal with the dogs; then they helped themselves. As they were leading them away, however, a man suddenly shouted behind them and they heard the sound of several people running in their direction. As one they sprang onto their horses' backs, grabbed them by the manes, and kicked them into a gallop down the road, followed by cries of "Thief!" And, before too much longer, the sound of more horses galloping after them.

"It's going to be a damn poor end to this journey if we end up hanged for horse thieves," Micum shouted to the others.

"Rhal should be back," Alec noted. "If we can just get there—"

If. Seregil tried not to think about what that turnip farmer had told them.

Suddenly he heard a horse scream and looked back over his shoulder just in time to see Rieser's horse throw him and stagger off on a broken leg.

Alec happened to be the hindmost and saw Rieser's horse step in the rabbit hole and founder. Rieser was on his feet already. Reining in, Alec gave the man a hand up. Rieser took it and sprang up behind him, then grasped the back of Alec's shirt as he galloped off after the others. Not a word of thanks, of course.

Micum was in the lead now, and Alec leaned over his mount's neck, urging it on to catch up. Seregil was looking back, gesturing for him to hurry. Alec checked back over his shoulder and saw the farmer and his men gaining on his more heavily laden horse.

"Oh, Illior, give this horse wings," he muttered, then started as he saw the foremost rider fall, then another. Micum had stopped and was shooting, his eye as sharp and his hand steady as Alec's. One by one, he picked off the lead riders until the rest turned tail and rode back the way they'd come.

Alec let out a triumphant whoop and urged his horse on to reach the others as Rieser clung on behind. "It's about time someone used that bow!" he called out with a laugh.

Micum slung it over his shoulder and took stock of the arrows left in the quiver as he rode. "Less than a score now."

"Well lost, though," said Alec. "I didn't much fancy getting hung from the nearest tree, or having my guts torn out back in the city."

"But there's some more people who've had sight of us," Seregil pointed out, not happy about that. As escapes went, this one was a mess. "We've got to get off the highroad. We might as well wear signs on our backs, otherwise."

They left the road and continued cross-country toward the sea, riding more carefully for the horses' sakes and eating the cheese and dry sausage Micum had thought to bring with him last night, knowing the rest might not have a chance to go back for their packs.

The sun was well up when they struck a track that ran close along the shoreline.

"This must be the other end of the fork we saw when we came in," said Micum.

"A way less traveled by the look of it," said Seregil. "What do you say?"

They took it, and found themselves on a winding track that followed the crenellated coastline. They passed one small fishing hamlet and a few lonely houses, but soon the dry, open countryside was deserted, sloping ever down to the rugged sea ledges where the glass-green waves came crashing in with great gouts of white spume. Gulls cried overhead and ospreys soared above, while sea ducks bobbed out beyond the breakers. Tiny yellow and white flowers blossomed along the ledges, and clumps of sea lavender, cling-

ing to what soil there was. The air was sweet with their perfume yet left the taste of salt on Alec's lips. But for the lack
of forests, it was hauntingly similar to the stretch of
Plenimaran coastline where Duke Mardus had brought Alec.

As they spelled their horses at a freshet by the roadside at
midday, Alec noticed that Micum dismounted a bit awkwardly and stood clutching the horse's mane a moment. Alec
had noticed signs of his leg paining him when they'd stopped
earlier, too. Riding without a saddle or stirrups put a strain
on anyone's legs. When Micum led his horse to drink, he
was limping noticeably, but he didn't say anything, so neither did anyone else.

Rieser walked over to Seregil and held out his hand. "I
want to see the books." Seregil unshouldered the bag and
undid the strings. Three large leather-bound books slid out.
Seregil, Micum, and Alec each took one. Seregil's shirt hung
awry and Alec saw an angry red line where the string had
rubbed Seregil's skin raw during their ride.

The slimmest of them was bound in worn brown leather
and stamped with faded gold. It was written in Plenimaran,
but Seregil and Micum could make it out. Seregil paged
through it to a picture of what looked like a winged naked
being, sexless like Sebrahn. "It talks of various elixirs you
can make with different sorts of blood, including rhekaro,
but I don't see any recipes."

"That's probably in this one," said Alec, holding up the
largest, bound in red leather, with a whole page filled with
drawings of winged rhekaros. "This is the book I saw."

Rieser leaned over Alec's shoulder and traced a line of text
with one grimy finger, not quite touching the page. "So this
holds the means of the making?"

"So does this one," Micum said, holding up the third, to
show them another engraving of a rhekaro. "Where were
they? How did you find them?"

Seregil looked up at him and sighed. "Ilar. Again."

"Him?" Alec felt a sinking feeling in his belly. "How did
he turn up here?"

"I don't know. He's under Ulan's protection now, but he
betrayed him to help me."

"Why would he do that?" asked Rieser. He might know nothing of Ilar, but betraying a khirnari was a serious matter.

Seregil and Alec both ignored the question.

Instead, Alec raised a skeptical eyebrow. "He told you, and then just let you go?"

"I told him he could come with me. He told me where the books were. I knocked him out and left him to explain himself to Ulan."

"He'll just lie his way out of it."

"Probably. But he's not our problem now."

Alec turned his book to show them elaborate engravings of alchemical equipment in various arrangements—flasks, athanors, crucibles, and the like. "I recognize some of these. I saw them being used in Yhakobin's workshop."

"It will be useful to someone," said Seregil.

"No, it will not!" Rieser snapped. "I am taking those back to my people, and no one will use them."

"We only have your word for that, don't we?" said Seregil. "I have a better idea. Micum, lend me your knife."

Taking it, he opened the brown book halfway through and sawed through the binding, splitting it into two parts. "You can have your pick of which half you want, Rieser, but you can't have it all. I get to pick the next one, and Alec the third."

Rieser watched in silence as he cut the others, then sighed. "I suppose it's as good a solution as any."

"Why not just throw them into the sea?" asked Micum.

"Because things like these have a way of surviving," Seregil told him. "Let's try something."

He gathered enough twigs and dry plants to start a small fire. When it caught, he held the corner of one page to the flame. It didn't catch fire. None of the books would. "As I expected, you don't keep such important information in an ordinary book." He put them back in the bag. "Half of these are yours. We won't fight you for them. But you know what we want in return."

Rieser gave them no reply, just walked off down the ledges.

"That was your best solution?" Micum whispered.

"It's better than fighting over them, assuming that the other Ebrados agree," said Alec.

Seregil gave them both a crooked grin. "I may not be able to read the code, but I can tell where one chapter ends and another begins. I wouldn't say I cut each one exactly in half, and I made sure we got what looked like the best parts. They may not be enough to tell us the whole story—"

"Assuming you figure out the code," said Micum.

"How many times have you seen me fail at that sort of thing?"

"Not often," Micum admitted.

"And if you can't, then perhaps Thero can," said Alec. "He's handy at that sort of thing."

"He should be," said Seregil, giving him a wink. "We had the same teacher. Let's go."

"Wait." Alec cut a piece from his saddle blanket, folded it into a sort of pad, and put it between the bag's strings and Seregil's shoulder.

"Thanks, talí," Seregil murmured.

CHAPTER 30

The Cottage by the Sea

BY LATE AFTERNOON they'd struck the highroad and Alec's belly was complaining loudly again.

Micum pointed forward to a familiar headland as they stopped by a spring. "I believe the cove is just beyond there." It was no more than a mile on.

"Good." Seregil yawned widely.

"Don't start that," said Micum, then succumbed to one of his own. "We don't have that much farther to go."

"I just hope Rhal is actually—" Suddenly Seregil went very still, head cocked slightly. "Do you hear that?"

The soft breeze carried the distant sound of riders—more than a few and coming on at a gallop.

"They couldn't have tracked us through the city," said Rieser. "Someone must have seen us at the gate. Micum Cavish is a hard man to mistake in this land."

"Too true," said Seregil. "Rieser, you ride with me for now, and give Alec's horse a rest."

Alec went to Micum's horse and laced his fingers into a stirrup. Micum's limp was more pronounced now, and a stiff leg could mean a bad fall.

Micum set his foot there and Alec boosted him up onto his horse's back.

"Can you ride hard?" Alec whispered to him, not wanting the others to hear.

"Of course I can," Micum scoffed softly, but his smile was tight.

Seregil mounted his own sweating horse. The Hâzad

jumped lightly up behind him and gripped the back of Seregil's shirt.

"We don't know for certain it's them," Alec pointed out as they forced their tired horses into a last gallop. "It could be the man we stole the horses from."

"It could be slave takers," said Micum.

"I'd rather not wait around to see!" Seregil replied, taking the lead.

Whoever it was, they couldn't be too far behind if Alec could hear them over the surf. Sure enough, when he looked back over his shoulder, he caught the glint of afternoon light on metal. "Damn!" Whoever it was behind them, their horses must be fresher, for they were steadily gaining. There were too many to be the horse breeder and his men, unless he'd raised the countryside against them.

"They're gaining!" shouted Micum, though it hardly needed pointing out.

Their pursuers were close enough now that Alec could make out the pale ovals of faces, but not features yet. Still out of bowshot, hopefully. He didn't fancy getting shot in the back again. Or anywhere else, for that matter.

And still the riders gained on them.

"We're not going to make the cove!" Micum shouted.

"No, but we can make it there." Seregil pointed to a nearby cottage above the ledges, one of the abandoned ones they'd passed when they'd first arrived here.

It wasn't the best of redoubts. The roof thatching was rotting away on one end, and several shutters were hanging on by a hinge. The remains of a fishing net hung sun-rotted over a drying frame. But there was nothing better in sight.

"Rieser, take the horses around to the back and tie them up somehow," Seregil ordered.

The door was blocked on the inside, but Seregil and Alec climbed in through one of the windows that flanked it and lifted the warped bar from the rusty staples. A table still stood at the center of the room, and there was one broken bench and an overturned sideboard. A rotting pallet lay in one corner close to the stone chimney.

They let the others in and barred the door again, then set

about using the broken furniture to block the windows with broken shutters as best they could. The shutters still on their hinges were warped by the salt air and wouldn't withstand much of an assault, but they'd be enough to shield them from archers, if it came to that.

"Look what I found," said Rieser, brandishing a rusty axe.

"Good man!" exclaimed Micum.

Rieser nearly smiled.

Seregil looked around, taking stock. "So, one bow—"

Alec settled the quiver strap over his shoulder.

"I hope you're as good as he says you are," Rieser told him.

"He is," said Seregil. Micum had one of the front windows half open now. "How many, Micum?"

"I'd say twenty at least."

"Closer to twenty-five," said Rieser.

"Damn, I don't like those odds, not the way we're armed," Seregil said.

"What about this ship you keep talking about?" asked Rieser. "Can't one of us go for help?"

Seregil exchanged a look with the others. "It's not that far. Half an hour round trip, at most."

"Longer, getting out to the ship to gather the men and get them organized," Micum pointed out.

"You're the fastest runner, Seregil," said Alec. "And the least likely to be seen."

He was right, of course, and there was no time to quibble.

"Give me the knife," said Seregil.

Micum handed it to him. "No lollygagging, you."

"Luck in the shadows," added Alec.

"And to the rest of you." Seregil gave him a quick kiss and ducked out the back window.

Seregil could have taken one of the horses, but that would have called too much attention, and at this distance he couldn't outrun the riders. He could hear them more clearly now, and could tell by their shouts that they were making for the cottage. Crouching as low as he could, he kept the house between them until he reached a shallow gully that took him toward the headland and down over the lip of a rise. Out of sight of the cottage at last, he fixed his eye on the distant beach and ran for all their lives.

As he rounded the base of the small headland, however, he found the cove aglow with late-afternoon light, and quite empty.

"No!" He sank to his knees in the dry bladder wrack at the tide line and stared incredulously out across the empty water. Had they gotten the day wrong? Worse yet, had something happened to the *Lady*?

"Lord Seregil?" One of Rhal's crewmen—Quentis, Seregil thought—emerged from a patch of bushes, brushing twigs and dead leaves from his jerkin. "Where's the rest of 'em? The captain set me to watch for you—"

"Where's the *ship*?" Seregil gasped, pushing himself to his feet and noting that Quentis was wearing a sword.

"It's the tide, my lord." The man hooked a thumb at the water, and Seregil cursed himself for a fool. The tide was out. "It'll be another hour before there's draft enough to float the *Lady* through the shoals."

"An hour? We don't have an hour!" The sun was sinking toward the western horizon. Squinting into the glare, he looked for some sign of the ship, but there was none that he could see. "Bilairy's Balls, man, the others are trapped. Besieged!"

"What are we going to do, my lord?"

Seregil walked down to the waterline and washed the dust from his face and neck, trying to collect his thoughts. Quentis appeared at his elbow with a waterskin. Seregil rinsed his mouth, then took a sparing sip and slung the skin over his shoulder; you couldn't run on a bellyful. "Do you have a boat?"

"Yes, hidden over there."

"Good. I need your sword." He glanced down at the smooth, egg-shaped rocks he was kneeling on. "And your shirt."

"I'm coming with you!"

"No, you're going to row out and signal the ship any way you can. You saw the direction I came from? If we don't come back, have Rhal send a force up the road to a little cottage over that rise, on the seaward side of the road. He can make up his mind what needs to be done once he gets there."

Quentis watched unhappily as Seregil buckled on the sword. "What are you going to do, my lord?"

"Whatever I can."

"How many do you make it now?" Alec asked, leaning against the barred door.

"Closer to thirty, and there are archers among them," said Micum, peering out. Their pursuers had reined in on the road. Some dismounted and came running forward with swords drawn. They made easy targets.

"All right, then." Alec threw open one shutter at the other window and set an arrow to his bowstring. He took down three before the rest retreated, and two more still on horseback. A moment later, an arrow sang past his cheek and embedded itself in the wall behind him. Others followed, and Alec stepped back into cover. Picking up a fallen shaft, he looked at it closely.

"What do you make of it?" Micum asked.

"'Faie made, I'd say. That's a relief of sorts," Alec replied. "If we are captured, I'd rather it be by Ulan." The head was chipped, but he sent it speeding back the way it had come anyway. His range was longer than they'd guessed. Another man fell. "That's six, but not a kill."

Micum grinned over at Rieser. "How does it feel, fighting beside a Tírfaie?"

Reiser hardly spared him a glance. "Necessary. They're flanking us."

He was probably right. There were more missing out there than Micum could account for by the dead. The archers were apparently well supplied, for they continued for quite a while. Alec finished the last of his arrows and those he could salvage, then slammed the shutter closed and barred it again. In the midst of it all they heard a commotion in back of the house.

"There go the horses," said Micum, checking through the shutters.

"Now what?" Rieser asked.

"Attack or parley, I expect," said Micum.

"Yes, here comes a man holding up a white scarf," Alec told them. "It's a parley."

A moment later a man called out to them, "You in the house. We outnumber you and have no desire to kill you. Surrender now."

"Who are you and why should we?" Micum called back.

"My name is Urien, captain of Ulan í Sathil's personal guard. I speak for Ulan í Sathil of Virésse."

"What does this Ulan fellow want with us?" Micum drawled back, stalling for time, trying to estimate if Seregil could possibly be on the way back yet. Most likely not. "We're just humble travelers making our way, until you lot put Bilairy's wind up our ass."

"If that is so, then you should have no fear of showing yourselves."

"No fear?" Micum scoffed. "With more arrows around us than sprills on a hedgehog's back? Oh, no! You'll kill us first and make certain of us afterward."

"If you are innocent, then why did you run?"

"Where I'm from, the only men who ride around in gangs are bandits and soldiers, and they can both be trouble to travelers. As you have only just proven, I might add. It's an outrage! And what, may I ask are Aurënfaie doing gadding about the Plenimaran countryside?"

"That's no concern of yours, if you are what you say you are," Urien retorted, sounding a little amused now. "You have some things that belong to the khirnari and he wants them back. Three books and a boy with blue eyes. Give those over and you're free to go."

"Books!" Micum feigned disbelief. "Who in their right mind busts into the house of a—what do you call it—Keer-nair-ey, and steals *books*? Don't tell me you mistook us for scholars, too? And boys?"

Darkness was falling and torches were being lit.

"Send out Seregil the Bôkthersan!" a different, slightly higher voice called out.

"No one here by that name," Micum called back. "Really, this is getting damned tiresome."

"I know that voice," Alec whispered, looking out through the shutters to be sure. "That's Ilar!"

"The traitor who fancies your lover?" asked Rieser.

Alec turned to him with a shocked, slightly chagrined look.

Rieser shrugged. "You think I haven't been paying attention?"

Micum took a peek himself, wanting a look at this mysterious man from Seregil's past. He didn't look like much—a thin, trembling man with a coward's eyes. "Well then, Captain, since you don't believe me, and I don't believe you, I'd say we're at a bit of an impasse."

Meanwhile, Rieser and Alec made the rounds of the room, peering out through the shutters.

"Well?" Micum whispered.

"We are surrounded," said Rieser, "but they're thinly spread, unless there are others still out of sight."

He was proven right in less than a breath. The shutters of the single window in the wall to their right cracked and groaned on their hinges and several swordsmen leapt in. Throwing the bench aside, they lunged at Micum and Alec. Micum had the sword at hand, so Alec grabbed the rusty axe. Unarmed, Rieser kept behind them, awaiting his chance.

The house was a small one and didn't leave a lot of room for swinging weapons around. Aware that more men were in the process of kicking the door in, Micum caught his opponent's blade with his hilt and lashed out with his left fist, hitting him squarely in the face. The man dropped his sword as he fell to the floor. Rieser darted forward and grabbed it as Micum jumped over the fallen man and took on another who'd come in through the window, ending up back-to-back with Alec. He could hear the crack of splitting wood as the brackets holding the bar across the door began to give way.

Seregil heard the sound of fighting before he was in sight of the cottage. At least it wasn't over, which meant his friends weren't captured yet, or dead.

It was easier to approach than it had been to leave, now

that it was dark. Or mostly so; Ulan's men—he knew them by their tack and coats—had very helpfully lit a few torches, making it a simple enough matter to knock down four men from a distance with the lovely rounded beach stones he'd collected in Quentis's shirt. Several of the men were Plenimarans—Ulan's hired dogs were relatively loyal, it seemed. He wondered which one of the bastards had been the one to spot them leaving by the city gate. Seregil sincerely hoped he'd brained him.

He slipped away in the shadows before anyone could tell where the stones had come from, dashing around to the other side of the house where he found half a dozen men all trying to get in through the same window. There was no sound of his friends inside except the clang and thud of a fight.

"I think they have enough people in there. Why don't we stay out here in the fresh night air?" Seregil called to the men, drawing the sailor's sword. They turned on him like a pack of wolves. Seregil could see chain mail glittering at the necks of their tunics. In a fight like this, you struck to break bones, not cut flesh.

"Micum! Alec!" Seregil shouted as he held off two swordsmen at once. "Rieser!"

"All here!" Micum shouted back.

Two men went down with broken pates, and a third with a shattered arm. The other two rushed Seregil at once, trying to bowl him over. He ducked, throwing one over his back, and vaulted in through the open window.

With his help, they managed to clear the last of Ulan's men from the room and prop the broken door back into place.

"About time you got here!" said Micum. He sounded winded.

"Did you find it?" asked Rieser, not sounding the least bit tired.

"Fight now. Talk later," Seregil gasped, locking blades with another swordsman who'd come through the open window. Alec took on a second man who'd come in at the far end of the room, bringing him down with a blow to the head with the hilt of his sword.

He doesn't want to kill them, either, thought Seregil, swinging his left fist at an unwary swordsman. He misjudged, striking him in the forehead instead of the nose, and felt the long bone in his middle finger snap. The pain gave him strength and he surged forward, taking another man in the face with his sword hilt and kicking him backwards out the window. Micum and Rieser tossed out the last three stragglers and slammed and barred the shutters. Alec wedged the table up against the door.

Thoroughly winded, Seregil took a drink from the waterskin he'd brought and handed it around. He wouldn't admit it, but he was exhausted, and he could see that the others were, too. "Rhal was delayed by the tide. He should be sailing in about now."

"If we run, they'll cut us down," Rieser whispered back, "but we've thinned them out. I count only eleven men left."

"Are you ready to stop this?" someone called.

Seregil went to the side of one of the front windows and looked cautiously out. A man with the look of a captain sat on horseback beside a hooded man. Almost a dozen men were still in front of the house, nearly all of them archers. As he watched, two more staggered out of the shadows, clutching their heads.

That's what I get for being merciful, Seregil thought— though he had rather assumed he'd killed them with his rock throwing.

Just then the mounted man next to Ulan pushed his hood back.

Seregil laughed. "Ilar! I didn't expect to see you again." Even from here he could see the dark, swollen bruise on his jaw.

Alec stepped in beside him, and for an instant Seregil was afraid he was going to charge out after him. Instead, he regarded the other man coldly. "You're worse than a stray cat at supper time. Always turning up when you're least wanted."

Seregil studied Ilar's face and the way he sat his horse. The library had been dark; now he had a better look at him, though, and it simply confirmed his impression. This was not the gloating man who'd made Seregil wash his feet and taunted him with fleeting glimpses of Alec during their captivity. Nor was this the same man who'd tried to seduce him once again during their escape. Even at this distance, Seregil could see fear in his face, and his stoop-shouldered, cringing posture. As their eyes met, however, he also saw the hunger in him. Ilar was Ulan's creature now; no doubt certain promises had been made, which almost certainly did not involve letting Alec or him go.

"Well now, where are we?" he asked, leaning on the window frame.

"Surrender, and I assure you, none of you will be killed," their leader replied.

"Those are your terms? Not very enticing."

"You're as foolish as your friends. Very well. The khirnari only wants Alec. You have his solemn word that he will be well treated. The rest of you can go."

"Even worse!"

Micum, who'd been standing just behind Seregil, disappeared for a moment.

"Well treated?" Alec laughed hoarsely. "Then he's either lying or he doesn't know what he's talking about. It's an abomination. How in Aura's name can you support this, Captain Urien?"

When Micum returned his face was dark with fury. "Rieser is gone, and so are the books. All of them."

Seregil kept his expression neutral and his attention on the captain.

"I was ordered to catch a thief and return what was stolen," Urien told him. "These are the terms I was given. Whatever my khirnari asks of me, I know it is for the sake of Virésse."

"Even if it means he becomes no better than a necromancer?"

"He's lying to confuse you!" Ilar told him angrily. "Remember your honor, Captain. And the khirnari said to bring Seregil, as well. He's one of the chief thieves. The others can be killed."

Just then they heard a low whistle from behind the house. Micum went to the window and looked out between the shutters. "Well I'll be damned," he whispered. "Rieser's back, and he's brought horses!"

"Captain, please grant me a few moments with my companions. They may take a bit of—convincing," Seregil said.

"Take all the time you like," Urien replied.

Seregil closed the shutters and went with the others to the back window. Outside two men lay on the ground, dead or senseless, and Rieser stood over them with four saddled horses and the bag of books slung from one of the pommels.

One by one they climbed out and took a horse, then began leading them away in the direction of the cove. They hadn't gotten more than a hundred feet, however, when someone shouted, "There they go! They're escaping!"

Seregil gave Micum a quick leg up onto his horse, then leapt into the saddle on his own and followed the others as they galloped for the cove, their starlight shadows coursing like pursuing dra'gorgos beneath them.

They had a head start and the element of surprise, but Urien and his remaining men were hard on their heels.

Rounding the headland for the second time that day, Seregil let out a victory cry at the sight of the ocean lapping at the high tide line and the *Green Lady* riding at anchor. Longboats were skimming in across the glassy surface of the cove, lanterns casting long spears of light toward the beach.

"Keep going!" Micum yelled as his horse lunged into the water.

Alec was close behind. "Look out! Archers!" he cried as he slid off his horse into the water, still clutching the pommel.

Seregil, for once in his life, was too slow. Something seared across his back like a hot whip, and then something heavy struck him in the side, knocking him off his horse into the water. His ankle caught in the stirrup and suddenly he was being dragged as the horse churned on, an arrow grinding between his ribs and water going up his nose. He won-

lered vaguely if he'd bleed to death or drown first. And odd-
est of all, someone was screaming something about him. It
was hard to tell if it was a man or a woman, with his head
bobbing in and out of the water, but they sounded hysterical.

Then a hand was gripping his arm so hard it hurt and
another was pulling his caught foot free of the stirrup.

"Hold on," Alec said against his ear. "The boats are coming. They're almost here."

Seregil coughed up salt water and gagged out, "Rieser—"
He had the books.

"Micum went back for him."

Back?

Arrows were still coming down in the water around them,
but now others were whizzing back the other way from the
boats.

Then rough hands and strong arms were hoisting them
both up into a boat, and the arrow was catching on everything until a ham-fisted sailor snapped it off and Seregil
allowed himself to scream just that once.

The voice calling his name was still carrying across the
water. "Seregil! Seregil, don't leave me here! Please! Come
back. Take me with you! You know what they'll do to me!"

Propped up against Alec's chest, Seregil saw Ilar pacing
back and forth at the water's edge, wringing his hands and
wailing. And that was the last thing Seregil remembered
before he fainted.

❧
The *Green Lady*

"THINGS went wrong, did they?" Rhal asked as Seregil and Rieser were lifted aboard the *Lady*.

"We ran into a bit of trouble," Alec told him, following close behind. "I hope your healer is a good one."

"He is." Turning to the crewmen gawking at them, he snapped, "Get these men below and find Konthus! Nettles, Skywake. Prepare to hoist anchor."

Rieser and Seregil were put to bed in their respective cabins as the ship got under way. Seregil was conscious now, but was having trouble breathing.

"Prop him on his good side," Micum advised.

Alec positioned several pillows behind Seregil's back to keep him lying on his unwounded side, then carefully began easing his wet, bloody shirt off. Seawater mixed with blood spread in a widening stain on the silk coverlet. In addition to the arrow in his side, Seregil had a thin, deep gash across his back where another arrow had clipped him, which would take sewing up. Seregil lay there, panting, but managed to push himself up enough for Alec to get the shirttail out from under him. Meanwhile, Micum rummaged through the clothes chest at the foot of the bunk and found a clean shirt. Alec pressed it around the remains of the arrow shaft to staunch what he could.

Seregil grimaced. "Missed my lung, but I think I have some cracked ribs." He held up his right hand, showing them his swollen middle finger. "This hurts like hell, too."

"You'll have plenty of time to heal up, my friend," Micum

said, patting his foot. "We're bound for home now, and well earned."

Presently a young man in a brown robe hurried in, the bronze serpent lemniscate of his profession swinging against his chest on its chain. "Lord Seregil, I'm honored—"

"Rieser first," said Micum. "He's hurt worse than Lord Seregil."

"Are you sure, my lord?"

"Go!" Seregil gritted out.

"I'll go sit with him," said Micum. He limped away after the healer, leaving the door open behind him.

Alec wrapped blankets around both of them and sat down on the edge of the bed. "How are you doing?" he asked, smoothing Seregil's wet, tangled hair back from his face.

Seregil grimaced, but it was mostly a smile. "Been better. Been worse. What happened to Rieser?"

"Shot in the chest. He saved our lives back there, not to mention the books. I have to admit, I thought he really had run off."

"So did I." Seregil closed his eyes, shivering. "It's a good thing for us he didn't. I wouldn't want to go back to the Ebrados without him."

"No. You're chilled." Alec got the rest of Seregil's wet things off him and got him under the covers, then found dry clothing for himself among the things they'd left on board.

Seregil was dozing when Micum and the healer returned.

"How is Rieser?" asked Alec as Konthus set to work looking Seregil over.

"Not well, I'm afraid," the young drysian replied. "The arrow struck under the left collarbone and went through to break his shoulder blade. It's a painful wound, and will be a slow one to heal."

"Konthus had to cut out the arrowhead, but Rieser never made a sound," Micum told them.

The arrow in Seregil's side had lodged between two ribs, breaking one but not penetrating to the lung. Seregil gritted his teeth as the drysian worked the arrowhead free and packed the wound with herbs and salved linen. When he was finished, he had Alec help Seregil onto his stomach and deftly sewed up the gash across his back with linen thread. He bandaged both wounds, then splinted the broken finger and said several healing spells over Seregil.

"That's all I can do for now," he said, washing his hands in the basin and going to the door.

"Thank you," Seregil murmured, relaxing as the magic took hold.

"Send one of your friends for me if you need help with the pain. Maker's mercy on you."

"Rieser wouldn't let the fellow magic him," Micum said when he was gone. "Wouldn't say why, but I suppose it was too Tír for his liking."

"No doubt." Seregil pulled weakly at the collar still around his neck. "This off. Now."

Micum drew his knife and carefully slid it under the edge of the collar at the flanges. Holding the collar steady, he sawed through the lead rivet and pulled the collar open far enough to slip it from Seregil's neck.

"A free man at last!" Seregil said with a hoarse laugh.

The metal had chafed a bit, Alec saw, leaving a band of reddened skin on Seregil's neck. It made him think of Ilar, who'd worn a collar so long the skin under it was worn white. They'd left him there in Plenimar without a collar, or any slave marks, but his scars would surely give him away.

You know what they'll do to me!

Alec knew. "Maybe we should have gone back for him," he muttered aloud.

"Ilar, you mean?" Seregil asked. "It would have been suicide. Why didn't he stay with Ulan? Or ride out after us?" He closed his eyes again, but not before Alec caught a fleeting look of regret. "I thought he'd be safe with Ulan."

"Perhaps he still will be," said Micum, but he sounded less than convinced.

Curious Allies

RIESER had left Nowen in charge. It should have been easy duty, watching Sebrahn and looking out for anyone traveling this way.

The last of the Tír magic had worn off; Sebrahn was as pale as Hâzadriën, with the same silver-white hair, neatly cut and braided now. She'd shaken her head over the ignorance of the ya'shel, to feed him every day. He was a beautiful little thing, but for the lack of wings, and seemingly devoted to Hâzadriën, as the older tayan'gil was to him. The two were inseparable. It was not uncommon for tayan'gils to flock together, but this one called Sebrahn was almost childlike in his manner. He climbed into Hâzadriën's lap whenever he sat down, and curled up next to him with his head in Hâzadriën's lap at night, saying "Sleeping," in his strange raspy voice. If anyone tried to make him leave the tayan'gil's side, he said, very distinctly, "No." It sent a shiver up Nowen's back every time he spoke.

Tayan'gils were—apart. Or they should be. Back home she seldom saw them, and when she did they were little more than a curiosity unless a healing was needed. The Hâzadriëlfaie valued them deeply for that ability, knowing the price. Every one of the creatures had been born of suffering and servitude, and no Hâzad liked being reminded of that. The fact that Sebrahn acted more like a real living being only made this more obvious.

But she had other, more troubling concerns right now.

"Did you see any of them?" she asked Rane and Sona, who'd just come back from a hunting expedition.

"Yes, and there are more today."

Day by day, the answer was the same. Nowen had never had any bad experience with the Retha'noi; they kept mostly to their peaks, and when they did descend to trade and barter, they were usually friendly and bothered no one. Turmay and Naba had been instrumental in their success so far, enlisting the aid of a local clan to fell those trees. But something had changed since Rieser left; Nowen was too experienced a tracker not to know when she was being tracked herself.

Naba had remained with them after the capture, and so had those he'd summoned. Now others were appearing on the heights. The smoke from their cooking fires rose against the sky by day, and the light of watch fires sparkled along the ridges through the night. Day and night they could hear the distant sounds of oo'lus; many oo'lus.

What could they possibly want? The Hâzad didn't carry more than they absolutely needed, which left little worth stealing, except for the horses, and these southern Retha'noi didn't seem to have any use for those.

Turmay came and went between the two camps freely and kept assuring her that they were in no danger, so long as they stayed down here by the waterfall.

"What do they want?" Nowen asked.

"They distrust outsiders and they want us to be gone. That's why they helped you, so that you would go away sooner."

"But they accept you."

"I am Retha'noi."

Turmay went to his southern brothers each night and played the oo'lu in the great circle while the witch women danced their magic around the fires. He made love to their women under the moon to put babies with northern blood into their bellies and shared his food and his healings with all who asked. Their two peoples might have been parted for more years than they could count, but the ways of hospitality still held strong.

The Mother spoke to them when they played and danced, repeating what she had told Turmay of the small tayan'gil and Alec Two Lives, of life and death and the immutable gate between the two.

Retha'noi had come from many miles away, answering the oo'lus' messages, and they came for their own reasons, as well. There were at nearly forty men now, and five of them witch men. They met around the fire and talked of the small tayan'gil and the man with two lives. Turmay listened and said little, but he taught them the song the Mother had given him.

Two days out from Plenimar there was no sign of pursuit, but Alec and Micum still walked the deck, looking back over the *Lady*'s wake. Ulan í Sathil could probably guess where they were headed, if he chose to pursue them. But the sea was empty again today.

Seregil was healing quickly enough to be restless, and they found him in Rieser's cabin, chatting with Konthus while the drysian tended to the Hâzad's wound. Rieser appeared to be tolerating both of them with an effort.

"I don't understand it," Konthus was saying. "This is infected, in spite of all my efforts. It must be from the shattered bone, or some bit of arrowhead left in the wound."

"I've suffered worse," Rieser told him. "Just do whatever you can, healer, and leave me in peace."

The drysian frowned but went about draining a little pus from the wound and packing it with fresh herbs and honey salve. "I'll give the cook the makings of a posset for the pain. That's all I can do for you, friend. And now for your you, Lord Seregil."

After a quick look at the splinted finger and Seregil's back, he set about unwrapping the bandages from Seregil's ribs and probed the wound hard enough to make Seregil hiss in pain. "This is healing well."

"I guess I just heal more quickly," Seregil gasped.

"You can thank the Maker for that. If the arrow had gone any deeper, you'd not be sitting here now." He wrapped fresh bandages tightly around Seregil's ribs to keep the bones stable, then placed his hands on Seregil's head and spoke a spell.

"Thank you, brother," Seregil said. "That's the best I've felt in days."

"I only wish I could do as much for your friend."

As soon as the drysian was gone, Rieser opened his eyes and rasped, "I want to see the books."

Alec went to his cabin and returned with them. He kept them wrapped in a cloak during the day, and spread out on the cabin floor at night to dry them. The pages were rippled and curling at the edges, and the writing in the halves of the red journal was smeared in places beyond recognition. The other two, the ones in code, were otherwise undamaged.

"You were right about not throwing them in the sea," Micum remarked, trying to smooth the pages of the brown book. "Who knows whose hands they might have washed up into."

"I haven't thanked you for saving these, and us, Rieser," Seregil told him. "But you have my gratitude. I'm in your debt."

"And me," said Alec.

"And I, and my family," added Micum with a half bow. "You'll always be welcome at my door."

Rieser looked up at him, face betraying little. "I'm told it was you who pulled me from the water after I was struck."

"That's right."

"Then we are even and there is no debt on either side."

Micum shook his head, grinning. "Well, you're welcome at my door anyway."

After a few days, Seregil's side still hurt badly enough by nightfall to keep him from lying down flat to sleep, but Rieser was in worse shape. His broken shoulder blade was a constant source of pain, and the arrow wound was still infected, the skin around it a swollen, angry red. Rhal's healer dressed their wounds several times a day and used his healing spells and potions, but they only slowed the infection spreading through Rieser's shoulder without curing it. The fever from it kept him in his bunk for the duration of the voyage. The others looked in on him through the day, though he didn't welcome their attentions.

"You've caught yourself a strange one there," Captain Rhal observed over supper one night. "Not a real friendly sort of fellow."

"Not really," Seregil agreed with a wry grin. "He's an interesting man, though, and a good fighter."

"What's going to happen when you get him back to his people?"

"We'll see, won't we? I'm prepared for a less than warm welcome, especially if Rieser dies on us before we get there."

"Sounds like you could use some help," said Rhal.

Seregil raised an eyebrow. "I was thinking the same thing. Could you spare me ten men? I'll do my best to get them back to you in one piece."

"Will ten be enough?"

"I think so. It will give us some protection without looking like we're declaring war. If it does take a bad turn, your crew are seasoned fighters."

"So are the Ebrados," said Alec.

"We don't know that," Seregil pointed out. "They used magic and trickery on us, not force."

Rhal scratched under his beard and thought a moment. "Well, I guess I'll come along with you. We've had some slack months and I don't want to get out of practice. Nettles, you'll be in command while I'm gone. Skywake, go ask for volunteers. And Dani isn't to be one of them."

"I'm going to enjoy having the odds more in our favor for a change," Alec said with a dangerous grin.

"Do they have any wizards we should watch out for?" asked Rhal.

"Rieser is the only one I know of, and he doesn't seem to have much power beyond simple transformations," said Seregil. "But there's a witch called Turmay who uses a long horn for his magic. If we can get that away from him, he may not be able to do any harm."

"Can he kill with it?"

"We don't know," Micum replied. "But he can put you to sleep better than a nursemaid's song, and that could be just as bad in the long run."

C H A P T E R   33

hard Choices

RHAL STOPPED at the same island to change sails. From here it was less than a week back to the waterfall encampment.

Alec hadn't slept much better than Seregil for the past few nights. In the dark, the thoughts that had been lurking at the edges of his mind since they'd burgled Yhakobin's workshop could not be kept at bay.

When they dropped anchor in the little cove, Alec turned to Seregil suddenly and said, "Are you up to a walk?"

"Yes."

"Let's go ashore. Just you and me, this time."

Alec was grateful that Seregil asked no questions as he rowed him ashore in one of the boats and put in at the same beach where the four of them had skipped stones together.

Alec was in no mood for that today. Taking the lead, he walked up the short beach and over the ledges beyond. Great flocks of grey-backed gulls rose with raucous screams of protest and circled stubbornly. Thick forest lay beyond, and as they made their way along a deer path that wended between the tall pines and oaks they found themselves stepping around stick rings of last year's gull nests, some still holding shards of speckled brown eggs in a bed of matted white down.

It wasn't curiosity or the pleasure of being off the ship that drove Alec deeper and deeper into the woods. The words he wanted to say were burning his heart, and once he began, there would be no taking them back. So he walked on, and Seregil followed in silence.

Birds chirped and sang overhead, and somewhere nearby an osprey was defending its territory with harsh cries. In the distance the gulls croaked and argued as they returned to their nests and ledges.

Alec had to remind himself to go slowly. Seregil didn't complain, but Alec caught him holding his side. Alec thought he'd pushed him too far when Seregil paused at the foot of an ancient oak and bent over, but it was only to pick something up. It was a long barred owl feather. He twirled it between his fingers, then presented it to Alec. "You have something on your mind, talí."

Alec took the feather and stared down at it. "I've been thinking about Sebrahn."

"I thought you might be."

This was more difficult than he'd feared. He sat down on a log and took a deep breath, owl feather clutched, forgotten, in one hand. His eyes stung and his throat felt tight as he said, "I think—I think you were right. We should let Rieser take him back to Ravensfell. He'll be safe there, and there are others like him and—" He fought back tears as Seregil sat down and put an arm around him. "If we keep him, he'll always be in danger. We'll always be looking over our shoulder for someone trying to take him."

"You're right, talí. I know you think I've been wanting to get rid of him—Oh hell, you know I have, but when the time comes, it's not going to be easy for me, either, if you can believe that. Whatever else he is, he's a part of you, and I owe him everything I have in the world for saving you. But it will be safer for him."

Alec took a shuddering breath as he struggled with what he had to say next. "Since we left him? I've missed him, but—well, we couldn't have done all we did with him there, could we?"

"No, talí."

"And that's what we're meant to do. When I met you and you brought me into your world, that's where I wanted to be. I still do."

"I'm glad." The emotion behind the words spoke volumes. "And once it's over and we're back in Rhíminee, I want to tay there. I want the Rhíminee Cat to hunt again, and visit our whores in the Street of Lights and play the nobles in Wheel Street and—"

"We will, talí," Seregil assured him, then laughed softly. "And I promise you, I'll never complain of boredom again!"

Alec managed a weak smile. "I doubt that."

They sat in silence for a little while with the sunlight treaming down through the branches all around them, listening to the sound of the birds and the breeze and the distant sigh of the ocean. Finally Alec stood up and said resolutely, "I'll tell Rieser when we get back to the ship."

Seregil gave him a sad smile. "I'm glad you came to it on our own, Alec. It had to be your decision."

Alec held up the bent feather. "Should we burn it?"

Seregil took it and tucked it behind Alec's left ear, then ouched the dragon bite there. "No, let's save it. A gift from he Lightbearer. I think Illior must be pleased enough with ou for now."

Alec's heart felt a little lighter, now that he'd voiced his decision. "I'm going to miss him," he said as they started back for the ship.

"I will, too. But who knows? Maybe he was meant to be with the Hâzad all along."

Alec mustered a shaky smile. "Are you talking fate again?"

"If I am, we'll never know what else might have happened. And I know what this means for you; I don't think the Hâzad are going to change their attitude toward uninvited guests in their valley. It's too bad, really, to come so close but not get to meet any of your mother's people."

"Why would I want to? I saw enough of them at Sarikali."

"You saw the ones who killed her. You don't know that hey're all like that."

"They're Hâzad. They wouldn't welcome a half-breed ike me."

"It doesn't matter. You're Bôkthersan now, and well loved here."

And I'll get a warmer welcome, next time, if I don't bring a threat with me, Alec thought. But right now that wasn't much comfort.

Aboard the ship again, Alec went straight to Rieser's cabin and found him awake.

"I have something to tell you," he said, standing just inside the door.

Rieser's eyes were dull with pain, but he lifted his head and beckoned him closer. "What is it?"

"I'll give you Sebrahn when we get back."

"Of course. But it's better that we aren't forced to take him from you, Alec Two Lives."

"But you would have, if I didn't give him up?"

Rieser closed his eyes. "What choice do I have? Can you get me some water, please?"

Alec filled the cup from a waterskin hanging on the wall and helped him drink. "I don't want to fight you, Rieser, but I'm not going to go with you."

"You could be with Sebrahn."

"Until someone sticks a knife in my back."

"I would present you to our khirnari. She's a wise woman and would see your worth, as I have come to. You and your companions could have killed me at any time, or abandoned me after I was wounded. You still could, but I don't think you will. You have great atui, all of you."

Alec's eyes widened at the unexpected compliment. "Even Micum?"

Rieser actually managed a strained smile. "Even Micum. If there were more Tír like him . . ."

"And me? I'm half Tír. I was raised among them. There *are* more like us, whether you want to believe that or not."

"But too many of the bad ones. Would you wish on any of my people what happened to you?"

"Of course not."

"Then believe me when I tell you that things are best left as they are. So far we have held our valley. If the Tír move north again, though? I think this time it will be war. Our valley is too precious to us."

Alec thought of the clan house at Bôkthersa, of the lake

nd the village and the people who lived there in peace and rosperity. "If it comes to that, you should fight. But then eople will know for certain where you are."

"We've grown in number since those early days. We could ake your town of Wolde with ease."

"I hope it never comes to that."

"So do I."

"But I'm still not going back with you."

Rieser sighed and would say nothing more.

As soon as the sails were changed, Rhal had the sailors oist all canvas and pounded on for Skala. Rhal either hared their concern over Rieser or was anxious to have him ff his ship; it was bad luck for a sick man to die on board. n the meantime Rhal's shore party made their preparations, rinding swords and cutlasses to a razor edge and checking he buckles of their cuirasses and chain. Chain mail shirts vere found for Seregil, Alec, and Micum, as well. This time ney were prepared to meet the Ebrados.

Nowen had stopped sending scouts into the hills behind he waterfall. Turmay had made it clear that it was an intru-ion into Retha'noi land and that the number of people up here had increased, though he could or would not say how nany, only that it was more than the number of Ebrados. All e would say was for them to stay out of the hills.

Owls hunted and hooted in the darkness close by. There vere so many here, for some reason. One little one had come lown and perched on Sebrahn's shoulder the other night. It ad even let him stroke its back and wings. When it flew way, he followed it with his eyes, then pointed after it and aid "aldrakin," whatever that meant. Some Tír word, probably.

She looked around the fire that night, listening to the owls unt and counting her people. Rane and Sona were on watch t the edge of the forest; the Retha'noi hadn't circled around here—yet. With Thiren dead and Rieser gone, that left only ight of them: Taegil, Morai, Relian, Sorengil, Kalien, Allia, nd Hâzadriën, who did not fight.

And there was Sebrahn. He'd used his song magic against

them once; would he do the same to the Retha'noi? She
doubted it, after the conversation she'd had with him that
afternoon.

Kneeling before him, she'd taken his hands and he did not
resist. He just stared up at her.

"Will you sing for us, if we need you?"

"Hurt?" he replied with no hint of expression.

"Hurt those who hurt us."

"Baaaaad."

"Yes, they are bad. Will you help us?"

"Help. No. Bad. Ahek no bad."

Whatever that meant, it didn't sound like a yes.

She scanned the heights, counting fires. There were six
visible, and she could see dark figures crossing the firelight.

*How many of you are there? How are we supposed to get
back through the mountains when the time comes?*

And then there was Turmay, who came and went between
the two camps, and seemed troubled. But he still would not
speak of what was going on. Nowen began to think of killing
him in his sleep. She wished Rieser were here to make such
a decision. The Ebrados did not take killing lightly.

Manab, an elder of Sky village, ran a hand down the
length of his oo'lu. "I say we kill them all now."

"No, we must wait until the ya'shel returns," Naba replied.
"And this book Turmay speaks of."

"What do we care for books?" Orab, chieftain of the Blue
Water Valley village, scoffed.

"They are powerful things, books. So Turmay says," Naba
told him. "This one tells how to make the abomination, and
the ya'shel with two lives carries the blood of abomination
in his veins. Turmay says to let the Retha'noi kill the ya'shel.
He says that the tayan'gil can kill, but only a few. Let it kill
them. Then we will strike."

"Turmay does not want any killing," the witch woman
Lhahana, reminded them. "They may be outsiders, but they
do not wish to stay, any more than we want them to. Why
spill blood on our soil unnecessarily? Do you want their
ghosts to take this sacred place? Bad enough that the low-

nders use our road. They do not come that often and they
o not stay. Ghosts will."

Naba nodded. "Better to see what the Hâzad people will
o. Turmay says they want the two lives dead, too. Let them
ke the wrath of his ghost."

And so the talk went on, into the night.

CHAPTER 34

❧

Mistrust

BY THE TIME the *Green Lady* made anchor at Beggar's Bridge, the flesh around Rieser's wound had turned dangerously dark and taken on a sickly sweet odor. Alec and Seregil sat with him while the drysian changed his dressings one last time before they went ashore.

Konthus shook his head. "You should be well healed by now, with all the broths and magic I've poured into you."

"You did the best you could, and I am thankful," Rieser replied, his cheeks pale except for the red fever patches. "At least I will live long enough to return to my people."

Konthus made a blessing over him and took his leave.

"I hope you do," murmured Seregil, wrinkling his nose at the foul odor of the wound.

"Just get me back to Hâzadriën."

"Or Sebrahn," said Alec.

"No, Hâzadriën!" Rieser gasped, and there was rare alarm in his voice.

"Why are you so scared of Sebrahn?"

Rieser stared up at the cabin ceiling for a moment before answering. "Because he's not a true tayan'gil. Please, honor my request. It could be my last."

"Suit yourself," Alec said.

They reached Ero Harbor in the morning, and readied to leave. The longboats were packed, and Rhal and his men were armed and ready. They took their leave on deck, shaking hands with Nettles.

"I'll expect the ship to be still afloat when I get back," Rhal said with a grin as he clapped the mate on the shoulder. "And provisioned. It's hunting season again."

"And I'll expect you to come back safe and sound, Captain."

I hope so, too, thought Seregil as he joined Alec and Micum in the longboat and helped lift Rieser onto a pallet spread in the bottom. He wasn't sure giving up Sebrahn would be enough to satisfy the Ebrados, and Rieser had refused to say one way or the other.

There was nothing Rieser could do about the sailors who were coming along. He hoped Turmay could handle that many people at once, if it came to a fight.

He held on in silent misery until they were rowed in, but collapsed as soon as they were ashore. He awoke in a clean bed in a sunny room with no idea how he'd gotten there. His shoulder burned like fire, and stank so bad it was making him even sicker.

"I think it's your Hâzad blood," said Seregil, the only other occupant of the room at the moment. He was sprawled in an armchair beside him, bare feet propped on the edge of the mattress.

"I think you may be right," he croaked. "These Tírfaie healers aren't much good to me. Are there any 'faie?" He was mortified to show such weakness in front of his companions, especially the Tír. It put him at their mercy, and that was something he'd never experienced before.

"They heal me well enough," Seregil told him. "But I'm not of your blood. Do you have healers among your people, or do you just depend on your tayan'gils?"

"Both. What the healers can't cure, the tayan'gils can."

"That must make you a very long-lived people."

"No more than you, I expect. We just don't die young as often."

The Bôkthersan was quiet for a moment. "It's a shame,

how they have to be made. In their way, the tayan'gils are a real gift."

"Our gift and our curse. It cut us off from your people long ago." He paused. "My ancestors were Bôkthersans." *Why am I telling him at all?* he wondered, even as he said it.

"So you said, soon after we met."

Did I? My mind is wandering. It must be the fever talking. It was far better to tell himself that than admit that he'd come to admire Seregil and his friends—even Micum Cavish. It was hard not to, when you'd fought for your very lives together.

He was beginning to doubt he'd live long enough to die among his own people.

Alec left Seregil to tend Rieser at the inn they'd taken for the night and went to the Sea Horse with Micum to see about the horses they'd boarded there. The stable hand had kept his word, or the fee they'd paid had been high enough. Either way, Patch and the others were sound and glossier than they'd been when they left. Seregil had offered to buy Rhal's men horses, but apart from their captain, none of them were horsemen.

Patch was glad to see Alec, and gave his belt a good nip before she nuzzled the apple from his pocket.

"There's a small cart out in back," Micum told him. "I don't think Rieser will make it any other way—What are you frowning about?"

"When we first met him, he'd have killed you without a second thought. I never expected to see you two friends."

"I wouldn't call us friends, exactly. But he's a brave man and a good fighter. I was glad to have him at my back when things got tight back at the cottage. What that will count for once we get him back to his people, though? I'm not going to assume too much."

"Did Seregil tell you what I decided about Sebrahn?"

"No, but judging by that long face, you've decided to give him up."

"Yes. So there's just the matter of whether they'll let me go. Rieser won't give me a straight answer about that, but maybe it's not completely up to him. It's a good thing Rhal and the others are coming with us."

Micum rubbed a hand over his short beard. "I've been wondering that myself. But I figure we'll have better luck if we show up with their leader alive."

Seregil had said the same.

The cart was cheaply got. Seregil put Star between the traces and saddled Cynril. The long rest aboard the *Lady* and the drysian's good care had him nearly mended, and he was able to ride without much discomfort.

They made Rieser as comfortable as they could with their packs and bedrolls, but every bump and jolt took its toll. Micum drove the cart and Alec and Seregil rode beside it, watchful for trouble. With Rhal and his men strung out behind them on foot, they made a respectable-looking force.

Rieser lay very still, his sunken eyes closed most of the time. As the day wore on he spoke less and less, and the fever spots in his pale cheeks spread in angry patches.

They made camp that night beside a stream, but Rieser wouldn't drink, not even the tinctures Konthus had sent with them to ease his pain. Seregil was sitting in the wagon with him late that night when the man woke with a start and grabbed his arm.

"Promise me—" he whispered through cracked lips.

"What?" asked Seregil, leaning down to hear.

"If I die—I had a dream. Don't let your tayan'gil bring me back if I die."

Seregil didn't bother arguing with him. There was a good chance the man wouldn't see another sunrise. "Why not?" he asked, curious.

"It's not—not meant to be that way. It's wrong."

"But why wouldn't you want to live if you could? Alec is no different than he was before."

Rieser stared up at him with fever bright eyes and rasped, "Honor this request. That's all I ask of you."

Seregil touched the man's hot hand. "You have my word, Rieser í Stellen."

He wasn't sure if Rieser heard him or not. Seregil sat with him for some time, pondering Rieser's words. He'd never questioned whether it was right or wrong to bring Alec back from Bilairy's gate. All he cared about was that Alec was still with him.

And let's not wonder if a tayan'gil's magic wears off, like Thero's did on Sebrahn.

Was there something more than simple superstition behind Rieser's request? He wondered if Rieser would tell him his dream. Of course, if the man died tonight, then he'd never know.

But Rieser did live through the night, though he remained unconscious as they set out for the Ebrados camp, rousing just often enough to take water to keep life in his body.

They approached the forest's edge late that afternoon and spotted masked riders. Instead of coming to greet them, however, they turned and disappeared up the trail to the waterfall.

Micum reined Star to a halt. "I guess they can count at a distance."

"Or they have a special welcome for us," Seregil said with a frown.

"We should ride ahead and explain," said Alec.

"Not you, Alec. Rhal, will you come with me?"

The captain drew his sword with a grin. "I'd be glad to."

"You'd better have Rieser with you," Micum advised.

"True. All right, you come with us. Alec, you and the rest stay well back from the trees for now. One of us will come back for you, or yell if we're in trouble."

Alec took an arrow from his quiver and set it to the string, resting the bow across the saddlebow. "We'll be ready, but I'll only wait an hour. It will be almost dark by then."

"Good. See you soon!" Seregil took the lead ahead of the wagon, with Rhal in the rear.

"I don't see any sign of archers," Micum said in a low voice, scanning the forest on either side as they entered the trees.

"It's the ones I don't see that I worry about."

No one challenged them until they reached the clearing at the waterfall.

Nowen and Sorengil came to meet them with swords

drawn. Behind them Rane, Relian, Morai, and Allia had bows at the ready, and Turmay stood by the fire, oo'lu in hand. The other four were missing. Seregil wondered how many other bows were aimed in his direction. There was an air of tension here that seemed out of proportion with the situation.

"Who are those men you brought with you, and where is Captain Rieser?" Nowen demanded.

"Those men are our bodyguard," Seregil replied. "We left them behind as a show of good faith, but I'd be happy to go and get them. As for Rieser, he's here in the wagon and needs your healer badly."

The archers he could see lowered their bows and followed Nowen to the side of the cart.

"Did they do this to you, Captain?" she asked, shocked.

"He's beyond hearing you," Seregil told her. "And if we had, we wouldn't be bringing him back to you, would we?"

Hâzadriën and Sebrahn climbed into the cart while the youngster named Rane fetched a bowl of water and a knife.

Seregil and Rhal dismounted and watched with the others as Hâzadriën drew his knife and slit his finger. He made half a dozen yellow lotus flowers and arranged them in a ring on Rieser's shoulder. Each one melted away in turn, and their sweet scent mixed with the rank odor of pus and proud flesh.

"By the Old Sailor!" Rhal exclaimed softly as he watched.

"But it's not enough," said Nowen.

Sebrahn reached for the knife, but before he could make his dark flowers, Seregil climbed in to stop him.

"No," he said firmly, holding Sebrahn by the wrist.

"What's this?" asked Nowen.

"Rieser told me he didn't want any of Sebrahn's healing. I gave my word. Let your tayan'gil go on."

Nowen motioned for Hâzadriën to continue. At last the flowers began to take effect. The infection began to fade from the flesh, and the wound opened and oozed bloody yellow pus.

"You're bringing those men here?" Nowen asked, still suspicious. "If you come in peace, then why do you need them?"

"They are my men," Rhal told her. "We're just here to ensure the safety of our friends. We mean you no harm."

"Is Alec with them?"

"Yes."

"Good. Go get your people and bring him with you."

Rhal exchanged a quick, questioning look with Seregil.

"It's time you went back." The sun was nearly touching the tops of the peak now, and long shadows were stretching across the clearing. Rhal mounted Windrunner and galloped off down the track.

A few moments later Rieser came to with a sudden gasp and stared up at Sebrahn crouched beside him with a mix of awe and horror. "Nowen! Was I—Was I dead?"

"No, but as good as," Seregil told him. "And don't worry. It was your tayan'gil who healed you. How do you feel?"

Rieser flexed his shoulder. More pus streamed from the wound. Rane handed him a cloth and Rieser pressed it to the wound with a grimace of disgust. "Better than I was, except for this mess."

Nowen felt his forehead. "The fever's gone down a bit."

Rieser smiled at Hâzadriën—the most genuine smile Seregil had ever seen on the man. "Thank you, old friend."

Hâzadriën just looked at him and twitched his shoulders slightly. Seregil could see the outline of the wings press out against the back of the rhekaro's tunic and wondered what kind of garment he normally wore.

"The small tayan'gil has great power," Turmay replied, "but Seregil would not let the little one touch you. Why not, if it can heal, too?"

"I prefer the tayan'gil who is my friend," Rieser told him. "Now let's see if I can hold myself up."

He climbed unsteadily from the back of the cart, then gripped it to stay on his feet.

"Good to have you back, Captain," Nowen said, helping him over to a log seat by the fire. It was clear he was in no condition to fight.

"How are things here?"

"Not good. Some Retha'noi are massing on the heights. I don't know how many, but more than we have, I'd say. They don't want us here and we won't get through without a fight. Kalien and the rest are on guard duty in the woods. That man Rhal has gone back for his men, and Alec. I hope I did right, letting him go?"

"You did. They only came to make certain of their friends' safety, which I have sworn to."

"Did you find the book?"

"We did, thanks to Seregil and Alec. Seregil, show them." Seregil pulled his share of the halved, salt-warped volumes from his pack.

"You have already tried to destroy them," Turmay said with evident approval.

"Not quite. We're splitting them," Seregil replied. "No one will have a complete book. We take half and the Ebrados take half and they'll never come together again."

"No, they must be burned!"

"They won't burn, thanks to the alchemist's magic. It's better this way," Seregil explained.

"Then cast them into some deep, dark place!"

"That's for our khirnari to say, Turmay. You know that," Rieser said.

"But the small tayan'gil? You will destroy it?" asked Turmay.

"No! That was never our intent. You know we honor tayan'gils."

"This is not like the others. You know what it can do. It's already killed one of your people."

"We're taking him back with us, to protect him, like the books," Rieser said firmly. "You've guided us well so far, but you have no say in this." He gestured at the heights where watch fires were burning. "What is the meaning of all this?"

"They don't like outsiders," Turmay replied, but Seregil caught the hint of untruth in his words, and the way he glanced around at the surrounding forest as he spoke.

"You've agreed to give up Sebrahn?" Nowen asked Seregil, evidently not noticing.

"It was Alec's decision," said Seregil. "It won't be easy for him, when the time comes, but Sebrahn will be yours."

"I see." Turmay was frowning now.

"There's one more thing, though," Seregil said, turning to Rieser. "You have the tayan'gil and the books, or parts of them anyway. In return, I need your word, on your honor, that Alec will be free to go."

Rieser hesitated, then nodded. "You have my word."

"Those were not our orders!" Nowen said.

"I am taking responsibility for that. I'd never have found the books without them. And they saved my life twice over. No, Alec will go his way in peace, and we will not hunt him again."

"What will you tell the khirnari?"

"Just what I have told you. It's a debt of honor and I take full responsibility. I have seen what these men are capable of. Alec will not be caught and used again."

Seregil looked around at the others, watching the different emotions play out there: doubt, anger, acceptance.

Meanwhile, Hâzadriën had made a few more flowers for Rieser's shoulder. Rieser waited until he was finished, then reached out and stroked Sebrahn's hair. "And this little one will be treated with honor and kindness."

"He's unnatural," said Turmay.

"Aura's white road runs in his veins, however mixed. He's not an abomination."

"That's for the khirnari to decide," Sorengil warned.

"No, it has been decided!" cried a voice above them.

The witch Naba stood above the waterfall with several other Retha'noi men, all with oo'lus poised to play. Behind him Retha'noi archers were taking aim, and two other witch men were there with their horns.

"This can't be good," muttered Micum.

"If any of you move, the archers will find you," Turmay warned. "Rieser í Stellen, you were sent to find this tayan'gil, and to destroy the ya'shel. I was sent to destroy both, and the Mother has given me the means and brought me to my brothers of the south."

"This is treachery!"

"Please, Rieser, you must listen to me," Turmay pleaded. "I have no desire to see Hâzad blood spilled."

"Then you have chosen the wrong friends!" Rieser growled.

At that moment the witches on the heights began to play. First Rane, and then Relian slumped to the ground, dead or unconscious; it was impossible to tell.

Micum fell to his knees. Seregil could feel the effects creeping over him as he knelt in front of Sebrahn and shouted, "Sing, damn it! Sing!"

And Sebrahn did.

Seregil carefully refrained from touching Sebrahn, but he still felt the rush of power strike through him, banishing the effects of the horns. A swirling wind blew up from nowhere at the center of the clearing, scattering gear and blowing the fire to pieces. Neither the Ebrados nor the Retha'noi fell, and Seregil guessed that the wind must be Sebrahn's magic colliding with that of the hill folk. He'd never seen anything like it, but the Retha'noi were still on their feet. Ducking a flying branch, he crawled over to Micum and felt for a pulse. He was alive, and woke when Seregil shook him.

The Retha'noi fell silent first, then Sebrahn. Seregil heard shouting on the heights, and a sudden scream from the trees behind them.

"They're flanking us," said Nowen.

"Aura's Light, that sounded like Kalien!" Morai exclaimed even as she took aim and let fly.

Nowen and several of the others who were still on their feet pushed the cart onto its side to shield them as the Retha'noi shouted what were probably war cries—he hoped to hell they weren't some new magic—and the Retha'noi archers shot back. Arrows thudded into the bottom of the cart and embedded themselves in the trees behind them.

"Will you be able to fight, if it comes to that?" Seregil asked Rieser.

The man shrugged. "I will do what I can."

Some of the Ebrados scrambled for their bows while Nowen and Sorengil chanced death to drag Rane and Relian to safety. They were nearly there when Relian was struck in the neck. Seregil and Micum ducked out and helped bring them in. Rieser quickly inspected Relian's wound and shook his head. Blood was pulsing out around the shaft and he was wheezing bloody foam. Sebrahn was with him in an instant, but there was no water for him to use.

Seregil pulled him away. "Leave him. There's nothing you can do for him right now."

"I wish Alec was here with his bow," said Micum, crouched beside Hâzadriën and Rieser, sword drawn.

"So do I," said Seregil.

Taegil burst from the woods at their back and ran for cover. "They're in the trees! I think they killed Kalien!"

"How many?" Rieser demanded.

"I don't know. At least a dozen." Taegil fell to his knees, gasping for breath. "We heard that awful noise, then suddenly they were there. We both ran but—"

"You have a bow," Rieser snapped. "Use it!"

Seregil looked up at the darkening sky. "Alec won't wait much longer."

It was only then that he realized that Sebrahn was gone.

Looking around frantically, he saw that the rhekaro had left the shelter of the cart and was making for the pool with the bowl Hâzadriën had dropped. Sebrahn filled it, but as he turned to come back, an arrow struck him in the side. He staggered, but kept going. Another struck him in the leg and this time he fell.

Seregil dashed out and grabbed him, pulling the rhekaro to safety. Ignoring his own wounds, Sebrahn immediately reached for the bowl and looked up at Seregil, the message plain. Seregil filled it from a fallen waterskin and helped him over to Relian. Sebrahn didn't have to cut a finger; using the white blood from his own wounds, he made a dark flower and pressed it to the wound in the dying man's neck.

"It's no use," Seregil told him, but Sebrahn made another, and another. His wounds were still bleeding, and Seregil saw that the rhekaro was taking on a shrunken look; his already thin arms were noticeably smaller.

He pulled Sebrahn away, and over to Rieser. "Sebrahn needs strong blood!"

The Hâzad cut his finger and stuck it in Sebrahn's mouth. The rhekaro latched on to his hand and sucked desperately.

Then the sound of the oo'lus began again. Dropping Rieser's hand, Sebrahn jumped to his feet and began to sing again.

"It's been too long," Alec said, watching as the sun sank toward the peaks in front of them.

"I don't like it, either," said Skywake. "We haven't heard a damn thing. I say we go find them."

Alec hobbled Patch and took up his bow. "Come on."

"Wait, I hear a horseman," said Skywake.

A moment later Rhal burst from the trees, an arrow bobbing from his horse's shoulder.

"The camp's under attack," he shouted. "I was on my way back for you all and suddenly someone was shooting at me!"

Just then they heard a distant droning.

"What is that?" Skywake exclaimed.

"Oo'lus. Lots of them," Alec began, then another piercing, unmistakable sound joined it. "And that's Sebrahn. Come on!"

"Don't run off alone," Rhal called after him. "Your man will never forgive me if I let you get yourself killed."

"Then you better hurry up!" Alec called back, sword in his right hand and his bow in the left.

Running in the lead, Alec was the first to see the body of a dark-haired man lying facedown in the road, two arrows in his back. The clothing wasn't Seregil's, but Alec still had to stop and roll him over, just to be certain. It was Kalien.

"We're deer in a meadow here," he told the others as they caught up. "Get into the trees. Rhal, you take that side of the road, I'll go left."

Five of the sailors followed Alec as he plunged through the shadowy wood. In a matter of minutes a small dark form leapt out at him with a long knife. Alec struck him down before he was in reach, and the one right behind him. There were more and suddenly he and his men were in the middle of a melee. From the shouts and ringing of steel nearby, Rhal had met with the same welcome.

They dispatched the men with knives, only to find themselves targeted by unseen archers. One of the sailors—it was too dark under the trees to be certain which one—was struck in the arm, and another fell.

"Keep going!" Alec shouted. They could hear more shouting from the direction of the waterfall, and now he could smell wood smoke.

Illior must have been still pleased with him; Alec reached the edge of the clearing without losing anyone else. A few trees on the far edge of the clearing were in flames, making it easier to see in the gathering gloom.

The droning started again, and Sebrahn's answering song rose to mingle with it. Alec gritted his teeth against the sound, watching a violent wind whip up near the waterfall.

Rieser and some of the Ebrados were just in front of him, hunkered down behind the overturned cart. A few others were in the woods, shooting at the enemy on the high ground above the falls. Micum and Seregil were in the act of chasing after Sebrahn, who stood in the open, singing.

There were a lot of men up there, and some of them had oo'lus, but they had gone silent when Sebrahn began to sing. "We're here!" Alec shouted to Seregil, then sheathed his bloody sword and raised his bow, aiming for the witches.

He struck two of the five in quick succession before the others ducked from sight, then turned his attention to the armed men streaming down through the trees in their direction.

"Over here!" Alec called over to the others as he took aim at the Retha'noi.

"How many?" asked Micum.

"Two score or more, but that's what I see."

There were short arrows scattered everywhere, and the cart looked like a tailor's pin pillow, but the archers had stopped. They were probably among those coming down after them.

Then the remaining witches began to play again and Sebrahn answered them with a new, even more earsplitting note.

Alec staggered toward him, then fell to his knees as the combined sound of Sebrahn and the horns threatened to overwhelm his senses.

They are going to kill us all, thought Alec. His head felt like it was going to explode and his vision went red. The mingled sounds of the oo'lus and Sebrahn's song were unbearable, and a sudden wind knocked him flat on his back, making it impossible to get to Sebrahn, who was exposed now, standing beside the cart, pale hair whipping wildly around his head.

Just when he thought he would die or go mad, the air was suddenly filled with the sound of wings. Looking up, he saw owls—hundreds of them—some swirling overhead while others dove toward the Retha'noi.

Sebrahn is calling them! His "owl dragons." Illior's sign. If only there were real dragons in this part of the world!

But the huge flock descending on the men on the heights might equal a dragon; the oo'lu song faltered and stopped and there were cries of pain and dismay from the forest to their left, some dangerously close.

Sebrahn stopped singing and fell to his hands and knees, his hair dull now, and dragging in the dirt. Alec crawled the short distance to him, aware that Seregil was shouting for him to get to cover. He grabbed up the rhekaro and staggered behind the cart with the others.

Sebrahn clung to Alec, croaking his name. Here in the shadow of the cart, Alec couldn't see Sebrahn well enough to be sure of any injuries, but he could feel how depleted that little body was. Cutting his finger on the edge of his sword, he fed him and was relieved when Sebrahn sucked eagerly.

The owls were still diving and clawing at the Retha'noi, looking like avenging demons in the glare of the spreading forest fire. But that didn't stop more armed men from bursting from the trees and falling on Seregil and the others. Entrusting Sebrahn to Hâzadriën, Alec waded into the fight.

The Retha'noi outnumbered them, but certainly couldn't outfight them. They were all small like Turmay, and were armed with nothing but knives or short spears. Alec cut down four of them, and then lost count. It was horrible, like fighting children, and all the while the owls swooped and tore at their scalps and faces. He could see Seregil and Micum a few yards away, and they both wore similar expressions of dismay.

But the Retha'noi kept coming.

The sound of oo'lus behind him startled Alec. Glancing back over his shoulder, he saw Turmay there, with Naba, and another witch he didn't know. They were all looking at him as they played.

An icy hand gripped Alec's heart and froze the blood in his veins. The sword fell from his numb hand and he staggered, vision going dim as Sebrahn began a song that Alec had heard only once before.

Seregil saw Alec crumpled on the ground and Micum kneeling beside him, pressing a hand to Alec's chest. Stanching a wound or feeling for a heartbeat? Just beyond, Turmay and Naba stood with another witch, but Sebrahn was there in front of them, singing.

Dropping his bloody sword, Seregil ran to them and fell to his knees beside Alec, hardly noticing when both songs ceased. He took Alec's face between his hands and felt blood seeping from the younger man's ears. More ran like tears from beneath Alec's closed eyelids.

"Alec! Alec, open your eyes, talí!"

After a long terrible moment, Alec's eyelids fluttered.

"Alec, can you hear me? Say something!" Seregil pleaded.

"Stop—yelling—at me," he mumbled.

Micum laughed in relief, and so did Seregil, but there were tears on his cheeks.

Alec reached up and brushed them away with one grimy, bloody thumb. "I'm all right."

"I told you no more dying, damn it!"

"I didn't, this time," Alec gasped, then pushed himself up on one arm. "Sebrahn—Where's Sebrahn?"

Retha'noi and some of the Ebrados lay scattered like forgotten rag dolls all over the clearing and at the edge of the forest. Hâzadriën knelt in the midst of them, tending Morai.

There were bodies floating in the pool below the waterfall and—

And Sebrahn lay in a heap near the bodies of Turmay and Naba and some other witch Seregil hadn't seen.

Struggling to his feet, Alec staggered over to the rhekaro.

The luster was gone from Sebrahn's pale hair, and when Alec turned him over and gathered him in his arms, Seregil saw that the color of those open, unseeing eyes was as dull as old lead.

Seregil drew his poniard and held it out. Alec drove the tip of his forefinger against the point, piercing it nearly to the bone, then put it between Sebrahn's slack lips. The rhekaro's whole small body was withered like a pumpkin vine after a frost.

"Drink, Sebrahn," Alec urged, squeezing droplets onto Sebrahn's tongue. "Please drink."

"Can't Hâzadriën do something, Rieser?" asked Seregil.

Rieser shook his head sadly. "Tayan'gils can't heal themselves or each other. Only—"

"Hâzadriëlfaie blood," Alec finished for him, pressing his thumb against his forefinger to make the blood come faster.

Seregil put an arm around him, saying nothing.

"Please don't die, Sebrahn."

Seregil was about to pull him away when Sebrahn's lips twitched around Alec's finger and his dull eyes slowly closed. Alec stabbed his left forefinger and squeezed out fresh blood for him. Sebrahn was sucking weakly now; blood ran in a thin trickle from the corner of his mouth.

Rieser knelt down beside him. "Thank Aura. I didn't think it was possible."

"Maybe you should feed him, too," said Alec. "Your blood is pure."

Rieser nodded and cut his finger, then fed Sebrahn as Alec held him.

Alec leaned against Seregil, not taking his eyes from Rieser and Sebrahn. "He saved us all."

"Not all," said Nowen, limping over to them, her sword arm bloody to the elbow.

"How many of us are left?" asked Rieser.

"Rane survived whatever those witches did with their cursed horns, but he's weak. Taegil has an arrow through his thigh. Relian is weak but alive, thanks to Sebrahn, though he can't talk. Allia and Morai are dead and Kalien is still missing."

"So many!" Rieser murmured grimly.

"Sebrahn's not strong enough to bring them back," said Alec.

"That's just as well," said Rieser. "It might be a temptation if he were."

Rhal came to join them, covered in blood and pressing a hand to a gash on his forearm.

"How many men did you lose?" asked Seregil.

"Not a man. There are some wounds, but nothing we need the rhekaro for. But we'd better get out of these woods. The fire's spreading."

The entire clearing was bathed in the shifting red light now, and smoke was drifting over them in a grey pall. The surface of the pool below the waterfall reflected the color of blood; Seregil suspected that it wasn't just a trick of the light. The wind was to the west, blowing away from the trail, but that could change in an instant.

"Nowen, get the dead tied on their horses," Rieser ordered.

"Is there time for that?" asked Rhal, and got a cold look from the Ebrados captain.

"Then my men will help," Rhal told him.

Rieser looked surprised, but nodded.

Hâzadriën tended the wounded while the others dealt with the dead. Rieser saw to it that some of the bodies were doubled on one horse so that Alec could ride out with Sebrahn. Rane, Sorengil, and Taegil slumped in the saddle and had to be tied on, but Nowen and Rieser made a quick job of it.

Meanwhile, Seregil and Micum went to where Turmay and the other witches had fallen. They lay just inside the trees, dead eyes staring up at the night sky, and still gripping the oo'lus. Seregil pulled Turmay's away and ran his hands over it. "It isn't cracked."

"He failed his destiny," Micum said.

Seregil gave him a tilted grin. "So much for fate. I think I'll take these with us. Thero and Magyana will find them of interest."

They left the smoke and firelight behind, moving as quickly as Rhal's men on foot could, their way lit now by the moon. They stopped only long enough to take up Kalien's corpse, then hurried on to the edge of the forest.

There was no question of taking the dead home, or burning the bodies without the proper resins and oil. Instead, Rieser and Nowen cut locks of hair for the families, placed the hunting masks each fallen comrade had worn in life over their face, and sewed them into their cloaks. Hâzadriën joined them as they carried the bodies just inside the forest and buried them side by side in the soft loam while the rest sat on the ground and wept. Seregil and the others had offered their help, but Rieser simply shook his head. When they were through, Sorengil and Nowen built tall cairns on top of each grave, then joined with the others in a keening song of loss.

Seregil and the others watched from a respectful distance, then headed back to the night's campsite.

"Do your people do that, Lord Seregil?" asked Rhal.

"Yes, but the songs are different. They're guiding the *khi* to their next life."

"Khi? Is that a soul?"

"Something like it, but not exactly."

"You believe there's something after this life, then?"

Seregil nodded. "I didn't, most of my life, but an oracle showed me glimpses of my lives to come."

"Really? And what were they like?"

Seregil gave him a wry smile. "I always have a weapon in my hand."

They set about making the evening meal. Alec had been silent, and he looked thoughtful as he tended the rabbits and grouse spitted over the fire.

* * *

The moon was setting when Rieser and the remainder of his people returned to the camp.

"Come and eat," Seregil said.

The wounded were healed enough to join them, and they all ate in silence out of respect for the dead.

"I don't think we'll be able to go back the way we came," Rieser said at last. "There will be more Retha'noi, and they don't count us as friends."

"There are most likely plenty more of them back in the hills," said Micum. "I've been thinking. It would make your journey home a good deal shorter if you sailed with us. It's no time at all to cross to Nanta from here, and you can make your way back up the river from there. What do you say, Rhal?"

The captain looked over what was left of the Ebrados. "As long as they leave Lord Alec alone, I've no reason to deny them. What say you, Lord Seregil?"

"I think it's a good idea."

Rhal offered his hand to Rieser. "Will you clasp hands on it, sir?"

Rieser took it with a weary nod. "You have my thanks."

Seregil exchanged a secret grin with Micum. Rieser's opinion of Tírfaie seemed to have softened just a bit.

C H A P T E R   35

❧

farewell

THE VOYAGE to Nanta took three days—three all-too-short days for Alec. He spent most of his time tending Sebrahn, and had him in the bed with them every night. Seregil made no complaint, but let him know with a silent nod that first night that he understood. They'd soon be saying farewell.

Alec grieved in silence; his decision back on the island seemed harder now that he was so close to losing the little rhekaro. Sebrahn wasn't strong enough to walk yet, and Seregil kept the Hâzad away.

They reached Nanta in the morning, and the time to part forever came at last. Alec said his good-byes to Sebrahn in the privacy of their cabin, with only Seregil there to see.

Seated on the bed with the rhekaro on his lap, he stroked that pale hair for the last time and whispered, "This time it's you leaving me."

Sebrahn touched Alec's cheek. "Leeeeving."

"That's right. But you'll be with Hâzadriën, and other rhekaros. You're happy with him, aren't you?"

"Haaaaa-zen."

"I'm sorry." Alec was fighting back tears now. "I wish—I wish things were different but—I want you to be safe and—" Overcome, he hugged Sebrahn close, wondering what Rieser would do if he refused to give him up.

Seregil sat down and put an arm around him. "It's time, Alec," he said gently. "Do you want me to do it? Rieser's just outside."

Alec wiped the tears from his cheeks. "No. I will." Rising, he carried Sebrahn across the room, committing the feel of those cool little arms around his neck to memory.

Hâzadriën and Rieser sat on the stairs outside, but rose when he came out.

"You're ready?" asked Rieser.

"Yes." It took all of Alec's will to place Sebrahn in the tall rhekaro's arms. "Take—take care of him for me. He trusts you."

"I'll see that they remain together," Rieser promised.

And then there was nothing left to say. Unable to watch them climb the stairs, Alec turned and walked back into the cabin. Head down, he mumbled, "I need to be alone."

"Are you sure?"

"Yes. Just for a while."

"All right then." Seregil paused and embraced him, and Alec knew how important it was for him not to pull away. Instead he hugged him back gratefully, then found he couldn't let go.

Seregil stroked his hair. "I know, talí. I know. It's all right."

"No, it's not!" He already felt the burning ache of loss in his chest. His "child of no mother" could not be his. Not if he wanted the life he had. Seregil's arms tightened around him; he knew loss, too. Somehow, that helped.

From Nanta, Rhal set sail for the Cirna Canal, and the little port of Ardenlee nearby. Seregil spent the first day in the cabin with Alec, and Micum let them be. When Alec appeared at supper the following night, his eyes were red and he was very quiet. Micum looked over at Seregil, but his friend shook his head. There was nothing anyone could say to Alec right now that would ease his pain.

Alec was a little better the next day, and by the time they reached Cirna, he seemed nearly himself again, though there'd been no singing or gaming this crossing. Seregil spent a great deal of time poring over the pieces of the stolen books, trying to pierce the code, but with little success. Micum suspected his heart wasn't really in the task just now. Sebrahn's absence was palpable between them.

They arrived at midmorning, guided in by twin columns of smoke from the beacon fires above the Astellus and Sakor columns. It had been a few years since Micum had sailed through the great Canal, which connected the Inner and Osiat seas. As they sat at anchor, waiting for the harbormaster to signal their turn, he stood on the deck with Alec and Seregil, taking in the sight of it.

"I'll never forget the first time I saw this, aboard the *Grampus*," murmured Alec.

"While I was busy dying in the hold," Seregil said with a chuckle.

The ships ahead of them disappeared one by one into the dark maw of the channel, each signaled in by a mirror flash from near the top of the Astellus pillar.

"That's our signal!" the lookout cried.

It was too dangerous to sail though the narrow channel, so ships like the *Lady* that were not fitted out with oars were towed through by large longboats.

It was just short of noon now, and they could clearly see the glassy places on the rough, towering walls, signs of the ancient magic used to make this wonder. Freshets of water flowed here and there, their tinkling splash sounding loud in the narrow space.

As they reached the halfway point, Micum saluted the statue of Tamír. "Thanks for the use of your road, Majesty."

Reaching the far end at last, the longboat cast off and they hoisted canvas and sailed down the rocky coast to Ardenlee.

They'd decided to put in here, rather than Rhíminee, and enter the city as quietly as possible, which for Seregil and Alec meant evading any of the queen's spies who might recognize them. There were still the pieces of the books to be dealt with before they made their presence generally known.

The sailors swam their horses ashore, and they followed in a longboat with their gear. Rhal came along to bid them farewell.

When they were ashore at last, he clasped hands with each of them and held Alec's the longest. "Take care, my lords, and see if you can keep out of trouble for a while."

"Good hunting," said Seregil.

"And a full hold," added Micum.

They stayed the night in a small inn, and set off the next day for the Bell and Bridle once again. "It's good not to be pursued this time," Micum remarked.

Seregil chuckled but Alec just looked away and said nothing. He'd been carrying Sebrahn the last time they came this way.

They spent the night at the Bell, and Seregil used one of the message sticks to let Thero know of their return. The following morning it was time to finally say another farewell.

"I could ride to Rhíminee with you," Micum offered as they stood together in the stable yard.

"You've made Kari wait far too long already," Seregil told him. "Give her our apologies, and tell Illia and the boys that we'll bring presents to make up for your absence."

"They'll hold you to that. And see that you come out to Watermead soon." He wagged a finger at them both. "I expect to see you before the spring foaling's done."

"You will," Alec promised. "I'll make sure of it."

Micum embraced them each in turn. "I'll miss you. I always do."

Mounting his horse, he turned and headed for home.

Alec and Seregil watched him out of sight, then headed for the stable to get their horses.

"What do you say, Cynril, my girl?" Seregil asked, rubbing the tall black's nose. "Ready to turn your head for home?"

Home, thought Alec. "The villa or the inn?" he asked, hoping for the latter.

"The inn, of course. I think we deserve a few days' peace before we plunge back into society."

"Good." After all the horrors and hardships of these past months, Alec wanted to hide away in their secret rooms for about a year before he even considered parties and intrigues.

❧
Rhíminee in the Dark

THEY ARRIVED at the north gate of the city just before midnight and rode through into the Harvest Market. The labyrinth of stalls was dark, and the great square was deserted except for a few sleeping beggars and a stray tomcat howling its lust somewhere in the shadows. From here they followed Silvermoon Street into the Noble Quarter, past the Palace grounds, and on to the walled grounds of the Orëska House. The soaring white palace towered above its walls, gleaming like pearl in the moonlight. The huge glass dome that topped it, and three of the four towers that stood at the corners, were dark, but light still showed through the dome of the east tower.

"Looks like we won't be waking Thero," said Alec.

"Perhaps he waited up for us." Seregil patted his saddlebag and the two oo'lus strapped behind his saddle. "This time we brought presents for him, too."

Guards in the red livery of the House stepped out to challenge them, but their names were password enough. They rode on through the dark, ever-fragrant gardens and left their horses with an attendant. Climbing the broad steps, they entered the huge, echoing atrium and strode across the great dragon mosaic floor to the stairway. Five stories of elaborately carved balconies and walkways were lost in shadow, except for lanterns hung at intervals along each.

Thero was uncommonly disheveled when he answered their knock. His blue robe looked slept in, and there were purple ink stains on his fingers and right cheek. "There you are! I didn't expect you until tomorrow." He looked them over, taking in their mud-spattered boots and trousers, and the saddlebag and oo'lus Seregil carried over one shoulder. "Where is Sebrahn?" he asked as they came into the workshop. The smell of a brazier hung on the air, and the stink of some spell.

"He's safe. I'll tell you the tale in a while," Seregil said quietly with a meaningful look in Alec's direction. "When we've had some wine."

"Very well. I've had some news of my own, today. Ulan í Sathil died in Riga."

"When?"

"Not long after you left, I'd say. He was carried back to Virésse in state with a boatload of ransomed slaves, a hero to his people."

"A hero?" Alec exclaimed.

"It's all right," Seregil told him. "He's more use to everyone that way. No good could come of the truth."

"But, still, it's sort of ironic, isn't it? Us keeping his secret for him?"

Seregil gave him a wry smile. "Life does tend to work out that way sometimes."

"Did you find the book?" asked Thero.

"Books, as it turned out," Seregil told him.

Seregil set the saddlebag down on one of the workbenches and took out the three halved volumes.

Thero looked at them in dismay. "What happened?"

"I split them with a Hâzadriëlfaie captain we got to know, with the idea that it was safer with no one having all of any of them. I did try to salvage the best bits, though."

Thero gaped at them. "Hâzadriëlfaie? Really?"

"That's who was chasing us when we met you at the Bell and Bridle," Alec told him. "It's a long, long story after that."

"Another one. Then you'd better come downstairs and tell them."

"Is Magyana still awake?" asked Seregil. "She'll want to hear it, too."

"She went down to Rhina to visit Hermeus. I'll send word to her tomorrow."

"Oh, and before we go any farther?" Seregil pointed to Alec's hair; Thero's magic had not worn off and it was still brown. "Will you please put this right?"

"Of course." Thero stood behind Alec and ran his hands over his head. When he was through Alec's hair was back to its normal honey blond.

"Ah, that's much better!"

"And these," said Alec, pushing his sleeve back to show him the slave brand.

Thero removed those as well, and led them down the back stair to his tidy sitting room.

The room hadn't changed since Nysander's day. There was still the band of mural around the room, magical as well as decorative, and the old comfortable furnishings. A dining table stood at the center of the room, with armchairs by the hearth beyond. The walls were filled with bookcases, scroll racks, and dusty objects of uncertain origin.

Thero wove a quick spell on the air with one finger and a burlap-wrapped wine jar appeared on the table, still crusted with snow from Mount Apos. He poured them goblets of the chilled Mycenian apple wine and they sat down at the table with the books.

Seregil took a long sip of the cold wine and sat back in his chair. "Oh, I have missed that!"

"The books?" Thero asked impatiently.

"I think you'll find this one of the most interest." Seregil said, showing him the one with the most drawings of rhekaros. "I don't know if the whole thing is about the making of them, but I tried to get as much of it for you as I could."

"Excellent!" Thero looked as happy as Micum's daughter Illia with a new necklace. "This is wonderful! Given Yhakobin's skills, this could prove very useful, even if it is incomplete. I'll need your expertise in figuring out the code, I'm sure."

"Once we get settled in again," Seregil promised, then presented Thero with the oo'lus. "I thought you'd like these, too."

"Also part of the long story," Alec told him.

Thero refilled the cups. "I'm ready to hear it."

It did take quite a while, even with two of them telling it. When they were done, Thero shook his head. "I'm sorry about Sebrahn, Alec."

"It was the best thing we could do," Alec told him, but there was still a raw edge of sadness in his voice.

"The things you two survive! It never fails to amaze me."

Seregil saluted him with his empty cup, then set it aside. "Where are you going tonight? You're welcome to stay here."

"Thanks, but we're headed for the Stag," Alec told him.

"Shall I send word to Runcer?"

"No, thanks." As much as Seregil trusted the man who oversaw the running of the Wheel Street villa, he didn't want to chance word getting out of their return.

"When will you see the queen? She's not very happy with me for coming back without you, or about your extended absence."

"What did you tell her?"

"That you were still in Bôkthersa, recuperating and visiting your family."

"Thank you. We'll send word to the Palace tomorrow after we've had a bit of a rest. And that's what I need right now. Come on, Alec."

Thero walked upstairs with them and saw them to the door.

"I know you'll guard those books carefully," said Seregil. "It's a relief to be rid of them."

"I'll take good care of them."

With that duty discharged, they backtracked through the Noble Quarter to Golden Helm Street and on past the round colonnade of the Astellus fountain and the arched entrance to the Street of Lights. The colored lanterns in front of the elaborate brothels were lit and there were still quite a number of people on the street, heading for the favors of a favorite courtesan, or the gambling houses at the far end. A good many were soldiers.

From here they entered a twisting maze of narrow streets toward Blue Fish Street.

They were nearly there when they heard the telltale scuffle of feet behind them. The lanterns were few and far between in this part of the city, but there was enough light from the nearest for Seregil to count five men. They were young and dressed like ruffians. He didn't see any swords, just clubs and staffs and a few long knives.

"And where might you be going?" asked one with a northern accent.

"Those are pretty horses you have there," said another with a head of wild curly hair.

Two of them were advancing, probably meaning to cut the lead reins of Windrunner and Star. Smelling the brandy on them, Seregil let out a heavy sigh. "You don't want to do this."

"I don't see the bluecoats anywhere," the leader said with a confident leer.

"He's trying to do you a favor," Alec warned.

The man laughed. "I think you two better come down off those horses. Now."

"Why would we do that?" asked Seregil.

The man swung his club in a vicious arc in front of him. "We mean to lighten your load, that's why! So you can stop acting so high and mighty, my lordlings. We'll take those bags, and your purses. And that's a nice bow you're carrying, too, Yellow Hair."

Moving as one, Seregil and Alec swung down from the saddle and drew their swords. The polished Aurënen steel caught the faint light.

Two of the men in front of them stepped back a little, but the three others rushed them, swinging their clubs. Alec ducked a blow from the fare most and slashed the man across the chest, striking to wound rather than kill. It had the desired effect; the man dropped his club and staggered back. Seregil struck the other one—the erstwhile leader—across the face with the flat of his blade, opening up his cheek and stunning him. The rest turned tail and ran.

Satisfied, Seregil went to the man who lay doubled up on

the ground and gave him a hard nudge with his foot, pushing him over onto his back.

"Please, sir, don't kill me!" the man pleaded, craven now.

"I did warn you." Holding him down with a foot on his chest, Seregil put the tip of his sword under the man's chin and helped himself to the thief's purse. "You really should be more careful about choosing your marks."

The man gaped up at him in terror. "Please sir! I'm sorry! Maker's Mercy, please don't—"

Seregil looked over at Alec, who was still standing over the other man. "What do you say?"

"Not worth getting our blades dirty."

"I suppose not. On your feet, you pathetic bastard. Take your friend here and run away before we change our minds."

"He's no friend of mine!" the coward exclaimed and staggered away behind the horses.

"No honor among some thieves," said Alec.

Seregil sighed. "That was hardly any fun at all."

Mounting again, they continued on, alert for reprisals.

The Stag and Otter was dark. Bypassing the front door, they led their horses to the back courtyard and left them with the sleepy stable lad, then went in by the kitchen door.

Seregil went to the mantelpiece above the broad hearth and took down the large painted pitcher that stood at the center of it.

"Well, well." He felt inside and held up three folded vellum packets and a small scroll tube, no doubt delivered by Magyana or Thero. "We've been missed."

Alec lit a candle from the banked coals and they made their way up to the second floor, where Seregil unlocked the door of an empty storeroom and locked it again carefully behind them. Crossing to the opposite wall, he spoke the ward that opened the hidden panel there.

"Do you remember the passwords?" he asked Alec with a grin. "It has been a while."

"I certainly hope so. It would be a shame to be killed on our own doorstep." Alec took the lead, whispering the current passwords—*Aurathra. Morinth. Selethrir. Tilentha,* the

Aurënfaie words for the four moon phases—for each of the four wards Magyana had placed here to deal with unwanted visitors, should anyone stumble onto their secret.

Seregil's cat, who had her own way in, stood up and stretched as they reached the door at the top of the stairs.

"There's my girl!" Seregil exclaimed, reaching down to scratch her behind the ears as Alec spoke the final password. Ruetha broke into a loud purr and rubbed around Seregil's ankles as he opened the sitting room door.

The room was dark and cold and smelled of dust, but they'd left a good supply of wood by the hearth. Seregil tossed his saddlebag into a corner and kicked off his muddy boots by the door. Alec did the same, then used a fire chip from the dish on the marble mantelpiece to light the fire. Seregil went around the room, lighting candles and lamps, then—sweeping the dust cover off the couch—he stretched out there and inspected the seals on the letters.

Two of them were simply drops of melted sealing wax; it was more prudent not to advertise who was sending certain letters in case they were intercepted. The third was from a duchess he knew slightly, and the scroll was from Magyana.

Alec pushed Seregil's feet aside to sit down and covered them both with his cloak as they waited for the room to warm.

"Let's see," said Seregil, breaking the first blank seal. "This is from old Lord Erneus. Seems his daughter has gotten herself—No, look at the date. She's given birth by now." That one was relegated to the fire. The second had been left for them just a week before. The scent of a lady's perfume still clung to it. Seregil held it to his nose, giving Alec a wink, then looked it over. "This one is from Duchess Myrian, Duke Norin's wife. It seems she's unwisely given a token to her lover—Bilairy's Balls, why do they always do that?"

"We'd be out of work if they didn't."

The third missive was from Tyrien, a Street of Lights courtesan Alec had met the first time he'd blundered under a green lantern. The young man wanted someone to rob the house of a patron who'd wronged him.

"I wonder what he'd think if he knew it was you he was writing to?" Seregil said with a grin.

Alec ignored him and picked up the scroll tube. Breaking the seal, he shook out the rolled letter. "Let's hope Magyana has something more challenging for us. This is dated just four days ago. She must have left it as she went out of town."

Seregil pulled the edge of the cloak up under his chin. "That sounds promising."

"'My dear boys, if you return before I get back, I have a small matter that might be of interest to you. Please visit Lady Amalia as your lordly selves as soon as you can. Tell her you are in my confidence, and know of someone trustworthy who can help her. It's a small political matter. I do hope you had a pleasant adventure.'"

Seregil grimaced. "'Pleasant' is not the word I'd use to describe it. What about you?"

Alec pushed Seregil's feet off his lap. Going to his discarded saddlebag, he took out the false slave collars they'd worn and propped them up on the cluttered mantelpiece between a box of loose gems and a broken lock.

"Are you sure you want to save those?" Seregil asked. How could Alec look at them and not think of Sebrahn?

"It's all right," Alec assured him as he sat down beside him again.

He didn't say more, and Seregil didn't ask. Instead, he made a show of weighing a letter in each hand. "What do you say, talí? The lady or the whore?"

"Magyana first, then the whore, and then the lady," said Alec. "On one condition, though."

"You're leveling conditions now? All right, what is it?"

The flickering firelight made Alec look a bit menacing as he grinned and said, "That I don't hear you complain about being bored for at least two months."

Seregil gave him a mocking seated bow. "You have my word. I'm sure this old whore of a city can keep me entertained for a bit. Besides, it's nearly spring, and people do all sorts of foolish things in the spring. Ah, Alec—a good honest brawl and jobs waiting." He yawned and stretched, then uttered the words he had not said since the Cockerel Inn burned.

"It's good to be home."